Sweet
Stuff

ALSO BY BEST-SELLING AUTHOR DONNA KAUFFMAN

BABYCAKES

SUGAR RUSH

OFF KILTER

SOME LIKE IT SCOT

A GREAT KISSER

LET ME IN

THE GREAT SCOT

THE BLACK SHEEP AND THE ENGLISH ROSE

THE BLACK SHEEP AND THE HIDDEN BEAUTY

THE BLACK SHEEP AND THE PRINCESS

BAD BOYS IN KILTS

CATCH ME IF YOU CAN

BAD BOYS NEXT EXIT

JINGLE BELL ROCK

BAD BOYS ON BOARD

I LOVE BAD BOYS

Published by Kensington Publishing Corporation

Sweet Stuff

DONNA KAUFFMAN

KENSINGTON BOOKS
http://www.kensingtonbooks.com

KENSINGTON BOOKS are published by

Kensington Publishing Corp.
119 West 40th Street
New York, NY 10018

All Kensington titles, imprints and distributed lines are available at special quantity discounts for bulk purchases for sales promotion, premiums, fund-raising, educational or institutional use.

Special book excerpts or customized printings can also be created to fit specific needs. For details, write or phone the office of the Kensington Special Sales Manager. Attn.: Special Sales Department. Kensington Publishing Corp., 119 West 40th Street, New York, NY 10018. Phone: 1-800-221-2647.

Kensington and the K logo Reg. U.S. Pat. & TM Off.

ISBN-13: 978-0-7582-6637-8
ISBN-10: 0-7582-6637-5
First Brava Books Trade Paperback Printing: February 2012
First Kensington Books Mass-Market Paperback Printing: September 2013

eISBN-13: 978-0-7582-9148-6
eISBN-10: 0-7582-9148-5
First Kensington Books Electronic Edition: September 2013

10 9 8 7 6 5 4 3 2 1

Printed in the United States of America

*For the friends and family
who provide the roots that bind us together,
and the foundation upon which is built
a happy and contented life . . .
no matter where we each lay our heads at night.*

Chapter 1

Later, she would blame the whole thing on the cupcakes. Riley glanced through the sparkling windowpanes of the hand-stained, sliding French panel doors to the extended, multilevel tigerwood deck—complete with stargazer pergola and red cedar soaking tub—straight into a pair of familiar, sober brown eyes. "I know that look," she called out, loud enough so he could hear her through the thermal, double-paned glass. "Don't mock. I can too do this."

She turned her attention forward again and stared at the electronic panel of the Jog Master 3000. "I mean, how hard could it be?" A rhetorical question of course. Anyone, probably even the sunbathing mastiff, could figure out how to push a few buttons and—

"Ooof!" The belt started moving under her feet. Really fast.

Really, really fast.

"Oh crap!" She grabbed the padded side bars, an instinctive move purely intended to keep from face-planting on high-speed rubber, with little actual athleticism involved. Okay, not a drop of it, but if she could keep pace long enough to get her balance, she could relax the death grip of just one of her hands and smack—press, she meant press—the electronic panel of buttons on this very— very—expensive piece of leased equipment. At which point her ill-advised, unfortunate little adventure would end well.

Or at least without the local EMTs being called. Or a lengthy hospital stay. She was way too busy for stitches.

"Yeah," she gasped. "Piece of cake." She managed a smirk at the irony of that particular phrase, but quickly turned to full panic mode as she realized she wasn't exactly gaining ground. Rapidly losing it, in fact, along with what little breath she had. "Crap, crap, crap," she panted in rhythm with her running steps. It had only been a few minutes—three minutes and forty-four seconds, according to the oh-so-helpful digital display—and she was already perspiring. Okay, okay, sweating. She just wasn't sure if it was from the actual exertion, or the abject anxiety that she wasn't going to get out of this latest catastrophe in one piece.

Where were those big, strong, Steinway deliverymen when you needed them, anyway? Surely they could race right in and save her, in blazingly heroic, stud-monkey fashion. And she'd let them, too. Just because she prided herself on her total I-Am-Woman independence thing A.J. (After-Jeremy), didn't mean she wasn't above a little Rapunzel fantasy now and again.

She'd been awaiting delivery of the elegant baby grand for over an hour. So, technically, it was all their fault. The baby grand in question was the final component, and the *pièce de résistance*, of this particular staging event. With every other remaining detail attended to, she'd foolishly given in to the urge to run a test check—all right, play— with some of the toys she'd had installed. Once again, she had managed to get herself into a bit of a pickle.

Enough with the food analogies, Riles. Eight minutes, twenty-three seconds. At a dead run. The only way she could have ever pulled that off was if she were being chased by zombies. With machetes. And the world as she knew it would end if she didn't get to the edge of the dark, scary forest in time.

Instead, all she had was her mastiff and his baleful stare. Not exactly adrenaline-inducing.

Ten minutes, thirteen seconds. She was well past sweating and deep into red-faced overexertion. She glared back at Brutus, who kept faithful watch, but otherwise appeared unconcerned with his mistress's current distress. "No gravy on your kibble tonight," she called out. Well, in her mind, she called out. She was so winded it was all she could do to think the words. But her expression hopefully conveyed the message to her mutant, one-hundred-fifty-pound dog . . .

Who looked completely unmoved by her menacing glare. He knew she was a pushover. She'd taken him in as a rescue, hadn't she?

The sweet sound of the cascading entrance chimes echoed through the room, indicating the deliverymen had, indeed, finally arrived.

"Thank God," she wheezed. She didn't even care what they thought of the situation, or how horrible she must look. She'd bribe them with a few of Leilani's decadently delicious Black Forest cupcakes, featuring raspberry truffle filling, and topped with fresh, plump, perfectly rosy raspberries. There were two dozen of them, carefully arranged on the three-tier crystal display dish in the beautifully appointed breakfast nook. That, and maybe throw in a few bottles of imported lager presently chilling in the newly installed, stainless-steel Viking fridge with handy bottom freezer, and surely they wouldn't say anything to Scary Lois about Riley's less-than-professional activities.

Lois Grinkmeyer-Hington-Smythe was easily the most intimidating person Riley had staged showcase houses for thus far, or worked for in any capacity, for that matter.

Given her former career as head food stylist for *Foodie*, the number one selling food magazine in the country, that was saying something. Even the most intimidating chef had nothing on Scary Lois, highest performing Realtor for Gold Coast Properties, and Riley couldn't afford to annoy the source of her best bookings.

The chimes cascaded again. *Oh, for God's sake, come in, already*! She tried to shout, but all she could muster was a strangled, guttural grunt. Why weren't they just coming in? Open house meant the house was open!

She could see the headlines now.

Riley Brown Found Dead!

SUGARBERRY ISLAND'S PREMIER HOUSE STAGER IN HIGH-SPEED TREADMILL INCIDENT!

BARRIER ISLANDS, GEORGIA—Piano deliverymen and part-time models Sven and Magnus claimed they had no knowledge that the front door to the island's newly redesigned, prime lease property was unlocked, and that they could have entered the home and rescued the lovely and talented house stager from escalating terror and certain death. They did, however, make sure the reporter got their names right and photographed them from their good side.

Meanwhile, poor, dead Riley Brown probably wouldn't even warrant a hunky CSI investigator, who—clearly moved by her still glowing, cherubic face and bountiful blond curls—would posthumously vow to go to the ends of the earth to find out who was responsible for this terrible, terrible tragedy.

Of course, you couldn't exactly arrest a Jog Master 3000.

Right at the point where she knew her sweaty palms couldn't grip the rubber padding one second longer and her gaze had shifted to Brutus out on the deck for what could likely be the very last time, someone with a very deep voice that carried the warm caress of a slight Southern accent said, "Beg your pardon. I thought this was the house being leased. My apologies, I—"

Riley jerked her head around to look at the intruder. That was no Sven. Or even a Magnus. He was way— way—better than any Nordic fantasy. Framed by what she knew was a nine-foot archway, he was a rugged six-foot-four at least, with shoulders and jaw to match. Even in his white cotton button-down shirt, faded jeans, and dark brown sport coat, he looked like he could have delivered a baby grand with his left hand, while simultaneously saving the world with his right. Thick, dark hair framed a tanned face with crinkles at the corners of the most amazing bright blue eyes . . . Wait—she knew that face! How did she know that face?

Her jaw went slack the instant she realized who was standing, live and in the amazingly more-gorgeous-in-person flesh, right there in her Florida room. Well, not *her* Florida room, but . . . that didn't matter, because unfortunately the moment her jaw had gone slack, so had her hands.

She let out a strangled shriek as the rapidly spinning rubber track ejected her from the back end of the machine as if she were a clown shot out of a circus cannon. Sans the acrobatic skills. Or clean landing.

The good news? The tastefully arranged indoor/outdoor cluster of salt-air tolerant baby cabbage and saw palmettos, cockspur prickly pear and Adam's Needle yucca kept her from being ejected straight through the sparkling clean, thermal double panes she'd spent a full hour on that morning. The bad news? Well, other than the part about saw palmettos and prickly pear not exactly being soft and cushy kinds of foliage? Yeah, that would be lying in a sweaty, red-faced, scratched-up heap . . . all while looking up into the breathtaking, turquoise blue eyes of the one-and-only Quinn Brannigan.

Dazed in more ways than one, Riley found herself thinking that if her life were ever made into a movie of the week, she sure hoped the screenwriter would give her some clever, witty line to say at that exact moment. One that would show her to be adorably spunky and utterly charming . . . despite her bedraggled, pathetic, utterly disastrous appearance.

Alas, she was more a visual person—which was why she was a stylist and a photographer, not a writer. Quinn Brannigan, on the other hand, was a writer. Of the number one with a bullet, *New York Times* best-selling variety. So, of course, he knew exactly what to say.

"I am sorry." That hint of drawl in his voice made him sound inherently sincere, while the concern etched in every crease of his perfectly gorgeous face only underscored the tone. "I don't know how I made such a mistake. I never meant to alarm you like that. Let me help you up, make sure you're all right." He extended a hand.

See? Perfect white knight, perfect amount of sincere contrition, perfect . . . well, everything. She'd always thought him handsome, staring back at her from the glossy book jackets of his many best sellers. What the photo didn't convey was the magnetism and charisma that packed an even bigger wallop in person. Not to mention his voice. Deep and smooth, with a cadence hinting at warm honey drizzled all over a hot, buttery biscuit. If they could package that voice along with his books, he'd double his already enormous sales.

"You know"—her words came out in more of a post-marathon croak—"you really should read your own books." She closed her eyes when his expression shifted to one of confusion. *I said that, right out loud, didn't I?* Another rhetorical question, of course. "On tape," she added lamely, as if that was going to clear matters right up. "You know, audiobooks." Riley let her head drop farther back into the sharp fronds. "Never mind. I'm shutting up now."

"Give me your hand." When he crouched down, his handsome face and hot-sex-in-a-summer-hammock voice were even closer to her. "Are you hurt? Did you hit your head on the glass?"

Given her random commentary, his concern wasn't the least bit surprising. It was an easy out that a lesser woman might have taken. No one had ever accused her, however, of being lesser. Too much, maybe. All right, definitely.

"No," she managed. "Just a few scratches. I'm fine, I just—" She broke off, and, with a little sigh and a not-so-little huff of breath, tried to struggle her way out of the forest of serrated-edge foliage by herself. Then just as quickly gave up as the plants seemed to want to suck her in more deeply. She'd lost enough skin already.

She couldn't lose any more of her pride, however. That was all gone. She rubbed her dirty, still-sweaty palm on her pant leg, then took the offered hand, steeling her already fluttering hormones against the feel of his skin on hers. Not that she was normally so overwrought about such things, but, at the moment, her defenses were abnormally low. As in, completely missing.

And . . . yep. *Pow.* Right in the libido. Wide palm, warm skin, strong grip.

He lifted her overly tall, less-than-lithe form out of the tangle of deadly blades as if she were nothing more cumbersome than a downy little feather. She'd never once been accused of being a feather. Of any kind. She had to admit, it felt rather . . .

blissful. So much so, that, if he'd asked her, she'd have happily agreed to strip naked, have his babies, or anything else he wanted, right there. On the evil Jog Master, even.

Because, oh yeah, that's what he's dying to do, Riles. Take you, take you hard.

Not that it mattered. Even if she had somehow managed to look adorably spunky and utterly charming despite the scratched-up flesh and blotchy red face, she'd sworn off men. Nineteen months, ten days, and dozens of cupcakes ago.

Not that all men were stupid, lying, cheating, ex-fiancé bastards like Jeremy. She knew that. And she hadn't held his actions against the rest of the male members of the human race. Most of the time. But given how thoroughly and completely duped and humiliated she'd been by the one person from that part of the population she'd most trusted with her deepest, truest self, not to mention all of her carefully guarded heart . . . yeah, she wasn't in a mad rush to find out if her judgment in that arena had improved. Hence the switch to baked goods for personal comfort.

Men were complicated. Cupcakes, on the other hand? Not so much.

"You've got a few scrapes," Quinn-the-hot-celebrity-savior was saying as he steadied her with a wide palm on her shoulder. *Rapunzel, eat your heart out.* Still working to get her heart rate back to some semblance of normal, she acknowledged that her studly savior was probably more to blame than the Jog Master.

After another moment passed, he carefully disengaged his hand from hers, which took a bit of doing as she'd apparently switched her Jog Master death grip to a Good Studly Samaritan one, but he kept the steadying hand on her shoulder for an additional moment before letting go completely. "Let me help you get cleaned up."

Riley belatedly realized she was staring at Quinn with God only knew what kind of glazed, starry-eyed expression plastered all over her blotchy and battered face. She might have sworn off men and wrapped herself in fiercely guarded independence, but that didn't mean she was quite up for inviting them to stare at her in abject horror. Or worse, pity. "I—uh, no, that's okay," she managed, finally pulling herself together. "That won't be necessary. Just a few scratches. Really. I can—I can take care of it. I'm . . . really sorry."

"*You're* sorry?" His eyes truly were the definition of piercing.

"To give you a scare like that, I mean. I was just . . ." She looked behind her at the Jog Master, which was still churning away. "Never mind. Not important." She turned and casually bent down, trying not to overtly wince at the parts of her that rebelled at being bent at that moment . . . and jerked the cord from the wall socket, using a wee bit more force than was actually required. Or perhaps a lot more force, as the plug snapped back and stung her ankle. Right in that tender, vulnerable spot that brought instant tears to the eyes. She dropped the cord like a live snake as she somehow managed to suck in every single one of the very unladylike, but totally appropriate-to-the-moment swear words, then forced herself to straighten, slowly, while giving herself a quick, silent talking-to. She could fall apart later, and swear to the heavens if she wanted to.

Right now, she had to salvage the few remaining bits of professionalism that hadn't been shredded along with the foliage. Only then did she turn back to face him, trying for a sunny smile, though that was likely ruined by the way the stretching of her lacerated skin made her flinch. "So, you're here for the open house?"

He was still frowning. The concerned, Good Studly

Samaritan. It made her feel ridiculous and pathetic, though she was certain that wasn't his intent. Not that he needed to try. She could feel ridiculous and pathetic with no help at all.

"I really think we should give those scratches some attention, and you might want to sit down. At least for a few minutes. Get your balance. Again, my apologies for startling you like that." His frown eased into an abashed half smile that kept her pulse humming right along. "What in the world you must have thought, a strange man walking right into your home. I guess it's good you recognized me. I can't believe I got the number wrong. The island's not that big—wait." He paused, the half smile turning back to a look of confusion. "Did you mean to say that this . . . *is* the house that's up for lease?"

For the briefest moment, Riley entertained the wild thought of pretending she was also there for the open house and had just made the unfortunate decision to give the Jog Master a try. But she ditched the plan almost as fast as she thought of it. Even if he bought the story, at some point, if he ended up leasing the place—which would be just her luck—he'd no doubt run into her around the island. Sugarberry was the smallest of the inhabited barrier islands and the only town on it was hardly big enough to be called a town. They couldn't help running into each other.

He'd quickly find out she was hardly in any position to lease the newly renovated and exceedingly high-end beach bungalow. The houseboat she lived on might give the impression of a decent annual income, but it was a loaner, and while nice, not exactly yacht club material. Not that Sugarberry had a yacht club. The *Seaduced* was presently tied up on the south end of the island alongside a bunch of commercial fishing trawlers, as it was the only pier that could take her.

For that matter, Sugarberry didn't have any other high-end beach bungalows. The old Turner place—bought at a bank auction by a pair of Atlanta investors looking to mine new Gold Coast development opportunities—was the first of its kind. And, if Sugarberry residents had anything to say about it—and they had plenty to say—the last.

Unlike Quinn Brannigan, who was exactly high-end, upscale bungalow, yacht club material.

"Yes, this is the one," Riley answered him, making a grand gesture to the room around them. Anything to take his concerned gaze from her face. "It's truly a gem. I'm so very sorry your first impression of the property was well . . . you know. Hugely unprofessional of me. Not the hoped-for introduction, I'm afraid." She deliberated a brief moment on asking him not to mention her little adventure to Scary Lois, but ditched that idea, too. Not a good idea to beg favors from the guy who'd just saved her life. Inadvertently, maybe, but still.

"You're not Lois of the multi-hyphenated last names, are you?"

That earned a real smile and a wince before she could control it. "No. No, I'm not."

Quinn gave her that ridiculously charming half smile again. "I didn't think so."

"You mean I don't look like the Gold Coast's most successful A-List Realtor?" she said dryly. "I'm stunned."

His half smile grew to a full smile and if she'd had any doubt her heart had fully survived her Jog Master marathon, that fear proved unwarranted. It was pumping just fine, thank you very much.

"I've not had the privilege of meeting her as yet," he said, a bit more of that honey-coated-biscuits-and-melted-butter tone flavoring his words. "But what communication we've had, well, let's just say you seem far more . . . approachable."

"You mean less scary?" Riley looked down at herself and sighed. "I don't know about that. I don't want to see myself in a mirror anytime soon."

"Come on. Let's find the kitchen and get you cleaned up a little."

A gentleman's way of saying, yep, super-scary-looking. Not that it would have made a difference either way.

"That's okay, really. I'll go take care of it. Why don't you have a look around? Lois has all the literature with her, but once I'm cleaned up, I can give you a tour. I'm familiar with all the upgrades and should be able to answer most of your questions, at least as they pertain to the house itself."

In actuality, Riley knew every last inch of the place, before renovations and after. She knew every gizmo and upgrade that had been installed, as well as what parts of the property had been preserved, and why. Not because she had personal knowledge of Sugarberry history—she'd only been living on the island for a little over a year. This was actually the first project she'd done on the island itself. She normally worked farther down the barrier island chain, where the money was. She'd simply made it her business to know everything there was to know about the Turner place, just as she did with all the projects she was hired for.

In many ways, staging an entire home or condo wasn't any different than styling food for an elaborate magazine layout. She used to learn as much as she could about the cuisine being presented, including the history, the traditions, and, in many cases, preparing the dishes herself, or as close an approximation as she could, in order to come up with the most unique, authentically detailed settings possible. Knowing the history and setting of the property she was staging was as important as all the more glamorous, flashy details.

Not that every client, or even most clients, were interested in half of what she took the time to find out. They might not care, specifically, about the fact that the refinished, hand-carved sliding panel doors were original to the house, or that she'd purposely matched the colors of the pottery and doorstops throughout the house to the terracotta shingling on the roof, but she knew it was that attention to detail that ended up selling them on the place. It didn't matter that they didn't appreciate why they loved it, just that they loved it enough to write Lois a big fat check. And, in turn, Scary Lois kept signing hers.

"Why don't you start with the . . ." She'd been about to say the deck, pool, and gardens, but remembered the sunbathing Brutus. *Crap.* Normally she and her faithful companion were no longer on the premises when the actual event began. That she occasionally brought Brutus with her while staging various properties was also a teeny-tiny detail she'd neglected to tell Lois. This project had been so close to home, and she'd known he'd love lolling out on the deck. And, frankly, she enjoyed the company. Obviously not for protection purposes.

"Uh, bedrooms," she improvised, careful to keep her gaze averted from the sliding French doors. "Just up the stairs from the foyer entry. You'll love the master suite." Too late, she remembered it had a second-story deck that looked right down on the first-story deck. "Though you might want to begin with the guest bedrooms along the front of the house. The, uh, lighting, right now . . . they have the morning sun. Truly spectacular."

If he sensed the slightly panicked edge in her tone, his affable expression didn't show it. "And risk my dearly departed Grams coming back to chase after me with her wooden rolling pin for being anything less than the gentleman she raised my pa and me to be?" The easy grin returned. "No, ma'am. Especially considering I caused the calamity in the first place." He gestured for her to lead the way to the kitchen. "Pretty sure she's capable of it, too," he added with a touch of dry reverence, as he followed her from the room.

Riley smiled, and didn't mind the wincing so much. It was impossible not to be charmed by him. But she needed to get him poking around upstairs as swiftly as possible. Not that she had any place in particular she could quickly stash a dog the size of a subcompact car, but she was due for a little luck.

She entered the kitchen, and if Quinn was impressed by the newly installed, state-of-the-art appliances, the marble-topped center island, or the array of terra-cotta-toned Calphalon pots and pans hanging from the hand-hammered silver overhead rack, he didn't mention it. Nor did he seem to even notice them. Of course, things like that were probably par for the course for his lifestyle.

He was opening cupboards and pulling out drawers, but she doubted he was taking inventory. "Not much to work with here," he murmured.

"I've got it." Riley stepped around the center island and walked over to the small breakfast nook table and the three-tier crystal cupcake display. She grabbed a few of the color-coordinated napkins that were artfully arranged next to the themed paper plates and plastic forks, then edged back around the center island to the twin stainless-steel sinks. "Really, you should take a look—"

"Here." He came right up behind her just as she'd turned on the water and shoved a wadded-up napkin underneath the steady stream.

As in, *right* behind her. Deep in her personal space. Like she hadn't just recently recovered her ability to breathe normally.

"Let me." Quinn put one broad palm on her shoulder and turned her to face him, relieving her of the soggy party napkins with his other hand, which he used to carefully dab at the scratches on her cheek and her forehead. And her chin. And her neck.

How lovely that must look.

She couldn't think about that. Unless she closed her eyes, there was nowhere else to look but directly into his, and though he was busy attending to her wounds and not really looking at her . . . she couldn't resist taking the opportunity to look at him. Really look at him.

And, up close? He looked even better. Every laugh line, every crinkle, even with a tiny scar just above one temple . . . he was truly and spectacularly gorgeous. So unfair. Even scratch-free, she wouldn't hold up to the same up-close-and-personal perusal. For one, she had freckles. And not that faint little scatter you got from being out in the sun. No, she had real freckles. Thirty-one years old. With freckles. Not adorable at that age. Then there was the whole mouth situation. Hers was wide and full, just not in that sexy and mysterious Angelina Jolie kind of way. Instead of a vampy pout that did wonders for selling lipstick and lingerie, Riley's was sort of perpetually curved in a big, goofy smile. At best, good for selling bubble gum.

She always looked like she was smiling, which shouldn't be a bad thing. But just try being taken seriously in an editorial meeting full of men when no matter how much you tried on your stern, I-mean-business face, you always looked like a brainless bimbo. Dolly Parton looked fiercer than she did.

And don't even get her started on being a natural blonde. With curls. Lots of them. Long or short didn't matter. Her hair fell in big, happy, springy sproings no matter what. No one took that seriously, either. No matter how sleek a bun she'd torture her hair into, curls sprang out to frame her apple-cheeked, freckled face. Throw in the bombshell-sized boobs, with a back porch to match and . . . yeah.

Maybe slim, perfectly coiffed ice princess blondes got respect, but she couldn't pull off even a hint of that kind of frost. Smiley, sproingy, and stacked never added up to frost. No matter how you did the math. And that had been before factoring in a year's worth of Cupcake Club get-togethers.

"There," he said, with a final dab.

"Thanks." She felt herself flush as his eyes finally met hers.

The corners of his eyes crinkled ever-so-fabulously as he smiled. "Least I could do."

"Right." She heard the breathy note in her voice. She needed to get out of his personal space, pronto, or get him out of hers, before she made an even bigger fool of herself. If that were possible. "I mean, no worries. It was just one of those things. Could have happened to anyone." She took a step back, banged her hip into the counter, then turned with the intent of putting herself anywhere but in proximity to him and caught the edge of the refrigerator handle where it jutted out just a bit farther than the cabinets and counters. "Oooh, ouch!"

And just like that, his hands were on her again. On both shoulders, as he guided her back to safety. Dear God, didn't he know he was the more dangerous thing? She was a natural klutz on her best days—yet another minus from the ice princess equation—and what he did to her equilibrium was downright hazardous to her health and well-being.

"I'm fine, really, I just—" She turned around, attempting again to put space between them, but somehow only managed to wedge herself, front-to-front, between him and the counter behind her.

His gaze caught hers and held for that moment. You know, that *moment*. Like the one that happened in the movies, where a hundred things are said, but not a single word is spoken. And the tension is so tightly wound it all but makes its own soundtrack with its taut silence, fraught with so much promise, so many possibilities, if only one of the couple would just . . . do something. One little move was all it would take, and you watch, and wait, dying inch by inch, waiting for one of them to make that oh-so-crucial, heart-pounding *move*. The moment stretches, and expands, until you think you'll scream from the sweet, knot-tightening tension of it all.

A small furrow creased the center of his forehead. "I do think maybe you should sit for a bit. You're still a little flushed."

She slowly closed her eyes, and felt her cheeks flame hotter. *So not what the movie guy would say.* "Thank you," she murmured, making a point to be looking anywhere but at him when she opened her eyes. She edged herself to one side, away from the Viking monster, and Quinn mercifully stepped back.

"Why don't you sit at the table and I'll fix you some water. Unless there's something stronger—"

"No, really. You've been more than kind. You really should take advantage and go look at the place before the event starts. Scary Lois will be here shortly and I—" She broke off when he stifled a laugh with a fist to his mouth, followed by a clearly faked coughing attack.

"What did I—?" Then she realized exactly what she'd said. *Wow, just . . . wow.* Apparently she really didn't want to work again. Ever. Except she did. She loved her job. Maybe not as much as the one she'd left behind in Chicago, but as close—closer, really—than she'd expected to find again. Groaning in ever-deepening embarrassment, she turned toward the pantry door and leaned her forehead on it. Any other time she'd have given her noggin a good rap, but she wasn't too sure, given how the day had gone so far, that she wouldn't end up in the ER with a concussion. Or in a coma.

"Are there any beds? In the bedrooms? Upstairs?"

"What?" She lifted her head and turned to look at him. Had she rapped her head anyway and hit it so hard she'd just forgotten? Clearly she did not just hear him say— "Beds? Wh-why?"

"I think maybe a little lie-down would be even better."

He didn't even give her the chance to respond. He gently, but firmly, took her elbow and guided her to the front hall and the staircase landing. Unfortunately not in that "Hurry! I must ravish you now!" kind of way. More in the way a person would when helping the frail and feeble-minded.

"And don't worry," he added dryly "I'll keep an eye out for Scary Lois."

Riley groaned again, her mortification complete. At least if she got him upstairs, she could redirect his attention to looking at the rooms, then slide back down, round up Brutus, and make her escape.

They were at the halfway landing when the entry chimes reverberated through the foyer, finally announcing the arrival of the piano delivery guys. How had she forgotten she still had a baby grand to stage? Not to mention there was foliage carnage to clean up.

It turned out the delivery guys weren't exactly Sven and Magnus.

More like Jeffy and T-Bone. Those were the names someone had actually stitched on their navy blue uniform shirts. She also doubted that either had enjoyed a modeling career. At any point in their lives. Though, with neither one of them clocking in at a day under sixty, who was to say that with less around the middle, and more on top of the head . . . and, well, teeth in the mouth, they might have, at one time, turned a lady's head.

Then Jeffy wedged a fingerload of Skoal inside his mouth and Riley thought . . . *then again, possibly not.*

"I'm—I need to go direct them to—" She didn't keep

explaining. She just turned to make her escape. "Go on up and look around."

Quinn shifted so she could pass by him to head back down the stairs. He put a guiding hand on the small of her back as she took the first step, which sent a delicious shiver over her skin she had no business feeling. *He is just being kind to the feeble,* she reminded herself. She put her hand on the railing, just to be safe. As she started down the stairs, she felt a tickling little tug at the back of her head and almost lost her balance all over again when she instinctively swatted at it . . . only to freeze momentarily when her hand came into contact with Quinn's. She glanced back to find him holding a small palm frond that he'd apparently plucked from her hair. He gave her the briefest of smiles as he tucked it discreetly behind his back.

Apparently her cheeks were never going to be any shade but flushed as long as she was around him. She managed to nod a quick thank-you before turning back to oversee the matter at hand.

Mercifully, the task quickly enabled her to get her footing back—and hopefully her equilibrium—as she directed the two men to put the piano in the space she'd saved in the Florida room at the rear of the home.

"What the heck happened to you, missy?" Jeffy asked, nodding toward her face.

"Slight mishap with the foliage," she said, which reminded her she still needed to clean up that mess. "Nothing to worry about. Here, this way," she directed, not even so much as glancing back at the staircase. She could all but feel that half-amused smile heating up the back of her neck. "Right through there."

The two men put down protective runners on the hardwood flooring and rolled the piano—frame-packed on its side—into the house and carefully angled it through the arched doorway.

Naturally, that was when Brutus's up-to-then nonexistent protective instincts kicked in. He didn't so much bark as emit a very loud *woofing* noise that came from somewhere deep inside his mutant-sized canine frame.

"Good gravy. What on God's green earth is that?" T-Bone paused in removing the packing from the piano legs to stare through the French doors at Brutus, who was staring directly back at T-Bone from his position on the other side of the dog-slobbered glass.

The same glass she'd spent half the morning cleaning. Lovely. "That's just . . . my dog. Don't worry. He's fine."

"I don't rightly know that it was his health that concerned me," T-Bone replied. With one eye carefully still aimed in the general direction of the deck, he went back to work.

"Must be like feeding a horse," Jeffy commented around the lump in his cheek, less worried than his partner. Actually, he looked like he was trying to gauge how many of his family members he might be able to feed hunting with Brutus.

"If you could just position it here, so it's out of the direct sun, but facing the windows and the ocean view, that would be perfect," Riley directed, trying to keep them—and herself—focused on the task at hand. She worked at setting the potted plants back to rights and sweeping up the dirt and plant detritus while they finished up.

"You know it ain't tuned or nothing," T-Bone said. "We just deliver. You want to play it, you'll have to get in touch with Marty and set up an appointment."

"Yes, thank you." She didn't need it to be in tune. It was just for show. She had specifically chosen some sheet music—Debussy's First Arabesque, perfect for sunsets—to place on the rack above the keys, but intended to keep the key cover down, so hopefully no one would actually touch it. Marty was one of her better contacts, and she didn't plan to do anything to change that.

By the time it was all said and done and she'd signed the paperwork stating she'd personally be responsible for any damage done to the piece before its return, Quinn was no longer in the immediate area. Assuming he'd gone off to look at the rest of the place, Riley took a moment, after ushering the men out the front door, to duck into the bathroom off the foyer.

"Yet another bad idea." She sighed as she catalogued the damages in the beveled vanity mirror positioned over the transparent glass pedestal sink. She hadn't thought it possible to look worse than she'd imagined, but she'd managed to pull that off. Making a stab at cooling off her face with cold water, she cleaned up the worst of the scrapes on her arms and hands. The dirt smears on her plaid camp shirt were beyond repair, but since it was still damp and rumpled from her sweaty Jog Master marathon, there was no point in trying to salvage it.

She smoothed her hair and rewound it back into the knobby bun she'd previously been sporting—before the palmetto fronds had yanked it down and to the side, like a drunken harlot's. She addressed her reflection as she snapped the puffy, sky blue braided elastic back into place. "This is your life, Riley Brown." Smirking at herself, she squared her shoulders and took one last inventory of the cuts and scrapes. It was either laugh, or cry. And she'd learned one thing for certain in her year on Sugarberry Island. "Laughing is a hell of a lot more fun."

Chapter 2

Quinn was standing on the back deck, with snapped-in-half pieces of a pretty decent size tree limb in either hand, when the curly-headed blonde found him. Well, them, really. "I didn't get your name, before."

"Riley," she responded as she crossed the deck. "Riley Brown."

"Quinn Brannigan," he offered in return, well aware she already knew his name, but being polite nonetheless.

That dry smile tugged at the corners of her outrageously compelling mouth. "A pleasure to make your acquaintance, though perhaps I'd have chosen a different way to greet you, had I to do it again."

"You do know how to make a lasting first impression," he said, hopefully appealing to her dry sense of humor.

The wry hint of a smile remained as she inclined her head and performed a quick curtsy, but it was the rather lovely shade of pink that suffused her freckled cheeks that ended up captivating him. "I'm quite the master of all-eyes-on-me entrances," she replied gamely, "just not always executed in the most preferable manner."

He chuckled at that, but not wanting to cause her further embarrassment, he shifted his gaze back to the beast. "He's not much for fetch, is he?"

"Search and destroy is more his idea of a rousing sport."

Quinn hefted the weight of the longer chunk of tree limb in his palm and looked to the far end of the property, past the small pool, toward the gardens and the dunes that lined up beyond it. "Yep. I'd say he's got scholarship potential in that department. What's his name?"

"Brutus." She held up a hand when he choked out a laugh. "I didn't name him. It really doesn't suit him at all."

"If you say so. Here you go, big fella." Quinn gripped the limb, pulled it back, then launched it like a javelin, in a high arc, over the pergola and the organic sea gardens, to the more sparsely designed pine-needle-carpeted rear of the property. Scrub-covered dunes formed the rear fence line, somewhere behind which, from what he could hear, was the ocean.

"Impressive." She followed the trajectory of the lofted limb with one hand framing her forehead to block out the sunlight. "High school quarterback, right? College, too, probably?"

"Nope. Too scrawny. Track and field. Decathalon." He smiled as he watched the limb sail. "Didn't know I still had it."

Quinn thought she might have muttered something under her breath after that last comment, but he didn't quite catch it. His attention was still on the beast.

Brutus remained seated next to him and calmly tracked the branch's entire trajectory along with them, not overly excited about the pitch or the game as far as Quinn could tell. Only after it hit the ground, stirring up a little cloud of pine needles and dried palm fronds, did the monster-truck-sized dog set off in a deliberate but unhurried trot down the tiled walkway.

"I guess I can see why he doesn't really feel the pressure to exert himself," Quinn commented. "Even if he's not first to the prize, who's going to keep it from him, right?"

"He's really a big, gooey sweetheart." Riley walked over to stand beside Quinn. "Wouldn't hurt a flea."

"Not unless the flea was trying to take away his big stick." Quinn waggled the shorter end of the limb he still held in one hand, before tossing it in the hedgerow that edged the deck.

"He only cracked the stick because he thought you were playing tug-of-war. He loves tug-of-war."

"I'll bet. It's always fun to play games you never lose."

She laughed. "I wouldn't know much about that." She turned to watch her pet beast trotting back, tree limb clenched in his mighty jaws, but Quinn hadn't missed the brief wince when she'd laughed, or the way she'd reached up to put her hand over the worst of the scratches on her face.

She'd gamely applied her sense of humor to the whole ordeal, taking her bad spill with a great deal of grace. It was pretty much the only thing graceful about her, at least that he'd witnessed thus far. Perhaps his reaction simply came from long-evolved instinct. Having spent most of his formative years as a fast-growing young man with an awkward command of his gangly body, he understood what it was like to wish gawky, long limbs would behave in a more coordinated fashion. Though she was obviously well past her formative years—as was he—just because he'd outgrown gawky didn't mean he wasn't empathetic to those who never did.

While she'd appeared to be a bit of an uncoordinated klutz, ditzy she definitely was not. Despite the bountiful blond curls and farm girl freckles framing that intriguingly deluxe set of lips, those big brown eyes of hers didn't miss much, he guessed.

Brutus trotted up and plopped himself on his butt right in front of Riley, dropping the branch on her toes, then looking up at her with what could only be termed pride and a great deal of self-satisfaction. "You're such a good boy." She rubbed his massive head, which leveled out above her hips, as if he were nothing more than a wriggling pup, needing approval. "Scoot," she told the dog, then bent down and picked up the stick.

Brutus instantly shifted his stance and faced Quinn, eyes alert, jaw tense.

"What?" Quinn said, holding up his empty hands, palms out. "I don't have the stick, she does."

Riley laughed. "Yes, but he knows I can't throw. He also knows, now, that you can."

"Ah."

She shadowed her eyes again when she turned and looked up at him. She didn't have to look up as far as most people, and he discovered he rather liked that about her. Perhaps still a bit gawky as a woman grown, her body was anything but. Lush was the word he'd use to describe the abundant curves that wrapped around her sturdy frame. Combine all that with the greater than average height, the equally lush mouth, and all those blond curls, and, klutzy or not, she was a definite attention getter. Actually, it was the klutzy part, and those farm girl freckles, that made the otherwise bombshell body all the more interesting. She'd gotten his attention anyway.

"Not much of a dog person, huh?" she said.

"I love dogs. Had them all growing up. It's just . . . been a while. Also, the dogs I had as a boy were a mite smaller than a half-ton pickup truck."

She smile-winced again, then looked away. "It's okay. Most folks don't look past the size to the heart."

She was talking about the dog, but something in her tone made him believe she meant something else entirely.

Herself maybe? He felt like he'd been judged, and found lacking. Or, worse, predictable. He wasn't sure why that stung—but it did—or why he cared what she thought, but apparently, he did.

Before he could decide how he wanted to respond, she dug into the side pocket of her bleached white khaki trousers and came out with the world's largest dog biscuit, then slapped her leg.

"Come on, Brutus, let's get you out in the Jeep." She started off toward a gate in the fence that framed the sides of the backyard. "I'll be back in. I've got to finish setting up the breakfast nook area with the food. Lois should be here momentarily, and he needs to not be here when that happens." She glanced over her shoulder as she opened the gate for Brutus. "I know it's asking a lot, but I'd really appreciate it if we could keep my catastrophe in there our little secret."

"Given it was my fault, I don't see how that's a favor."

Her lips curved briefly. "You're being very kind. It was going to have a bad end, no matter what. I just—well, thanks. I owe you one." She let herself out the gate and trotted after Brutus, who was already out of sight before Quinn could reply.

She really was the damnedest thing. And despite her attention-getting frame, not at all his type. That thought annoyed him. He liked to think he didn't have a type, that he took everyone he met as he found them. Maybe it was just that he'd never met anyone quite like her. He didn't know what to think about that.

Not that it mattered. He wasn't there to socialize. He was there to focus, to get a firm handle on his next book. The last thing he needed was Claire making her politely professional but pointed phone calls as the publisher started pressuring her for a due date, or worse, for his agent, Lenore, to start in. *If they only knew the depth of the concern they should already be having.*

The real reason he'd come back to Sugarberry Island was in hopes it would remind him of the handful of summers he'd spent there as a teenager with his grandfather, and, more important, the wisdom his grandfather had passed down to him. Quinn had to figure out what direction to take, not only with the manuscript in question, but with his career. He wished his grandfather were still alive, but hoped just being back would give him the balance and perspective he needed to think things through and make the best decision possible.

And to get on with the damn book. One way or the other.

Did he take the path he always took, the one he knew his readers wanted him to take? Or did he risk everything, and continue down the new, tantalizing trail that was calling to him, the one he had no idea if anyone would take along with him? He smiled at that and shook his head. "Being predictable. Good or bad? Right or wrong?"

He went inside and found Riley in the breakfast nook, putting the final touches on the crystal display stand filled with amazing-looking, heavily topped cupcakes. He didn't have a huge sweet tooth, but looking at them made his mouth water and his stomach grumble a little with the reminder that he'd only fed it toast and coffee thus far that day. "Those look incredible."

She squealed and dropped the cupcake she'd been carefully sliding onto the top tier, which in turn, hit the cupcake on the tier just below it . . . and, of course, both plopped down to wipe out the entire side of the bottom tier.

"Oh, no. I'm so—"

"Sorry," she finished for him, sighing as she stared at the cupcake catastrophe. "Now I know why you write mystery novels. You're naturally stealthy."

"I like to think it's more about being observant, but I suppose if I truly was, I'd have noted your focused concentration and done something to announce myself before I spoke. The cupcakes just got my attention." He entered the nook area and stepped over to the display. "I am sorry, though."

Reaching out, he scraped a dollop of frosting from where it had been clinging to the side of the middle tier and licked it off his finger. "Wow"—he groaned a little as he swallowed—"if the cake part tastes half as good, you can leave them all right there in a pile. I'll just get a fork."

"Unfortunately, I can't leave them looking like that. The open house officially opens in"—she glanced at the clock and blanched—"fifteen minutes. I've got more of these stashed in the fridge, but I'll have to clean off—" She stopped talking and started moving.

He was savoring another scraped-off dollop of the rich, creamy frosting, so he stopped her the only way he knew how. He reached for her arm, turning her back to face him, belatedly realizing as she looked in surprise to where he held her, that he'd reached for her with his frosting-fingered hand. "Oops," he said, when she lifted her disbelieving gaze to his. He tried out his best disarming grin. "I don't suppose you have any ice-cold milk to go with these?"

Her mouth dropped open, and suddenly he forgot all about the cupcakes, distracted once again by her mouth. It matched her body, but was so incongruous with the splashy freckles and big, brown doe eyes.

At the moment, all he could think was how incredibly decadent those lips would be with frosting tipping the bowed curves in the middle and . . .

Still holding on to her arm, he impulsively reached out and snagged another cupcake—a perfectly intact one—and held it up to her mouth. "Have you tried one?"

"Mr. Brannigan—"

"Quinn. Please. And I'm not kidding. Try this." He nudged the cupcake closer to her mouth. "I'll replace the shirt. And the ruined cupcakes. Did you make these?"

"No, my friend Leilani Dunne made them. She owns the Cakes by the Cup bakery, in town. Now I really"—she tugged at her arm, gently but firmly—"need to get this display finished before—"

"What you really need is to try this." He drew her and the cupcake he'd proffered closer. He had no idea, less than zero, actually, why he was doing it, but couldn't seem to stop. The more annoyed she became, the more determined he grew. "After the day you've had, you've earned it." He nudged the frosting to her lips, leaving a chocolate smudge.

He'd been teasing, telling himself he'd wanted to make her smile again. He hadn't meant to smear frosting on her lips, but tell that to his body, which jerked instantly to attention. When his gaze shifted to that sweet little dab of chocolate fascination clinging to her lips, he was gripped by an almost overwhelming urge to take another little lick of frosting. A very specific little lick.

Her tongue darted out to remove the temptation, increasing his discomfort . . . and his impulsive urges.

"Why are you—"

"I honestly don't know. But you've got frosting on you now." He nudged the cupcake toward her again, careful not to leave any traces. He smiled as she narrowed her gaze. "Might as well, right? It's incredible, I promise."

"Mr.—Quinn—I really have to—" She broke off, and looked back at the wrecked display. "Lois is due any second, and I don't want her to find me standing here in the midst of cupcake carnage, sampling the wares, so to speak."

His body jerked to renewed attention, needlessly reminding him of just whose wares he'd really rather she sample. "She won't. I mean Scary Lois won't. Be coming. Not today."

"But, how is that possible? I can't run the open house, it's not my function. Besides, she has all the—is she okay? Has something happened?"

"She's fine, and yes, something has happened. While you were setting up the piano, I called my manager and had him make an offer on the place. A very nice offer."

"You—did what?"

"Leased the place. I believe there is a flurry of faxes going on between Scary Lois and even scarier David as I speak. I'm sure I'll have to sign something at some point, but the deal is done."

"So . . . no open house."

"No open house."

"But . . . it's been advertised. People will show up."

"Then they'll be disappointed to find a sign on the front door telling them the property is no longer available. I suppose I should go take care of that."

"Right, but—"

"But first . . . honestly, try this."

She stared at him over the top of the cupcake. "Are you always like this?"

"Like what?" He grinned. "Unpredictable?"

He watched as her gaze darted from his eyes, to his mouth, and back to his eyes again. Her pupils expanded, her brown eyes growing darker and deeper as her throat worked and the muscles in her arms tensed—quivered, actually. He wrote, in great detail, about all those little, tell-tale signs that took place when someone was aroused. Though, admittedly, it had been a while, a good long while, since he'd had an opportunity to personally observe them.

"That's not entirely a bad thing, is it?" he asked.

"Uh, no," she managed, still all hung up in his very direct gaze. "No, I guess it's not."

"Good. Now . . . lick."

She did—which surprised him, though he wasn't sure why. He'd expected an eye roll. Or a cupcake shoved into his face. Either of which he'd have deserved. Having brought her up earlier, he absently wondered what Grams would say about his rather . . . assertive behavior. But those fleeting thoughts vanished when Riley immediately closed her eyes and made a sound in the back of her throat as the rich chocolate coated her tongue, in that instinctive way a person did who was naturally, even viscerally connected to the sensuality of experience. Smell . . . taste . . . touch . . . Watching her, he felt a very distinct, deep-in-the-gut quiver of his own.

"Lani," she murmured. "Once again, you rule."

"Possibly the patron saint of baking," Quinn agreed, almost reverently, as he continued to watch, fixated, as she finished enjoying every last creamy bite.

She opened her eyes, and caught him watching—staring, really—and her cheeks bloomed once again. "I—" She tugged her arm free and took a short step back. "You—just, uh, let me know when you'll be moving your stuff in and I'll make sure to have all the staging furnishings and decor out of here. I, uh, it will take at least two days, but I could easily have everything ready for move-in by the weekend."

She jerked her gaze to his hand, which still held the cupcake, then back to his face again. He couldn't tell what was behind the hunger clearly written on her face, but it didn't seem to matter to every inch of his anatomy. Some inches more newly invigorated than others.

"I just have to make a few calls."

"I offered for it as is," he said, not any more in control than she appeared to be. Perhaps for entirely different reasons, but still proving that while unpredictability might be exciting, it wasn't exactly without risks. A point to remember.

"Oh. Oh! Well . . ." She gazed around a bit wildly.

Maybe it was just his interpretation. His own pulse was like a jungle beat at the moment.

"I guess I should just . . . uh, go then. I'll go." She looked back at him, and smiled brightly, though it didn't reach her eyes, which were still kind of half glazed. "If you have any questions, Lois can just—or you could call me. Or—David, was that his name? He could. Actually, you should. Call me, I mean. I'm the one with the contacts for the furnishings and I'm here on Sugarberry, too. Full-time. So, anything you don't want, I can just—do you want me to clean this up?" She gestured haphazardly toward the mangled display. "No," she answered herself when his gaze dipped to her mouth again. "Okay, I'll just—I'll go. Now."

He was still standing by the ruined cupcake display, cupcake in hand, as he heard the door shut and the crank of her Jeep engine a moment later. He rather thought the sound of sprayed gravel, indicating she'd torn out of his driveway like the proverbial bat out of hell, was perhaps a bit of an extreme reaction to the situation. Until he tried to take a step and realized he was so hard and his jeans so accordingly tight that he could barely move without risking damaging something . . . and decided maybe she'd had the right idea all along.

"Focus," he said. "You came here to focus." He promised himself he'd get on with it . . . just as soon as he finished every last bit of the cupcake in his hand. The one with the dollop of frosting missing. And that's exactly what he did, without questioning why, right down to the last swirl, fleck, and crumb. Savoring each bite, he stared at the ruined cake display, imagining how differently the afternoon might have gone if he'd simply pushed her back onto the breakfast nook table, peeled open her blouse, and drawn one of those frosted cups of heaven over the rosy tips of what he knew would be lovely, lush breasts . . . then followed up with his tongue. He wondered if her senses were engaged so rapturously when involved with pleasures of the flesh, rather than the decadent results of cleverly combined amounts of flour, butter, and sugar . . . and already believed he knew the answer to that question. A sensualist was a sensualist.

He groaned at the new round of images that idea brought to mind, tossed the crumpled paper on the table, and went off to find out how well the advertised drenching showerheads worked when they were set on ice cold.

Ten minutes later, when that hadn't worked, he switched to steam heat. At least, for the following ten minutes or so, he remained focused on something.

Chapter 3

"Land sakes! What on earth did you get tangled up with?" Alva Liles, the most senior member of the Cupcake Club, didn't add *this time,* but it was implied.

"Whatever it was, I think you lost." Young Dre, whose hairnet-draped purple Mohawk never failed to make Riley smile, immediately hunched back over a white fondant-draped layer of cake, intently focused on squeezing out perfect rose petal after perfect rose petal along the curved edge. Four more individual tiers were on the stainless-steel table behind her, each covered with hundreds, if not thousands, of roses in all shapes and sizes. Dre took the practice-makes-perfect mantra to new and dedicated heights.

Riley hung her purse up on one of the apron hooks, and slid her HELLO KITTY apron off another, quickly looping the neck strap over her head and tying the dangling waist straps behind her hips. She liked the whimsical aprons that every Cupcake Club member adopted, inspired by Leilani's lifelong collection. It was certainly more fun and more comfortable than the chef's jackets she'd often worn in her previous life.

"What are you working on tonight, Miss Alva?" Riley

knew full well the entire story of her lacerated self would come out, but she wasn't quite ready to entertain the troops with her latest misadventure. Actually, she didn't want to talk about Quinn Brannigan at all. He might not be able to read her thoughts—or maybe he had—but she knew her fellow baking buddies never missed a thing.

"Hey, you're here," Leilani said, as she bumped open the swinging door leading from the shop front of the bakery to the decently sized kitchen area, where they all gathered every Monday night after the shop closed early. She was around the same age as Riley, much shorter but sturdy, with light brown hair, usually pulled back in a haphazard ponytail, and a calm, competent demeanor that somehow managed to keep everything controlled and sane, even in the midst of chaos. "I have a new cake flavor I want you to try," she told them. "It's my take on a Dreamsicle."

Everyone let out a collective "yum."

"They just need to rest another five minutes, then I'll frost and we're all doing a taste test."

"Once again it does not suck to be us." Riley hauled her toolbox and quilted supply tote over to an empty space on the far stainless-steel worktable to set up shop. The bakery was situated on the main floor of an old rowhouse style shop, with the retail area out front taking up only slightly more than a front room or parlor's worth of space. The lion's share of the first floor was dedicated to the kitchen. Riley had initially questioned the inequitable division of space, thinking it made more sense to put on a splashier display up front, but, of course, that was her styling background speaking. For her, it was all about the presentation.

For Lani, it was all about the preparation. As Riley's friendship with Lani had developed, she'd quickly come to learn, the former Leilani Trusdale had been a James Beard–nominated executive pastry chef at New York City's famous Gateau patisserie. The pastry shop was still owned by her now-husband, Baxter Dunne, the famous British pastry chef seen weekly by millions of adoring fans—Riley included—on his network television cooking show, *Hot Cakes.*

Lani and Baxter, who'd gotten married just before Riley had moved to Georgia, were quite happily ensconced islanders now—Baxter taping his show in a gorgeous plantation house just over the causeway on the outskirts of Savannah, and Lani running her own little cupcake bakery on Sugarberry. When the big-city girl had initially designed her new little rural island shop space, she'd given in to her penchant to retain the one thing from her former life that she truly hadn't wanted to give up—the fully locked and loaded, professionally appointed kitchen her former profession demanded.

"Where's Franco?" Riley asked, referring to Leilani's swarthy, Bronx-born Italian pal, whom Lani had known and worked with, back in New York. He and their mutual friend, Charlotte, had also migrated south and set up a catering business in Savannah. Charlotte was involved with Carlo, one of Baxter's prep chefs from his television show. Franco was big, gorgeous, gay, and spoke with an affected French accent that made absolutely no sense, but was utterly and exactly Franco.

"He's in Savannah for the next few days, helping Baxter finish up the last part of this season's shoot. They're trying to piggyback the final three episodes and get them done in the time it normally takes to do one, so Bax can have a little extra time to finish up his next cookbook. With the first one out for over a month now, he was supposed to already have this one in to the publisher. But with the show moving to a major network after last season, and all the press he was asked to do for that and the cookbook release, well . . . you've heard me bitch about it all before. I swear, the man is superhuman. But now, added to that, one of Baxter's chefs is out with the flu. So Franco is stepping in to help."

Riley looked concerned at the news, and Dre noticed. She looked up long enough to say, "Don't worry. The son-of-a-bitch traitor is gone."

Riley's brows climbed halfway up her forehead, which made her flinch. Resisting the urge to press a cool palm to her scratched-up face, she said, "Brenton's gone?" referring to Franco's soul mate life partner. His *former* soul mate life partner. The son-of-a-bitch traitor. "As in *gone*-gone?"

Dre nodded, making her newly installed eyebrow ring—a bit bigger than her other two—jiggle with the motion. The weight of what looked like a tiny dragon charm hanging from a tiny loop on the ring added to the sway.

"Got an offer two days ago from a new place out in San Francisco," Dre explained. "Took it."

"Baxter was relieved when he turned in his notice," Lani added. "Told him he didn't need the two weeks, to just head on out. Brenton was gone that day. If Baxter could have fired him for what he did to Franco, he would have, but it wasn't business-related and—"

"We know. No one blames Baxter." Riley said. "I don't know how Franco managed to help out on the show as much as he did."

"Baxter tried to mitigate that," Lani said. "It wasn't fair to not give Franco the work, especially since Carlo has partnered in with them to launch Sweet and Savory. We all know Franco's still doing a lot of work with the catering business, but I think, with Brenton out of the picture, he was feeling kind of homeless. I was honestly worried he might go back to New York.

"Baxter offered him a full-time gig with the show almost before Brenton had left the building, but Franco hasn't agreed to take it yet. I think for the time being he's planning to bounce back and forth from his continuing work with Char and Carlo to helping Bax out when he can."

"As long as Brenton is gone and Franco is still here, I'm happy," Riley said.

"Damn straight," Dre muttered, then groaned. "God, no pun, no pun."

Everyone groaned with her, then Lani added, "Franco will be here later, though. He's coming back with Baxter this evening. And guess what?" Lani wiggled her eyebrows. "I think he had company night before last."

"He did," Alva confirmed. "The kind you cook breakfast for," she added, in case anyone hadn't picked up on the inference.

Everyone turned to look at Alva, eyebrows lifted in question, but she merely lifted a shoulder. "We talk." She beamed at the assembled group. "I told Franco to bring his friend along so we could meet him."

"When did you talk to Franco?" Lani asked.

"Never you mind, missy. Franco and me, we're snug."

Riley and Lani laughed at that. Even Dre's lips threatened a smile.

"Tight," Dre finally offered when Alva looked surprised by the laughter.

"What's tight?" Alva patted her perfectly teased and lacquered bouffant of white hair, while looking down at her expertly pressed and color-coordinated hot pink tracksuit. Riley was pretty sure the feisty octogenarian was the only woman who could wear pearls with a tracksuit and make it work.

"You and Franco." When Alva merely looked confused, Dre sighed. "Never mind."

"I don't see what's so funny," Alva said, clearly a bit miffed. "Franco is family and we look out for family. We don't know anything about this new young man. Who his people are, where he's from, what his designs are on our boy."

"If anyone is doing the designing, I'm pretty sure it's Franco," Dre offered in the kind of laconic drawl only a twenty-one-year-old, disaffected art school student could pull off with any real authenticity. Dre nailed it regularly.

"Be that as it may, I still say we should meet this young man sooner rather than later."

"I'm sure if shared breakfasts become a regular part of Franco's routine, we will," Lani said.

Riley began unpacking her supplies for her evening's baking endeavor, happy not to be the focus of the conversation. She'd gotten a workstation that would keep her back conveniently aimed at the kitchen's occupants, as opposed to her scratched-up face.

"Well," Alva said, "if he doesn't, I'll just drop by unannounced with a pan of my blueberry crumble." She smiled the innocent, twinkly smile of the elderly that everyone in the room knew to be a blatant and utterly false cover for her devious and perfectly sharp eighty-three-year-old mind, and went right back to work, humming as she triple sifted another two cups of cake flour.

Riley smiled to herself, privately hoping she'd be half the woman Alva Liles was by the time she reached the woman's advanced age. Half her age, even. Heck, given Riley's propensity for causing herself personal harm, she'd be thrilled to reach Alva's age at all.

Just then Franco swung through the back door, with all of his typical "making an entrance" insouciance. "*Bonsoir, mes amies!*" he announced cheerfully. "How are all the lovely bakers of *les petites cakes* this fine, fine hot August night? Speaking of hot August nights, Lani, do you have any old Neil Diamond on hand? I think we need a little 'Cracklin' Rosie' or 'Sweet Caroline.'" He grinned and made a show of primping his hair. "You can skip 'Solitary Man,' though."

"Wahoo!" Lani hooted. "You know, I think I might be able to accommodate you." It was well known, at least among the group, that when alone in her kitchen, Lani often baked while shaking her groove thing to old movie soundtracks, hard-driving rock and roll, and dance music. On many occasions, they "pumped up the jam," as Charlotte put it, her proper Indian dialect making the eighties song phrase particularly amusing, at least to Riley, who laughed every time Char said it.

As yet, no one had turned on the stereo that particular evening. Last time they had was two weeks prior when Alva had brought in her latest contribution, a CD from that "very nice-looking boy" Justin Bieber.

Riley tried not to smile and make her scratches sting again, but remembering Alva waltzing about the kitchen while lip synching "Baby, baby, oh," made it pretty much impossible. Of course, considering Alva's previous offering had been the *Best of John Denver*, she'd be happy to keep the Bieber on permanent rotation if it meant they never had to listen to Alva actually sing along to "Thank God I'm a Country Boy." Ever again.

"Let me see what I've got." Lani tipped up on her toes to buss him loudly on the cheek as she passed by on her way to the stereo cabinet. "Where's Baxter?"

Even though she'd been married for over a year now, Lani's eyes still sparkled like a newlywed's whenever she so much as said her husband's name. If possible, Baxter was even worse. Or better, depending on how you looked at it. Riley looked at it happily, for the fairy-tale-come-to-life that it was. So what if she suffered a few incredibly selfish pangs of envy? That was her problem, not Lani and Baxter's.

"He told me to tell you he was going by the house first,

toute suite, then will be by with some leftovers from today's shoot." Franco folded his arms and smiled a very smug smile. "And it won't be Baxter's baking, either. Guess who dropped by today?"

Lani turned around. "Who?"

"Let's just say somebody wanted a little throwdown with Chef Hot Cakes."

Lani's mouth dropped open. "No way! My TV chef boyfriend, Bobby Flay? Right in our Savannah house kitchen? And no one called me?" She made a little squeaking sound of outrage.

"Calm down, sister," Franco said, the accent disappearing, as it often did when he was giving Lani a hard time. "It wasn't a real throwdown. He was in town to see Miss Paula and came by to check out the setup, have a little chat. And, you know how it is . . . cooking happens." He went over to Lani and put a consoling arm around her shoulders, though his shameless grin was anything but. "You get to eat your TV chef boyfriend's amazing barbeque, so all is not lost."

Lani groaned. "He made barbeque." She dragged out the last word on a deep sigh of abject appreciation mixed with a healthy bit of envy.

"It was the end of the day. That's why we're late. He wasn't there long enough for you to get across the causeway."

"Fine, fine. But I'm like an elephant," she said, tapping her forehead. "I don't forget these things." She poked Franco in the chest. "You get to be the one to tell Char what she missed when she gets back." Lani took smug pleasure from Franco's blanched expression. "And no Neil for you. Tonight, we bake along with . . ." She whirled around and punched the play button, then spun back as the opening strains of "Ice Ice Baby" smoothed into the room, making Franco groan, as she'd known it would. As they'd all known it would. "Oh yes, my smug, Bobby Flay barbeque-eating friend, it's harem pants on the dance floor night!"

Riley barely swallowed her smile as Franco spun away in aggrieved disgust.

"Does that mean it's going to be Hammer Time?" Alva asked. "Oh, goodie." She wiggled her hips as she spun the sifter handle, spraying a fine mist of white flour all over her workstation.

It was at that point Riley lost the battle entirely. Scratched face be damned. She loved these people. She laughed and boogied herself as she continued to unpack her supplies, humming with the bass line as she unrolled her knives.

"I hope he's bringing enough for everyone," Alva said.

"*Oui, oui, mes amies,*" Franco said, his joie de vivre making a swift return. "Have no fear. And it is, I must say, *que magnifique.*" Franco kissed his fingertips.

Lani rubbed her hands together in anticipation as she boogied her way back to where she'd prepped to frost her Dreamsicle cakes. "MC Hammer, eat your heart out. Are you baking tonight," she asked Franco, "or just playing taste tester after being in the studio kitchens all day? Eating barbeque, and making goo-goo eyes at my TV boyfriend."

"May I respectfully remind you that both you and your TV boyfriend are happily married? To other people. As for me"—Franco's accent thickened—"tonight I will be baking zee perfect petite red velvet cakes, as I am in need of sweets for serving." He turned and shot a wink at Riley, who, still in her happy Hammer Time place, winked right back.

"Sounds like we all have a plan then. Oh, Dreamsicle taste test in five minutes," Lani told him. "New flavor I'm thinking of adding to the shop menu."

"I vote it's dreamy," Franco sang, giving in and moving to the beat as he shook out and put on the required crazy apron. Tonight he was sporting one of his standards, the always amusing Charlie's Angels apron that Dre and some of her graphic artist cohorts had made for his last birthday.

"But then"—he assumed, as he did each and every time he donned the apron, all three Angel poses, with amazingly accurate precision—"everything in my world is dreamy." As soon as he finished the Farrah pose—always the last one—Franco twirled around and placed his tool tote perfectly at the empty space right next to Riley.

Riley marveled, as she always did, how a man his size could be so utterly graceful. If she'd tried even a fraction of that move, she'd have taken out half the kitchen and sent at least three of them to the ER. On a good night.

She wrapped an arm around his waist and leaned in to give him a quick squeeze. "It's so good to see you like this."

"It's good to be like this, *mon cher*." His deep, basso voice, was sweet and ardently sincere.

So many times, especially right after it had happened, when Franco had been at his lowest, Riley had wanted to meet with him privately, to commiserate. But nothing was private on Sugarberry, and though she knew Franco had a great big wonderful heart, she also knew he couldn't keep a secret to save his own life. So, she'd done her best to be there for him in every way she could, but had always felt a bit guilty for not being more open with him. God knows they'd all been open about all sorts of things. She was so thankful, so incredibly thankful, for their friendship and the sisterhood that had evolved—Franco included—during the time they'd spent together.

She'd come to Sugarberry essentially to hide out and lick her wounds, with no real idea of where she'd head from there. She'd only known the one place she didn't want to be. What she'd found instead, without even looking, was so much greater than anything she could have ever hoped for. Almost thirteen months later, it was no longer a temporary port of call. The island had become home.

"What on earth?"

Riley jumped as she suddenly found her chin gently but firmly cupped in Franco's very broad palm as he turned her face to his.

"Who did this to you, *mon cher*?"

"Who do you think?" she said, through distorted lips.

He turned her head to one side, then the other, before letting his hand drop away.

"You know me." Using her fingers, she made a quick *L* on her forehead. "I . . . kind of fell off a treadmill into a bunch of plants, okay?" She spoke quietly, so as not to alert the rest of the gang.

So much for that. Eagle ears Alva turned right around. "What's going on? What were you doing on a treadmill?"

Dre and Lani looked up then, as well.

Riley sighed. "You know the Turner house—"

"Don't get me started on the Turner house," Alva said. "Monstrosity. I can't believe what they did to that place."

"Looks pretty awesome if you ask me," Dre said.

Everyone looked at her in surprise.

"What? Just because I dress like a street orphan doesn't mean I don't appreciate the finer things of life. I happen to appreciate comfort, that's all. I went by the place back when they completed the exterior. They expanded the rooflines, added the sunroom, but maintained the traditional style . . . and the landscaping is stellar. Shows what you can do with a little ingenuity in this scrubby, sea-salted wilderness. Even though it's upscale, it's really modestly done, not so gaudy and obvious like the ones in the lower islands. I thought the concept was respectful of the traditional, yet celebrated a unique vision." She shrugged. "Just my take."

Alva harrumphed. "We'll see how unique you think it is when the other developers start crawling all over the island, trying to get us to sell our properties so they can flop them to some of those country club snoots."

"Flip," Lani said. "Flip the houses."

"Flip houses, flop houses, I don't care what you call it. I think it'll be the ruination of our little island, and our quiet way of life. We like things peaceful and slow. We don't need fancy-shmancy. And I'm not afraid to say that I was a bit surprised you took the job." Alva looked right at Riley.

"She has to work." Lani tossed an apologetic look Riley's way.

"She's got a whole slew of islands south of here that love nothing more than to play Out-Jones-the-Joneses. We don't need to encourage it here."

"The house had already been renovated when I was offered the job to stage it," Riley reminded her mildly. "All I did was help get it back off the market and into the private sector as fast as possible."

"And did you?" Lani asked. "Was there a taker today?"

"Um, yeah, as a matter of fact, there was." To Alva, Riley added, "You'll be happy to know they didn't even end up holding the open house. It was snapped up beforehand." She made herself busy taking out the ingredients she'd brought along. "No one else traipsed through it, no investors pretending to be buyers. Hopefully this will be a one and done."

"Really?" This from Lani. "Wow, that's kind of unexpected. Who would take a place sight unseen?"

"I'll tell you who," Alva said. "The Jones-busters, that's who."

Dre snickered, but swiftly returned to her so-bored-too-cool expression when Alva spun her sifter in Dre's direction. Lani and Franco snickered at that. A little. Alva just gave them the eye.

Lani looked at Riley then. "Do you know who rented it?"

But it was Franco, standing right next to her, who spoke first. "Ooh, la la, *ma chère*, is that a blush *la rouge* I see blooming on those lovely luscious cheeks?"

Riley smacked away Franco's hands, but he was still beaming. "Do tell, my sweet. We'll find out soon enough anyway." He rested his hips on the edge of the worktable and folded his arms across his expansive chest. When she didn't immediately comply, he scooted a bit closer, then a bit closer still, until he could bump hips with her—which he did. Repeatedly.

"Franco." Riley knew she was doomed. So, after a brief sigh, she turned to face the room, reminding herself again how great it was to have such close friends.

"Oh, good." Franco clapped his hands together. "Leave out nothing juicy. And it's juicy, am I right?" He looked at the assembled group, each one of them having completely abandoned their baking projects. "It's juicy," he assured them. "Spill it."

"You're the one with the secret boy toy news," Riley retorted. "You spill it."

"The difference, *ma fleur hauteur,* is that *I* want to share my news. Fair to bursting with it I am. But I promised myself I'd go slower next time, moderate my enthusiasm. You, on the other hand, don't want to tell us a peep—which automatically makes yours far more delicious." He crossed his ankles and batted his insanely luxurious and enviably naturally thick black eyelashes. "You know me, dog with a bone. I could put Brutus to shame. We're going to find out anyway." He warbled the last word.

"Okay, okay." Riley nudged him back a little. But she still took another moment to figure out how best to share only the parts she really wanted to share. She wasn't going to humiliate herself all over again by explaining the whole Jog Master thing. She was taking the rest of the day off from abject mortification. And she certainly wasn't going to talk about what she'd come to think of as the Cupcake Moment. She still had no idea what to think about all that.

But Franco was right about the rest not staying a secret. "It's Quinn Brannigan."

Alva and Dre frowned, but Lani and Franco's mouths dropped open.

"Seriously?" This from Lani.

"As a heart attack," Riley said. "Which is what I almost had when he came into the house early and startled the daylights out of me."

Franco laughed, but then reached out to gently touch her cheek. "Ah, now I understand." His eyes twinkled affectionately, even as he tsk-tsked.

She swatted his hand away anyway. "Quinn took one look at the place and called his manager. Done deal." She shrugged. "End of story." She turned back to her bag and began unpacking her supplies.

" 'Quinn,' is it? End of story, my saggy senior patootie," Alva said.

Everyone spluttered a laugh at that, even Dre.

"Honey, you have a very fine senior patootie," Franco said, slipping into the Bronx borough dialect of his birth, except he sounded like gay Rocky. "Ain't nuthin' saggy 'bout that, sister."

It made everyone laugh even harder, except for Alva, who preened a little bit.

"Why, thank you, Franco, dear." She gave him her sweetest smile. "What can I say?" She turned to the rest of them, patting her coiffed curls once again. "The French know how to appreciate a real woman."

Not a single one of them attempted to correct her. About most things, Alva was one of the sharpest tacks on the board, but there were rare occasions when she was delightfully clueless in the way most would associate with someone her age. Or at least she did a damn good job of pretending to be. Riley was never quite certain.

"Now, Miss Riley May," Alva said, "are you going to tell us the rest of the story?"

Alva added "May" to everyone's name, except Franco and Baxter, especially when she wanted something from them. Riley had learned it was sort of a Southern endearment, and had never minded it much. In fact, it was rather sweet. If you overlooked the whole underlying manipulation part.

"There is no rest, Miss Alva. It's a six-month lease. He's here, I assume, to get some peace and quiet to work on his next book. There's really nothing more to add. He's taking the house as is, so I don't even have to ship back the staged furnishings. Win-win."

Alva merely folded her arms over her My Little Pony apron—the very same one Lani had saved since childhood, and which also happened to be the only one that would fit Alva's tiny-as-a-bird frame.

Riley sighed again. "I don't think he's going to be throwing any swanky parties with snotty guests, if that's what you're worried about. In fact, it's my guess he'd like nothing more than to be left alone while he's here."

"So, you talked to him." Lani inched closer. "Tell us, is he as dreamy as he looks on the jackets of his books?"

Riley gave up. "Dreamier," she admitted. Every last person in the room sighed.

"Do tell," Franco said. "Details. The eyes?"

"Yes, they are that blue. Bluer, if possible."

"I bet he's shorter in person. Those movie stars always are," Alva said.

"He's a writer, not a movie star, but no," Riley assured her, "he's not at all short. Quite the opposite. Quite," she added, before she could stop herself.

"And?" Lani begged her to continue.

"And, that's pretty much it. He's tall, tanned, gorgeous,

with just a flavoring hint of a Southern accent. And a really deep voice."

"My, my." Alva fanned herself with her recipe card, sending a coating of finely sifted flour all down the front of her apron.

"Do you read his books?" Lani asked Alva. "I didn't think you recognized the name when Riley said it. I'm not surprised, though. He writes some pretty gritty stuff."

"Some pretty sexy stuff, too," Dre murmured.

Lani turned back around, and Riley looked at Dre, as well. But Dre was busily making more roses. A lot more roses. Like it was her damn job.

"So, you know who he is, too." Lani said to her.

"Duh," Dre said, not looking up. "He's a household name. Like Grisham, Patterson, and King. Who hasn't? I was just surprised he'd come to Sugarberry."

"How do you know about the sexy stuff?" Lani asked her.

Dre looked up, and blinked through the hot-pink-and-black leopard-print cat-eye cheaters she'd put on, the girlishness of which was in complete contrast to the overall goth-darkness of the rest of her ensemble. Riley was fairly certain that was exactly why Dre had chosen them. She was nothing if not a fan of incongruity, two thousand identical paste roses notwithstanding. Perched on the end of her nose, they only partially hid the four rings now piercing her left eyebrow, but left entirely visible the diagonal lines she'd shaved across the other.

With great patience, Dre tipped her head back so she could look down her nose through her crazy eyeglasses, which, Riley had to admit, did go with her much-favored Johnny Depp Mad Hatter apron. "I realize I have the body of a twelve-year-old boy, and the relative height of said twelve-year-old boy's ten-year-old brother. But I assure you, at the age of twenty-one, I do know about the sexy stuff. In fact, I know where babies come from and everything."

"Come on, we know you date and all," Riley said, not wanting her to feel awkward. "I simply meant—"

"No, I do not date," Dre corrected her, clearly not needing the save. "I'm focused on my studies, and learning all things pastry from the master chefs Dunne and Dunne." She turned and performed a from-the-waist-up abbreviated version of the "I'm not worthy" bow in Lani's direction.

"What about Andrew, from your graphic illustrations class?" Lani said, giving her a quick salute back. "You've been to a couple things with him recently, right? Lectures and stuff?"

"Right. As friends. Colleagues. We share similar interests. We do not share a bed. Much less the clichéd backseat of a car."

Lani and Riley might have swallowed a little hard at that.

Dre rolled her eyes. "What? You can't have it both ways. You say you're cool that I'm dating, which implies I'm having sex, but then you seem all weirded out by the idea that I might actually be—never mind. I'm not having this conversation. Or sex. There. Happy now?"

Lani was too busy coughing—it had been that or choke—so Alva said, "You're a good girl, Missy Dre. I'm proud of you. Stand up for what you want, and don't lie down for anybody you don't."

It was Riley's turn to choke a little, though on laughter. To hide it, she ducked her chin so she could twist her hair up into a knot before she started working.

"As long as you're happy, you go girl," Franco told Dre. Then he turned right back to Riley. "What else?"

"Nothing else," she said, exasperated, as she snapped the hot-pink scrunchie into place.

"Well, I love his books," Lani said, turning back to her rack of tester cupcakes and picking up the pastry bag she'd filled with a creamy sherbety orange frosting earlier. "How he writes such gritty, horrible crime dramas, but wraps them up in such powerful love stories"—she sighed and fanned herself with the flap end of the pastry bag—"gets me every time."

"I bet he's good in the sack," Alva said, then turned back to her sifting. "I just read them for the sex. You can skip right past the gory parts if you don't like them. The sex parts alone are worth the price. I buy them in hardcover."

It was pretty much a group choke that time. Riley recovered first and grinned broadly, not caring that it pulled at the tender skin around her scratches. "Power to you, Miss Alva."

Franco started humming "Sisters Are Doin' It for Themselves," making Riley nudge him in the ribs.

But she was grinning. She did love this group, nosy busybodies, fake accents, mandatory crazy aprons, and all. They had no idea how much they'd done for her.

"Okay, everyone, taste test time!" Lani lofted the tray of freshly topped cakes. "I give you Leilani's Dreamsicle cakes, featuring mandarin orange–soaked butter cake with cheesecake filling and sherbet whip frosting."

Everyone *ooh*ed together, sounding exactly like the little green men in the *Toy Story* movies.

As they shuffled over, still replicating the LGMs in the movies, Riley quickly took the butter out of the cold pack she'd stored it in before heading to Lani's table.

Franco swung back and cut her off, then leaned down close. "We're not done talking, you and me, *mon amie*."

She looked up at him. "Franco, I swear, there's nothing more."

Instead of a teasing or pleading look—he could teach master classes in both—his expression was uncharacteristically quite serious. "You've been there for me, Riley." When she started to brush that off, he placed his big hand gently on her arm. "You've been there. You don't have to confirm it, okay? I know. Those of us who've been there . . . we know. It's time for me to return the favor and be there for you. So . . . we're going to talk, *Mademoiselle* Brown."

Riley was surprised into momentary silence. She appreciated that he'd understood her desire to be there for him, and perhaps she really had been more of a help than she'd realized, just by providing a shoulder and words of comfort. It was a little disconcerting, though, that he'd ferreted out just how much she had understood about his pain. "I don't need a return favor, Franco. Not in this instance. I was glad I could be there for you. That's what friends are for."

"I know. And friends return favors." He bent down and looked into her eyes, then smiled broadly. "I saw the stardust in your eyes, *cherie.* And that's something I know a little about." He looped an errant curl behind her ear. "Just know, I'm here."

Chapter 4

Quinn stepped from the fixed pier onto the floating dock situated at the very back of the commercial moorings. It was where fishermen, commercial and local—he knew from past experience—could tie up temporarily without having to navigate through the maze of permanent slips, so they could run into Biggers' Bait and Tackle for supplies or a bag of ice. Old Haney Biggers had run the place back when Quinn's grandfather had run his trawler out from those very commercial piers. Other than a few fresh coats of paint, and an ATM parked out front, it looked much the same as it had fifteen or sixteen years ago. Quinn doubted Haney, who'd been older than his grandfather, still ran the place. Probably a son, or grandson by now.

Quinn wobbled a step or two as the dock dipped and swayed in the wake of an incoming slow-chugging trawler. It had been a very long time since he'd needed his sea legs, but he was happy to discover, as he gained more consistent balance, that it was apparently much like riding a bike. Something else he hadn't done in ages, he thought absently, as he made his way down the lightly swaying row of weathered planks. Maybe he'd pick up a bike while he was here and tool around the island. He knew many of the residents did, or had when he was younger.

He shifted his gaze past the bait shop to the boats tied up to the bigger, sturdier piers. Gavin Brannigan had kept his trawler there. He'd also harbored a little centerboard, single-keel sailboat back on a tiny pier behind the house on the sound that he and Quinn's grandmother had lived in, on the west side of the island. Not too far from his beach bungalow in actual distance, but a lifetime away now. The house was no longer there; it had surrendered its weathered clapboard planks to a hurricane—what had it been, at least seven, eight years ago? Fortunately it had stood empty, both Gavin and his grandmother long deceased by then. The owner had been using it only as a summer cottage.

Quinn had gone by there yesterday, out of curiosity and sentimentality. A relatively new, modest lodge stood there now. He'd thought about knocking on the door and introducing himself, asking if he could walk the grounds around the sound for old times' sake. There was no little pier behind the house, and the rest was so different, it hadn't seemed worth the intrusion. He had his memories, and looking across the calm, smooth waters of the inlet brought them back as clearly as if he and his grandfather had set out on a sunset sail the evening before.

Gavin had been a fisherman by trade, operating a commercial vessel for work purposes, along with many other merchant vessels. Those days were long, hot, sweaty, and reeking of fish stink, filled with some of the most demanding physical labor and extreme tests of Quinn's patience the then fifteen-year-old boy had thought he could possibly endure. The former had taught him a lot about what kind of man he could be. The latter was the skill that would come in most handy for the man he had become.

Gavin Brannigan had lived to see his only grandson graduate from college, only the second, after Quinn's father, in their branch of the family to do so. By the time Quinn had published his first book a few short years later, Gavin had already joined his beloved wife, Annie, in the "great and grand beyond," as he'd called it, his rolling brogue always making it sound like the best adventure destination in the world. And perhaps it was.

Quinn thought about the summers he'd spent here, from the age of fifteen until just past his twentieth birthday. He'd worked the trawlers for the income, lending a hand where it was needed . . . and because Quinn had come to understand that what his father had wanted most was more time alone. Even from him. Maybe especially from him. Quinn had never been entirely certain. Still wasn't. As if the long, eighty-hour workweeks his father put in hadn't isolated him enough. Quinn's mother had died in a car accident just after his thirteenth birthday. His father had never been particularly geared to parenting, though he wasn't openly averse to it. But Mary Elizabeth had been born to the role, and he'd gladly left her to it, taking on the traditional patriarchal role, which was providing for his family. A role Michael Brannigan had taken seriously. They didn't live in the lap of luxury, but they'd never gone wanting.

His father had loved his wife, that much Quinn knew, if by nothing other than the depth of his father's grief. He wasn't a demonstrative man, even with her. Not that Quinn had seen, anyway. And Mary Elizabeth's death had pushed him to some place he'd never quite come back from, even now. So that had to speak of a deep bond.

Quinn didn't know for certain. It remained a subject that, to this day, he and his father didn't speak of.

He shifted his thoughts purposefully back to the handful of summers he'd spent on Sugarberry. When he'd been younger, his grandparents had lived farther south, and he'd rarely spent time with them. It hadn't been until their move to Georgia, and his mother's death, that he'd been shuttled off to their care, at least for the summer breaks. He smiled, remembering coming in from the backbreakingly long days, thinking there was no way in hell he'd be able to rise again the next morning and do it all over again. That if he never touched or smelled, much less ate, another fish for the rest of his life, he'd die a happy man.

Only to sit down to a solid, hot meal, lovingly and always deliciously prepared by his Grams, and discover, to his absolute and continued amazement, that by the time the relaxed meal had been concluded, when his grandfather asked if he'd like to head out on a little sunset sail around the sound in the single keel, man against the sea and wind—rather than against what swam beneath it—Quinn had actually thought it sounded like a good idea. And it had been, every time. The leisurely loops around the inlet had provided opportunity for the two of them to talk, shooting the breeze and the bull. Workdays didn't allow for conversation of any kind, and the young man Quinn had been looked forward to those long, rambling conversations as the favorite part of his day.

Quinn could hear his grandfather's hearty chuckle as clearly as if he stood before him. He knew the pride that would have shone in his bright blue eyes upon hearing the news of his grandson's accomplishments. Quinn's smile spread to a grin. Along with it, the old man would have delivered a healthy dose of ribbing that his only grandchild had chosen to earn his keep making up stories rather than using his hands and back for what Granda Gav would deem an honest day's work.

There weren't too many Irishmen plying the Southern shores back then, or likely now, for that matter. His grandparents and their families had come over from Doolin, a small fishing village on the west coast of Ireland, to build a fresh life in New England, where the hardier Brannigan souls continued to eke out a living fishing. It was only after he'd met and married his wife, the former Annie O'Sullivan, and they'd begun their small family that Gavin had pulled up stakes and moved south. The warmer climate was beneficial to Annie's poor health. First to the shores of the Gulf, and only much, much later, after Quinn's own father had grown up and gone on his own way, had they come to Sugarberry.

Quinn had never known, exactly, what had ailed her. He knew it to be something with her breathing, but Annie Brannigan was a proud woman and the very last to allow anyone to see that she might be running on less than full steam. It simply wasn't discussed outside what was held private between her and her husband.

Quinn's smile turned wistful as he thought about the two of them, how they'd been with one another. For all that his mother had been loving and warm, making him feel very loved, his parents' relationship had always been somewhat austere and reserved. Given his mother's predilection for hugs and kisses, Quinn had assumed she'd taken those cues from his father. Actually, he hadn't thought much about it one way or the other—his parents were his parents—until his mom had passed and he'd come to stay with his Granda Gav and Grams. Theirs had been an entirely different sort of relationship, the likes of which he'd never known could exist.

They were always as happy to see each other as if they'd been apart ages rather than hours. They were truly the light in each other's eyes, even when they were squabbling, which was done with more affection than anger. He'd come to know theirs had been a love story of epic proportions, one Quinn had never been able to come close to writing about. No one would quite buy just how inordinately and blissfully happy the two of them made each other.

It had been the best thing Quinn had ever learned about the capacity of the human heart, and one of the hardest, as well. Finding a partner who could be to him all that he'd witnessed them to be to each other had proven elusive. Quinn often wondered if he'd have been happy settling for less if he'd never known what could be. If he'd only observed his parents' kind of love.

Of course, he liked to think if he hadn't, he wouldn't be the writer he was, either. Although he couldn't completely capture the depth and breadth of his grandparents' love for one another on the pages of a book, the absolute knowledge that love like that existed was a large part of why Quinn wrote the kinds of stories he did. Not the murder, the grit, and the horror . . . that was the grip, the grab, the thing that pulled his readers in. But what kept them in, what made them invest more than their curiosity, wondering how he was going to solve the crime, was his ability to make them care—and care deeply—about the people he put at risk. Would they triumph?

Of course. They *had* to triumph. And the why of that was always—always—love. Love was the foundation that motivated his protagonists to fight off the evil that other men do. It gave them the will and strength to do whatever it took to win out, and why, in the end, they always—always—did. To that end, the love affairs he wrote about were epic as well. Perhaps not in as grounded and real a way as his grandparents' love—fiction demanded something of the tempestuous and fantastical—but his characters experienced love as deeply and fully as Quinn was capable of writing it.

Love was also the very reason he found himself at a crossroads. "What should I do, Granda Gav?" he murmured, looking out over the waters to the hazy blue horizon beyond, though his thoughts were much, much further away. "What would you do?"

On the surface, it seemed easy. Go with his heart. His grandfather would tell him that much, Quinn knew. On a certain level, he knew that was the right decision. Maybe even the only one he could make. But there were other considerations. Not the monetary ones. In fact, money was the least of it. It was more that he felt an obligation to his readers, to the ones who had made possible the life he was so fortunate to have, the career he so loved and enjoyed. He didn't take lightly the idea that he would be potentially snubbing all that goodwill and trust. And for what? A self-indulgent choice that would possibly make only him happy?

His grandfather might not understand that specific commitment, the pact Quinn felt he'd made with each and every one of those readers who'd chosen to give him their loyalty and their hard-earned dollars. But he would have understood the emotion behind it. Commitment to the well-being and happiness of others, even at the detriment of your own success or happiness, was why Gavin relocated himself many hundreds of miles away from his own family and all they'd built on these shores. For the love of his wife, and her welfare, he'd started all over again. More than once. He'd never achieved a fraction of what he would have had he stayed north, where the strength and bond of their numbers alone had built a much sturdier trade.

His grandparents' lifestyle could be described as simple, basic, but Quinn had absolutely not a single doubt that his grandfather would have done any differently, given another chance. Granda Gav would have made any sacrifice if it meant keeping his beloved wife happy and healthy. He would have even said it was a selfish choice, not a noble one. Because he'd been rewarded with her companionship and love for all the additional years the move south had awarded her. Them.

Quinn sighed and rubbed a hand over the back of his neck as he felt the tension begin to creep in again. It seemed so ridiculous on some levels. Just write whatever damn book he wanted. It wasn't life or death. Not like with his grand-parents' choice. But this was *his* life. In the absence of what his grandparents had, at the age of thirty-four, this was what fulfilled him and made him happy. This was what he invested his passion and energy in. This was what he stood for, what mattered. So, in that regard, it was a very big deal. To him.

He rubbed the same hand over his face, then raked his fingers through his hair . . . and laughed. "Damn, Branni-gan. Maybe you just need to think about getting a life."

No sooner had the words left his mouth than the entire dock shook and rumbled under his feet, followed by what could only be described as an inhuman-sounding bellow.

He actually knew that bellow. One glance over his shoulder proved that he'd guessed right.

Barreling toward him, jowls flapping, was all one-hundred-and-God-knew-how-many pounds of Brutus.

Quinn stood frozen for a moment, stunned that the be-hemoth was capable of such speed. He had just enough time to glance skyward and murmur, "Sometimes you have a really twisted sense of humor," before sidestepping out of the way, up onto the tips of his toes like a matador, so Bru-tus could skate right past him without taking them both into the water.

Unfortunately, with his intended quarry suddenly no longer in front of him, Brutus tried to scramble his huge, hulking frame back around with a skidding, surprisingly agile slide. But he didn't quite make it, and off the end of the pier he sailed, making a huge splash in the water. The cascading fountain naturally sheeted back over the dock . . . doing a decent job of soaking a good part of the front of Quinn's polo shirt and khaki shorts.

"Brutus!"

Quinn felt more dock vibrations and turned to see the star of his cupcake fantasies running down the pier, blond curls bouncing. Well, more than just the blond curls, if he were honest. And it might have been the other bouncing things that distracted him momentarily from responding.

Yeah. Definitely need to get a life.

Of course, if he knew how, wouldn't he already have one? Perhaps he should tell Finch to put it on the schedule. If anyone could figure it out, it would be his PA—who was, for all practical purposes, more like his manager David's PA—since Quinn didn't work well with people actually underfoot. All he knew was, between the two of them, they expertly handled all the career and business stuff that didn't involve actually writing the books. Maybe they could arrange a social life for him while they were at it.

"I'm so sorry!" Riley called out, huffing a little as she also skidded to a stop a few feet from his damp form. "I was putting my bags on the pier back there, only took my eyes off him for one second. He usually doesn't go after anyone like that. I'm not even sure how he knew it was you, all the way down here." She framed her forehead to shield her eyes from the sun, so she could smile up at him. "He likes you."

She had dimples. How had he missed that the other day? Of course she had dimples. They suited her completely. They also made his body stir, which was nuts. Sunny freckles, apple cheeks, ringlets and now, dimples. Not remotely his speed. At the very least, she was definitely not the type of woman who might actually follow through on that fantasy he'd had in the shower. Much less the one he'd had later that night. Or the following morning in the shower. Again. Not because he wanted to have them, they just kept . . . appearing. It was the other part of having a very vivid imagination. Sometimes it handed him things he didn't ask for.

With this added detail, he had a strong suspicion his vivid imagination wasn't done toying with his subconscious quite yet.

Yeah. Really bad idea, remembering the cupcake fantasies. The way that delectable dab of chocolate had clung to those ridiculously earthy lips she had, smack in the middle of that girl-next-door face. And there was the matter of that body. That body could fulfill dreams he hadn't even thought up yet. As long as they didn't try anything particularly acrobatic, he amended, recalling her less than graceful treadmill dismount and general banging about in the kitchen.

He shifted his stance and looked out across the water, to where Brutus was presently paddling around. "Is he going to be okay out there? Do we need some kind of doggie life preserver?"

"He'll be fine. He'll come back over and I'll haul him up. The floating docks are good that way."

Quinn slanted her a look. "You *pull* him up? How many times do you end up in the water with him?"

The dimples deepened when she laughed. "Pretty much as often as you think I do. But he doesn't dive in often." She glanced up at him. "What brings you down here? Did you get the notes I sent to your personal assistant? Mr. Fincher? He's very nice, by the way. Super . . . efficient."

Quinn smiled. "Yes, Finch is definitely that." He might have phrased it as anal-retentive perfectionist, but, as he directly benefited from Finch's retentiveness, it didn't much matter how it was described. "And yes, everything came through fine. I appreciate your getting the necessary approvals and whatnot, so that I could keep the contents of the house for the duration of my stay. And so quickly. I was able to move in day before yesterday, ahead of the weekend schedule."

"Good. I'm glad it all went smoothly."

"I also made sure Finch and my manager, David, mentioned to Lois how pleased I was with your work and your help. I didn't realize you'd staged the house."

She tilted her head slightly to one side, clearly bemused. "What did you think I did?"

He smiled. "You mean after I realized you were work-jogging?"

He watched her cheeks bloom, and thought she might be the first woman he'd met who couldn't hide a single thing she was feeling. Her fair skin acted as a veritable bulletin board for her thoughts. She probably hated it. He found it rather tantalizing. And maybe a little adorable. She'd probably hate that last thought, too. Something about how she carried herself, the alertness that was always there in her eyes, and the bit of a shield she kept up, despite her sunny and outgoing nature, told him her waters ran a lot deeper than the dimples and freckles, curls and cleavage combination that what likely led most people to believe.

She cleared her throat. "Um, yes, after that part."

"Well—and don't take this as an insult—but initially I thought maybe the superefficient Finch had set up a maid service for me."

She frowned. "Really. Before you even got there?"

Quinn flashed a grin. "He is amazingly efficient." She wasn't smiling. "Not that you looked like a maid! Anything but," he hurried to say.

"I've got nothing against maids," she said.

"It's just, Finch is also something of a . . . uh . . . caretaker, constantly nagging me to get more life in my life, if you know what I mean. So . . . at the time, it didn't entirely surprise me that perhaps he'd set up something like that because you're . . . uh—" He stopped, somewhat mortified to realize the hole he'd somehow dug for himself. He was usually the observer, watching other people chatter on. He was never the guy talking. Always the guy watching. The guy watching never got in trouble for opening his big, fat mouth, and inserting his foot.

"I think I get where you're going." Her tone was more acerbic than insulted. "And, clearly, I wasn't that."

"Right." He was relieved that she seemed to be taking his unintended slight with grace. "No, that I knew, obviously. Don't worry. I just wasn't sure what it was you did do."

That made her cheeks darken further, only he wasn't sure it was due to embarrassment. Not if the quick flash he'd seen in her eyes was any indication.

"So, after you safely determined that your PA couldn't have possibly hired me to see to your . . . personal needs— and by the way, is that a service he performs often for you? Because I have a really hard time believing, even if you were stranded in the remotest part of the desert or at the ends of an arctic tundra, that somehow, someway, you wouldn't find a willing partner, all on your own."

"First, no, he never has. He's just been more than typically concerned about me lately, and . . . well, his skill set runs more to the logical, linear solution than to the more socially acceptable ones. And, secondly, thank you. I think." Quinn had no idea how he'd arrived at this particular conversational juncture, but knew he had only himself to blame for the understandably wary concern still on her face. So maybe Finch wasn't the appropriate go-to guy for Quinn's Getting a Life campaign after all.

"So, when you ruled out the Julia Roberts *Pretty Woman* gig, and the J.Lo maid gig, what did you think I was doing there?"

"Working for Lois, I guess, in some capacity. Assistant? I wasn't certain. But I wish I hadn't brought any of this up, because clearly I've offended you and I sincerely didn't mean to. All I wanted to tell you was how impressed I was with everything you've done. I hadn't looked at the entire house while I was there—"

"Wait, back up." She frowned as if something had just occurred to her. "You sort of fudged over it, but how could Finch have already reserved some kind of 'maid service,' "— she used air quotes around that last part, and for the first time in pretty much as long as he could remember, his cheeks were the ones growing warm—"and had me already there before you'd even decided to lease the place? Didn't you put that into motion while I was getting Jeffy and T-Bone to set up the baby grand?"

"Right. That. Well, actually, I'd already put David in touch with Scary Lois. He handles all the personal contracts, my regular agent only handles dealings that directly relate to the work itself."

"You know, you really have to stop calling her that or somehow, someway, it will come back to bite me. I can't believe I ever said that out loud. Only, of course I did."

He smiled at that. She was such an unusual woman, this odd mix of someone with easily tweaked red cheeks but otherwise outspoken and pretty direct about most everything else.

"I'll do my best. And if I screw up, I'll take the blame. Just tell her I'm developing this amazing real estate character or something."

"I don't know that she'd be flattered to think you'd be making her some kind of intimidating villain—wait a minute, what am I saying? She'd be all over that."

Quinn laughed. "Then we're covered."

"So, then, you'd just leased the place sight unseen?"

"Well, I'd seen the brochure photos and write-up, but, to be honest, I would have taken any place available on Sugarberry where I'd have unlimited privacy. You can't get that at a bed and breakfast, which was all that was available."

"It's true. Once folks come here, they tend to stick around. I can speak to that personally."

"I was excited when I found out there was a place available. When you were with the movers, I confirmed with David and Finch that after seeing it, I hadn't changed my mind. I told them to finish up the paperwork."

"And to politely decline the maid service." She didn't use air quotes that time, and her self-deprecating smile had returned in full. "Thank you. For the good review to Lois. Your endorsement means a lot. Especially considering the . . . uh, work-jogging."

He grinned and her cheeks warmed a bit again. She felt it and purposefully turned around, ostensibly to keep track of Brutus, who had paddled around to the other side of the dock, but Quinn was pretty sure it was to hide her face from him.

Given his cloddish, ungentlemanly commentary, he could hardly blame her, but he wished she wasn't self-conscious about the blushing. It wasn't like she could help it. It was the contrast between the old-fashioned courtesan curves and straight-shooter personality that made her all the more interesting to him.

"The good review was sincere," he said, shifting so he stood beside her. He noted she kept her face framed from the sun as she looked over the water, but switched to using her left hand, to block her face from him as well. It shouldn't have bugged him. He shouldn't have cared if she wanted to hide. From him, or anything else. But it did bug him—which meant he did care.

He should probably cut that out. Any time now.

"The thing I made sure David mentioned to Lois specifically was how much the house felt like a home, like someone had already been living in it. You did a wonderful job keeping it sophisticated enough to match all the over-the-top upgrades, but you did an even better job of keeping it comfortable. I've rented other places that looked great in a magazine layout, but I couldn't sit anywhere, or touch anything for fear of leaving footprints or fingerprints. Those places leave me feeling like an intruder. But the bungalow . . . I really like it."

He hadn't mentioned to Finch or David that perhaps he really liked it because he knew she'd had a hand in designing the decor. Or because his recollections of her being in the house made him smile. Mostly because he hadn't been aware that was true until this very moment.

"Why do you lease places that leave you cold?" she asked, still without turning to him. "At the very least, why not refurnish it to your own taste?"

He laughed at that.

"What's funny? I mean, I don't want to be rude or indelicate, but I'm guessing it's not a financial worry for you. Is it that you don't stick around long enough, so it's not worth the effort?"

"Sometimes, but it wouldn't matter. Because I haven't the first clue what my style is. Other than I know it—"

"When I see it," she finished, nodding. "It always amazes me how many people are like that. I mean, I guess I understand it doesn't matter to everyone, but, speaking for me personally, I can't imagine not being influenced by my surroundings. As a writer, I'd think it would be imperative to be comfortable, or to set a certain tone or vibe. Or whatever it is you need to get your head in the space it has to be in."

"I don't know if that's so much a thing for me. All I really need is quiet. When I sink into the work, the world around me goes away. All I see is whatever I'm writing. The rest of the time . . . yes, I guess I do notice. And I want to be relaxed, comfortable. But I don't know that I've put any real energy into figuring out what works best or why. All I can say is, I knew I liked the cottage the moment I saw it."

She glanced up at him, then back at the water again. "Even the baby grand?" she asked. "You don't strike me as a baby grand guy."

"Why not?"

"No particular reason. I guess it's that comfortable, lived-in vibe you spoke of. If that draws you, then I'd think the baby grand would be a little over the top. I worried about putting it in there, but Lois was adamant about having a few big statement showpieces. I was going for something more like a pool table or even foosball, but she—"

"Foosball," he repeated, with fond reminiscence. "Haven't seen one of those, or played on one since college. That would have been classic."

"I could have the piano removed. Put the foosball in, or the pool table, or maybe some more workout equipment. It shouldn't take more than a day or two, to—"

"No, no, I'm good. Actually, I like the piano. Statement piece and all." He grinned and looked more directly at her. "Does that change your opinion of me?"

She looked right at him then. "No."

He laughed outright.

"What?" she said. "I said it didn't change my opinion. My opinion wasn't a bad one."

"You just said it straight out, like having an opinion of me doesn't come into play because that's not part of the job."

She eyed him. "You got all that out of a simple no?"

He studied her face for a long moment. "I'm pretty good at reading people."

She started to turn away from him again just as the pink rose to her neck, but he found he really didn't want her to escape. So, without thinking, he reached out and touched the side of her cheek, turning her face back to his.

"Mr. Brannigan—"

He rolled his eyes, but didn't take his hand away. "We're not business associates. Quinn. Please."

"As long as you have leased furniture in your bungalow, you're a client."

"I signed waivers on all of that. If anything happens to any of it—"

"That's not what I meant. I just meant . . . you're a client. You leased a home I staged, with pieces I'll still be responsible for again at some point, and that's business, so—"

"So, you can still call me Quinn. Unless you really want me to call you Miss Brown." He tilted her cheek a little. "The scratches have healed up fast. Doesn't look like they'll leave any permanent marks."

She shifted away from his touch. "They have, thanks, and yes, it's all going to be fine." She turned again, watching Brutus as he came toward the dock.

"So, it's just the business thing, then?" he asked.

She looked back at him. "Is what just the business thing, then?"

"You retreat if I get close."

"You're right, I do. Partly because it's a business thing, but mostly because . . . well, I'm otherwise not—"

"You're not available," he finished for her. Of course she wasn't. He thought about his behavior with that cupcake. He was lucky she hadn't pushed it in his face and kneed him in the groin. Wow, he normally wasn't so slow on the uptake.

It shouldn't matter. This was the wrong time to play anyway, and she was the wrong woman to play with. He should be relieved. Game over. Back to work. "I'm sorry, I shouldn't have assumed otherwise. You're clearly—I mean, any man would be lucky to—"

He broke off as her cheeks bloomed anew. Her pupils slowly dilated—like they had over the cupcake in his dining room. Yeah, he definitely didn't need that to be happening, especially knowing she wasn't available. To him, that put her off-limits even for fantasizing—which he really had to knock off. If he was going to fantasize about anyone getting any, it should be his characters. His needs could wait. As usual.

"I'm shutting up now," he said with a small grin, wondering if she remembered saying those same words to him, post-treadmill launch.

She smiled briefly, letting him know she did. They didn't need things like in-jokes and meaningful looks between them. Not when he had a book to write and an entire career path to figure out.

And she had some other man to go home to.

They fell silent, and then Brutus hit the dock, making them wobble on their feet. Riley was still wobbling when she awkwardly knelt to heave the beast's hulking wet frame onto the dock, prompting Quinn to kneel beside her. "I can get him. Will he let me?"

"If he wants to get out, he will. You take that side, I'll take this side."

Quinn grabbed the side of the dog's collar with one hand and braced the other behind his front haunch and pulled as Riley did the same on the other side.

Brutus grunted, then scrabbled once his front paws hit the dock, half climbing, half leaping out of the water. It sent Quinn and Riley sprawling onto their backsides, where they got to suffer the further indignity of Brutus extensively and quite enthusiastically indulging himself in a rather long, full-body shake, sending a cascade of seawater all over them.

"Brutus!" Riley spluttered, blocking her face from the spray. "Seriously?" She spit out the briny seawater and clambered to her feet, slipping a bit as she did. Quinn, having just made his feet, grabbed her elbow to steady her.

They stood like that for several moments longer than either of them needed to. *Drop your hand, Brannigan*, he thought, while simultaneously very aware she hadn't shrugged him off as she had before. *Spoken for*, his little voice reminded him, and he let his hand fall to his side, dismayed at how reluctant he was to do so. *Relief, Brannigan. That's what this is supposed to feel like. Relief.*

She stepped back, but not before he noticed the flash of color on the back of her hand. He reached for it without thinking, lifting it between them, holding on when she would have pulled it back as he saw it was an oversized Band-Aid. "What happened?" he asked, smiling briefly when he noticed the bandage sported Minnie Mouse faces all over it. "Are you okay?"

She slid her hand from his, but her smile was a rueful one. "Kitchen burn. Hit the back of my hand on an oven rack. It's fine. Happens. More often to some of us than others," she added dryly. She took the dog by the collar, turned to go, then glanced back at Quinn. "You really are soaked. And I know he got you when he first went in, too. Do you want to come aboard? I have dry towels, at least. Wash seadog off your hands? I'll be happy to have the shirt cleaned. The, uh, shorts, too, if you want." She looked him up and down, as if noticing the rest of him for the first time. "He really did get you. I am very sorry—"

"Aboard?" Quinn asked, as her words sank in. It had taken a moment because he'd been distracted by the fact that her shirt was soaking wet, too. If he'd thought her body distracting when it was clothed in dry, dirt-smeared cotton, well . . . he'd yet to understand the true meaning of the word distraction. Other than the fact that he was a guy, and therefore appreciated the female form, he otherwise wasn't typically a fan of women who were . . . generously endowed. Mostly because he wasn't a fan of plastics mixing with God-given body parts. But there was nothing plastic about Riley Brown. In fact, every last thing about her was about as non-plastic and God-given as possible. In fact, the big man upstairs had been most generous.

All that, Quinn thought . . . plus a gaze he recognized. Maybe he had from the first moment. He understood exactly what it was he saw there now—aware, attentive . . . observant—because he'd been recognizing the very same things for the better part of the past thirty-four years. Every time he looked in the mirror.

"My boat." Her gaze grew quizzical the longer he looked at her. Then, just like that, she shifted it away, but not before he saw the guards go up again. "Oh." She sounded . . . disappointed? Or maybe embarrassed again, though he couldn't, for the life of him, imagine why. "You didn't know I live here. I thought when I saw you on the dock, you'd come down here looking for me because there was a problem—or because, ah—" She abruptly waved that away with her free hand. "Never mind. None of my business. I do have towels though, if it would help. Again, Brutus and I are sorry." She tugged on the collar and gave the beast a pointed look. "Aren't we, big guy?"

Brutus actually looked slightly abashed. He hung his head a bit lower.

"Apology accepted," Quinn said. "And don't worry. About the rest. It's hot, so it felt good. I was heading back to the house anyway." Because the very—very—last thing he needed to do was climb on a boat with her, into a small confined space, with them both wearing wet clothes clinging to every inch of her body. Er, their bodies. But mostly her body. Yep. Definitely a bad idea.

Quinn reached out, started to give Brutus a pat on the head, then decided not to risk getting the dog wound up again, and sketched a quick salute to them. "Thanks, though."

"Okay, then," she said, as he moved around them so he could head back down the dock. "Dunking notwithstanding, it was nice to see you again. I mean, it's good to know that everything worked out okay with the house, not because it was nice to see you because I thought—" She stopped and he glanced back to see the blush—hot this time—creep up her neck. She made a self-deprecating face and ducked her chin. "Yeah," she said quietly, then lifted her head with what he knew was her fake sunny smile. He'd seen the real one. That one came with dimples. "Drive carefully," she said.

"I will," he replied, wishing she didn't feel so flustered around him. Not that he supposed it mattered. He wouldn't be seeing any more of her. The thought drew his gaze down, whereupon he jerked it right back up again. Nope, definitely didn't need to be seeing any more of her. He'd seen more than enough. He nodded again and started off down the dock. With every step, his shoes made a rather comical squishing-squirting-squeaky sound, like something out of a cartoon. He grinned, which changed to a laugh when he heard her snicker behind him.

"You sure you don't want a towel or something to at least put on your car seat?" she asked. "You're pretty wet." She smiled when he looked back, a truer one this time, though dry rather than dimpled. "I saw your ride when I left the bungalow the other day. Nice rental when you can get it. I know it's just a short hop back home, but I'm pretty sure those were hand-tooled leather seats."

"You made a pretty quick exit." If she'd been in even half the state he'd been in, the last thing she should have noticed was what kind of seats he had in his old Carrera. "How did you notice that?"

"I'm a stylist. I pay attention to details. The smaller, the better."

"That's a skill set I can appreciate."

"Yes, I guess you would, given what you do. It's an entirely foreign concept for most people. I will say, I didn't realize they rented out vintage sports cars."

"They don't."

Her eyes widened slightly at that. "It's yours? You drove all the way here from—well, again, I speak without thinking. I don't even know where you drove from because I don't know where you call home, if that's even where you were. With your accent, it might only be Atlanta for all I know."

He tried not to grin, but she was babbling a little, as if she was nervous. The kind of nervous he was beginning to understand—intimately—when he was around her. Not that he had any business understanding it. Or enjoying it. "I guess maybe my accent has peeked out a bit since I've been back. Normally, I never notice it. My dad and his parents are from down this way, but I spent most of my life up north. My father has been up there for eons, since before I was born anyway. I have a place just outside D.C., in Old Town. Alexandria. That's in Virginia."

"Yes, I'm familiar with the name. That's where Lani's from originally. She owns the cupcake shop. And I meant D.C. Her dad was a police detective there, but her mom was from Georgia. They moved down here after he retired. He's our sheriff now. Leyland Trusdale."

"Doesn't sound all that retired," Quinn said.

"You probably don't really want to know all the details. Anyway, very nice ride. That's all."

"Actually, I love hearing about the people here. I have sentimental ties to this place, but people always interest me. And the car was the first one I ever bought and paid for, which I did right after I signed my first big book deal."

"That wasn't all that long ago, was it? I mean, I've read all your books. You were young to publish your first. That was what, ten years ago at the most?"

"Close, nine. But you're right, the car is a model from the mid-eighties. Neighbor of ours had one when I was growing up, and I've always liked the body style. Plus, to me, it symbolized success. Our neighbor was an attorney, middle-upper class, and well . . . we weren't."

She nodded, then smiled. "So, how did it feel, when

they handed over the keys? Did it feel like you thought it would?"

He grinned. "Better. Way better. But that was pretty much all I wanted, or at least the only statement I felt personally compelled to make."

"But you kept it. That statement."

"I did. Mostly because I really ended up loving that car."

She grinned. "You're such a guy."

He lifted one hand. "Guilty as charged."

They stood there another drawn-out moment, grinning at each other, then she cleared her throat and said, "Sure I can't get you that towel? Protect those beloved, statement-making leather seats?"

He opened his mouth to say no, thank you. Because, pleasant conversation aside, that was the only real option. At least that was the one easy decision he could make. So, no one was more surprised than he when what came out was, "To be honest, I'd really appreciate it, if you don't mind. I'll make sure you get it back."

It was at that exact same moment he realized just how much trouble he'd already gotten himself into.

She nodded, then moved past him and motioned him to follow her. He did, fully and utterly mesmerized by every voluptuous inch of her as she strolled ahead of him in what looked like soaking wet men's long, black basketball shorts. They should have been the definition of anti-sexy, but they so incredibly weren't. They rode low on her naturally swinging hips, and it was her beautiful heart-shaped backside they were clinging to. If he dragged his gaze off that view, it was only to collide with the equally sodden, mango-colored tee that clung to her waist and rolling hips, which brought him to the mass of wet and wild blond curls tumbling down the center of her back that would easily be the envy of mermaids the world over.

He found himself clenching his fingers into his palms,

but that didn't keep him from wondering what it would be like to sink his hands into those curls, to wrap them around his fingers and gently tug her head back so he could reach the creamy skin of her neck. That couldn't happen. She was not his to touch. Or taste. Not now. Not ever. *Taken, Brannigan.* Why was that so hard to imprint on his suddenly hormone-jacked brain? He'd never, ever, not once, pursued anyone who was otherwise involved. Beauty, body, brains, or any combination thereof, no matter how alluring, didn't matter. The instant he discovered a woman was otherwise involved, it was like an instant off switch for him.

The woman he'd been looking for, waiting for, would only have one man on her mind. Him.

He watched as Riley's mutant pet trundled easily along beside her, though she kept her hand on his collar anyway.

Quinn thought he might as well have been the one with the collar around his neck. But she wouldn't have to tug him along beside her. The way he was feeling right at that moment, he'd have trotted along, panting, right behind her.

Yep. He was in deep, deep trouble.

Chapter 5

"It's just over there." Riley walked up the ramp to the fixed pier, and over to the far side of it. "Home sweet home." She gestured to the forty-five-foot Cruiser Craft.

"You live on a houseboat? Cool. I didn't even know they docked pleasure boats here. I thought it was all commercial."

"It is, but the place where my friends had this docked, a few islands down the chain, charged a pretty steep monthly fee, so I checked around. Someone mentioned Sugarberry was more rural, less resorty, which suited me, or my finances anyway. It's quiet and off the beaten track, and, most important, they don't mind Brutus. We just sort of . . . fit in here. I am still close enough to the rest of the Gold Coast properties to make the staging job work out." She shrugged. "So, I kind of persuaded them to let me lease a spot, temporarily."

"How long have you been here?"

She smiled. "Little over a year."

"Nice. Nice friends, too. Portable house loan. Not a bad deal."

"Yep," she agreed, thinking how Greg and Chuck had,

for all intents and purposes, saved her life. Or had certainly provided the means to escape her old one. She let go of Brutus's collar and grabbed the railing that ran along the side of the boat. "You can step onboard here, then walk around to the back." Brutus led the way, and when she turned back to grab the bags she'd put down earlier when she'd had to go dog chasing, she found that Quinn had already picked them up. "Thanks—you didn't have to do that."

"You didn't have to offer me dry-cleaning service," he countered, watching Brutus nimbly maneuver the narrow alley between railing and boat to head straight over to his big water dish for a healthy slurp, before collapsing under the aft deck awning in a boneless heap. "Looks like he's taken to shipboard living."

"That he has. I'm not sure how he'd have done on a different kind of craft, but this isn't so much different from life in a tiny Chicago apartment. Easier, actually. Certainly a far more direct route to being outside than a twenty-two-story ride down in a small elevator." She took two of the bags from one of his arms and he reached around her to slide open the back doors. She stepped through and into a tidy little dining area, but walked past it, straight to the small galley tucked just beyond it. She set the bags on the stubby little counter that formed half of the U-shaped space, then turned to get the remaining two bags, only to find Quinn had followed right behind her.

"Oh." She stepped back slightly, only there was nowhere to go. "Sorry. Didn't know you were right behind me. Thanks," she added, when he set the bags down on the counter.

"No problem." He turned and checked out the rest of the main cabin, which formed the entire back half of the boat. In addition to the tiny dining area and galley, there was a small living room space, complete with recliner chair, short couch, small desk, and an entertainment center that held a state-of-the-art flat screen.

"Pretty cool use of space," Quinn said. "And very bright, sunny, with all the windows and the back being all glass."

"Thanks. It's actually surprisingly practical. I thought it would be harder to get used to, not that there wasn't a learning curve." Some parts of it more expensive than others, though she was mercifully and finally all caught up with the repairs now, and hoped the curve was complete. "Once you get used to it, it's kind of nice not having a lot of space you just clutter up anyway. Sort of makes you think more about impulse buys."

"I bet. Nice setup," he said, motioning to the flat screen.

"Yes, well, Greg likes his creature comforts. The satellite dish is hooked up top off the fly deck."

"Ah, right," Quinn said, in a slightly smoother, though still friendly tone. "Greg."

Since his back was to her, Riley smiled, and briefly debated about letting him think . . . what he was thinking. But she was already feeling bad about letting Quinn believe his assumption about her relationship status was true. Subterfuge of any sort was not her thing.

"Greg and his partner, Chuck, own the boat, though they've used it a whopping two times since making the impulse buy almost five years ago. Greg is a self-admitted gadget guy and Chuck indulges him because, well, he can. They both can. They're the most highly sought after food photographers in the country."

"Ah," was all Quinn said. "Well, these are some nice toys." He stepped a little bit out of the galley as he continued to look around the cabin.

Not enough to let her squeak by, but enough so that she had a prayer of getting her equilibrium back. Even her first few nights of bad storms while living aboard hadn't made her feel as off balance and light-headed as being in close proximity to Quinn Brannigan did . . . right in her own galley.

"I take it you worked with them, back in Chicago?" he asked.

"I did, yes. In fact, we were assigned to the same project my first time out of the gate. They're known for being rather . . . outlandish, I guess is the best way to put it, and not a little eccentric. But, for whatever reason, they took a liking to me and, well, they became mentors of sorts, certainly helped shepherd me through the earlier trials and tribulations of getting into the frenzied world of print work. I owe a great deal of my success to them."

"So . . . you worked as a photographer, then?"

"Oh, no, sorry. I worked with them as a food stylist."

"Makes sense. I'm sure you were very good at it."

"I did okay for myself." She braced herself for the inevitable question of why she'd made such a huge geographic and career change.

Instead, he turned around, neatly boxing her right back in between counter and appliances again. "I don't know how your friends had the place decorated, but I can already see your influence."

Surprised, she momentarily forgot about her sudden need to escape. "You can? I haven't really done that much." With her various learning curve catastrophes and the sporadic nature of her job assignments, she couldn't afford to.

"The throw pillows on the couch—I'm thinking those are you. You like rich jewel tones. You also have some of the same kind of prints on the wall here that are in the bungalow." He smiled. "Give me a few more minutes and I could probably list a half dozen other things, but those were the first two I noticed."

"I'm sure you could." Suddenly she didn't feel so bad about letting him think she was involved. He had a way of making her feel so . . . tended to. The center of his attention. His interest in her always seemed so . . . paramount and honest. Clearly she needed all the help she could get in regaining her perspective where he was concerned. "I, uh . . . let me get that towel for you."

He shifted slightly, to keep her from passing. "Wait."

"What?" She wasn't sure why he was making her so nervous. She'd already convinced herself that the "moment" she'd sworn they'd had—the whole cupcake thing—had just been her overactive imagination kicking in after the treadmill trauma had lowered her defenses.

He smiled, and there was a bit of a daring twinkle in his eyes. Just what she did not need him to be . . . more devilishly handsome.

"Was I right?" he asked.

"About—oh, the pillows, and . . . yes. Yes, you were. Apparently you weren't kidding about having an eye for detail."

"No. I wasn't kidding."

She was almost sure there wasn't some underlying . . . tone, in his voice, just then. She had no trauma to blame it on, unless she considered Brutus's belly flop off the pier a trauma—which she didn't. So . . . "Towels," she repeated, almost desperately. "If you'll just—"

Quinn slid easily to one side and immediately began walking around the cabin as if nothing had happened. *Because nothing had happened*, her little voice supplied, a tiny bit waspishly.

She was a complete ninny. An apparently sex-starved, hormonally overloaded, reality-challenged ninny. It confirmed her earlier suspicions that she'd romanticized the rest of their time together as well. And that meant the faster she got him off the boat, the better.

"I'll be right back." She quickly ducked down the narrow passageway to the master stateroom. Another, smaller stateroom with two twin beds was opposite the master. Another space above deck, something called a cuddy, was where people could also sleep, if they lay flat on a floor mattress and didn't sit upright. Greg and Chuck had never entertained anyone on the boat but her, and she was hardly planning to have sleepover company, so she'd used it as storage.

Her thoughts went straight from sleepovers to the man presently inhabiting the main cabin. She felt more than a little ridiculous, letting herself get caught up in the nonsense she'd let herself believe, to the point that she'd lied about something—by omission—but that didn't even matter. Considering the fact that, on her best day, she'd be unlikely to attract a man like Quinn, it was rather pathetically comical she'd ever allowed herself to entertain such an idea.

She could blame that on the cupcakes, too, but it was time to put the blame where it resided.

On her, Riley Brown, klutz extraordinaire with the proportions of a sturdy English peasant—which was her heritage. Men like Quinn Brannigan, a studly Southern gentleman with crazy good genetics and a healthy dose of sexy Irish ancestry thrown in, didn't generally get the hots for peasants.

She rummaged in one of the roll-out drawers under the queen-sized bed anchored into the space, requiring a step up in order to climb under the sheets. The step up provided the storage underneath, which essentially made up what would have been a dresser and a walk-in closet in a regular bedroom. She grabbed the remaining two clean towels and reminded herself—again—she really needed to get to the laundry. One of the things about living aboard she'd learned right off was the constant salty spray in the air was hell on clothes, skin, and hair. She did her best to keep up with at least two out of those three, but was forever behind on the laundry.

She slung the towels over her shoulder and slid the

drawer back until it latched shut, then turned around just as Quinn was ducking down to step inside the stateroom door.

She squealed in surprise. Okay, yelped might have been a better description.

He immediately raised his hands, palms out, in front of his chest, "I swear, I don't make a habit of sneaking up on people. I'm sorry. I was just—" He took the towels from where she was clutching them in both hands, and slid them free. "I thought I could help, so I could leave you to get on with your day. Not to mention I'm sure you'd like to change, too. In fact, let me duck back out and—"

"No, that's okay, really," she assured him. "I'm sure you'd like to get going, too." The open space in the stateroom not occupied by the bed was narrower than any other space onboard, except maybe the shower. At the moment, it felt about a hundred times smaller. And a million times more intimate.

"There's two towels. Use one to dry off if you'd like, and take the other for the car." He really did fill the space right up, including that space she'd so recently cleared out in her head. "I'll, uh, just get out of your way and let you clean up."

She gestured to the tiny bathroom as she stepped past him. "Sink is through there if you need it." Greg had kept insisting she call it the head, but she just couldn't; it sounded like a guy term. She had managed to get the big three—cabin, galley, and stateroom. But don't ask her about aft and starboard, and all of that. She didn't see why they just couldn't say front and back, left side and right.

His voice halted her just outside the door. "You wouldn't by any chance have a T-shirt I could borrow, would you? Promise I'll get it back to you along with the towels." He smiled. "Polo shirts hold a lot of water, as it turns out." He was holding the hem edge of the stretched-out wet shirt in a ball in his cupped hands. "I'm dripping on your floor. I'm sorry."

"It's made to get wet," she said, somewhat absently,

briefly transfixed by the way balling up the front of his shirt had managed to pull tight the fabric over his chest and the sleeves. She couldn't believe his claims that he was ever too scrawny. His shoulders and arms alone . . . made her want to fan herself. "Shirt," she said, belatedly remembering what he'd just asked her. "Right. Uh . . . I don't know." She turned back and started pulling out drawers and fishing through one, then another, still seeing the outlines of his broad shoulders and bulgy biceps in her mind's eye.

She wasn't finding anything. It wasn't like she was some perky little size six, or eight, but none of her T-shirts would fit his bigger-than-life, archway-filling frame. Not to mention he'd look ever-so-cute in melon pink sorbet or sherbet orange. From the corner of her eye, she caught him glancing around the stateroom, much as he had the main cabin, and it struck her that if she were, indeed, in some kind of committed relationship, as she'd allowed him to believe, wouldn't it stand to reason she'd have at least one or two of her partner's big ol' manly man–sized T-shirts laying around? Left behind after their latest round of rambunctious, three-times-a-day, crazy-hot boat sex?

Possibly, she was just projecting. Then she remembered. She did own one oversized man's shirt after all. "I do have one that might work. I just need to get around to the other—" They once again did their do-si-do so she could squeeze past him and his shirt of amazing balled tightness, to get to the foot of the bed, where there was one more, wide drawer in which she stored her off-season clothes. She dug under the top few layers of long-sleeved Henleys and sweaters. "Here," she said triumphantly as she slid out a clean, but very old and worn, oversized White Sox baseball jersey. She shook it out, then tossed it to him. "That might work." He didn't have to know it was one of her sleep shirts. Let him think what he wanted. Not that it mattered, but it was a point of pride that he believe she was actually capable of having a man living onboard who would leave old jerseys strewn about.

"Thanks." He snagged it in one of those big hands of his. One of those same big hands that had framed her shoulder back in the kitchen of the open house—well, his bungalow, she supposed it was now. And again, on the stairs, and . . .

"Sure," she managed, her throat tight and dry all over again—because she was an idiot. She ducked her chin slightly as they did one last do-si-do. "I'll just be in the galley, putting stuff away. No hurry on getting the shirt back. Actually, if you want, you can just leave it at Lani's shop in town. I can pick it up next time I'm in for club night."

"Because coming all the way out here would add so much time to the trip."

She heard the dry, teasing note in his voice, knew there was no underlying message, just amusement. But tell that to her hammering heartbeat.

Before she could think up a suitable response, he said soberly, "I can leave it at the bakery, Riley, no worries. But, just so you know, I wouldn't have dropped by unannounced. I appreciate the loan. I'll leave it and the towels in town with Lani."

She felt foolish for trying to play it oh-so-cool, instead being oh-so-ridiculous. "I appreciate it." She turned back to the door, escape attempt number two the next thing on her immediate agenda.

"What's club night?" he asked.

She'd made it to the passageway, and debated pretending she hadn't heard him, then paused. She'd like to think she really wasn't that ridiculous. She braced her hand on the doorway as the boat swayed and dipped, then gripped it tightly after she turned back. It was that, or prove just how ridiculous she really could be, by face-planting at his feet.

The same bare feet that were covered with the wet shirt he'd just pulled off.

She should turn back around. Decency demanded it, despite the fact that men on Sugarberry went shirtless more often than not this time of year. It was just . . . none of the men on Sugarberry looked like this. For that matter, none of the men in Chicago did either. And before she knew it, she wasn't turning around at all, she was staring. Gawking.

Giving herself lecture after lecture as she let her gaze travel ever-so-slowly up his still wet, khaki shorts-clad legs, to the belted waist and the expanse of flat, very male and muscular bare skin that extended upward from there. There was a dark, sexy swirl of hair patterning across his pecs, then arrowing down, oh so tauntingly, until it disappeared behind the buckle on his belt. She about swallowed her tongue.

Even being in imminent danger of death by choking apparently wasn't enough to abort the rest of the full-body sweep. He had his arms over his head as he was pulling the shirt on, so she got to watch the riveting display of pectoral and shoulder muscles at work and play. Then, like the curtain at the end of a performance, the Sox jersey fell down into place over all that gloriousness and the show was abruptly over.

Like a tractor beam of shame, her gaze lifted that fraction higher until it locked right into his. It was probably just the dim, shadowy interior of the stateroom that gave those crystal-blue eyes of his the dark, dangerous glint she saw there. Surely, that was it.

"I'm sorry," he said, though not exactly sounding at all put out. "I thought you'd turned your back."

"You asked . . . something." It was a damn good thing she'd already come to terms with the very—very—different leagues the two of them played in. If she'd ever allowed herself to seriously think about what it would be like to get naked with him, that little display had just guaranteed she would never—ever—be disrobing in front of this gorgeous specimen of man.

Yeah, she thought. Good thing she'd cleared that up.

"You have a club thing? At the bakery?" He smiled. "If it's a secret society, complete with a special handshake, forget I asked. I was just trying to think what kind of club meets in a bakery."

Was he seriously making small talk? "We, uh, that is, a group of us get together and . . . we bake. Cupcakes."

"To help the owner—Lani, right? To help her out with stock?"

"No. Just to bake. It's like . . . you know how guys have poker night? We have bake night. Lani teaches us stuff. She used to be a pretty big deal of a pastry chef in New York, and her husband is—"

"Baxter Dunne. I know." Quinn smiled when Riley sent him a questioning look. "Scary Lois name-dropped him as a way to sell me on the finer points of Sugarberry's hidden celebrity allure."

Riley found herself smiling at his continued use of the dreaded nickname. "Anyway, we learn, enjoy each other's company, share what's going on." She managed a smile then. "And donate a lot of sweet stuff to the Senior Center, the Moose Lodge, and other unsuspecting groups all over the greater Savannah area."

His smile flashed wider and the exponential speed at which Riley's pulse rate zoomed told her it was time to end their little chitchat.

"Sort of like a book club for bakers?"

"Exactly. And you don't have to read the boring stuff you'd never normally—" She broke off, then shook her head. "Good, Riley." She looked at him. "I didn't mean your books. I meant the stuffy ones that book clubs think they should be reading because someone, somewhere said that reading dysfunctional stuff about miserable people where it always ends badly somehow makes you a better person. I never figured that one out. I want the book club where everyone reads fun fiction." She smiled again. "Yours would fall in that group."

He sketched a little bow. "Thank you. Much appreciated. And if it makes you feel any better, I don't get highbrow, stuffy literature, group-read think, either. Well, that's not true. I understand why the genre exists, just not why there aren't at least an equal number of reading groups engaging in discussion about more popular fiction. I mean, it's called popular for a reason." With that, he bowed again. "Allow me to step down from that particular soapbox. You don't want to hear me pontificate."

"Actually, it's refreshing and relieving to hear you say it. I thought it was just me being shallow and superficial." Riley squeezed her eyes shut. "I really need to stop talking. You know I didn't mean that your books were——"

"I know what you didn't mean."

Her eyes flew open. The voice was much closer. In fact, he was standing right in front of her, just inside the door. The door she belatedly realized she was blocking.

"Thank you for the shirt," he said amiably enough, but his gaze was searching hers.

For what? she wanted to shout. "I'm sorry my dog is a bit . . . exuberant." She was completely hung up on that deepening sea of turquoise blue.

"Please let . . . whoever he is, know that I said thank you as well."

"What?"

He plucked at the jersey. "The owner of the shirt."

"Oh. Right. I . . . will."

"Will you tell him one other thing for me?"

Riley nodded, held there by the steady gaze, the deep

voice, that hint of accent . . . and the way he made her feel like the only woman in the universe.

"Tell him he's a very lucky man. And that I hope like hell he knows what he's got here."

"Got? Oh, you mean . . . the old White Sox jersey? It's not a real—"

Quinn grinned then, and she added *dazzled* to the list. "You, Riley," he said. "He's got you."

"Oh. Right." She wished she could somehow be at least slightly less banal. But that was not her karma. Not around him, at any rate. "I—thank you."

He kept smiling.

"I should let you get out of here." But turning around and having him follow her down the snug passageway . . . that she didn't need. "I'm—I think I'm just going to trade places with you and change out of my wet—uh, change. My clothes."

His eyes had flashed on the word wet for the briefest of seconds, and she found herself holding her breath. For what, she didn't know, but there seemed to be some kind of anticipation . . . building. Surely that wasn't all in her mind? But then he backed up, slinging the spare towel around his neck, and the damp one, along with his wet shirt, over his arm, which he swung wide, gesturing her inside. Ever the gracious Southern gentleman. His Grams would be so proud.

Riley tried not to let that depress her.

"I'll launder and bring both towels back, if that's okay."

"You really don't need to." Against all odds, she managed to not trip over herself or in any other way cause further embarrassment as she got out of his way and let him out of the room. It was something, anyway.

"I don't mind," he said, as he stepped into the passageway.

She stopped him with a question. "Why were you down here?" she blurted out. "At the docks, I mean?" *Good God,*

Riley. He was one step and a hop away from being back on the pier, on the way to his car.

He turned back, and paused in the door opening. "I spent my summers here as a teenager, fishing, working for my grandfather. He moored his big trawler on these docks."

Her eyes widened. "Your family is from Sugarberry?"

He shook his head. "Extended family on both sides are from New England, then Ireland the generation before that. My grandparents moved south out of consideration for my grandmother's health issues. Dad was born down on the Gulf. My grandparents moved here to Sugarberry after my father had gone off to college, married, and started a family, which began and ended with me."

"Why Sugarberry? The Gulf would seem a more prosperous place for a fisherman."

"Looking for less challenging competition as my granda got older and my grams' health was worsening. My father's career ended up keeping us around D.C.; work keeps him there still. So, I guess I'm something of a mutt, of sorts, geographically speaking."

"Your grandparents, they're gone now?"

"Yes, long time. Their house here is gone, too."

"I'm surprised with the way island lore is passed around down here, that there aren't stories about the famous writer's grandparents."

"My grandparents were both gone before I'd published my first book. I doubt anyone would have made the connection after the fact."

Riley smiled. "You seriously underestimate the depth and breadth of the local gossip mills. Your mom and dad are still in D.C.?"

He shook his head. "Actually, my mom passed when I was thirteen, which was right around when I started spending summers here. Kept on with it every summer until I was in my junior year in college. I had an internship that summer, in journalism, which was where I thought I was headed at the time."

"I'm sorry about your mom."

"Thank you. My dad . . . well, he had a pretty hard time of it. But it ended up giving me the gift of time spent with my grandparents, for which I'm forever grateful."

"He must be proud of your successes. Your dad, I mean."

Quinn smiled, but for the first time, Riley noted it didn't quite reach his eyes. "Yes, he is. Well, I won't make you stand around in wet clothes any longer. Do you need any help unloading that stuff? From the bags we carried on-board?"

"Oh, no, that's okay. I've got it." Surprised to realize that their short chat had relaxed her once again, she was relieved when her smile came naturally, with no dry throat or heart-pumping side effects. "It would take longer to tell you where it all goes."

"Okay then, I'm officially getting out of your hair." He turned to go, but she stopped him one last time.

"Thank you, Quinn."

"For?" he asked, leaning back to look through the open doorway.

"Sharing. I'm sure you get asked endless curious questions about your past. I just . . . I appreciate hearing about it. I'm glad you had the chance to connect with your grams and granddad."

"Thank you. I'm not usually all that keen to talk about it, but this was nice. It felt . . . normal. I appreciate that."

"Good." Her smile spread. "I feel less guilty for being nosy, then."

"Nothing nosy about making neighborly conversation."

She laughed. "You might want to rethink that before stopping in at Laura Jo's diner or Stewie's pub."

He grinned. "So noted."

"Be careful getting off the boat. It's tied securely, but it still bobs."

"I will." But he stood there a moment longer, then another moment still. "Good-bye, Riley."

"Bye," she said, thinking he'd made that sound rather permanent. Wishing the idea didn't make her so sad.

She heard him talking as the rear glass door slid open, presumably to Brutus, and quickly shrugged out of her wet shirt and bra, pulling on the first thing she yanked out of the open bench seat. She frowned as she heard something—or, more to the point, someone—on the outside stairs that led to the upper fly deck. The weight of the steps were heavier than any noise Brutus would make, not that he could climb the ladder anyway. She figured, given his earlier curiosity about the boat, Quinn had probably decided to take a quick peek up there, which was perfectly fine. It was another guy thing. A fixation with all things transportation. She certainly didn't mind.

But as she pulled her hair from under the back of her shirt and grabbed her heavy comb, she found herself spending a moment or two wondering what it would be like to have someone else's footsteps echoing in her living space again.

She entered the galley just in time to see Quinn hop from boat deck to pier, and watched him, thinking about all kinds of things she had no business thinking, but mostly about what he'd said about her when she'd thought he'd meant the old jersey.

Then she was sliding the rear door open, almost falling over Brutus, who was sitting like a sphinx, watching his now-beloved Quinn walking away, leaving him behind. If she hadn't been so busy gathering the courage to follow up with one final question, one she knew would plague her overactive mind otherwise, she'd have been a little wistful about Brutus's obvious bout of lovesickness. He'd never once, as far as Riley had ever seen, looked after Jeremy that way. She rubbed his head. "I'm sorry, too, big guy," she said, admitting that much was true. "Quinn," she called out, before she lost her chance. "Wait. Can I ask you one more thing?"

He turned around. If he was surprised, or annoyed, he surely didn't show it. His smile was as easy and amiable as ever. "Sure." He raised his voice just slightly to be heard over the sudden whip of wind, despite only being a few yards down the pier.

She walked to the side of the boat and looked up at him as he moved a few yards closer. "You said you hoped my . . . um . . . partner, knows what he's got. I know now that you meant me, but I still don't know what you meant. Not specifically. I realize you were probably just being polite and charming, but on the off chance you meant it . . . can I be horribly gauche and ask what is it you think he's got in me?"

A slow smile curved Quinn's lips, and even with the short distance between them, there was no doubt the warmth in it invaded every speck of those crystalline eyes. "A woman who can ever-so-sincerely ask that very question . . . and honestly not already know the answer."

And with that, he turned and walked away.

Brutus's head bumped her hip as he ambled over to sit beside her. Riley draped a hand over his neck, rubbing his still-damp fur as she watched until Quinn was no longer in sight.

"I wish I knew what he meant by that," she told her faithful, currently sorrowful companion. "But maybe it's just as well I don't."

Chapter 6

Quinn wanted her so bad he could taste her. He'd written books around the theme of forbidden fruit, but he'd never once been tempted by it himself. Yet, he couldn't seem to get Riley Brown out of his mind. Not to mention her lingering impact on other parts of his body. All he had to do was walk into the damn breakfast nook and he got a hard-on. It was insane.

Quinn flexed his grip on the handle of the paper shopping bag he carried and glanced up at the shop signs as he walked past the row of stores circling the small square in the middle of the tiny town of Sugarberry. Other than the docks and Biggers' place down on the pier, it was the only commercially developed area on the small island. Even with houses lining the streets extending out from the square, and those scattered along the loop road that circled the entire island, it was still largely marshland, dunes, and beach.

The streets that weren't paved, or set with bricks as they'd briefly been in some generation gone by, were most often composed of hard-packed sand and dirt, with a healthy layer of crushed shells ground in for good measure.

The town itself was an odd amalgam of rural Southern charm and the more bohemian lifestyle often found in island culture. Sugarberry was only connected to the mainland by a single causeway over Ossabaw Sound, and even that was a relatively new development. As a teen, he'd had to take a ferry over. He couldn't recall seeing any ferry signs now, so maybe it didn't exist at all anymore. Understandable, though sentimentally speaking, somewhat disappointing.

Quinn also noted some of the shops had changed ownership over the years. More surprising were the ones that still remained the same, all these years later. There was some comfort in seeing the town square was still much as he remembered it. The grassy park in the middle, with the large fountain at its center. That much hadn't changed at all.

He spied the colorful and whimsical sign for Cakes by the Cup and slowed his steps. Hopefully just the sight of the cupcakes wouldn't have the same effect that thinking about them in the privacy of his own home had. Maybe he should have considered that before deciding to drop by. He'd come to Sugarberry with problems that needed solving. Thus far, the problem that was Riley Brown was preventing him from getting on to anything else.

After another fruitless morning alternately spent staring at his computer screen, or at the waves crashing against the dunes behind his bungalow . . . or her baseball jersey . . . he decided it was time to drop the damn shirt and towels off and cut the strings once and for all. Not that there were any real strings left between him and Riley. He could have dropped the stuff off at any time over the past week and that would have been that.

The borrowed items had made it from the dryer to the back of the chair across from where he sat to work. The really pathetic part was it wasn't even her damn jersey. Worse, it likely belonged to the man who got to see her in it. Nightly, for all he knew. But that wasn't what he'd been thinking about as he'd pondered the shirt.

It was the only tangible thing of hers still in his home. The bigger issue was how much he felt her presence without any tangible representation. How someone could have imprinted herself so viscerally into his thoughts, in a space they'd shared for less than an hour, he couldn't say, but he felt her there all the time. In the Florida room, the kitchen, the foyer, the breakfast area . . . his shower. And he didn't want to. Not any longer. He hoped the act of getting rid of the shirt and towels would somehow symbolize the total disconnect he needed to achieve so he could get on with more important matters.

"Right," he said under his breath while jiggling the bag in his hands, still staring up at the sign and not entering. Yet. "Good luck with that."

It would be one thing if it was just the farm girl freckles sprinkled across those often blushing cheeks, or that mouth, those lips, all abundant and beckoning, like ripened fruit begging to be suckled and savored, or the siren curls of gold that made him want to tangle his fingers in them, or the God-given curves that filled out her lush body. A body made for a man to sink himself into, to find pleasure in, and to pleasure in return. She was all fresh-faced innocence mixed with pure, molten carnality, in one unexpected package.

And yet that wasn't what made his body behave like a randy fifteen-year-old. Or certainly not all of it. It was the direct talk despite the pink cheeks, the vulnerability so clearly present in her big brown eyes despite the dry, often acerbic humor. She spoke confidently about her work, yet was openly self-deprecating. There was the natural openness, her vibrant buoyancy, the inquisitiveness that had her sincerely asking about his family. And, most perversely, it was the way she moved through the world like a woman on a mission, but was a bit of a goofy klutz. She accepted those shortcomings with humor, which was its own brand of dignity, and also happened to be endearing as all hell.

She was unique and fascinating and he wanted to know more, to talk to her, to watch her move, to find out what she thought about . . . everything. She would be a woman with opinions. He wanted to know them all, to debate them, to laugh with her, kiss her inevitable boo-boos . . . then make wild, passionate love to her, and revel in all she would be capable of giving in return.

His hands tightened on the handle of the shopping bag until his knuckles hurt. He forced himself to relax his grip, the tension in his neck and shoulders, and all the rest in between. Maybe even more, the part between his ears.

She'd come into his orbit less than ten days ago, had crossed his path only twice in that time . . . so how was it that he'd found himself where he was? Maybe he was so wrapped up in the direction his book was taking him that he was projecting raw emotion on her. Or maybe he was merely using her as a distraction to keep him from thinking about the bigger thing, the major issue he'd come to Sugarberry to resolve.

But he didn't think so. He really, truly didn't want any distractions. He wanted to figure things out, make some hard, very serious decisions. Taking on new problems had been nowhere on his agenda.

It didn't matter why she fascinated him. Couldn't matter. What mattered was finding his way past the initial little buzz of fascination and getting back to his original purpose.

He pulled open the door to the bakery and stepped out of the sultry midday heat, into cool air redolent with the rich, buttery scent of baking cakes, the darker pull of melting chocolate, and an unknown variety of other treats that combined to make his mouth water. It was a decadent, multifaceted assault on his senses and he couldn't help pausing to breathe it all in.

"Well, hello there, young man. Something I can do for you? Our fun special today is the Dreamsicle cupcake—mandarin orange–soaked cake, a cheesecake filling, and orange whip on top. Our indulgent special is a truffle-infused chocolate pumpkin and ginger cupcake with mascarpone and cream cheese frosting."

Quinn hadn't initially noticed anyone in the shop when he'd first entered, so the friendly welcome caught him slightly off guard. "They both sound fun and indulgent to me," he said, running his gaze along the taller counters to the gap where a much lower counter held an old-fashioned, antique cash register.

It was there, behind the oversized register, that he finally spied the tiny bird of a woman. Her white-blond hair was set in a beehive of perfectly formed, meticulously preserved curls . . . and she was wearing what appeared to be an apron featuring a puffy white horse with purple neon mane and tail, over what otherwise appeared to be a sensible blouse. Pearls circled her neck and were clamped to fragile-looking earlobes. He smiled, charmed and a bit flummoxed.

"You look like the indulgent type to me." She eyed him up and down. "Perhaps a mixed set? We have our standard menu as well, each and every flavor combination guaranteed to make you sigh in pleasure with every bite. Can I fix you up a box?" Her blue eyes twinkled merrily as he stepped closer to the counter. "Well, my, my." Her eyes widened as she got a better look at him. "Look at you, all grown up." Her gaze skimmed over him and up until their eyes met. "You're Gavin Brannigan's grandson, am I right?"

Quinn grinned. Apparently she wasn't done surprising

him yet. He couldn't recall the last time anyone had recognized him for being a Brannigan first, and anything else second. "I think that's the nicest thing anyone has said to me in quite some time," he told her sincerely. "Yes, I am Gavin's grandson, Quinn. It's a pleasure to be back."

"I remember you from those summers you used to come down to fish with your grandpa. Didn't come around town much while you were here." A hint of scold was there, despite the merry twinkle, as if it were still something of a personal affront, all these many years later.

Given what he knew personally about some Southern sensibilities, especially in small towns, that wouldn't be entirely out of the question.

"Granda Gav kept me quite busy, sunup to sundown. On the rare occasion we didn't head out, Grams had a long list of chores for me to help her with." Quinn grinned. "I would have much rather been sampling the penny candy in those jars on the counter of Caner's Hardware, but I never had the time."

Her smile said he was forgiven and likely always had been. He suspected the pint-sized oldster just enjoyed being feisty. Of course, if he made it to her age, he hoped he'd enjoy indulging in a bit of that himself.

"He was so proud of you. Talked about you all the time. Track star, I seem to recall. Or something like it." She eyed him again, and the twinkle took on a clearly more feminine spark. "I must say you've filled out—and up—quite a bit, since those days."

"Yes, ma'am," he said, still smiling. He hadn't thought, given what little time he'd spent mingling with the locals, that anyone would really remember him. "I believe maybe I have. You, however, look exactly as I remember you, and as lovely as always. Mrs. . . . Liles, am I right?" He reached way back, proud and relieved that he was able to pluck the name from the flotsam and jetsam comprising his vast stores of beloved Sugarberry memories. "I remember you used to come down to the docks and buy fish for your husband's supper."

She beamed and the warmth in her eyes lent her rouged cheeks some natural color. "Why, aren't you a charmer! And please, you can call me Alva."

"Why, thank you, Miss Alva. I'm honored." He'd always considered himself a polite gentleman, but it was amusing and maybe a bit poignant how swiftly the Southern rules of etiquette his Grams had taken such great pains to endlessly nag into him rose straight back to the surface, almost as if they were second nature. "And how is Mr. Liles?"

"Oh, my Harold passed on some time ago." Her smile didn't fade a bit as she spoke of him, but rather an affectionate spark flickered to life instead, tugging at much the same place in Quinn's heart that his grandparents' affection for one another always had. He knew that look well.

"We had a good life, we did," she said, a bit mistily. "Still miss him. Old coot."

Quinn's smile softened. "I'm very sorry to hear of his passing, and yes, I'm sure you do."

"You know," she said, sparking right back up again. "We were just talkin' about you at last week's bitchy bake."

Quinn's gaze had begun to drift toward the amazing works of cupcake goodness lining each of the display shelves, but shifted straight back to hers at that. "The—I beg your pardon, the what?"

"Every Monday night after we close, a bunch of us girls, and Franco, of course, get together, and we bake and we bi—"

"Right," he said, smiling because it was impossible not to. "I think I get the drift."

"Now, what happens in Cupcake Club is supposed to stay in Cupcake Club"—she lowered her voice to a more conspiratorial whisper as she leaned across the counter—

"but I don't think it's really talking out of school to mention that you've been the hot topic the past two weeks running." She straightened and primped her hair, smoothed her skirt, as if nothing untoward had happened. "And now, here you are, paying a visit to our little shop, so I've a feeling that streak might just continue."

Despite the fact that bit of news was a little disconcerting, he found himself still smiling. "Well, I can't imagine there's anything of interest to discuss, but I appreciate your letting me know."

"Oh, don't sell yourself short. You're successful, talented, famous, and very good-looking these days."

"I, uh, well, thanks." He tried gamely not to chuckle. Alva Liles had had something of a reputation for being a firecracker back when he was a kid, though he couldn't recall much of what was said specifically. He hadn't paid a lot of attention to local gossip and his Grams wasn't one to wallow about in it, either. But it appeared that nothing much had changed since then. "I appreciate any good word you can put in for me. In fact, that's kind of why I'm stopping by today."

Her expression fell a bit. "Not to buy cupcakes? You really must give at least the chocolate buttercream a try. Although, if you want my personal opinion, it's the red velvet that really steals the show. Lani's recipe is the moistest you've ever tasted. Add a cold glass of milk and you'll think you've been transported to heaven."

Do not think about cupcakes transporting you to heaven, he schooled himself. Heaven and cupcake in the same mental place made it all but impossible not to think of Riley, a certain breakfast nook, and many subsequent showers. "Actually"— he gamely kept the conversation moving forward—"I had the chance to indulge in Mrs. Dunne's amazing cupcakes a week or so ago. Heavenly is a good word, indeed. I came by today to return some things I borrowed from Riley. Miss Brown," he corrected. "She said it was okay to leave them here with you. I hope that's all right." He lifted the paper bag.

Alva eyed the bag, then him, with a considering gaze, for a moment or two longer than was comfortable.

"If not, I can . . . come back another time. Perhaps when Mrs. Dunne is here?"

"Oh, Miss Lani is here. She's back in the kitchen. And no one calls her Mrs. Dunne, though it is exciting, her marrying Baxter and all. He's a famous pastry chef, too, don't you know. It's been all the talk for ages now. You'd think we'd be used to it, all the fuss, with him living here, and filming his fancy TV show right over in Savannah, but then his cookbook came out last month, and, well, it's brought a whole new round of attention. We're actually getting phone calls for long-distance orders, can you believe that? From all over the country. Personally, I think it has a lot to do with the fact that they're just so darn cute together, not to mention so talented." She placed a hand to her heart and sighed. "We're real proud to claim them both."

"I'm sure you are, as well you should be."

She proudly pointed to the shelves behind the counter. "We have signed copies of the cookbook for sale, if you're interested."

For all the sincere pride she had, he hadn't missed the bit of a gleam amid all the twinkle, and had a feeling she might be one of Lani's more successful salespeople.

She eyed him up and down again. "Of course, now that you're here, we have something new to talk about."

"I assure you, there won't be much to say. I'm just here for some peace and quiet, working on my next book."

"Well, we're really happy to have you back. You're a Brannigan, so, of course, you're family here. Your grandparents are missed in these parts. Miss Annie made the best cobblers for our fall festivals, and Gavin could always be counted on to contribute to the big annual fish fry we had as part of our Independence Day festivities. Put in quite a good performance as part of our Christmas caroling group, too. Fine voice he had, solid baritone. Do you sing?"

"Ah, no, I'm afraid I don't." Quinn hadn't known about his grandfather singing carols, though he could well imagine it. It occurred to him some of the older locals on Sugarberry could probably share numerous stories with him about his grandparents, adding to his own memories. He was excited to spend some of his time pursuing exactly that.

"'Course, you could have come back sooner," Miss Alva went on to say. "We'd have kept your privacy private."

"You know, since coming back, I've wondered why I didn't come back sooner. My memories here are all good ones."

"Well, now you've got that fancy place and all, don't know what more you could want." She leaned forward and dropped her voice again. "You're not planning on having any of those wild celebrity parties, are you?"

He covered her hand with his own. "I can assure you, that's not anywhere in my plans."

She looked relieved . . . and a little disappointed.

Quinn swallowed the urge to grin. "And the house, yes, it's very nice, but I'd have been at home in my grandfather's old place, if it were still there."

"Real shame when the storm took it out. But Ted Rivers, the man who owns the property now, has done it up real nice. You should go over, say hello. He'd get a kick out of showing you around. 'Course, the rest of us will never hear the end of it, but it might do you good, visiting what was once the family home."

Quinn grinned. "I've been by, but haven't said my hellos. Didn't want to disturb anyone. Maybe I'll go ahead and do that, then. Thanks."

She gave his hand a little pat before he slid it away.

"We're all glad you're here, and I'm happy to be the one to welcome you back." The merry twinkle appeared in her eyes again, the one that looked innocent enough at first glance . . . but made the back of his neck itch a little.

"So, can I just leave this with you?" he asked, offering her the bag.

"Certainly. If Riley asked you to leave it with us, you can be sure we'll see that she gets it." Alva took the bag, set it on the counter between them. "Of course," she added with such studied innocence his neck immediately started itching up a storm, "if you just hang around a few more minutes, you can give it to her yourself."

"Oh," he said, trying, and failing, to find the appropriate facial expression or response to that bit of information. His heart had instinctively leaped at the news, which was why his mind had immediately started running through the very long list of reasons why he shouldn't wait. "Well, I don't want to be in your way, or hers, so, if you'll just make sure—"

"Nonsense," Alva said, and he realized the twinkle-twinkle meant danger-danger. She was at full sparkle, and he knew damn well those wheels were turning up there under that scrupulously sculpted beehive bonnet. "In fact, you could help us out while you wait. Lani is back there right now, testing out a new recipe, and she's always wanting feedback. I'm sure she'd love to have your opinion." Alva beamed. "Play your cards right, maybe we'll name it after you. Our newest island celebrity! Or should I say our latest? Maybe you and Baxter will start a trend. Though I certainly hope it doesn't mean more house renovations. No offense. But we like to keep things simple around here."

"None taken. Simple has always been good enough for me. And please, pass along my hellos to Miss Lani, but I should really be getting—"

"Just wait right there. Now don't you move." Alva

pointed a finger. "Miss Lani," she called out as she headed
to a swinging door leading to the rear of the shop. "You'll
never guess who's dropped in for a visit. Come on out and
say hello, if you can."

Quinn shook his head and smiled. Wily, that one was. It
would do him well to remember it. Since there was no es-
caping without appearing rude, which he wouldn't do for a
multitude of reasons, he took a closer look at the shop. And
hoped like hell he'd manage to get out the door before
Riley made an appearance. More time with her meant more
things he'd be able to recall about her when he least wanted
to. Danger, danger, indeed.

He glanced away from the cases of cupcakes. More
temptation was the last thing he needed at the moment. His
attention was drawn to the framed photos lining the front
wall on either sides of the front door. On one side was a
black-and-white picture of the bakery in a former incarna-
tion. Judging from the car parked out front, he guessed the
photo had been taken sometime in the late 1930s or early
'40s. Beneath that was a bright, cheerful photo of the shop
on grand opening day with a beaming woman he assumed
was Leilani Dunne—or whatever her name had been
then—standing arm in arm with an older gentleman wearing a local sheriff's uniform. He knew from Riley that
would be her father. Leyland, he thought he recalled her
saying.

Smiling, he took in several more *then* and *now* photos
taken around the town square. The older photos were all
from the same era as the old bakery photo, before either his
time on Sugarberry or even his grandparents' time. He
thought for all the progress that had come to the small island over the years, keeping it a thriving community, not
much seemed to have changed regarding its charm. The
pace was slow now, as it had been then; the islanders were
a close-knit community, yet welcoming to new arrivals.

They had sustained a self-sufficient, modest economy that didn't rely on the tourist trade as most of the other, more populated islands in the chain did.

He'd noted the signs in the window of Laura Jo's diner that Wi-Fi was available, and the GO GREEN! flyer encouraging islanders to attend the meeting at the community center on proposed steps to keep the island environmentally friendly. And another announcing the upcoming annual fall festival coming in October, complete with a variety of carnival races and contests anyone could enter, and a pie-eating competition. So, progressive, yet protective of their more traditional, if not old-fashioned Southern sensibilities and way of life.

He shifted over to the other series of small photos, framed and mounted in a mosaic pattern on the other side of the door, tucked into the narrow strip of wall between the doorframe and the big display window. Some were in color, some black and white, but they were all current, he thought. All were scenes taken from various points on the island outside the immediate town square. There were some from the docks, which he recognized, but most were dunes, sand, beaches, or marshes. He had similar prints in his bungalow, though most were somewhat larger. There were small ones, too, tucked into alcoves and used as accent pieces on various walls here and there throughout the place. Riley had had some on her houseboat as well. A local artist, he thought.

He slid his hands into his back pockets and rocked slightly on his heels as he let the photographs' natural beauty draw him in. The photographer had captured the serenity and the wildness. He could actually hear the waves, and feel the breeze that moved the dune grasses, smell the salt and brine in the air.

While the town photos had captured the people, the community, these captured the uniqueness of Sugarberry. For all that it was simply another small Southern town in so many ways, it was also an island community, with all the distinctive elements that set it apart from any other town or place.

"They're good, aren't they?"

Quinn glanced over his shoulder to find a pretty brunette standing behind him . . . sporting an Alice in Wonderland apron. He smiled and turned. "Yes, they are. Hello, you must be Leilani Dunne. Your cupcakes are incredible." He put out his hand. "Quinn Brannigan."

"Thank you!" She took his hand in a firm, quick shake. "Yes, Mr. Brannigan, I know who you are. Though may I say that while the photo of you on your books is quite good, you're a great deal more . . . charismatic, in person."

His smile deepened. "Very kind of you." He nodded toward her apron. "I noticed Miss Alva's apron, too. I like the whimsy. Suits the place."

She beamed, maybe flushed just a bit pink. "Thank you. I've collected them since I was little. It's been fun to have someplace to trot them all out."

She lifted up a tray with cubed pieces of cake arranged on it. A brown-flecked cake with melted caramel oozing out from the center. "I'm working on new recipes for the fall festival. These are my reverse caramel apple in spiced cake, with the caramel on the inside. Care to try a bite and give me an honest opinion?"

"I think I'm sold just looking at them, but certainly." He took one of the toothpicks, pierced a cubed piece, and cradled his free hand under it to catch any of the drizzling caramel.

"Still warm, but okay to bite into," Lani said.

He popped it in his mouth and immediately closed his eyes as the flavors of apple, cinnamon, nutmeg, and creamy caramel burst and melted on his tongue at the same time. He groaned, just a little.

Lani laughed. "Okay. I think that's all the opinion I need. These go on the DEFINITELY CONSIDERING IT list."

All Quinn could do was nod.

Lani started to turn away, but not before Quinn shot her a fast grin and speared one more piece. She laughed and carried the sampler tray over to the counter.

After another moment spent contemplating how one bite of anything could be so decadently delicious, he said, "Would you happen to know who the photographer is who took the beach scene photos? I think I have some by the same person in my bungalow."

"I do," Lani said, then lifted the handled bag sitting by the register.

"Good. I'm interested in buying some prints." He pointed to the bag. "That's for Riley. Uh, Miss Brown. Towels and a shirt I borrowed after Brutus and I did a little dance on the docks. All laundered and clean."

Lani laughed. "We heard about that. Brutus really is just a big lump of love."

"So I keep hearing," Quinn said with a smile. "Will you make sure she gets that? She said it was okay to drop it off here. I hope you don't mind."

"Not at all, I'd be happy to, but you can just give it to her yourself."

"Oh, that's not—"

Lani inclined her head in a nod toward the front of the store. "She's coming in the door, as we speak."

Quinn, still standing in front of the door, turned just as Riley passed by the big front display window. "Right."

"You can talk to her about the prints, too."

Quinn glanced back at Lani. "She knows the photographer?"

Lani smiled as she bumped the swinging door to the kitchen open with her hip. "She *is* the photographer."

Chapter 7

Riley pulled the shop door open and stepped inside just as Lani was pushing through the swinging door to go back to the kitchen. "Hey," she called, and Lani paused halfway through. "I'm here—I just had to come in the front. Shearin's produce truck is blocking the back alley. Again."

"I saw." Lani smiled. "Alva went over to talk to him."

Riley smiled back. "Really," she said with heightened interest. "Did she take her apron off this time?"

Lani nodded. "And refreshed her lipstick."

"Ah, taking one for the team. Admirable. Poor man won't know what hit him."

"I know. Poor Sam. Here he's been angling for one of Alva's home-cooked meals for as long as I've had the shop open, and she just isn't interested."

"I know. She told me Harold ruined her for all other men." Riley sighed and fanned herself as she said it.

"I know," Lani said. "Have you ever seen a picture of Harold?" Riley nodded and they indulged in a short burst of laughter.

"It is sweet, though," Riley said.

"All I know is if she can get Sam to stop parking his

truck diagonally across the alley every time he makes a delivery, I'll cater a dinner for him myself."

Riley wiggled her eyebrows. "Somehow, I'm not thinking Sam is going to want extra company. He only has eyes for Alva."

Lani laughed. "Despite what she says, I'm not so sure Alva minds as much as she claims to. Hey, could you flip the sign for me? But leave the door unlocked, just in case. Franco isn't here yet, and Charlotte phoned and said she'd be in at some time tonight."

"Really? They're back?"

Charlotte and Carlo had gone back to New York so she could meet his giant, extended Puerto Rican family.

"That's great! Did she say how it went? How did the big introductions go? Is he going to go back to New Delhi with her to meet her folks?"

"She didn't have time to say, but she sounded happy. We'll get the nitty-gritty tonight. If we have to drag it out of her."

"I'll help pull," Riley said with a laugh. She piled her toolbox and quilted tote on the counter, then leaned down and took an appreciative sniff of the sampler plate. "What's on the tray?"

"Oh, right. I forgot I put those there. Inside-out caramel apple." There was a little quirk to her smile. "You'll all get to taste test tonight. I just brought them up front to get an outside opinion from a new customer."

Recognizing the quirk in Lani's smile, Riley's grew more bemused. "Really. Anyone I know?"

Lani motioned to a point behind Riley. "I believe you may have met once or twice." Then she pushed the rest of the way through the door. "Don't forget to turn the sign! He's distracting like that," she called out as the door swung shut behind her.

Riley frowned, completely confused, then popped a tester cupcake cube in her mouth, and promptly forgot everything else as she groaned in abject appreciation. She remained where she stood, enjoying every last bit of the entire flavor experience, then sighed in pleasure before turning to get her stuff. "Oh, right. The sign." She turned back to the door, only to jump back a half step, then stop dead in her tracks.

Quinn lifted his hand and gave her a short wave.

"It's like you were put on this earth to give me repeated heart attacks," Riley said, dropping the hand she realized she'd clasped to her chest like some fluttering heroine in a sultry, Southern drama.

"I didn't want to interrupt, that's all. Sounds like an exciting evening ahead. I didn't realize it was closing time. I can see myself out."

There hadn't been a trace of sarcasm in his voice, so she kept her tone politely casual as well. "We close early on Mondays, at six. It's usually the slowest business day."

"We? Do you moonlight for Lani?"

"No, I just—we're family here. Of sorts."

"Right." He smiled. "So this would be bitchy bake night, then."

Riley rolled her eyes, but couldn't help laughing. "I see you've met Miss Alva. She does help out in the shop from time to time."

"Wise choice. She's a good salesperson. I don't know any of the other members she mentioned, but it sounds like you've assembled quite the group. Sounds like fun."

Riley lifted an eyebrow. "It is—if you enjoy baking, anyway. Somehow I don't see you frosting little cakes, but—"

"My skills are many and varied," he said. "But, you're right. The only thing I ever baked was biscuits with my grandmother, and that was ages ago. I'm not sure being the designated biscuit cutter really qualifies me even as that. I had to stand on a stool."

Riley's smile warmed, even though she was determined not to soften toward him. She needed to stop thinking about him. All the time. He needed to stop being charming. And memorable. More Quinn Moments she definitely did not need. And right before Cupcake Club, too. She needed him gone before Franco and his all-knowing eyes and ears strolled in. "I think that sounds rather sweet, actually. I'm sure she loved the help."

"She did. It's a good memory. Actually, when I walked in here and took in how good everything smelled, it brought back all kinds of memories of being in my grandmother's kitchen over the years. Many that I'd forgotten."

"Scent is a powerful trigger," Riley said.

"Yes," he agreed, and somehow those crystal blue eyes of his grew fractionally darker, and a lot more focused. "It certainly is."

Riley felt her skin come alive, but not in an embarrassed flush this time. More like a sudden, intense awareness. Their parting conversation the last time they'd crossed paths echoed through her mind. *A woman who has to ask what she's worth . . . without already knowing the answer.* Or words to that effect.

"How did you and Lani come to know each other?" he asked.

"Why?"

His smile spread to a grin. The kind of grin that did nothing whatsoever to help her maintain her equilibrium.

"Just making conversation, that's all. I'm a writer. We want to know everything. I like knowing more about people. I enjoyed the things you shared about some of the folks here, who've come to be your friends."

Yet another reason she needed to get him out the door.

"I, uh, well, there's not much to the story, really. I had just moved here, and I was exploring the town square, checking out all the shops." She edged past him to flip the sign. "While working as a stylist for *Foodie*—that's the food magazine I was on staff with back in Chicago—I'd heard about Lani's shop, and the whole story with Baxter bringing his show here to woo her and . . ." And she'd thought it ridiculously romantic. But she wasn't going to share that with Quinn. "So, I made a point to stop in. We're both tied to the same industry, or were anyway, in my previous life, so I wanted to say hello. She was in the kitchen, so I poked around while waiting for her to come up front, and, I guess I found myself rearranging things—just a little."

Quinn lifted a brow. "Rearranging things? Like the displays?"

"Her window treatment was all wrong. The cases were good, but they could have been improved, and the shelves behind the register weren't really being put to the best possible use." Riley smiled and shrugged. "I can't help it. I'm a stylist. It's how my brain works. Anyway, I was just sort of moving things around a tiny bit in the big display window, nothing major, just . . . little adjustments, waiting for her to come out."

"And she caught you, red-handed? Or cake-handed, as the case may be?"

Riley laughed at that, and felt the guard she'd tried to keep up collapse like so many cupcakes on a three-tier crystal display stand. "More like frosting-fingered. I sort of knocked one of the little signs over and it snagged the display tablecloth and—"

Quinn lifted his hand. "I think I've witnessed this first-hand."

Riley did flush then, but it wasn't so embarrassing anymore. He knew about her klutz tendencies, and apparently found them amusing, or at the very least not off-putting.

She found herself laughing as she once again owned her shortcomings, and he laughed along with her. Of course, defenses down, their gazes happened to catch, as they always seemed to do at some point when they were together and . . . *dammit*, she was sucked right back into another one of those moments.

At least they were moments to her. She'd swear they were for him, too. That whole deepening blue thing happened as his pupils expanded, and her throat went dry and her palms grew damp. Their laughter faded, but somehow, the goofy smiles did not, and for some reason she couldn't explain, that made the moment even hotter, more intense, than all the previous moments combined. Maybe because they had a shared history, now that they knew more—and liked more—about each other.

"Anyway," she managed, pushing gamely past the sudden tightness in her throat, "I apologized for the wreckage, explained what I was doing, and made a few suggestions. We got to talking about my background, and we knew some of the same people." She lifted a shoulder. "It happened to be a Monday, in fact the shop should have been closed. She'd just forgotten to flip the sign, which was why she'd been in the kitchen as long as she had. Some of the gang started showing up, and she introduced me around, and somehow I found myself back in the kitchen, and . . ." She smiled and shrugged.

"Baking happened," Quinn finished.

"It did, indeed. I've been part of the bitchy bake group ever since."

"I would imagine it's been a nice tie-in, between the work you do now, and what you did before, working with food and all. Why the change?" he asked. "And the migration?"

Her defenses down, Riley wasn't prepared for the question. Something of that showed on her face, and he lifted his hand to halt her response. "You know, none of my business. Even writers don't get to know everything. I didn't mean to pry."

"Fair's fair," she said, "I asked about your family and history here." Riley smiled briefly . . . but didn't exactly get around to answering the question.

"Do you enjoy what you're doing down here? Staging homes? I guess it's a much grander scale than styling food, bigger platform, bigger challenge. Bigger payoff?" He held her gaze for a moment, then let out a short, self-deprecating laugh. "I'm doing it again."

She couldn't help it, she laughed, too. "You just can't help yourself, can you? If you were a cat—"

"I know," he said with a fast grin. "I'd be dead right now. Usually I'm less impulsive about it, but what you did in Chicago, what you do here . . . I find it all fascinating. We're both in creative fields, but so very different in what we draw from, how we build our respective scenes, so to speak." He shrugged. "It's compelling and interesting and makes me want to know more."

"Well, I'm flattered," she said.

But it wasn't by accident that she changed the subject. "Lani said you were a new customer. Did you come by to pick up some cupcakes? They are addictive."

He hesitated, then said, "Actually, I was just dropping off the towels and your shirt." He pointed to the shopping bag, still sitting on the counter by the register. "All freshly laundered, good as new."

"Oh, thanks. Although nothing can make that jersey good as new again." It had been bugging her, the whole subterfuge thing, so she added, "I've had it since I was in high school." She smiled. "But I appreciate the effort."

Quinn's smile returned, too. The kind with crinkles

around the eyes and that honest warmth filling them. "High school, huh?" He exuded all that charisma as naturally as most people breathed air.

"Actually, it's Tommy Flanagan's jersey." Her smile turned dry. "I'm just not as good at returning things as you are."

"High school sweetheart?"

Riley laughed at that. "Only in my desperate little schoolgirl dreams. Tommy was the football quarterback, debate team captain, and senior class president, all rolled into one."

"I hate him already," Quinn said.

Riley grinned. "He made it hard to do that. He was the kind of guy everybody loved. But when it came to girls, he was the head cheerleader type, and well . . . I was definitely not that."

"So, how'd you end up with the jersey?"

Her smile turned rueful, and a tiny bit of heat infused her cheeks. "Let's just say the less than graceful moments you've had the pleasure of witnessing when you've been around me had their roots very early on in my childhood. By high school, I was a full-fledged dork. In this case, it involved a ridiculous attempt on my part to impress him with my pre-track warm-up skills—of which I had absolutely none, by the way—and the very unfortunate timing of the track field irrigation system flipping on."

"Aw. I'm sorry. Though I'm sure you made a very charming drowned track dork."

She laughed. "I don't know that Tommy shared your vision, but he was a gentleman. My track suit was white. Opaque when dry, not so much when wet. When wet, it showcased the little yellow ducks on my matching cotton bra and underwear."

Quinn closed his eyes and shook his head, trying not to laugh.

"Don't hold back on my account," she told him. "I mean,

any sixteen-year-old girl who has ducks on her underwear deserves what she gets." She waited a beat, then added, "Soooo sexy."

He opened one eye, caught hers, and they went off in peals of laughter. "I'm sorry. That's just . . . so wrong of me," he finally managed, wiping the corner of one eye. "I'm sure you were adorable in ducks." That sent them off all over again.

"Sadly, they were utterly me," she agreed, trying to catch her breath.

"Well, if it makes you feel any better," he said as they struggled to get themselves back under control, "we share track and field attempts to impress gone awry. I think I told you, I was a skinny kid in school. I really loved sports, but I was too small for football, and not tall enough at that point for basketball. Baseball wasn't my thing, so I went out for track. In the case of my brutal downfall, it was the state championship meet, my first year on the team, and I was going to impress Amy Sue Henderson, star distance runner from our crosstown rival, with my mad pole-vaulting skills."

Riley covered her mouth to keep the laughter from starting all over again. "And?" she said, the word muffled behind her hand.

"You know how you run down the lane, plant the pole in the pit, then launch yourself over the bar to the big mat on the other side?"

All Riley could do was nod at that point, tears of mirth already forming at the corners of her eyes.

"Well, I took off running, and made the mistake of looking over, midstride, to see if she was watching. And when I saw that she was, I got all hung up in those pretty green eyes, and it threw me off count. I planted the pole on the track, missed the pit entirely, tried to launch myself any-way—"

Riley covered her open mouth.

"—snapped the pole in half, and landed in a skinny, crumpled, disgraced heap in the pit."

Riley's hand dropped away. "Were you okay?"

"My body was fine. I would have sworn then, though, that my ego would never recover. Or my self-confidence."

"What did Amy Sue do?"

"Let's just say she wasn't raised with the same admirable traits as Mr. Flanagan. She and her teammates were highly amused."

"Bitch," Riley whispered.

Quinn grinned. "It was painful, but a lesson was learned that day."

"Which was?"

"Run softly and be careful where you plant your big stick?"

Riley spluttered a laugh. "I can't believe you just said that."

"Sorry." A mischievous twinkle glowed in his blue eyes as he laughed along with her. "Actually, I learned to be more realistic in my goals. On and off the field. And to stay focused on the more important ones."

"How did you get yourself back in the meet? I mean, could you?"

"I stumbled through the three other events I was in. It's mostly a mortifying blur. Unfortunately there was no Hollywood ending where I went on to dominate in all the other disciplines and take home multiple golds. But by the time track season rolled around the following year, I'd gained some size along with a lot of height. I worked really hard, and I got pretty good at it."

"Decathlete, you said. That's impressive."

He shrugged, his smile self-deprecating and far too endearing because of it. "By my senior year. Maybe I was just trying to prove myself to the Amy Sue Hendersons of the world."

"Maybe." Riley understood the feeling. "Maybe we're always doing that, in one form or another."

His expression sobered a bit, and their gazes connected again, but, for once, he didn't probe, didn't push. And she was more grateful than he could possibly know. The whole fiasco with Jeremy had brought a lot of her insecurities crashing back, and though she was dealing with them, it was still a sensitive topic.

Quinn turned and nodded toward the photos framed on the wall by the door. "Lani tells me this is your work."

"It is," she said, thankful for the shift in topic once again.

"They're really good. I'm assuming the prints in the bungalow are yours, too? And obviously, the houseboat. I guess I should have put it together."

She shrugged. "I don't see why you would have."

"David handled all the paperwork for keeping the furniture and things, but I did go over the inventory list to make sure we hadn't missed anything. I didn't see you listed as a lease or buyer contact."

"Since most of my jobs are somewhere along the chain of barrier islands, I use my prints in some of the houses I stage."

"So, were some of the shots taken on the other islands as well?"

She glanced at the photos that Lani had chosen for the shop. One in particular was a small print of a picnic table in the wilderness park just down the road from Lani's place. It had played an important role during Lani's courtship with Baxter. She'd talked about it once at Cupcake Club, so Riley had done some exploring, found the place, and shot it as a gift for the couple's first anniversary. A larger print of the same shot, matted and framed, hung in their home.

"Occasionally, but these were all taken here." Various other memories flitted through Riley's mind, of time spent wandering with her camera. Brutus often forged the way. That made her smile. She had albums full of photos of him, discovering his place in island life, too. "Taking them was a large part of how I came to fall in love with the island," she murmured, then realized she'd spoken the musing out loud.

"I can see why." He came to stand beside her.

She kept her gaze fixed on the prints, but there were a lot of other images crowding her mind. None of them framed and on the wall.

"I didn't mean to keep your work from you," he said. "I'm guessing you usually take your prints back down after the homes are done being shown. If you want me to return them, I will." He shifted his gaze to her. She could feel it, like a warm caress. "But I'd prefer to keep them, or at least some of them. I'll get David to work out whatever compensation—"

"They can all stay. No compensation required." She wished like mad every little glance and word from him didn't affect her so acutely.

"Well, if you ever need them for a job—"

"I'm good," she assured him. "I have plenty. And I'm always taking more."

"Thank you. I appreciate it. They're a big part of why the bungalow feels . . . right to me." He made a soft snort. "How's that for a descriptive turn of phrase?"

She smiled. It made perfect sense to her. "I'm glad you like them."

"Does Lani sell your prints? Are they for sale, I mean? If so, I'd—"

Riley shook her head. "These were gifts to her, mostly because she kept bugging me about them after seeing a few I'd put up on the houseboat. She's offered, many times in fact, to put more in here on a commission basis. But I don't want to . . . I don't know, commercialize the work, if that makes any sense. I take them because what I'm looking at makes me want to capture it, for my own pleasure. If I think it will move someone else, then I give it to them. But that's all the satisfaction I need or want, really. It's just something I do for myself. A hobby, I guess. I don't want it to be work."

"Well, as hobbies go, it's a spectacular one. If you ever change your mind, the offer stands."

"Thank you. I'll keep it in mind."

"What about the older prints?" he asked, motioning to the black-and-whites on the other side of the door. "There are some of those in the bungalow, too."

"Lani came across them when she was cleaning out this place after buying it. It had stood empty for some time and there were boxes of stuff left behind long ago."

"Nice find," he said. "I like the historical bookends. Old and new, then and now. So the older prints in the bungalow, they wouldn't have come from here?"

"No, they didn't. I don't know how much you know about the place, but the bungalow had been unoccupied for a very, very long time. The older gentleman who owned it had apparently used it as a summer place decades ago. He had been in ill health for many years, and left it to sit, mostly neglected. When he passed away a few years back, his executor put it on the market. Two investors finally bought it, had it completely renovated and updated, and really made something of the place, as you've seen. It's quite a showpiece, especially here on Sugarberry. The pictures you have were either already on the walls, or found in storage boxes. Fortunately, the new owners didn't ditch them. I found them stacked up in one of the upstairs bedrooms, and decided to use them. So, they go with the house."

"That they do," he agreed, though she knew he under-stood she'd meant they were conveyed with the lease agreement. "Your work complements the vision of whoever took them. Your viewpoints are much the same. Kind of interesting, when you think about it. Two people whose paths never crossed, from different eras, both moved by the same setting in much the same way, both documenting it in their own way."

She smiled at that and found herself nudging his arm with her elbow. "You're such a writer."

"Storyteller," he corrected. "And yep, I can't help it. That's how I see things, I guess. How I document what I see. I think about the story that goes with them, or that might have gone with them. If I were telling it."

"Have you always known?" she asked. "About being a storyteller?"

"Um . . . my understanding of the calling developed over time, but looking back, there were clues all along. What about you? Have you always had an eye for setting? Either behind the lens, or staging and styling the things in front of it?"

She smiled. "I was forever rearranging my stuffed animals and I set a mean tea party table, even as a five-year-old, so . . . yes, you could say that."

He grinned at that. "Did you head straight into that field?"

She glanced up at him again. "Yes, Curious George, I did."

He laughed. "I've gone from dead cat to curious monkey. But I'm done apologizing. I can't help it. The subject matter is very interesting to me."

"Interior design?"

"No." His gaze landed very squarely on her own. "The woman doing the designing."

She hadn't been prepared for that. For the intensity of his gaze. Or the way it tied her tongue right up.

"*Bonsoir, ma petite* bakers," Franco called out as he

sailed into the shop. "Oh." He stopped short as he almost stumbled straight into them. "Didn't see you there." He ran his gaze openly over Quinn. "Well, 'allo, *Monsieur*... Brannigan, I presume?"

Quinn kept his gaze on Riley's for a fraction of a second longer, then glanced up at Franco. "Quinn," he said. "Please."

"Franco." He stuck his beefy hand out and they struck a quick shake. Franco glanced between the two of them and Riley could see the struggle between the knowing smile and the frown of concern.

"Lani is in the back," Riley said. "Alva is next door." She wiggled her eyebrows, hoping to distract him. "Dealing with Sam. And Charlotte is back! She'll be in tonight."

Franco clapped his wide palms together. "A tasty evening menu, for sure." He kept his gaze straight on Riley's. "Will you be joining us?"

"I will. Quinn—Mr. Brannigan, was just dropping something off for me."

"Ah, the borrowed shirt," Franco said, his openly curious gaze moving back to Quinn. "I see."

"I've taken up enough of your time," Quinn said to Riley, then looked at Franco. "A pleasure to meet you." He turned back to Riley. "Thank you for the loan, and for indulging the dead cat. And the curious monkey. Both are greatly appreciative."

She couldn't help it, even with Franco sucking in every blink, she grinned. "Did I have a choice?"

"We all have choices." He smiled at them as he sketched a slight bow, and let himself out.

Riley immediately lifted her hand, blocking Franco's handsome face. "Don't start. Do not even start. I can't. Okay?"

She looked up, expecting to find either a pout or a devil-ish smile. Instead, his expression was completely unreadable. It was so unlike him, she wasn't quite sure what to think of it.

"Okay." He put his hand at the small of her back and guided her to the counter where her baking tote and toolbox still sat.

"That's it? Are you feeling all right?"

"Better than I have in a very long time." He surprised her by leaning down and planting a kiss on top of her head. "Just remember, I'm always here if you need me."

She surprised them both by turning and hugging him tight. "I know you are." She looked up and smiled. "I'm a lucky girl."

He leaned down and kissed her nose. "You don't know the half of it, honey." They laughed as they headed to the kitchen.

Chapter 8

"It's coming along fine," he lied. Quinn tucked his cell phone between his ear and shoulder as he shifted gears and pulled his Carrera into the narrow, crushed shell and gravel lot behind Laura Jo's and parked. He didn't immediately get out, wanting to finish the call with his editor first.

It was already humid and, even though the calendar had finally turned the page to September, he knew the day would be a scorcher. At the moment, there was a steady, early morning breeze. It carried the rich, mingling scents of sizzling bacon and fresh roasted coffee wafting out the screened kitchen door, straight through the open windows of his car, making his stomach grumble in appreciation.

He'd started something of a habit, indulging himself with a hot breakfast a few mornings a week. Those delectable smells didn't begin to promise what they actually delivered, providing another reason to end his call as swiftly as possible.

"Good, great! So . . . can you give me a delivery date? Pretty please," Claire begged. "Just so I can keep the wolves at bay. They're starting to circle."

"I'm sure they are, and I'm sorry for that. I am. But it's not like we're behind schedule."

"I know, I know. We just usually have a publication date all picked out by now. Can you give me even a whisper of a general idea?"

Quinn sighed. He'd known the pressure would start sooner rather than later, but he hadn't expected the Big Push this soon. He should have, he supposed. With the industry struggling to find its way in an era filled with new gadgets and an ever-widening variety of publishing formats, all the New York publishing houses were feeling the pressure to do whatever it took to ensure their upcoming release lists remained strong and vital. He was at the top of his publisher's list in that department. An announcement of a new release from their best-selling author would go a long way toward quieting the wolves, from the publisher, to the distributors, and on down the chain, to the most important element . . . the reader.

No one was more keen on satisfying that particular link in the chain than he was.

"Claire, as soon as I feel I can give you a target, you'll be the very first to know. You know I'm consistent, I'm never late, and I don't let you down. So just tell everyone to calm down. They'll have another Brannigan title for next year's schedule. Sitting on my shoulder is not helping the process."

"I know, I know. You know I wouldn't be making a peep unless I really had to," she said, all contrition now.

"I do. Just glad we're on the same page. I'm looking forward to some uninterrupted writing time," he added pointedly.

"Of course," she said, though they both knew his uninterrupted time had been officially marked as limited now. "So, how is it down in Georgia?" she asked, which translated into *Is migrating to the middle of nowhere making you write any faster?*

"It's great, actually. Better than anticipated."

"Good, great!" she said, overly excited by the news. He knew she'd take that and run with it. *He's on a roll!,* she'd tell them.

"Always good to talk with you, Claire." He seized the chance to end on an enthusiastic note. "I'll be in touch." She should hear those words as *don't call me, I'll call you,* but they both knew she'd ignore them.

"It's good to touch base with you, Quinn." Sincere affection mixed in now that her official duties were complete. "You know, if you want to send me a partial, so I can start the marketing ball rolling—"

He rolled his eyes even as he smiled. Claire, after all, would always be Claire. Her professional duties were never really complete. He didn't fault her for continuing to push. Her bulldog-in-a-poodle-suit tenacity was what made her the successful executive editor she was. It worked to his advantage when she was fighting in-house to get him every possible edge in promotion and placement.

There was sincere warmth in his voice when he continued. "You know I don't write that way. I'm all over the place until the book is finished. That hasn't changed."

She laughed. "Can't fault a girl for trying. Besides, you know at heart I'm just a fan who can't wait to see what you're up to next."

If you only knew, he thought, feeling a different tug in his stomach.

The shame of it was, Quinn knew her statement to be utterly true. In addition to being savvy about marketing, branding, placement, and the business side as a whole, she was keyed in on an intimate level with his work. She didn't just get his work as it pertained to current marketing trends.

She truly understood and enjoyed his stories purely as a reader. She was his target audience.

It was that very duality that made them such a good team. He valued her input on all things, especially on story, more than she knew. However, the politics of the game didn't make that easy to express. Over the past few months, he'd been sorely tempted to pick up the phone, wanting to pick her brain about the new direction the current work was pushing him toward. Not to get her blessing, or force the panic attack such a revelation might induce, but to discuss the work itself. More than current market analysis, that was what he needed to help him decide what to do.

The problem was, she played for both sides. A fact he could never forget. There was no way to talk with her about his idea, without simultaneously announcing the same news to his entire publishing house. He couldn't ask her to keep it a secret until he decided, and he wasn't ready to make any kind of public announcement yet. It was the same reason he hadn't bent the ears of any of his fellow authors. Not that he couldn't trust their discretion, but this was not a typical brainstorming session. The idea that someone so successful in one genre was even contemplating switching it up would be too juicy a tidbit to keep under wraps. Especially in the current writer-eat-writer economic environment.

If and when he decided to change it up, he'd need to control the big reveal as best he could. He'd have to tell Claire immediately. It would be career suicide, on many levels, to just spring the manuscript on her, fait accompli, then let the chips fall where they may. But when—and if— he did tell Claire, he needed to be damn sure of what he was doing, so he could defend the book as thoroughly and enthusiastically as possible, ensuring to the best of his ability that it would be well received, with everyone on board his new train and thrilled to be there.

"We'll talk soon," Claire was saying.

Once again, he bit his tongue and kept his tumultuous thoughts to himself. "I know we will," he said dryly, accepting the inevitability of that. "Take care." His smile faded as he clicked off the phone. He groaned as he slid his sunglasses off and hooked them on the rearview mirror. The dragons were officially breathing fire.

Climbing out of the car, he pushed the aggravation away, focusing instead on the pleasures of Laura Jo's bacon and egg sandwich, the world's best coffee, and the friendly smiles and hearty welcomes of the locals who also made the diner part of their morning routine.

He'd wondered at first if he was making a mistake, if bumming around the island would end up inviting more distractions than he already had. Thanks to a small write-up in the local paper announcing he'd leased the old Turner place, and mentioning his ties to his grandfather and the island, everyone knew who he was, even those who'd never heard of him three or four weeks ago.

Although his ties were tenuous at best, it was precisely that connection to Sugarberry that had made him an instant local to the other islanders; welcomed, accepted, and, other than a nod and a friendly hello, largely left alone to his own devices. He appreciated both. More than he could have imagined. They also took a sense of pride and ownership of his accomplishments—local boy makes good—which could have come off as a bit of latching-on, but felt like a warm, supportive embrace.

He hadn't realized how un-embraced he'd felt, or just how solitary a life he'd led over the years. He considered himself social, and involved. He did charity work, played a round of golf with a few fellow writer buddies when he could. David and Finch were always about or in contact, and there was rarely a time when he wasn't traveling to see places he wrote about, or tracking down, meeting, or talking and listening to the broad range of people he interviewed and came to know while doing research for his books. He'd have said he had a full, vibrant, interesting life.

Yet, in a very short time, the span of a single month, the whole island had become as comfortable to him as his bungalow had been the moment he'd set foot in it. It felt like home. Or certainly a place he'd like to call home. Even with the monumental decision he had to make, he couldn't remember ever feeling so . . . grounded. Centered. As if rooted, toes in the sand, island breeze on his skin, and the quiet, loyal support, so good-naturedly offered up by everyone around him . . . he could free the rest of himself up to think, to ponder. To plot and plan—which would be ever-so-glorious . . . if he could just decide which version of the story he was going to tell.

His problem wasn't that he didn't know what to write next. He wasn't blocked. Quite the opposite. There were two stories dueling for supremacy in his head. The one he knew he could write, because he'd written it, or some version of it, a dozen times before. The one he knew, hands down, was a solid, marketable, exciting idea that would produce a great story once it was all done and told.

And the other one, the tantalizing one, the one luring him down a path that was dark and shadowy, where there was no rich experience, accumulated knowledge, and certainty to fall back on. That story was all but bursting inside his head, luring him like a seductive siren. Promising heat and fun and heady anticipation, even though he knew there was a better than average chance his career would end in one huge, crashing, explosive ball of flames.

The only real question was . . . did he risk the flaming ball of destruction for the chance to achieve what might be a slow, steady burn? One that could keep him in a heady, exciting place for many years to come?

"I wish to hell I knew," he muttered as he climbed the

short set of steps to the rear door of the diner. He'd needed to escape the four walls of his house . . . and the four sides of his beckoning computer screen. *Write what you know . . . make everyone happy . . . keep your day job.* Those were the words echoing in his ears when he sat down to work. As was often the case of late, it had driven him straight out the door through the dunes and to the beach.

But a long, limit-testing run or punishing sea swim hadn't done a damn thing to silence the voices . . . or convince him to embrace them. He knew the creative process was unpredictable at best, so he remained hopeful every time he set off down the sand, that the epiphany would come, that some thought or idea would signal to him why he should turn his back on the seductive siren call torturing him, and stick to the steady reliable companion he'd worked so hard to cultivate. To believe in. To trust. He'd already achieved that with his publisher, his editor, and most important, his readers. Was he tossing those relationships away, like a sorry bastard who cheated on his spouse?

But that wasn't even half his problem. Half his problem—hell, it felt like all of his problem—was those long runs that were supposed to promote clearheaded, rational thinking . . . did nothing of the kind.

No sooner would he settle into a nice loping stride than his thoughts would trip away from the dialogue his characters should be having to echoes of other conversations, real ones, of laughter shared and insights revealed . . . and a pair of devastating dimples bracketing a mouth he'd spent far—far—too much time wishing he'd already tasted.

What should have been a brief, inconsequential run-in at the bakery the previous week had turned out to be neither brief nor inconsequential. Every time he was with her, he learned more . . . and the temptation grew. He'd first told himself he was using his attraction to distract himself from the confusing and challenging choices he had to make. It wasn't the first time his head had been turned. He'd been writing long enough to see a distraction for what it was.

Riley Brown was in a whole new category. He couldn't truly imagine that he'd ever forget her.

Quinn opened the screen door to the kitchen and gave a small salute and smile to Laura Jo and her line cooks, who were busily plating and serving up dishes, sliding them across the top of the half wall that divided the kitchen from the front diner counter and the tables lining the walls beyond it. He'd come in through the kitchen door by mistake his first time, thinking it was merely the rear entrance, since that was where the parking lot was. But he'd learned most everyone either lived within walking distance, or worked around the town square, so they came on foot. A few tourists or island wanderers would park along the curb out front, in the few spaces available. Typically, the other cars in the rear lot belonged to Laura Jo and her staff.

She'd thought he was sneaking in due to his celebrity status, which had made him laugh. Despite his sales numbers and his smiling face plastered on book jackets around the globe, he was like the rest of the best-selling authors out there—household names no one would recognize in person.

At best, he got the "where do I know that guy from?" look or a head scratch. It was amusing when Laura Jo had seated him discreetly in the back of the restaurant, right by the kitchen door, thinking he wanted privacy, and then had snuck samples of all kinds of heavenly goodies to him. He'd appreciated her sensitivity even if, normally, it would be unwarranted. With Sugarberry being so small, and folks knowing everything about each other's business, he'd accepted the privacy she'd offered, simply for the chance to think and plot without interruption.

But on Sugarberry, there really was no such thing as privacy, no matter where he sat. On the other hand, because he'd been so quickly and warmly adopted by the islanders, rather than finding their smiles and jovial hellos and hey, how are yas intrusive or suffocating, he found them welcoming and heartwarming.

He felt like the Norm character from the iconic *Cheers* television program, with everyone raising a mug or tossing out a friendly hello whenever he wandered in. Sometimes the islanders engaged Quinn in conversation, other times they'd leave him to his thoughts, but he was always greeted warmly and openly. More surprising to him was that, rather than sit back and keep to his own thoughts, or observe and listen, he found himself actively engaging in the conversations that sprang up around him, as most of the other diners did, everyone talking over each other and any number of conversations converging, dividing, then converging again. He'd immensely enjoyed the give-and-take, learning more about his new neighbors, and finding himself sincerely and actively getting caught up in their lives.

He still used the back entrance, though more as an amusing tradition, one he and Laura Jo enjoyed . . . and he still took the rear table by the kitchen door. Mostly because Laura Jo still spoiled him with tasty tidbits.

He pushed through the door to the diner that morning and was greeted by a wave of "Hey," and "Mornin' " and nods or coffee mug salutes all around. He gave a short wave and a smile to everyone, then settled in at his table, which already had a well-thumbed copy of the *Daily Islander* on it, even though it was barely past nine in the morning. He'd also discovered islanders were an early rising lot, and knew he was easily the fifth or sixth occupant of that table that morning. Not being a morning person, his leisurely mornings were one of the things he enjoyed best about writing for a living. That had shifted a bit since his arrival on Sugarberry. He wasn't entirely certain why, but when the sun came up, he generally followed close behind it.

He was getting more regular exercise now than he ever managed in the city . . . which he was doubly thankful for. He'd relearned the joys of the slower-paced, Southern lifestyle . . . most especially as it pertained to the utter pleasure to be found in lingering over a well-prepared meal and a good cup of coffee. To that end, he settled back in his chair, the tension from Claire's call already easing out of his neck and shoulders, then smiled broadly as he picked up the paper and realized it was Thursday.

Miss Alva's advice column ran on Thursdays.

Laura Jo popped out with a fresh cup of coffee, two creams, one sugar, which wasn't at all how he'd taken it in his former life, but how he always had his coffee now. "Thanks," he told her, wondering how he'd ever enjoyed the brew bitter and black. "That bacon smells incredible."

"Good. You're about to get some with an egg, sunny-side up, on two slices of grilled toast."

Quinn closed his eyes in anticipation. "My heart and soul thank you, even if my arteries do not."

"Come now, a finer specimen of a man I don't recall I've ever seen. Except, of course, for my Johnny. Rest his soul."

"Of course," Quinn agreed with a smile, "and thank you kindly." She spouted some version of the same sort of flattery every time he came in, and he was quite certain did the same with every other customer as well, sounding just as sincere, which was a large part of her charm. And why his cheeks warmed right up, every time.

"I'll be right back out," she said with a wink.

He grinned and shook his head, taking another sip of the sweet, creamy, aromatic brew as he flipped the paper open straight to "Ask Alva." The column was purported to be an advice column, but was, in fact . . . nothing easy to label. Folks did send in letters, and they did ask her advice, but that only seemed like a flimsy excuse to gossip about everyone on the island. She didn't name names, but there was no doubt to anyone who lived on Sugarberry—which comprised the entire readership of the daily paper—whom she was referring to as she spun her tales of "advice." She always managed to include a colorful story about how someone of her acquaintance had once done something similar to someone else. The end result rarely was a flattering portrayal, but was always told in such an entertaining manner, it never left a bad taste. Well, other than perhaps to the person being scolded for their bad behavior. But since they generally appeared to deserve it . . . Quinn didn't judge himself too harshly for being amused.

It did make him wonder why anyone would send a letter in and assume they'd retain any sense of anonymity, which led him to suspect the actual validity of those letters . . . but as a born storyteller, he'd immensely enjoyed the few columns he'd read thus far and settled in with the happy anticipation of another round of entertaining anecdotes over breakfast.

Laura Jo popped out a moment later and slid a steaming plate in front of him. It was like a mini buffet for one. He loved the South. In addition to the egg and bacon grilled sandwich, there was a side of pan-browned, hashed potatoes, a small bowl of buttered grits, and what he knew was going to be a melt-in-your-mouth flaky, buttermilk biscuit. Add to that the little bowl of apple butter, another one of sausage gravy, and a second mug of coffee to replace the one he'd already drained, and it was his own personal definition of the "great and grand beyond"—which was where it would likely send him, if he kept eating like this, he thought with a chuckle . . . then dove right in.

When Laura Jo stopped by to top off his mug again, Quinn looked straight into her lively gray eyes. "Will you marry me?"

"Well, now that my sweet Johnny has met his maker . . . I am available," she responded, without missing a beat. "Of course, I'll expect you to take me away from all this."

He gave her a look of mock horror. "Why would I want to do that?"

She leaned down and propped her ample frame on the table with one hand, while the other expertly kept her serving tray aloft. "If I can put out that food you're devouring from my little, sorry excuse of an aging kitchen where half the stuff don't work unless you kick it, pound it, or swear at it, imagine what I could whip up for you on that brand-new Viking I hear you have." She fluttered her lashes as she straightened. "I'll consider that your dowry."

Quinn laughed outright, then took her hand and kissed the back of it. "Take me, I'm yours!"

She tugged her hand free, then swatted him with the towel she kept tucked in her apron pocket, but not before he spied the bit of pink in her cheeks. "Scoundrel."

"Saucy temptress."

She laughed even as she snapped the towel at his leg and stepped back toward the kitchen. "Just because you have a way with words, don't think you can woo me."

"Good thing Johnny's not around, or I'd have to tell him to keep an eye on his back," he called out as the door swung shut behind her. Still grinning, he continued his meal with renewed energy, like a man starved, knowing it wasn't so much his belly but his battle with indecision fueling his need for biscuit-and-gravy comfort. There were few forms of comfort more satisfying than a home-cooked Southern breakfast.

His mind immediately skipped from Alva's sermon on the evils of coveting your neighbor's wife and how she once knew a certain tackle shop owner who should really have kept his bait on ice . . . to a different kind of comfort food. Riley Brown came directly to mind, full lips parted, blouse opened, with chocolate frosting smeared all over her—

"Well, look who's up early and eating like a man should first thing in the morning."

Quinn startled guiltily from his little reverie, so much so that he rattled the table and almost knocked his coffee mug over. He quickly steadied everything, then looked up to find all five-foot-nothing of Alva Liles smiling straight at him. "Good morning to you, Miss Alva. What has you up and about this fine morning?"

Quinn shifted uncomfortably in his seat, thankful for the linen napkin covering his lap, certain that, like his body's current condition, his thoughts would somehow broadcast themselves like a neon sign. But that was Alva's influence on folks.

Eighty-three or not, ol' eagle eye immediately spied the column he'd folded the newspaper to. She beamed. "Are you enjoying today's column?"

"I am. Always do," he said, happy and thankful to direct his thoughts away from Riley and on to anything else.

As if Alva had some kind of Vulcan mind meld with him—the more he got to know her, the more he wasn't too certain she wasn't at least part alien; it would explain so much—she took the seat across from him. "Can I ask you a nosy question? And you can just tell me I'm an old busybody who should mind her own business. I won't take offense."

Quinn, who couldn't imagine anyone saying that to Alva's face—certainly not him—simply nodded. And braced himself.

"I was wondering if you were . . . involved. With a woman, I mean." She placed her tiny, birdlike, blue-veined hand on his arm, and gripped it with surprising strength. "I don't want any details, you know, just a simple yes or no. Are you available?"

Quinn instantly thought of Riley again, and was surprised. More from panic than plan, he flashed Alva a grin and covered her hand with his own. "Why, Miss Alva, are you askin' me what I think you're askin' me?"

She swatted at him much the same way that Laura Jo had. And blushed much the same way, too, he noted, charmed by the notion that anything could make the tiny octogenarian blush.

"Now, now, Mr. Brannigan, what kind of woman do you take me for?" She smiled at him, that devilish twinkle back in her eyes. "On second thought, be the gentleman I know you to be and don't answer that."

He laughed, and her eyes twinkled.

"So"—she said, not letting him off the hook.

"Is this going to end up in your column?" he asked.

"That depends. Are you asking for my advice?" She leaned a bit closer. "Perhaps you'd like some guidance on how to approach a certain someone who might have caught your eye?"

He saw the speculative gleam behind the deceptively sweet twinkle. In his head, he heard the *danger, danger* sirens go off, but somehow managed to smile. "I'm usually pretty good at that sort of thing, once I set my mind to it."

Alva slid her hand free, and thanked Laura Jo for the mug of coffee she slid in front of her before trotting off once again with a full tray. "Well, then, I suppose the only other question left is . . . what are you waiting for?"

Quinn was amused by her endearing question. Speculation and potential gossip fodder aside, he knew her interest was sincere. Perhaps not so much on his behalf, as that of her fellow Cupcake Club baker.

"I wasn't so much waiting as being respectful," he said, not bothering to confirm they were talking about Riley. Alva was no dummy. Other than Laura Jo and Miss Alva herself, Quinn hadn't spent any real time chatting with any other woman on the island.

"Well, that's a measure of what a fine Southern gentleman your mother raised you to be—"

"And grandmother. My mom passed when I was young, and Grams picked up the project from there." He smiled. "And what a project I was. But I'd like to think they'd be proud of how I turned out."

Alva's smile was warm. "I'm more than certain of that. But I'm not entirely certain what it is you think you need to be respectful of?"

Quinn was amazed he was even having this conversation. He was always the questioner, the seeker of information, never the one being questioned. "Well, not to speak out of turn, but, assuming we're talking about Miss Brown, I was being respectful of her current relationship."

Alva's carefully penciled-on brows—works of art in and of themselves—furrowed delicately, though her magnificently rendered bouffant of blond and silver curls didn't so much as quiver. "What relationship?"

It was Quinn's turn to frown. He didn't think it was possible that anyone on Sugarberry could have a relationship that wasn't known to the rest of the population. Especially the member of said population currently seated across the table from him. But Riley did a lot of work in the lower islands, and it was quite possible that she was able to keep her private life discreet and at a distance. She was from the city, too. Perhaps she wasn't comfortable conducting her romance in a fishbowl.

In that case, he definitely didn't want to be the one to out her to her friends. He gave Alva a half-abashed smile.

"Perhaps it was simply her way of letting me know she's not interested. Please, don't mention it to her. I appreciate her kindness in letting me down gently."

To his dismay, Alva's frown didn't ease, nor did the speculative gleam in her eyes diminish.

Wonderful. Now what had he done?

Chapter 9

Riley plopped her tool bag and supplies on the work-table next to Charlotte, then gave her a quick hug. "If it's any consolation, boys are dumb."

"Hey now," Franco said, stationed at the table just behind them.

Riley looked over her shoulder at him and made a kissy face. "Not you, my sweet baboo," she crooned, "never you."

"Damn straight." Delivering the words in his full-bodied, Rambo-from-the-Bronx voice, he then executed a perfect curtsy and twirled around back to his table. "Carry on, *ma petite mes amies.*"

Charlotte rolled her eyes, but she offered Riley a short smile. "Why does it have to be so complicated?"

"Because your fiancé is Puerto Rican and you're from New Delhi. Even though the two of you are poster children for the rainbow coalition, your parents are from different cultures and different generations. Take heart, Carlo's folks loved you."

"As a business partner and potential career stepping-stone for their son, yes. As his wife? Don't fool yourself, Riley." Charlotte laid her hand on Riley's arm. "We knew it would be far from easy. With that as a given, our visit to his family went very, very well. I think that's why I was so surprised to hear they have no interest in meeting my family when they come to visit next month. I thought I was being accepted into the family circle, but I was just being accepted into the one-of-Carlo's-nice-friends circle."

Riley frowned and lifted up Charlotte's left hand—the one with the beautiful diamond and antique platinum setting adorning her ring finger. "They do know you're engaged. Wasn't this his grandmother's ring? I'm sure they didn't miss that."

Charlotte looked away, but only for a moment. Riley tightened her grip on Char's hand when she tried to tug it free. "Tell me you did not take this ring off when you met his folks."

"Okay, I won't tell you. We wanted to test the waters first, see how they liked me. We were going to have a little dinner party later on, and make the formal announcement to them then."

"Your parents know, right?"

Charlotte shot her a dark look. "Why do you think they're traveling here? They didn't come to see me graduate from culinary school. They didn't come to see me accept any of my awards. But I announce I'm engaged, and suddenly they're booking flights. I honestly didn't think they'd care."

"Really?"

Charlotte squeezed Riley's hand, then let it go. "We haven't been any kind of actual family for a very long time. I don't know why they're suddenly being traditional about things. Possibly they want grandchildren. I haven't a clue. But it won't change things between Carlo and me, no matter how horrid they are. And they will be horrid. At least I'll defend him to them, if it should come to that. We're not asking them for anything to do with the wedding, or anything else. Neither are we asking anything from Carlo's family. So there's no dependency on either side. I just wish . . ."

"That he'd been as willing to face the fire as you are?"

Charlotte nodded. "It's unfair, I know. He's close with his family. All five million of them—which is why I left it to him to handle however he saw best. But now . . ."

"Now you want him to stand up for you."

"At least stand with me. He's . . . waffling. Not about us, but about how to blend me into his family. He doesn't want any strife, and I know that's not possible."

"You don't think he'd end things with you because of family pressure, do you?"

Charlotte shook her head, but her eyes told another story. "I wouldn't think so. Or I hadn't. Before. Everything has gone so well. Amazingly well. It's truly like a fairy tale. Not that it hasn't taken a lot of work on both our parts. We work together now, and live together. All that togetherness brings many challenges, but they're the kind you want to tackle, relish tackling, and figuring out. Because the reward is so worth it. Worth ten times more. A hundred. Any number to infinity. We both know what we have is special. We've been around long enough, dated enough, hurt enough, and loved enough, to know that this kind of relationship comes along once in your life. We're not going to mess this up. Do you know what I mean?"

"I do, yes, very much." Riley, moved by Charlotte's avowal, answered without thinking.

Charlotte took both her hands. "I suspected so. Will you tell me?"

"Us," Franco chimed in, not even pretending he wasn't hanging on their every word.

"What happened to your fairy tale, Riley?" Char asked. "It wasn't long ago, was it? Is that why you came to Sugarberry?"

Regrouping quickly Riley turned Charlotte's hands over in hers, squeezed back gently, then let go. She turned away to fiddle with her tools, but wasn't paying any attention to what she was unpacking. "You're in a really good place, Charlotte. You and Carlo. You're so lucky. Even better, you both know how lucky you are." Riley sent her a brief glance. "Hold on to it, do whatever you can to nurture it. Don't take it for granted. I know you're struggling right now. Talk to him. Honestly. Openly. Tell him what you're feeling. Don't make him guess and don't sweep it aside."

Franco came around the table and gently pulled her against his side with a brawny arm over her shoulders. "You should take your own advice, *ma belle.*"

Riley snorted, but it caught on a sob in her throat. "You don't have to tell me that. Trust me, if I ever get the chance again, I will."

He turned her to face him and Char joined in their little circle. "You have the chance now. That rule doesn't just apply to partner relationships, but to friendships as well. Both require trust and commitment, after all."

Riley blinked away the sudden sting behind her eyes. "You're right. Don't think I don't love and appreciate both of you. I know I'm new to your group, that you both go way back with Lani, but—"

"It's not about time spent," Franco said. "Paths cross, some briefly, and others stay connected forever. Ours will."

"Thank you," Riley said, deeply sincere. "You all don't know how much your friendship has meant to me."

"You have friends back in Chicago," Char said. "Have you at least been talking with them?"

She looked first at Char, then at Franco, then down at her hands. "I do. A very few. But . . . not like the three of you are with each other. It's complicated."

Riley had long ago shared with the group that both her parents had passed away. She'd never really known her father, who'd died in combat when she'd been barely a toddler. Her mother, in the same branch of the military, had died of complications from pneumonia when Riley was in college. Hers had been a nomadic life. Her mom was often gone and Riley stayed with this family or that one on whatever base they were stationed, until her mom returned. There had been nothing traditional about her upbringing, but it had been the only life she'd known. She'd been independent very early on, and hadn't thought that was so bad.

While her life had prepared her to fight her own battles and fend for herself, it had taught her little to nothing about how to put down roots, much less make and sustain lasting friendships. She had no immediate family, just a string of cousins scattered all over that she'd never really known or been particularly close to.

Char one-arm hugged Riley, too. "I've been going on and on about my bliss, then whining about little things. You must think me a ridiculous fool."

"No, I think you're madly in love and you want to hold on to that forever. You should want that." Riley looked at Char. "And you will hold on to it. So will Lani and Baxter. You guys are doing it right."

Franco gave her a supportive smile, but there was sadness in it. "Not all of us get a real chance to fulfill our dream." He was referring to the painful end of his relationship with Brenton.

"Exactly." Riley still hoped she could escape without rehashing the entire humiliating ordeal of Jeremy.

But Char pulled up a work stool and Franco pulled up two more. "Sit," he commanded. "No one else will be here for at least an hour. Alva is helping Lani cater the Kiwanis community garden fund-raiser, and Dre isn't coming tonight."

"I know, she told me her fall semester schedule is still all screwed up." Riley smiled. "I'm so proud of her. It's her last year."

"We are, too." Char rubbed Riley's arm. "You don't have to share if you don't want to."

Franco shushed Char with a *"shh"* and a glare, then gave Riley his most earnest and supportive look. "You'll feel better. You remember how long it took you all to pull the story out of me—"

Char snorted. "Right. I believe it was, oh, approximately sixty seconds after you came storming in the back door." Then she relented and rubbed his arm, too. "And it was horrible. We were all devastated for you. You know that."

It had been horrible. And no one had understood the depths of Franco's pain brought on by that kind of devastating blow more than Riley.

Franco had moved to Savannah from New York to stay with his newly committed partner, Brenton, a PA on Baxter's cooking show. For Franco, Brenton was the love of his life, and everyone who had seen them together would have agreed the feeling was mutual—right up until ten months ago. Franco had surprised Brenton on set to celebrate the anniversary of the purchase of their condo where they'd first lived together as a couple, only to discover Brenton locked in an embrace with another PA—a female PA, at that—in the prep kitchen.

It had shattered his entire world, and the whole Cupcake Club had suffered right along with the brokenhearted Franco.

"I know you were, and it meant the world to me." Franco looked back at Riley. "Trust me, honey." All traces of France were gone. "Never underestimate the power of collective disdain and loathing on the one that done you wrong. It's so much better than a pity party for one."

"I know, I just don't want to dwell on it anymore. I've moved on. Rehashing it won't help me now. A group bashing session would just feel . . . petty."

"Did you think I was petty for wishing bad things on Brenton?" Franco spit the name out like he'd just tasted something bitter. "Or worse yet, pathetic?"

"No, no, not at all. But it had just happened to you. It's expected when you're raw from being so badly hurt. It's been almost two years for me. I have no excuse."

"That depends," Char said. "What did he do?"

"Why do you think he's the one who did anything?"

Char and Franco gave Riley a quelling look, then Char added, "It doesn't take two years to get over it when you're doing the dumping."

"Maybe I deserved it," Riley pointed out.

Instead of admonishing her, Franco stroked her hair. "Oh, *belissima*, is that what you think?" It was such an instinctive, heartfelt gesture of comfort, hot tears instantly gathered in the corners of Riley's eyes. "Bastard," he added, with just the right amount of French-accented disgust to make her go from the verge of tears, to half-snorted giggle.

"Well . . . he is that," she agreed. "But it sounds so much better when you say it."

He hugged her again, then pumped his fist in the air. "*Solidaritie!* See? I told you, ees much better, this beetching with friends." All he needed was a French flag to fly over his head.

"Will you tell us what happened?" Char asked.

Riley sighed. Somehow, telling them didn't seem all that bad. Maybe Franco was right. When you knew the people you were sharing difficult news with would have your back, no matter what . . . telling became almost a relief. Determined not to get sniffly again, she took a breath, squared her shoulders, and smiled at them. "You know, maybe if I'd spent my time cultivating true friendships and not just work relationships, things would have turned out much differently. But I had no time for real friends. I was too obsessed with the amazing bliss that was my relationship with my fiancé."

"Possibly. I know it's helped having all of you keeping me grounded when I feel like I'm floating five feet off the ground." Charlotte smiled dryly. "I was never a floater. Ever. In fact, I was always the lead balloon in the room. If you'd told me I'd ever be in this situation, a ring on my finger, and fighting mad about families blending and still wanting this partnership so badly, the cynic I used to be—"

Franco snorted.

Char elbowed him, not gently. "And am not any longer, would have had a very good, very long laugh. In fact, it's a good thing I met Carlo about the time Lani and Baxter figured things out, because I don't think I'd have been the friend she needed, otherwise."

Char made a face at Franco, who bussed her noisily on the cheek, making her smile sincerely. She looked at Riley then, with all that honest affection still clear in her dark eyes. "I shamelessly need you to help me navigate this, so please let us help you navigate, too. Even if it's in the past, some waters stay dark and run too deep, until you cross them and realize it wasn't so bad a crossing after all."

"Maybe." Riley was heartened by the steadfastness she saw in both their faces. She huffed out a sigh. "Okay. His name is Jeremy. He's a journalist, a very good one, magazine articles mostly, and a trained chef, so his work was all food-oriented. We both worked for *Foodie*." Char and Franco knew that was the magazine she'd styled food for back in Chicago. "It was love at first sight. We were disgustingly inseparable when we weren't dragged apart by work, which wasn't often, but you'd think we'd been cast off to the desert for months after just a day spent apart. Yes, our bliss was that disgusting. I knew I was, hands down, the luckiest girl in the world. He made me feel like the only woman who'd ever existed in his."

I'm not going to sound wistful, dammit. "It's funny, you know. I don't miss him. Not the man, anyway. What I miss is how I felt when I was falling in love, knowing that the person I loved was falling, too. Being around you all, even listening to Alva share her stories about Harold . . . that's the part I wish I still had, that sense of being connected to someone in the way you can't be with friends or family, no matter how strong the ties. I don't miss Jeremy, but I do miss having that one person who is all the things your nearest and dearest can be . . . who is the one no one else can be. Your lover. Your mate."

Out of nowhere, an image of Quinn's sexy, smiling face popped into her thoughts. She blinked it away, disconcerted, and tried to stay focused on the story. She'd been struggling to kick him out of her fantasy life since he was not going to be in her real one. It couldn't be healthy to allow herself to daydream about what might have happened with that cupcake in the breakfast nook . . . if she hadn't been sweaty and scratched up, with random foliage sticking out of her hair. Or, on the boat . . . when they were both drenched and smelling like wet mastiff.

Surely it was a bad sign when she could make a fantasy out of even that.

"Riley?" Char touched her knee. "If it's too painful—"

"What?" Riley snapped out of her reverie. "No, that's not it. It's just like I said. I miss the feeling of it. Of being in love."

"I know." Real sadness tinged Franco's voice.

Riley leaned her head on his arm. "I know you do. And it sucks to have it taken away. Ripped away, really. Especially when you don't see it coming."

"Oh." Char spoke softly. "I'm so sorry."

"I was, too," Riley said, simply and honestly. She glanced at Franco, who was nodding. He might not have been involved with Brenton for a fraction of the time she'd been with Jeremy, but none of that mattered if you'd gotten to the part where you trusted the person you were in love with to take care of that special bond. To treat it with the dignity and respect it deserved, even if the bond was going to be broken. "It's not that I couldn't have gotten past it if we'd fallen out of love, or had problems we simply couldn't surmount. Even if only one of us was having those issues. But when one person wants out, there are ways to end things, and ways not to."

"Hear, hear," Franco said, a bit of mad edging out the sad.

"Did you know he was—that he wanted out?" Char asked.

"Not a single clue. I mean, in retrospect? I realize ours was not necessarily the utopian bond I'd imagined it to be. But we weren't arguing, or having any concerns or stresses we didn't always have. We were happy, in that settled way you are when you've been together a long time. None of our coworker friends, who were with us for long hours every single day, noticed or knew anything was off. No one suspected, least of all me."

"When you love someone, and are loved in return, you trust each other to respect your relationship," Franco said, mirroring her thoughts exactly. "You become the easiest one to dupe, because it would never occur to you to think otherwise."

"Exactly," Riley said. "I get that I was easy to fool . . . but how do you look your best friend in the eyes, and play them for that fool? Knowing you're doing it? That I will never get."

"Me, either," Char said. "I've never experienced that kind of betrayal, because until Carlo I never allowed myself to be vulnerable to anyone. But I've watched it so many times. Breaking up seems hard, not wanting the scene, the drama, but the alternative, is so . . . cowardly."

"That's the other thing," Riley said. "On top of being bludgeoned with the revelation that the person you loved and thought the world of clearly didn't hold you or your love in the same esteem, you also have to admit he's a lying, cheating bastard. In one swoop, Jeremy destroyed every single attribute that made me fall in love with him in the first place—which made me feel even more ridiculous. On top of being sad, and horrified, and heartbroken because I chose to love a man who was capable of doing that I ended up wondering how much of an idiot am I. How did I not know he was capable of that?"

"How do any of us know?" Charlotte said. "We're each evolving all the time. I'm a great testament to that. I was always attracted to men who would certainly never love me back the same way. Self-inflicted relationship sabotage. But we do grow, hopefully in a positive way. I believe that I have. But sometimes it's not positive growth. Life brings new things, new experiences, and a gradual building of events can change people from who they were before."

Char squeezed Riley's arm again as she continued. "But that's just the thing, Riley. You came through it, and you can look yourself in the mirror, and know who you really are. A woman capable of loving fully, with all her heart. Capable of giving herself completely to someone, and cherishing the sanctity of that bond. Jeremy also gets to look in the mirror and see exactly what kind of man he turned out to be."

"Not that he'll ever allow himself that kind of honest assessment."

"You never know what lies in store for him. I'm a great believer in karma. But even if he never holds himself accountable, look at it this way, at least you're no longer accountable for him. Or to him. You're free of his selfish, cowardly, thoughtless acts. Free of having anything to do with his damaged self. You fell in love with something good. It's not your fault he allowed himself to sour into something bad. No matter the dynamics, everyone can choose how to handle life's hurdles. That's how he chose to handle his. Better you knew before something really important happened. Like marriage. Illness. Hardship. *Children*. He deserved to lose you. And you deserve someone who would do anything not to."

"I love you," Franco blurted out, and hugged Charlotte hard. "That was beautiful. That will stay with me forever, I think. I hope. So wise."

"It's simply how I see things now. I couldn't have said those things even two years ago—which is a testament to my growth," she said tearfully.

"Thank you." Riley sniffled, not even trying to stop. "I—that helped me, too." She laughed through the tears. "It really did."

"Good." Charlotte smiled. "You know what, putting all that into words helped me, too. I know now what I want with Carlo. What the 'small stuff,' as you call it, is . . . and what's worth waging war for. So, thank you, too."

They shared smiles for another moment, then Franco pulled them both in. "Group hug." They hugged and laughed, and there was more sniffling. Setting them back on their stools, he crossed his legs and folded his arms over his knees as he swung to face Riley. "Okay, Dr. Phil is over. Now it's Oprah time. What did the rat bastard do? And where can we hunt his ass down?"

Chapter 10

Riley burst out laughing, and so did Charlotte. "Say it again," Riley urged Franco. "You know."

"*Bastarde!*"

She grinned. "I know it makes me seem small, but I don't think I will ever tire of that."

"I'll have shirts made," he said. "We'll get Dre on board."

Riley's laugh turned to a groan. "I can only imagine what she'd do with it. Goth bastarde!" Riley pumped her fist. "You know, though, that might work," she said thoughtfully. "A few tasteful skulls, some blood . . ."

Char shuddered, but they were all laughing.

"No more ducking," Franco said. "You've come this far, just air the rest of your laundry, missy, and we'll be all done with it."

"It was the sitter," Riley said bluntly. Surprisingly, there was a twinge of sadness, more than a twinge of anger, but an even bigger one of disgust. "We were together seven years . . . and he dumped me so he could boink the hot sitter."

"Seven years? That's a long time, *mon amie*. I'm so sorry."

"Yep, the better part of my adult life, up to that point."

"We're going to need to add a few more lines to those T-shirts," Franco said, making Riley smile, and nudge him again.

"You know you want to."

"Oh, I do. *Bastarde*," he said again, in a growling, hissing kind of way.

"Oooh, I like that one, too."

"Wait," Charlotte said. "Did you say the sitter? You had—he had, children?" She looked appropriately aghast.

"Thank God, no. I can't imagine how awful it would have been if he'd dragged children through all of that. I was a fully grown adult and it leveled me. She was the dog sitter for Brutus." Riley smiled. "I remember the day I got Brutus. I knew Jeremy would kill me when I brought him home from the pound. He was a bit of a neat freak. Jeremy, not Brutus."

"Brutus was a pound puppy?" Franco asked.

"Is that really surprising?" Riley asked dryly.

"Well, when you put it that way . . ."

"Some family got him as this adorable big lug of a puppy, then he grew into a mammoth lug of a dog and they couldn't handle him, so off to the pound he went."

"Why were you there? Did you two want to get a dog? From what you've told us about your schedule when you were a stylist—"

"No, we'd never even so much as breathed a whisper of it. We'd talked marriage, we were engaged then—"

"You were engaged?" Charlotte asked. "It just keeps getting worse."

"I know. We dated for two years, then moved in together, got engaged about eighteen months later, but never could set a date because our schedules were so crazed. But that didn't matter to me. I've never been the type to dream about my Big Day."

"Me, either," said Charlotte. "Probably because it was all my mother talked about. I was betrothed at birth to a boy from a very good family and my whole life was geared toward the Big Day, as you call it. I couldn't wait to get out."

"I've always dreamed about mine." Franco sighed wistfully. Riley and Charlotte smiled, but Charlotte took his hand and squeezed it.

"If it helps, you're more than welcome to plan mine. Of course, you'll have to deal with two families hell-bent on making sure it never happens. We should just elope." Charlotte's eyes lit up, but it was short-lived. "His family would really never forgive me then. He has all sisters. Five of them."

"Yikes," Riley said. "Well, we had no pressure either way. We had a life together. I was where I wanted to be, with the man I loved. I had no family hounding me to set a date, and his parents spent most of their time bickering despite being divorced for more than twenty years." She shrugged. "We both knew we wanted kids, somewhere in the distant future, so I figured marriage would happen when it finally mattered. At the time, we loved our jobs, loved the lives we had, so . . . children were not imminent. We were both in agreement on that. I knew he'd always had dogs growing up, and I'd always wanted one, so I guess whenever we did have that hazy future family, I always pictured a dog in it. I suppose I figured Jeremy would, too."

"But this wasn't some hazy future time," Franco said.

"Well, yes, true. That was the day, or one of them, when the future stopped being quite so far away. I mean, it has to happen at some point, right?"

Charlotte's eyebrows climbed. "You just . . . came home with a dog? A very large dog?"

"No, no. I wouldn't have done that. It was going to be a monumental change, so I talked with Jeremy first. It was rare that I asked for anything, really rare, so Jeremy had a hard time saying no to me about it. Even then, I wouldn't have insisted if I thought he was really against it. He seemed more concerned about the logistics, though, than about having a pet, so I asked, if I could get all the care and feeding issues worked out with our schedules, would he be on board, and he agreed. In fact, once I did get it figured out, he was excited about it. I was the same kind of marshmallow with him when he really wanted something, and he had taken advantage of that fact, many times."

"You two were disgusting," Charlotte said.

"Back in the day, yes. But you're one to talk," Riley shot back.

"So . . . did he love Brutus on sight as you did?" Charlotte asked.

"And you never said, but why were you at the animal shelter in the first place?" Franco put in.

"Mrs. Stroeheimer. In 4B. Her cat was forever getting out, getting into scrapes, and usually ended up in lockup at the local shelter. They all knew him there, so they'd call her up and I'd take her down to pick him up."

"Why didn't she get him fixed so he'd stop fighting and well . . . catting about?" Charlotte asked.

Franco groaned at that. "Women always want to cut off a man at the—"

"If it kept him from catting around," Charlotte said, looking him dead in the eyes, "then, perhaps, yes."

Franco considered that, then nodded. "You may have a point."

"Oh, Mr. Bumpers was fixed. He just liked to fight. Usually over Dumpster food. It had to be some sort of king kitty complex, because Mrs. S. fed him like royalty. He didn't need to dive for food, much less fight over it. Anyway, whenever we went down to spring him from lockup, I usually waited in the car, but that day she was feeling a bit light-headed, had complained of being a bit dizzy, so I helped her inside."

"And then, the Hallmark moment." Franco fanned his hands out in an arc as he hummed a tune, then clasped his palms under his chin.

"Maybe not quite like that. I knew it was a mistake to go inside the minute I stepped through the door. I can't stand misery—I mean, who can?—but it wrenches me. I know I can't save them all, and that there are many animals out there in that same situation. But I also knew I could reduce that number by at least one."

"And there was the childhood dream," Char added.

"Exactly."

"But wasn't there some small, lap-size dog that needed rescue?" Franco asked. "You lived in an apartment in the city, right?"

Riley nodded. "A tiny one. Yes, there were dozens of other dogs, all of them smaller than Brutus, of course."

"Of course," Char and Franco said together. Neither of them was really an animal person, but they had taken to Brutus. Eventually.

"He was lying in a run in the back, chin on his paws, not even trying to get my attention. It was as if he knew there was no point in it. The shelter was in the middle of the city. Who was going to be looking for a dog his size? He was just so . . . defeated."

"Oh boy," Franco sighed.

"Exactly, right? I didn't have any intention of adopting any of them, though I admit at that point the seed, at least, had been planted. When that hazy, future day came, I knew right then I'd adopt rather than buy. But when they brought out Mr. Bumpers, I asked about Brutus. I was worried for him. He wasn't even trying. I had such a feeling of . . . dread for him. I guess I expected something like that same attitude from the woman who worked there, but her face immediately lit up and she went on and on about what a doll he was, how charming he was, and how they all loved him to pieces and he was such a gentle giant."

"Sucker born every minute," Franco said, shaking his head. "She was envisioning how much more dog food they'd have to spread around."

"Come on," Riley said. "You know him. That's exactly how he is."

Char and Franco shared a look, then nodded toward her. "Of course he is," Char said, in the same tone one would use to placate the mother of an unruly child.

Riley stared them right back down. "Then I saw the sign that said they only hold dogs for sixty days. This was not a no-kill shelter. And I noticed on the card next to Brutus's cage how long he'd been there." She gave them a solemn look. "Just a few days shy of two months."

Char's and Franco's expressions fell at that.

Riley nodded. "I know. But, even then, when I left, I wasn't planning on anything. When Jeremy got home, of course I told him all about taking Mrs. S. down there, and, well . . ."

"You took Brutus home the next day."

"I got him a stay of execution the next day. There was a lot of advance planning required. We brought him home ten days later. We had to pass a home inspection and interview."

"Seriously?" Franco asked. "I'm surprised they didn't drag him out and stuff him in your car before you could change your mind."

"It's the law. Anyway, I thought for sure they'd turn us down for being apartment dwellers, but it turns out mastiffs aren't all that athletic or physical. They don't like to do more than take a short walk, maybe chase a ball in the park, but that's about it. So, we were approved."

"Who ended up hiring the dog walker? You or him?" Char asked.

"I did." Riley sighed. "I know. Can you believe that? But Jeremy was too busy and he trusted my judgment."

"He did a hell of a lot more than that," Franco muttered.

"To be honest, I never thought of him in context with her. For all I knew, their paths would never cross. I was more worried that she couldn't handle Brutus."

"You liked her?" Charlotte asked, her mouth all pinched up as if she'd just tasted something really, really sour.

"Sure. If you can really like super perky, five-foot-nothing, ridiculously fit, zero-body-fat women with thick, television-commercial-worthy straight glossy hair, perfect teeth, and a Lithuanian accent I found challenging to understand. As I found out much later, Jeremy apparently found it mysterious and sexy." Riley looked at Char. "So, tell me, how bad is my karma going to be if, even before everything happened I admit I pictured her aging like Mrs. Pachulis in 2A? I'd seen photos of Magda when she was younger and she was quite the looker. At seventy-five, not so much. She had this big, pointy mole, right here." Riley pointed to the side of her chin. "Is it small of me to picture Camalia with a big hairy mole? At age twenty-three?"

"Not small," Charlotte assured Riley. "God, she's only twenty-three?"

"*Bastarde*," Franco hissed again.

"Now. She was only twenty-one then. Maybe that's it," Riley said. "I made it happen because of my less than charitable thoughts. It was karma coming to get me."

"You don't honestly believe that," Franco said.

"No," she admitted, "but it did cross my mind that day. It was New Year's Eve—"

"New Year's Eve? Seriously?" Charlotte asked.

"As a heart attack," Riley responded. "Which was what I almost had. I ended up coming back early from the mani-pedi-massage Jeremy had booked for me as my Christmas present. I skipped the massage because they were running behind, and we had a huge industry shindig to attend that night, lots of power players. We were really amped for it, so the last thing I needed was to be a limp, relaxed noodle. I rebooked that part, thinking it was something to look forward to after all the holiday stuff."

"You're not saying he got you a spa day, specifically for you to use on New Year's Eve in preparation for this big party, so he could . . ."

Riley nodded. "Oh, that's exactly what I'm saying."

"And then you skipped the massage." Franco sighed and stroked her arm. They could see the train wreck that was about to happen. "You had no warning."

She shook her head. "Nope. I even stopped on my way back to pick up something to wear under my dress to surprise him. Only, I was the one who got the surprise."

"I'm so, so sorry," Charlotte said.

"Me, too," Riley said. "They were both naked. Right on my dining room table. With Brutus watching. I was jealous of her effortless perfection. We'd even made jokes about it, like couples do about people. She was so young, more than ten years younger than he was. He talked about her like she was a kid."

"Because she was a kid."

"I know. And he was madly in love with me, right?"

"Maybe it was just crazy temptation. Like you said, boys are dumb," Charlotte offered.

"I don't know if I could have forgiven that either. It would have been easier, I guess. But that wasn't it. They didn't even know I was there, because they were so . . . enthusiastic."

"Oh, dear," Charlotte said.

"I threw my Victoria's Secret bag at her. Clipped her on

the cheek. She may never have a hairy mole, but she'll probably have a little scar to remember me by."

"That's the least of what I'd have thrown at her," Franco said.

"They were startled, of course." Riley blew out a heavy sigh, prepping herself to go through it one more time. "Jeremy was contrite—not so much because of the cheating, but because I'd caught them at it. He had the nerve to be worried about covering her up, about her modesty. On my dining room table—*my* table—and he was more worried about me seeing her naked than—" She broke off, composed herself. "Once they were adequately covered, Jeremy proceeded to apologize that I'd found out that way. I asked how long it had been going on. He didn't answer, but he put his arm around her—not me. He never even touched me, or tried to—" She stopped. Reliving that exact moment didn't make her mad, it just broke her heart all over again. In that one moment, her entire life, everything she thought she had, thought she was, believed, and trusted in . . . fell apart. "He told me he loved her. And that he'd been trying to find a way to tell me, for a whole year. A whole year, and he couldn't find the right time to say, 'By the way, I'm boinking Camalia all over our apartment. Happy New Year.'" She stifled the sob clutching at her throat, pissed with herself for letting it get to her again. "They wanted to keep Brutus."

"Oh, honey." Franco stood and pulled her into a bear hug. "Now I am going to shoot him dead."

"I told Jeremy if he so much as laid a finger on Brutus, I'd cut parts of his body off and feed them to Mr. Bumpers," she said, muffled against Franco's chef coat. "While he watched."

Charlotte rubbed her hand on Riley's back. "I'd have held him down for you."

Riley gave a watery laugh and shifted from Franco's hug back to her stool. "My mad didn't last long, at least not right then. It took a while to get back to that. I was just . . . so devastated. Before that, I didn't know what it felt like to be heartbroken. It's this huge, clutching chasm in your chest. All the time. I wanted to get past it, to move on. To get mad again." She half sniffled, half snorted. "And I did. At least the mad part. I used up all my sick leave and my vacation time because I couldn't face the chance of seeing him at work."

"Oh God. You still had to work together."

"I didn't know what I was going to do. But I had to go back or risk being fired and I loved my job."

"But you ended up leaving Chicago," Charlotte said.

Riley nodded. "I lasted five months, three days, and one hour. And I'm proud of that. But even I can only take so much. No career, no matter how hard you've worked to achieve it, or how much you love it, is worth everything. No matter how much you deserve to think you shouldn't have to lose that, too, there's only so much you can do. Sometimes, you just don't get to win."

She slumped on her stool. "The first day I went back to work, I was freaked out about getting through the day without falling apart, not knowing what I was going to do when I saw him—it had only been two weeks—and I was still raw. Just . . . raw. Like a giant exposed nerve. I was a walking disaster. I had no business trying to do anything for a client, but I knew I couldn't sit at home and think about chopping my dining room table into kindling and setting it on fire, in Jeremy and Camalia's front yard. That probably wasn't healthy."

Drawing herself up, Riley took a steadying breath. "What I hadn't counted on was arriving at work to find out Jeremy had never missed a day. In my absence, he had actually gotten Camalia hired."

Franco and Charlotte gasped.

"Apparently Miss Perky Perfection had graduated with her degree in journalism right before Christmas. She was going to work with us, right in our department. Not a single person had thought to call and warn me—not that I had been taking calls. When I walked in, there they were, all gathered around the meeting table, drinking coffee and laughing. Laughing," Riley said, as if the concept was so foreign to her, she simply couldn't fathom anyone wanting to do it ever again. Of course, that was exactly how she'd felt at the time. "I was this pathetic, shattered shell . . . and there they were, all happy and . . . laughing. With my friends. Our friends. Well, our coworkers anyway. How could they? You know?" She laughed, but it was hollow. "The laughter died as one person spied me in the doorway and slowly everybody turned and stared at me. I don't know which was worse, the look of regret on my coworkers' faces, or the pity on Jeremy and Camalia's. Humiliating doesn't begin to cover it."

"And he's still anatomically intact?" This came from Franco. "Because I might have had to . . . do some rearranging."

"I don't really remember the next few minutes, but everyone started to walk toward me, like they were going to what? Hug me? Say they were sorry? One guy—Ted, from graphics—lamely apologized and said he thought I knew. I think I laughed, before I turned around and fled. Just . . . ran out."

"But you went back," Char said. "My God, how?"

"You know, I don't really know. I was like a zombie, but I felt I had no choice, and that by plowing through, I was being the bigger person, the better person. But I sure didn't feel bigger or better. In fact, it was probably the unhealthiest thing I ever made myself do. It was like working in a toxic cesspool every day. I didn't trust anyone there, no one—"

"Of course you didn't, they all betrayed you."

"Why did you finally leave? What happened?"

"Oh. I found the announcement. By accident, someone left it on the conference room table. Or maybe it wasn't by accident. I don't know, don't care."

"Announcement of what?" Char asked.

"Jeremy and Camalia's wedding."

"*Five months later?*"

"Well, you have to remember, for them, it had been more like a year and a half."

"Still. You'd been engaged longer than that."

"I guess the future wasn't as far off and hazy for them. Whatever. If I thought the looks of pity I'd been getting up to that point had been gross, I could only imagine where it was going to go from there. Not to mention the endless talk of wedding dresses, wedding cake, photographers, and food—" Riley made a sound of disgust. "That was it. I surrendered. I saw the future and wanted no part of it. I walked straight to my office, dropped the announcement in the shredder, packed up my tools and whatever I could haul out on my person, and left. Didn't say good-bye to a single person."

"Can't blame you," Franco said. "Then what did you do? How did you quit?"

"I sent in my resignation by e-mail. And told them to go to hell when they didn't even try to get me to stay but offered to give me good references. I was damn good at my job, the best stylist they had. I didn't need their damn references. They should have at least pretended they wanted me to stay, though I wouldn't have. They just . . . chose Jeremy, I guess." She shook her head. "No one picked me. I know that sounds so . . . pathetic."

Riley lifted her shoulders, then let them slump. "I lasted

one whole day at the apartment, but I'd wallowed enough by then and even I wasn't that pathetic. I packed some things, got Brutus into my car, and we drove east. I had two friends, Chuck and Greg, who I'd worked with on several shoots earlier in my career. They'd become mentors and friends to me. They'd looked out for me, professionally, and I knew they'd probably help me figure out the next step. At that time they were living in the Hamptons, so I called them and they invited me out, told me I could stay as long as I wanted. They had a houseboat they were always planning to wander the ocean blue on, though they never did. I don't remember who first had the idea I should live on it, but I do know there was a lot of wine involved. Anyway, Chuck has an uncle who lives on Jekyll, so that's where they had the houseboat docked. I couldn't afford to keep it there, so I had it moved up here, thinking I'd stay until I figured out what I was going to do next." She smiled then, pushing the ugliness away. "And here I still am."

"We choose you," Franco said. "I'm glad you're here."

"I am, too," Charlotte agreed.

Riley took a deep, deep, breath, and let it out slowly. It felt good. Cleansing. "Okay, so that's it, right? I don't ever have to talk about this again?"

"*Non, mon amie*, of course not," Franco said. "Unless you need to bash him. Then we'll all jump in and help. With great enthusiasm."

She grinned. "Thank you. And thanks for dragging it out of me. For obvious reasons, it's not something I like to talk about or even think about, but it's good to have it all out there. I'm happy here. Truly happy. I choose you all, too."

"Do you miss Chicago?" Charlotte asked.

"At times. Not so much the city. I've truly embraced island life. I love it here. I'm at peace here, and, more important, I feel like I fit in. I don't think I realized how much I didn't fit in, in the city. It was the job that took me there, and my life with Jeremy kept me there. Magazine life is pretty bohemian in a lot of ways and I loved so much of it, but I didn't really fit in with the movers and shakers, suit and tie stuff. Here . . . I'm accepted for who I am. Maybe because I can finally just be myself, I've figured out how to have—and to be—the one thing I've never really had in my life." Riley smiled at them. "Friends. True friends."

Charlotte nodded. "You do. I'm glad you know that. We've always been in your corner."

"I know, and I should have confided sooner, it's—"

"No, that's no one's business but your own," Charlotte said. "But I'm glad you felt like you could finally trust us enough to share. It makes sharing back that much easier."

"Not that it's a real struggle for us," Franco said dryly, earning a nudge from Charlotte.

"We've had each other for a very long time, so we're used to it," Charlotte said. "Do you miss your work, styling food?"

Riley nodded. "I do. A lot, actually. That was the one thing that did fit me. I think that's why I love getting together with you all so much. Jeremy and I were big foodies, too, so I guess I miss that part a little bit, the restaurants, trying new chefs, new dishes. Working at *Foodie,* there were always events and things. I miss that part. Not so much the social game, or the power plays, but the food. It's always been about the food for me."

"You'll have to come into Savannah for more than just shopping," Charlotte said. "Carlo is an amazing chef, and between us we've already met many of the local chefs and industry people. I think you'd really be surprised by the level of sophistication in their food. We go out all the time, doing exactly what you said, tasting, trying new things, getting inspired. We'd love to have you join us."

"Thank you," Riley said, loving the idea, but not so sure she wanted to be the third wheel to the giddy couple.

"I'll invite myself along," Franco said, so good at picking up on her every mood. "We'll double-date."

"Deal." Rather than feeling as if she'd given a chunk of herself away, Riley felt she'd received a very big gift. She knew her new friendships had been cemented with the exchange of trust.

She supposed the next thing would be figuring out where she wanted to go with her other relationships. Of course, Quinn's sexy grin popped to mind, but this time she didn't automatically try to block it.

Was it time to hang out her dating shingle again? She smiled, and tucked the thought away to ponder later. She'd done enough emotional dredging for one day.

"Let's make some cupcakes," she announced. "I could use something decadent and sinful." As they fell into the rhythms and patterns they'd established over the months of baking and working together, she realized she was happy. More important, for the first time in a very, very long time, she felt . . . hopeful.

She had no idea what the next step on her path would be, but she figured hope was a pretty vital ingredient to have. And, for now, that was enough.

Chapter 11

Hannah looked up, grooming brush in hand, as she heard the footsteps entering the stable. She stroked the mare's neck and mane, more to gather herself than to settle the startled horse. She should be more surprised to see him again. Maybe, in some part of her, she'd always known she would. She took a step away, and faced her intruder. "What are you doing here?"

If the lack of a warm welcome bothered him, he didn't let it show. Not surprising. "To be honest, I don't know."

"Then, perhaps you should head on out. Come back when you do know."

He cocked an eyebrow at that. "Is that an invitation?"

She allowed herself a moment to drink in the sight of him. It had been, what . . . five years? Six, now? It might as well have been twenty, for all that had happened in their lives since.

It might as well have been yesterday, given the way her heart was pounding. "I don't know what it is," she said, deciding honesty was the only way to handle this. Handle him. "What made you drive all the way out here? Did something happen on an old case?" She didn't bother asking how he'd known where to look for her. He'd once been the best detective the Denver Police Department had ever had. Colorado was a big place, easy to get lost in, which was precisely what she'd done after leaving the medical examiner's office over half a decade ago. But if Joe St. Cloud wanted to find someone, he usually did.

"I'm not with the department any longer."

"I know," was all she said, and found herself enjoying the way his eyebrow lifted again. She'd surprised him with that. Good.

He walked closer then, and she had to work at not taking a physical step back. It would have been better—smarter—if she could have taken an emotional step back. Just as she'd done the entire time they'd worked together.

"Some things you can walk away from and never look back." He stopped right in front of her. His piercing blue gaze, the one she'd seen pin down the most heartless killer and make him beg for mercy, pinned her now. "Other things . . . not so much."

* * *

Quinn abruptly closed his laptop. *Dammit.* He'd promised himself he'd stop doing that. Stop giving Joe and Hannah a voice, until he figured things out. But he'd been doing exactly that. He shoved away from his desk. A good hard run, that's what he needed.

Because today was going to be D-Day. Decision Day. He couldn't put it off any longer.

Already in running shorts and a T-shirt, he put thought to action and headed straight out the back, through the dune trail. Kicking off his flip-flops, he tucked them between the blades of a palmetto bush so they wouldn't blow away. He wasn't coming off the beach until he'd committed himself to figuring out the lives, and eventual epic love story, of (maybe retired) homicide detective Joe St. Cloud, and (maybe former) forensic analyst and (now full-time?) horse rancher, Hannah Lake.

Quinn had been on Sugarberry for thirty-six days. October loomed less than a week away. He'd taken reams of notes and plotted out both versions of the story, wanting—needing—one of them to grab him and not let go. Problem was . . . they were both good. Any other time, he'd have had his hooks deep into the homicide detective and forensic analyst partnership, pushing, dragging, propelling them through the paces of another gritty, grisly string of murders . . . and letting them burn off the tension and screaming stress with steamy hot, bodies-up-against-the-wall and down-on-the-floor, mind-blowing sex. He knew exactly how he'd tell their story, how they'd work together, play together. He liked these two. A lot. And they were going to like each other a whole lot more.

It was why the other story idea kind of pissed him off. He should already be knee-deep in brain matter and severed body parts, relishing the difficult path he was going to force those two down, if they had any hope of solving the murders. He'd even started the opening chapters, more than once.

But snatches of other dialogue, the kind that happens long before a partnership is solidified, kept whispering in his head. Images, ideas teased and tantalized. His captivation with the two people he'd created grew by leaps and bounds . . . but in the reverse direction. His characters usually had a backstory, how they'd come to be who and what they were as the story opens. His problem was, the backstory was as tantalizing as the current one he'd had in mind for them. So much so, his mind kept going there . . . and sticking around for a while.

The more he thought about what they could give each other, the more tantalizing that story became. To him. Question was . . . would anyone else care? He simply had no answer for that.

Quinn started off down the beach right along the water's edge, enjoying the feel of the cool, wet sand under his feet. The nights were cooler, but the days were still climbing to a pretty blistering average temperature. He enjoyed the chilled feeling he got while running on the cold wet sand, knowing it would be too hot to walk on barefooted, much less run on, by midafternoon.

The high tide was ebbing as the sun rose slowly above the horizon. New day. *The* day. There wasn't anything else his two characters could teach him, say to him, or persuade him to do. He had to pick. Would the murders be the story, and their past history already defined? Or would the murders be their past history, and their coming together define what happened next?

He'd settled into a particularly punishing pace, when out of nowhere, something clipped him hard on his right hip, sending him careening left, across the remaining narrow strip of sand, and into the water. He managed to catch himself before he went face-first into the surf, but not before getting soaked by an incoming, late-breaking wave. It was only as he shook the water from his hair and wiped his face that he spied Riley, about ten yards down the beach, running toward him.

Them, actually. Just above the safety of the waterline, Brutus had planted his massive, muscular butt in the sand, and was presently drooling all over an impressively large hunk of driftwood clenched in his mighty jaw.

"I'm sorry. I'm so sorry!" Riley called, out of breath from the run. She stopped at the water's edge in front of him, and tried to say something else, but ended up putting her hands on her thighs as she bent over to catch her breath.

"I'm starting to sense there's a pattern where water and Brutus are involved," Quinn said as he strolled from the waves swirling around his calves and walked toward them. As soon as his bare feet hit dry sand, Brutus dropped the driftwood right on top of them, then looked up expectantly, tongue lolling.

Wincing, Quinn bent down and hefted the log off his toes, then turned to loft it into the surf, only to have Riley spring into action, and grab his arm at the last second. "No, wait! Don't throw it in the water." Her voice was almost back to full strength.

Quinn turned to face her. The moment he'd realized who was running down the beach, his heart had literally leaped in his chest. Leaped. He felt foolish. And giddy.

Her cheeks were flushed, her eyes sparkling, and her blond curls danced about her head in a happy halo. Her lips were moving as she said something, but he was too busy corralling every ounce of his control to keep from hauling her into his arms, right up against his drenched frame, and kissing her until she lost her breath all over again.

"He's afraid of the water," she was saying when he finally conquered the beast of temptation.

"What? Wasn't he the one who went for a swim last time?"

"That was different. He didn't exactly go in willingly."

"But he stayed in there and paddled around like a champ."

"That was the channel. No waves."

"Oh." Quinn said, as if that made perfect sense.

Tired of waiting, Brutus leaned in and head-butted Quinn on the thigh, then looked up at him again, eyes shining in anticipation.

Quinn staggered a step, leveling a look at Brutus. "Patience, buddy."

Riley chuckled. "If this were a cartoon, there would be little hearts and birds floating over his head right now."

"I'd hate to see what he does to his enemies." Quinn flexed the sting out of his toes. He took a few steps farther up the beach, then turned to look down the shoreline. Brutus scooted around on his butt and followed Quinn's every move. "Don't get up on my account," Quinn told him, then cocked his arm back and did his best to launch the log as far down the beach as he could, which was maybe twenty or twenty-five yards away. It was a big log.

As he'd done in Quinn's backyard, Brutus watched the sailing hunk of tree without moving so much as a muscle, but Quinn noted he was tense and on full alert. As soon as the log hit the sand, Quinn expected him to explode like a coiled spring of action. Not so much. Brutus eased up off his haunches and sauntered down the beach at a slow trot toward his quarry.

Smiling, Quinn shook his head, then turned as Riley came to stand next to him.

"He follows his own drummer," was all she said.

"I can respect that."

She looked him up and down, which did absolutely nothing to support his struggle to keep his hands to himself.

"I'm really sorry. You're all wet. Again. I swear, I didn't see you, then suddenly Brutus took off. He never runs, so I had no idea . . . but I should have known, I guess. The last time he took off, it was to run to you." She looked up at him and smiled. "Just another Quinn Brannigan fan, I guess. A really big fan," she added, as Brutus trotted back toward them, tree chunk clenched in his jaw.

"As long as he doesn't start his own fan club, with more just like him, I think I can handle it."

Riley laughed. "When I came around the bend and saw you running, I called out and tried to warn you, but with the wind and the waves, I was too far away. I tried to catch up, but you were running like . . . well, like the hounds of hell were on your heels."

"If I'd only known," he said, and they laughed.

"I'm really sorry."

"Don't be. I'm sorry I made you run."

"That's okay, clearly I could stand to do more of it." She grinned, and her already wind-pink cheeks pinkened a bit deeper.

It wasn't the sort of thing he'd have thought would be a turn-on, but with her, the blush did amazing things to his circulation, too . . . just a bit farther south.

Brutus dropped the log on Quinn's feet, again. Quinn tried not to flinch as he bent down and scooped up the log again. "You're a menace," he told the dog. "Here you go."

"He'll want you to do that all day if you let him," Riley warned.

Quinn launched the log anyway. "How exactly do you not let him do whatever it is he wants?"

"Just rub his head, scratch his ears, and tell him you're all done. He'll understand. He's just a pussycat, really."

"Right. I can see that about him." Quinn started to walk toward the dog as Brutus got closer to the driftwood, and Riley fell into place beside him.

"I'm sorry we interrupted your run. You looked very . . . dedicated. Let me get Brutus and we'll leave you to get back to it."

He wasn't going to tell her that running in clothes soaked in salt water and sand was probably not the best idea if he wanted to keep his skin intact. "That's okay, I don't mind. I was just . . . running from frustration, really."

"Was it helping?"

He chuckled. "No, but at least it felt more productive than sitting and staring at my computer screen."

"Oh. Are you having problems with the book?" She waved her hand in front of them. "That's none of my business. Sorry."

"Don't be. Dead cat." He winked at her when her gaze flew to his, and they chuckled. "To answer your question, no, I'm not having problems coming up with the story, I'm having too much success coming up with a story. That's the problem."

"Too much story is a problem?"

They caught up with Brutus, but rather than plop the log in the sand again, he kept it and fell into step in front of them, leading their procession down the beach. Quinn kept walking . . . and so did Riley. He decided, sandy, wet clothes or not, it was a much better way to spend the morning.

"Too *many* stories is the problem."

"Huh. I guess I never thought of that. I always pictured writers bent over their keyboards, struggling to come up with the perfect line, the perfect way to set the next scene. I guess it never occurred to me you might have too many ideas and have to figure out which one fits the story best."

"Well, you're right. That's generally not the problem. You have it more accurately with your first assessment." He slowed his steps and shifted his gaze to her. "In this case, I actually have two story ideas for the same characters and I'm struggling to figure out which one to tell. Both are good, both compelling, and I don't know which one better serves them. And me."

"Can't you give one story to a new set of characters? And write both?"

"I don't work that way, but I did consider it. In this case, however, they simply are these people with these stories. No one else's. There are two different universes I can have them inhabit, either one of which they'd rock, but they can't inhabit both, and the universes can't collide, not as I have them, in my head. They compel me in a way no two characters ever have before, at least not before I've even begun. They're important to me now that I've spent so much time with them in my head."

He chuckled. "It sounds a little crazy, or a lot crazy. Normally I have a general feel, then dive in and get to know my protagonists as I go. But I know these two better already than I do most characters at the end of five hundred pages. They are fully fleshed out, developed people who feel as real to me as any characters I've ever devised. I can't let them down by giving them any less than a rocking, compelling, engaging, and fulfilling story that lives up to the epic potential they have."

"Wow."

"Exactly." He laughed. "No pressure."

"No one else can solve the crimes in these stories but them? And the stories can have nothing in common?"

"In my head?" He grinned. "No. I have to pick one. I feel like it's *Sophie's Choice* or something. Once I commit, that is their story. There's no giant erase, and start over. It's who they become. To me."

"Why can't you make it a series or something?"

"I thought about that, but that won't work, either. The stories put them together at two different times in their lives. They can have one life, or the other, but they can't have experienced both, not together." He slowed his steps, paused a moment, then stopped walking altogether. "Can I ask you something? Hypothetically?"

She turned to look up at him, then shifted so his body blocked the sun from her face. "Sure."

"And can I trust your discretion?"

She frowned slightly. "Of course. Why?"

"First, let me ask you this. And be honest. Brutally, if needed. What is it that draws you to my books? I mean, when you sit down to read, what's the thing you hope to find, the element that makes you anticipate the story most?"

"That's easy, though you might not be happy about it. It's the relationship between the two leads. Always."

He folded his arms. "Really?"

She smiled and lifted one shoulder in a half shrug, as if to apologize. "Really. I know you're a crime novelist and you do an amazing job with all the gritty, gory stuff, and I'm sure most people read your books to get their murder mystery suspense fix. But, since you're asking me, I can only tell you that I put up with the gory, grisly stuff so I can get my relationship fix from the leads. You always have such powerful couples and they're so unapologetic in their commitment to one another. I love that." Her smile turned dry. "Gee, aren't you glad I'm the one you asked?"

"Actually, I am." He started walking again, his mind spinning in a new direction. "You said unapologetic. What is it that couples who love each other should apologize for?"

"Absolutely nothing," Riley said. "That's what makes your books so great. You totally get that. Despite all the tragedy they live with every day, they're allowed to be happy. Most books—mystery books, anyway—have the lead detective, be it man or woman, leading some miserable or deeply conflicted life and they're never allowed to get the girl—or guy—and live happily. Or if they are, it's short-lived and their new love must die or dump them, so they can go back to being an even more tragic figure. I enjoy a well-told mystery, and I like trying to figure out who did it, but isn't it bad enough that some poor soul, or souls, died and some horrible monster is on the loose, without making the lead guy who catches him miserable, too? I mean, after a while, it's just depressing. And hopeless. Like, we caught the bad guy, so everyone can sleep a bit more easily, except of course the guy who did the catching, who is still deeply conflicted and wretched." She shrugged again. "I guess I don't get why it all has to be so dysfunctional and tragic, in the guise of making it more like 'real life.'" She punctuated the last two words with air quotes. "Real life has joy and love and happiness, too. And fun, and humor, and . . . well, you get my meaning. I love that you show the gritty, all-too-real side of what can happen in this world, what human beings are capable of perpetrating . . . but you show both ends of that spectrum. Maybe it's the balance, or the contrast, that makes the horrible things that much more horrible. When characters love like your people do, you—meaning me, the reader—are that much more petrified something bad will happen to them, too. That would be just too tragic. So it makes my heart pound harder when you put them in jeopardy than when some sadsack detective puts his neck on the line." She stopped walking. "I'm sorry. I'm probably sounding like a crazy stalker fan, and you just have your couples in love so they can have hot sex." She grinned. "I like that part a lot, too."

Quinn grinned back. "I'm glad. So do I. To answer your other question, no, that's not the reason why I develop my crime-fighting couples the way I do. I do it . . . well, for exactly the same reason you enjoy it. I'm glad to know readers are getting that. Well, one reader anyway."

"Oh, I'm sure it's a whole lot more than one reader. I think that's why your stories have such universal appeal. I don't know what the breakdown of your readership is by gender, but I bet you have pretty deep hooks into both groups."

They walked down the beach in companionable silence, Brutus still leading the parade, as Quinn's thoughts eddied and swirled.

"So . . . what was the hypothetical question?" she asked.

He glanced up. "Oh, right. Actually, I think you already answered it."

"Oh." She looked a bit deflated. "Okay."

"All right," he said, grinning, "here it is, but again—"

She made a lip-locking motion with her fingers, then threw the imaginary key away. On impulse, Quinn darted out a hand and made an air grab, as if catching the imaginary key. He curled his fingers into a fist, and smiled at her.

She smiled, too, and her cheeks warmed again. He got all caught up in watching her pupils expand and her gaze drop to his mouth, before she looked away, back to the shoreline in front of them.

And the question just popped out easily, without hesitation. "Would you be interested in reading a book from me that might leave out the grisly, gory, psycho killer part?"

She stopped walking again, and turned to look up at him. "Yes." She said it instantly and decisively.

And it was exactly what he'd wanted her to say. "Okay," he said. *Okay*, he thought. They started walking again. He expected her to pepper him with questions, but she didn't, respecting his silence and need to think as they continued on down the beach.

Brutus suddenly made a turn up the sand to where a cluster of trees provided a swath of shade, and plopped himself down under them.

"I think he needs a break," Riley said. "This is a lot of exercise for him. I know he looks big and strong, but a lot of extended motion is hard on his hips and back."

Quinn nodded and followed Brutus's path up the sand. "I think there's room here for all of us."

"You don't have to wait, you can—"

Quinn sat just in front of the shady part, so the sun beat down on the damp front of his clothes. He smiled up at Riley, then patted the sand next to him.

"Okay." She sat down next to him. Past the edge of her loose-fitting, knee-length, light tan khaki shorts extended the whitest legs he'd ever seen.

"Do you want to sit in the shade?" he asked.

"What?" She noticed where his gaze had gone. "Oh, no. I have like 4000 level sunscreen on. The only way I'd tan is if all my freckles converged, and since that would just be oh-so-lovely, I opt for the Casper approach."

He looked at her. "I think you have beautiful skin. So you're probably the smart one."

He knew the skin in question would turn bright pink at the compliment, and she didn't disappoint him. Feeling utterly content and happy, he smiled and turned his gaze to the water, but not before noticing the bright pink toenail polish she sported . . . and the delicate silver band circling her pinky toe.

Just like that, his body leaped to life all over again—with a vengeance—causing him to cross his ankles and shift his weight in the sand. Sitting more upright, he plucked his damp shirt away from his skin so it hung looser.

Riley wore a melon-pink tank top covered with an unbuttoned, short-sleeved pink, orange, and white plaid camp shirt. Her loose-fitting shorts rode low on her hips, drawing his eye when she'd walked toward him earlier. The whole outfit was perky and cheerful and suited her blond curls and ready smile. Styled more for comfort than to show off her figure, it certainly wouldn't be deemed overtly sexy. Nor were her freckles and pale skin. Not overtly.

Yet, something about the feminine tipped toes, and the earthiness of that tiny band of silver, combined with the comfortable way she dressed and the even more comfortable way she inhabited her lush, curvy body . . . pretty much drove him mad with the need to pull her under him . . . and find out what was beneath all that cotton and color.

He dug his fingers into the sand and wondered again about Alva's remark regarding Riley's availability. He'd thought about that more than once the past week or so. Many more times than once. And had come to the conclusion that it ultimately didn't matter. If she was unattached and he'd just assumed otherwise, she'd let him run with that assumption. Meaning she was okay with his believing it. Obviously, she did not want to let him get any closer.

He'd decided to respect that, and her, and just get the hell over it.

But that was decidedly more challenging to do at the moment.

Quinn decided to simply keep his focus on the sound of the water, the feel of the sun soaking through his damp clothes, warming his skin . . . and not on his simmering awareness of the woman sitting beside him.

Right.

"So," she said at length, "and you don't have to answer, but following your hypothetical question . . . is that the problem you're having? You have a murder mystery story for your couple to solve . . . but you also want to just spend time telling your couple's story? No murders. Is that it?"

He shot her a quick glance, intending to look straight back to the water, but he instantly got caught up in the sincere, direct gaze she'd aimed his way, and he replied without thinking. "I think their love story would be less than it could be if it came before they grew into the characters they are now. It's not the right time for them to have the love story I know they'd have later. But later . . . there are no murders to solve because he can't deal with any more death. They will have solved all the ones they're capable of."

"I get it now. So it really is either or. They either love each other while fighting crime . . . or find each other after they've fought all the crime they can handle and fall in love then." She sighed. "I can see the dilemma. Either way, they are who they are right now. So now is when it has to happen."

"Exactly." He felt as if an enormous pressure had been removed from his psyche. It wasn't a solution, but it was a huge help to know someone at least understood the dilemma. "Thank you."

"Why? I didn't do anything."

"You got it, and that's more than I'd hoped. I had begun to think I'd gotten so far into the forest I'd totally lost all perspective on the trees."

She shook her head. "I don't think so. You just want to do them justice. And you don't know which way will do that best." Riley shifted in the sand and rolled to one hip so she could face him more directly. "I will say this. I really do love your suspense, purely for the complex plots you come up with. I can rarely ever figure out all the twists and turns. But . . . and I mean this as a compliment, there are times in every single book that I wish I could spend more time with your characters, away from the crime stuff. Of course, that's not what the story is about, so there is no time for that. I understand that it wouldn't make sense . . . but I feel a little left out, every time. Not let down, really, because your books are always wildly satisfying, but . . . maybe you know what I mean."

"To be honest, I always thought the balance was right where I wanted it. I liked contrasting big love against big tragedy, but I was always comfortable with the balance."

"So, why are these two different?"

He lifted one shoulder. "I don't know. I really don't. They just are. I see them, I listen to them, and there's just so much more to tell. I've tried to relegate whatever brought them together to something that's already occurred when we meet them, and I know they'd do a hell of a riveting job as my crime-fighting duo for the murder mystery I want to tell . . . but I just—I couldn't make the balance work for me. I feel like it wasn't right, or fair to them. I wasn't giving them all I could allow them to have, when I know they are capable of having so damn much more."

"So, doesn't that answer your question?"

"What do you mean?"

"If telling their story that way feels like you're letting them down . . . then you probably are."

"Okay, but following that . . . if their careers are done, over, for whatever reason, and it's from those ashes that they come together . . . if I'm not giving them anything else to do, and there aren't all those other extra crazy twists and turns . . . does it become dull and not so passionate and epic after all? Do I need that contrast of murder and mayhem in order to make their love story compelling? This would be a huge departure for me, so I have no sense of how it would fly. If I'm going to make that huge leap, risk pissing a lot of people off, then I feel like I have to be damn sure I know what I'm doing, that I can pull it off, make it work."

"Well, I'm the wrong person to ask, because that story seems just as compelling to me as the thriller. Mayhem that scares the crap out of you doesn't have to include murder. There are many terrifying things out there. I think falling in love is dangerous territory for two people who are a little flawed, and a whole lot damaged, to find themselves suddenly traversing. Especially just when they thought it was safe. You know? They walk away from the murder and mayhem, the bullets flying, because they can't risk it any-more . . . only to find they haven't ever risked the thing that puts them in the most personal danger they've ever been in. Murder happens to other people, and they pick up the pieces. But what if the pieces might be theirs? And the bul-let they end up dodging is coming from a shooter they never saw coming? Because there are no more shooters, right? Except . . . uh-oh."

She smiled. "We know the shooter is out there, just like in the murder mystery. *We*—meaning the readers—we see the bullet coming, we see the big looming threat that is going to be them being tempted by each other, them falling in love, but they don't. They're going to be completely blindsided by that shooter. I don't know how much more on the edge of your seat you can get than that. If, at the eleventh hour, they screw it up, and they don't figure out how to conquer the shooter—who is love—they're the ones who lose it all. Can't risk much more than that."

"Well," he said thoughtfully, "when you put it like that." He grinned, but there was already a swirl of thoughts liter-ally bombarding his brain. He finally—finally—felt that inexplicable knot in his gut, that snap, crack, and sizzle that made his fingers twitch to type, that sent his brain to racing . . . that *thing* that told him he'd found it.

He'd contrast the cases they'd solved in their respective pasts, the very ones he'd have had them solve if he'd gone the other way, against the danger they now found them-selves in when pitted against each other, fighting against an entirely different kind of mayhem, just as Riley said. The mayhem that comes internally when two people are fight-ing against falling in love. He could even plot it like a mur-der mystery as they discovered the clues and, ultimately, solved the case. The case being coming to that place where they could commit to loving one another. Maybe they'd crossed paths professionally—no maybe about it, they had—so there would be some joint knowledge of their respective pasts. They applied what they knew, what they had discovered, in completely different ways. They'd struck sparks before, good and bad, but it's only with all the rest done that the real conflagration would begin.

"So, do you get what I mean?" She looked at him uncertainly.

"Not only do I get what you mean," he said, the excitement juicing him up higher, faster, "I can write what you mean. And, going one better, I can sell what you mean." He grabbed her face and planted a big, noisy kiss on those big, juicy lips, then hooted so loudly he startled Brutus into looking up to see what all the excitement was about. "Oh my God, Riley. You did it. You nailed it." His hands still framed her face. "*Nailed* it!"

He scrambled to his feet, pulling her up along with him, straight into his arms. He spun them around, laughing, sounding like a wildman. The relief was so profound, he hooted and spun her around again. "You saw the trees. You saw the whole damn forest."

Her eyes were wide, like huge pools of melted chocolate, as he set her feet down on the sand, but he kept his hands on her arms. "I can't believe I didn't get it," he said, laughing again. "But you have it perfectly and exactly right. It fills the exact same bill, but with entirely different stakes, scarier stakes. Why didn't I see that? It's both, and it's more. So much more. You're a genius."

"Oh, it was nothing," she said, but she was as breathless as he was, and she looked just as dazzled and excited as he felt.

She grinned, and her eyes lit with that always present light that seemed to be constantly inside her. Her lips parted on a breathless laugh, drawing his gaze . . . and his attention.

The sizzle in the air changed abruptly from exuberant

celebration and relief, to something decidedly more . . . elemental.

His hold on her arms gentled as he realized his excitement had him gripping her rather intently. He rubbed his fingers absently over the place where he'd held most firmly, but his attention was drawn from parted lips to darkening eyes, then back to her mouth again. "I've thought a lot about what you would taste like," he said, giving up entirely on censoring himself. He was giddy for all sorts of reasons, and it was just too damn good. Too damn good. Mayhem, indeed. "And I kissed you so fast, I didn't even get to savor it."

He saw her throat work. "Is there a rule about do-overs I don't know about?" She tried for casual humor, but the way she was looking at him was anything but casual.

That was also damn good . . . because he'd hate to be the only one feeling this way. "The only rule I have is that I don't kiss someone who is regularly kissing someone else." He smiled. "Spontaneous kisses of profound gratitude notwithstanding."

"I like that rule."

"Good," he said.

"Yes, it is," she agreed. "Very."

"You're not going to make this easy, are you?" But that was okay, because he was done worrying about easy. "Down at the docks that day, by your boat, you said you were involved with someone."

"No, I didn't."

"Okay, you're right." Fair was fair, after all. "I said it. You didn't correct me."

"I . . . thought it would be easier that way."

"Easier for who?"

"Me. I didn't think you would really care one way or the other."

That pissed him off a little, because it wasn't true, and

because he was pretty sure it was herself she was judging and finding lacking . . . not him. "But you did. Care, I mean."

"I like you. And I'm a sucker for caring about people I like. My defenses in that area stink, and, try as I might, there doesn't seem to be much I can do about it." Riley held Quinn's gaze for a long time, then said, "Can I ask you something? And I want an honest answer. Be brutal if necessary," she added, echoing his earlier request.

Normally he would have grinned, but the stakes felt suddenly high. Really high. And decidedly personal. He frowned. "Okay."

"You've been struggling to figure out your book. I'm guessing from your profound gratitude it's been more than frustrating. Maybe even a little frightening. And you've come here, to Sugarberry, because you wanted some time to focus on that. And . . . well, I'll be honest, I've followed you a little bit in the media, and I know half that stuff is made up, and the other half probably grossly exaggerated, but . . ." She trailed off, then said, "I guess I want to know if this interest you say you have in kissing me is based on a sincere interest in getting to know me."

She paused, and he realized this was harder for her than she had allowed him to realize. "Or because I'm here, and convenient? Because I'll be honest," she added, not letting him reply, "I don't strike me as the kind of woman you'd normally go for, and that's fine, no judgment, no harm, no foul. I get the attraction of hassle-free convenience. I'm probably the last person you'd see as a threat to complicate things. It's just I stink at that kind of thing. I wish I didn't, because it would most likely be a wonderful way to spend some time. I just . . ." She lifted her shoulders, then let them drop, along with her gaze. "It's not a good fit for me. It's not what I would want, or choose."

He started to say "me, either," with absolute sincerity, except, the truth was, she'd pretty much described exactly how his relationships had gone. He'd done that very thing in the past, enjoyed that exact kind of easy, breezy, no-demands relationship. Too many of them, in fact. He'd told himself if they were meant to be more, they would be. But how often had he set them up, subconsciously, or chosen women, specifically, knowing the chance of getting tangled up was unlikely to happen? He'd never wanted to hurt anyone, least of all himself.

He was pretty sure the "me, either" response absolutely applied. It was just . . . why would she believe that? Why did he?

"No, I wouldn't think you would," he said, instead.

She looked up. "But you would," she said, not quite making it a question. "Choose that."

"It has been a choice I've made in the past, yes," he said, giving her—and himself—the brutal honesty she'd asked for.

She looked disappointed. But not nearly as much as he was in himself. She wasn't wrong to feel the way she did.

"But I am also being honest when I tell you that's not why I said what I did. To toy with you, or play you. I said it because it's true. You couldn't be more wrong about your ability to complicate things. You drive me crazy. You're forever in my thoughts. That wasn't something I expected, not because it was you, but because that traditionally would not have been me. It just seems to be me . . . where you're concerned. And I honestly don't know what to do about that."

She frowned, then smiled that dry smile, making one dimple wink out . . . all but begging him to get the full grin out of her. "So, then, I think I'm flattered. Maybe. I guess."

He grinned at her unexpected response. "You should be. Maybe. I guess."

They laughed, and the tension eased just a little. It was

still there, simmering below the surface. It probably always would be, as long as it wasn't tended to.

"Thank you," he said, at length.

"For the story idea? No problem. Sounds like you'd already done all the heavy lifting. You just needed someone on the outside looking in to see where to place it all so it looked real pretty"—she grinned—"which, of course, is my specialty."

"It certainly is." He softened when he looked at her, despite the still sizzling sexual tension. "Maybe I should be brainstorming with stylists and stagers instead of other writers and my editors.

"But that's not what I was thanking you for. I meant for your frankness and your honesty. It's not what I want to hear, but it's what I need to hear. I never want to take advantage . . . but I might have with you. I don't seem to have much control over what I'm thinking or what I want, where you're concerned."

She smiled brightly then—too brightly—and let him the rest of the way off the hook. "Well, now neither one of us has to worry about that." She patted his arm, in a friendly, end-of-conversation way. "It's good that we talked, and aired it all out." She started to ease out of his hold, and he was pretty sure if he let her, she'd have taken off back down the beach. Never to be seen again.

He tightened his hold instinctively, keeping it gentle, but not ready—maybe never ready—to let her go. "So . . . that do-over . . . it's off the table, too. I guess." It was a ridiculous thing to say, he knew that, but it was all he had left.

She looked at him, and her smile faltered—badly—even if the spark in her eyes did not. "Quinn . . ."

"I know. I just . . ." He trailed off. "I know," he repeated. "We don't always get what we want." He held her gaze, hard as it was to see the desire there, and know he couldn't act on it. "It just . . . God, this sounds like a corny line from some fiction novel," he said with a short laugh, "but it just feels wrong. Walking away."

"What does it normally feel like when you walk away?"

It stung, her presumption that he was always the one to do the walking. It shouldn't have, because she was right. But it did, because she was right. "That's just it," he said, feeling more exposed than he'd ever allowed himself to be before. "It normally doesn't feel at all."

Her expression sobered as she looked as intently at him, into him, as he was looking at and into her. "You . . . really mean that."

The corner of his mouth lifted. "I wish that wasn't so hard to believe. I'm not a thoughtless jerk. I don't set out to hurt people. I'm always honest."

"I never thought you were a jerk, thoughtless or otherwise. You strike me as exactly the kind of man who says those kinds of things all the time, because you don't want to hurt anyone. I think it's second nature for you to soften the blow, to say things that make others feel good about themselves, to take the blame all on yourself for things ending when they end."

"Maybe." He never really thought about it that way. "But I didn't keep you from walking away just now because I didn't want to hurt your feelings." He slid his hands down her arms, and tucked his fingers through hers. "I kept you from walking away because I really don't want you to go. It's as simple and as complicated as that. I don't have anything else to offer. There are no promises I can make, so it's a purely selfish thing, and I'd like to think I'm not a purely selfish guy. It's just . . . the truth."

He broke off, looked down at their joined hands, sighed, then made himself look at her again . . . and laid the rest of himself bare. It was the least he could do, the least she deserved. "You make me feel, and think, and want things that aren't typical for me. I don't know why, and I don't have the slightest clue what it would mean, or where it would go. You're probably right not to take that risk, right to turn around, and walk down the beach, and not look back. All I have is the truth that I don't want you to, that it's not what I would choose. For the first time, it will make me feel something, when you leave."

She held his gaze steadily, for what felt like an eternity.

Until, finally, he let go of her hand. "This isn't fair to you. You've told me what you want."

"No," she said, suddenly finding her voice. "I told you what I can handle. Or, more to the point, what I can't." She took his hand back in hers. "I never told you what I want."

His heart started pounding hard. He'd never reacted like this to anyone, had never felt such a simultaneous wrench of anticipation and abject fear. His characters had . . . but not him. He realized he hadn't come close to doing that feeling justice when he'd described it. He'd sure as hell be able to now. "What"—he had to stop and clear his throat— "what *do* you want, Riley?"

Her lips, the very ones he was dying for, curved slowly, followed by the wink of one dimple, then the other. The warmth of her smile infused her skin, and reached all the way to the very depths of her deep, brown eyes. "What I want, Quinn Brannigan . . . is that do-over."

"Riley—"

She put her fingers—trembling fingers, he noted—across his lips. "Just kiss me and put us both out of our misery, will you? We'll plot the next scene when this one is done."

"Well, when you put it like that . . ."

Chapter 12

Riley closed her eyes. How was it she'd ended up on a long, quiet stretch of beach, standing under an Indian summer sun . . . and asking Quinn Brannigan to please kiss her?

"Riley?"

She blinked her eyes open. *Oh, right . . . he hasn't actually kissed me yet.* And all of her bravado fled. "I knew it," she whispered. Not accusatorily, more dispiritedly.

The corners of his eyes crinkled as he smiled, and she wanted to think that was affection she saw in those blue eyes, sweetly concerned affection. For her. But what were the chances of that? She should have run when she had the chance.

"Knew what?"

"I'm either dreaming this, and right now is when I'm going to wake up, because that would so be my luck, or you're about to tell me some really good reason why you changed your mind."

"Why would I do that?"

"Because this doesn't happen for me. I mean, once upon a time, a long time ago, it happened for me, but I didn't know then what I do now. Granted, I haven't been trying, or willing to even give it a chance to happen again. In case you haven't noticed, I'm kind of a disaster, so what were really my chances anyway? I mean, what guy really wants someone who lives on a borrowed houseboat, and at any given moment is sporting at least three bruises and two Band-Aids, has a dog who, even though he means well, is kind of a one-person wrecking crew, and—"

"This guy." He cut her off by taking her face in his hands, and kissing her. Really . . . kissing her.

At first she just stood there, hands out at her sides, stunned into inaction, simply letting him.

Then he lifted his mouth just slightly from hers, enough to look her in the eyes. His still had those endearing smile crinkles at the corners. And there really, truly was affection there . . . for her. "The reason I stopped before was because I didn't want you hiding behind closed eyes when we kissed for the first time. Now, kiss me back." He urged her arms around his shoulders, then pulled her fully into his own.

"Oh," she gasped in surprise. When their bodies finally made contact, she breathed a much softer, "Oh."

"Exactly." Easing his mouth back onto hers, he said against her lips, "Kiss me, Riley,"

So . . . she did. She hadn't kissed anyone since Jeremy—a lifetime ago. So long ago she had no other point of reference from before him. She had no sense of what it would be like when and if she ever kissed someone again.

She'd been head over heels in love with the last man she'd kissed, at the time she'd kissed him, and had felt loved every bit as much in return. And that had all been a lie.

When Quinn tucked her more firmly against his body, all big and dry and warm from the sun, and coaxed her lips apart, then groaned in the back of his throat like a long, satisfied growl as he slid his tongue into her mouth, she could never have anticipated it would be anything like this. Because she hadn't known there were kisses like this.

Quinn's kiss was slow, and unhurried, exploratory and, well . . . fun. He kissed her like he had all the time in the world, and planned to take every advantage of it. What pulled at her, what tugged someplace deep she didn't know she had, was that it wasn't artful seduction. The sounds he made, the way he encouraged her to kiss him back, then took such clear pleasure in it when she did, told her he wasn't in any more control of how this made him feel than she was. It was heady and intoxicating.

Her body flamed, and muscles long out of use clenched and tightened in that blissful, achy way, as slow and steady need began to build. It felt good to know she wasn't broken. She'd certainly felt that way. Empty, switched off.

Everything was switched on now . . . and it all worked just fine. If she hadn't been so caught up in kissing him back, she'd have let out a little shout of triumph. Her own little hoot and holler of relief. If she'd felt empty before . . . a few of Quinn's kisses were doing a pretty good job of filling her right back up.

She slid her fingers into his hair, and urged him to go deeper. She was purely in the moment. She had no past, and didn't care about the future. Just that exact moment. She would be quite happy to stay in that moment forever. She wanted to remember everything about this.

Quinn lifted his mouth from hers, then kissed the side of her jaw, then her temple, and pulled her into his arms, tucking her head under his chin. "That was . . ." He didn't finish, but the way his heart pounded under her cheek said it all.

Riley smiled against his chest. "It sure was," she agreed. She closed her eyes with the intent of going back over each delicious moment in her mind, willing it to permanent memory—the look in his eyes when he told her he wanted to kiss her, the taste of his mouth, the shape of his lips, the way he'd kissed her like tomorrow would never come. She wanted to remember every sensation, every feeling, to be relived whenever she desired.

Would there be others to store away? She had no idea, and Quinn had admitted he didn't, either. He'd admitted he didn't usually get involved, or get serious, or even know why he'd been interested in her. So, she'd take the one memory they had made, and hold it close. It felt good to have a sweet, wonderful memory to think about, and remember with nothing but joy. And that was enough.

A start, a first step up and out. Something.

Quinn tipped her chin up, shifting back so he could look into her eyes. "Thank you."

Surprised, she said, "For?"

"The do-over." They laughed. "Can I ask you something?"

"Of course." She liked—a lot—that he hadn't let her go. Staying like this, half wrapped around him, now that the mindlessness of their kiss was over, was . . . comforting. Like they wanted to linger in the moment a little while longer . . . before whatever happened next, happened.

That was nice. Really, really nice.

"Earlier, when you were releasing me from my apparently misguided desire to kiss you, you said a guy like me wouldn't normally choose you." He caressed her cheek as he said it.

She smiled up at him. "If you recall, you agreed."

"Much to my shame, if you also recall." He grinned then. "And which, I believe, we've now aptly disproved."

She liked that grin. It started that fluttery business all over again in her stomach. "Well, it's possible it felt like you might have, you know, enjoyed it," She teased him back, then smiled. "A little."

"So . . . let me ask you this. Strictly in the fair's fair category, when you kissed me back, were you kissing that successful guy on the back of the book covers? Or were you kissing me?"

She'd had no idea where he'd been headed, but that definitely wasn't it. In fact, the question surprised her. Greatly. Because he wasn't just teasing, or flirting. He was serious. She knew him well enough to know that—which, more or less, answered the question. She just wasn't sure how to explain that to him. "Well, it wouldn't be completely honest of me to say there isn't a certain surreal factor to all of this, because I have looked at your picture many times, and probably all of your readers feel some kind of connection to you from reading your books. It's an intimate act, in some ways, peeking into your mind like that, though one-sided since you don't get to peek back. And you telling me you wanted to kiss me . . . some part of me had a bit of a dork-out moment. Okay, a big dork-out moment. I'm human."

His lips twitched, but he was still serious when he said, "Riley—"

"No, wait, let me finish. I am a dork, at heart. We both know that. And that's just it. Straight off, you knew that about me. It's pretty much the only part of me that's been on display every time we've crossed paths. I never had a chance to show myself in a better light. So, when you kissed me, I had no doubt you knew exactly who you were kissing. I might not have believed you'd want to, but when you did . . . I knew it was honest, and real.

"You're exactly right. Fair's fair. You deserve to know what's honest and what's real, too. Unlike with me, initially what I had to go on with you was the book jacket guy, and book jacket guy always struck me as someone completely at ease with himself, who knows exactly who he is, is very comfortable in his own skin. Meeting you didn't change that impression. If anything, you enhanced it. So, at first, sure, I probably was superimposing the book jacket guy onto the actual guy. And if you'd kissed me the day we met, yes, I'd have been starstruck. I wouldn't have been able to help it. That's all I knew of you, all you were to me."

"But?" Quinn looked partly amused, but more curious . . . and maybe a little uncertain. "I can hear the *but.*"

"Don't worry, it's a good one. Well, it is to me. The day we talked on the houseboat, and again at the bakery, I felt I had gotten to know a little more about you, but it wasn't until today, walking on the beach, talking, that I felt I was meeting the real you. The uninhibited you, the writer, the man who is passionate about his work, focused, worried about it. Your work fascinates me. I could be ten dead cats and a dozen curious monkeys about it and still just scratch the surface. But that's more about me being a reader, a lover of your work.

"When *you* talk about your work, though . . . suddenly you're not polished and effortlessly charming guy, you're . . . I don't know, more real. Vulnerable, unsure. When you shared your frustration about the story, and how you've been agonizing over it, you're . . . well, it turns out you're a lot like me. You worry, you think too much, you spend a lot of time in your head, and you're way more concerned with doing something the way it should be done because that's what is satisfying to you, than just making everyone happy. I can't tell you how many photographers I drove absolutely bonkers with my insistence on getting the food styled and displayed just so for a camera shot. I had this idea in my head and I knew it would be the most tantalizing, mouth-watering presentation, and it mattered that I achieved the image in my head, or as close to it as I could. I'm the same way now with staging houses."

She smiled and shook her head. "So . . . you're kind of geeky about your work, like I am about mine. Beneath all the success and polish, good looks and charm . . . you're just a writer guy struggling to tell a story, a little off the beaten path, maybe a bit nerdy about it—which is great. I totally get that guy. And that guy, I might even believe, gets me, too. That guy I can almost believe would want to kiss dorky ol' me." She felt her cheeks warm a bit, but she said the rest of what she wanted to say. "So, when I kissed you back just now? That's who I kissed. That guy. You."

His expression was one of surprise, maybe even a little shock, and she was afraid maybe she'd insulted him. "I think that might be the best thing anyone has ever said about me. And it's good to know you like that guy"—he pulled her close again, so she had to tip her head way back to look into his eyes—"because that guy does get you, and he is exactly the guy who wants to kiss you. And maybe now I get that, too."

When he took her mouth, it wasn't gentle, or coaxing, or exploratory. It was that ardent, passionate kiss she'd thought about the first day they'd met, the one up on the big screen that happened when someone finally made that move, in that moment. Only way—way—better.

He didn't kiss and coax, he claimed. Even then, he wouldn't simply take. He wanted her to take him back, challenging her to a duel of tongues, of heat, trading his groan for her gasp, until she was close to begging him to just pull her down on the sand and get on with it already. Those newly invigorated muscles had long since gone from clenching to aching, and her fingers were digging into his chest, grasping at his shirt, wanting nothing more than to pull it off so she could feel the heat of his skin directly under her touch. She wanted to taste him, lick the salt from his skin, she wanted—"Oof!"

A split second later, they were sprawled in the sand, but not in an amorous tangle of arms and legs as she'd hoped . . . more in a heap of tangled limbs courtesy of Brutus, who had his front paws planted on Quinn's chest and arms, so he could stare him down . . . and drool on him.

"Holy Cr—Brutus!" Riley called to the dog, when she got her wits back enough to realize what had happened. "I don't know what's gotten into him. He's not the protective type. He's never—Brutus! Get down! Off!"

She started to scramble to her knees, intent on dragging him off Quinn if she had to, when Brutus leaned his big old head down . . . and gave Quinn a huge swipe of his tongue, right across his face.

"Gah," Quinn sputtered, but pinned as he was, by Brutus and Riley, he couldn't do much about it.

Riley sputtered, too, but with laughter.

"Easy for you," Quinn said, still spitting. "You're not the one that just got slimed."

"Oh my God. I'm so sorry." Riley scrambled off Quinn as best she could without adding injury to insult, though he did groan a few times as she managed it. "But it is kind of funny."

"He's probably jealous," Quinn forced out from lungs half crushed by the weight of the dog's paws. "I get it."

"Get off him, Brutus," Riley said, breathless from her efforts and the laughter that kept spluttering out. "He's jealous, but not *of* you. I think he just wanted some loving, too." She grinned as she tugged on Brutus's collar. "Come on, big guy. It's okay. Quinn likes you, too. Let's go find your stick."

Brutus didn't budge. He was still gazing at Quinn, tongue lolling, like a starry-eyed fan dog.

"Brutus!" Riley commanded, finally getting her wind and getting past her case of the giggles. "Off!"

Grudgingly, Brutus stepped off Quinn's chest, then plopped his butt in the sand next to him, still staring adoringly.

"I've never seen him take to anyone like this, and so fast, not even Jeremy. Are you okay?"

Quinn rubbed at his chest, coughing a little as he sat up. "Who's Jeremy?"

Riley's mouth fell open, then snapped shut. Had she really said that out loud? She closed her eyes on a silent groan. *Wow. Idiot.* She opened them to find Quinn standing, brushing the sand off his shirt. Thanks to Brutus. Again. "My ex-fiancé."

Quinn stopped brushing in mid-motion to look at her. "Fiancé?"

"Ex," she repeated. "We broke it off the year before last. The beginning of the year before last."

"How long were you engaged?"

"Four years." She laughed then, but there was little humor in it. Nerves got the best of her, and she suddenly couldn't seem to shut up. "Who stays engaged for four years? And that was after dating for another three and a half. I didn't think it mattered. We were together, you know? But I should have known he was never going to stick with me, right?" She shook her head, then busied herself brushing the sand from her shirt and shorts, more to give herself something to do, and anyplace else to look but at Quinn's unreadable expression. "It's ancient history."

"Right," he said. "And how long have you been on Sugarberry?"

She looked up then, serious, too. "A couple years. Yes, the same exact couple years, okay? Do you really want the whole pathetic story? I told you I was a dork."

Quinn took a moment to give Brutus a hearty pat on the head and scratch behind the ears, then walked over to her and took her arms in his hands. His grasp was gentle, but firm, as was the look he was giving her. "Maybe. But you're also strong, funny, sweet, and kind. And sexy as hell. You're utterly and completely yourself at all times. That's one of the things I find most attractive about you. You're exactly who you are. Band-Aids, monster dog, and all. And I seriously doubt there is anything remotely pathetic about whatever happened back then, especially if it made you leave a job you obviously loved, to move this far away, to start over. Painful, hurtful, and probably a whole lot of other things, but pathetic? I doubt it. Unless maybe we're talking about him." He shrugged, but his gaze stayed, laserlike, on hers. "Just a guess on my part, but probably a good one."

She stared back at him, totally taken aback. He'd stood up for her, just like that. "You don't even know me."

"I do know you. You just got done telling me how much we're alike. I know you, Riley. At least I know that much."

"I—thank you. For saying that. All of that. It means a lot."

"I meant every word. That's who I kissed. And it has a lot to do with why I kissed. And want to keep kissing."

"I—" She broke off, looked away. "This . . . is a lot." Suddenly she felt vulnerable and shaky and not necessarily in a bad way—which just made getting the hell out of there so she could regroup and think all the more imperative.

"Is that bad?"

"No. Not at all. In fact, it's very . . . very good."

"Too good? Is . . . are you nervous? Because so am I, believe me—"

"Exactly. All the more reason to retreat, regroup a little. It's been a big day, and there's a lot swirling around here, and"—she slid her arms from his grasp and stepped back, brushing her hair from her face, though the wind kept blowing it right back—"I'm sure you want to get back to your book, now that you have an idea of what you want to do."

"It was your idea."

"It's yours now. So, maybe it's best for you to just go do . . . what you do. And so will I. And . . . we'll see. About what happens next. We'll just . . . see."

"Riley—"

"I just need a little space, okay?" She was trying not to

panic, but this was too much. Way too much. It was one thing to kiss him, to fantasize about doing a whole lot more with him. But she hadn't counted on the whole emotional vulnerability part. She thought she'd have more time to figure that out, or at least how she felt about being so . . . so exposed to someone again. "I'm not running," she told him. "I'm—that's not me. But this is happening very fast. It was just supposed to be a kiss."

Quinn didn't say anything to that, and his expression was completely unreadable. She didn't know if he was pissed, disappointed, disgusted, or all three.

"It was," he said finally. "The best damn kiss I've ever had. And yes, I guess that is a lot. It is for me, too. And no, I didn't see that coming either. That bullet. But, unless you tell me otherwise, at some point, I'm going to want another kiss. I'm also going to want to know more about you. And want you to know more about me—which is terrifying . . . and exciting as hell. You're not the only one exposing your soft white underbelly here. But . . . wherever that path leads, I want to follow it. I have never been that guy who wanted to know where that path goes. But I want to know now. Because I'm very definitely that guy with you. You just have to decide if that's the guy you want to know, too."

"Quinn—"

"It's a lot. It might be everything. So take some time. Figure out what you want . . . and what you can handle. I know what I want." With that, he turned and took off down the beach at a steady lope.

He didn't look back.

Chapter 13

"Well, the wolves are wary . . . but excited!"

"I'll take it. Just as long as you trust me that this is going to be amazing, we're good." Quinn pulled into his spot behind the diner. "I know it's a gamble, Claire, but—"

"Stop selling me and go write the damn thing. I'm on your side." She paused a moment. "You know, you're excited about your books and I know you put your heart into everything you write, and that this will be no different. But . . . I've never heard you quite like this before."

"I've never written anything like this before."

"I know, but there's something else. You have this . . . energy about you, or something. What are they feeding you down there, anyway?"

Quinn tried like hell to picture Laura Jo's bacon and egg sandwich, but his autopilot brain took him straight to Riley. "You and your nice, clean, marathon-running arteries don't want to know."

She laughed. "You're probably right. Whatever it is, keep doing it. I've never heard you sound this . . . well, happy. Settled. I'll talk to you later. And thanks for the due date. That helped a lot, in all corners."

"My pleasure. Truly." He signed off, climbed out of the car, and headed through the back door. Laura Jo wasn't in the kitchen, which meant she was out front serving. He nodded to Petey and Magro, then ducked through the door . . . only to find someone else was already occupying his regular table.

"There you are." Alva tapped on the table with the corner of her menu, clearly annoyed.

"A pleasure, Miss Alva," he said, the smile sincere. He had no idea what she was up in arms about, but he was certain he was about to find out. One thing about Alva, you didn't have to be a mind reader. "Mind if I join you?"

"You're usually here earlier," she said, by way of a response. "I've been here twenty minutes."

"I was working. Got on a roll." In fact, if Claire's call hadn't disrupted the flow, he'd still be hunched over his laptop. "I'm sorry, but were we supposed to meet?" He took a seat across from her, still smiling. "If so, my apologies. I never like to keep a pretty woman waiting."

Two spots of pink bloomed in Alva's cheeks, but she was having none of his charm. The twinkle in her eyes ran more along the edge of dangerously glittering. "Well, you have an odd way of showing it. You know, men might like it when women play hard-to-get, but we women don't need any such foolishness. When we're interested, we're interested. Is that so hard a thing to comprehend?"

"No, not at all. I prefer the direct approach myself." Quinn was more confused than concerned, and his smile when he leaned forward and covered Alva's hand, came quite naturally. "Are you trying to tell me something of a . . . personal nature, Miss Alva?"

She snatched her hand out and swatted the back of his with it. "Of course I am. Why do you think I'm here? And if you'd stop fluttering those baby blues and trying to seduce me, I'd tell you about it."

He subverted his choke of laughter into a brief coughing spell, causing Alva to push her water glass to his side of the table. "Take a sip," she ordered. "And see if you can stop flirting for five seconds so I can say my piece."

"Yes, ma'am." Dutifully taking a sip, then another one, he put the glass down only when he was certain he could maintain a sober, considerate expression. She was a pip, though.

"Of course, maybe that's the problem," she said.

"The problem?"

"Oh, don't try and act all innocent with me. I'm sure you've left a string of broken hearts from Hollywood to New York City."

"Actually, I don't spend much time in either of those places. I have a place in Alexandria, just outside the nation's capital."

"Another town where sex is about power."

Quinn shoved the water glass away. He knew Alva could be a real pistol, but he'd never seen her worked up like this. "Speaking for myself, I don't trade sex for anything. But as long as the two people having it are satisfied with what's what, then I don't see the problem."

Laura Jo had stopped by the table just then, heard his comment, and suddenly got busy taking an order at a nearby table. He could see her straining to eavesdrop.

"What's this all about?" he asked.

"What it's about is you leading on our sweet Miss Riley Brown, then casting her aside like yesterday's newspaper. I don't need to know the details, but we're a close-knit community here and we stand up for each other. We had it in our hearts to stand up for you, too, but if you think, for one minute, that gives you blanket approval to just waltz in here and—"

"Whoa, whoa." Quinn covered her hand again. "Before I end up in your next column as the What Not to Do lesson, let's talk this over. First of all, no one has led anyone on. Riley and I are very direct people and I doubt there's been any kind of misunderstanding on where we stand. I'd be very surprised to hear she's said otherwise."

"It's not what she's saying," Alva said, a bit of the wind out of her sails. "It's what she's not."

"Well, that's a little different. Friends looking out for friends isn't a bad thing. Not at all. What makes you think whatever she's not saying has anything to do with me?"

The answer to that interested him more than it should. He'd spent the three days since their time on the beach all but umbilically attached to his laptop, partly because Joe and Hannah's story was gushing out of him and he had the power to make them do what he wanted them to do . . . and partly because it kept him from hunting down whomever Jeremy was, and punching the son of a bitch for putting that look in Riley's eyes. Considering Quinn was a man who believed in using words rather than fists, that had been a rather surprising revelation. Mostly he'd kept himself tethered because it prevented him from doing something he'd actually regret, like trying to make Riley do something she didn't want to do. He'd pushed her quite enough. Maybe too much. The next step was hers to take. Or not. She knew, quite clearly, where he stood.

"Well, for one, the expression on your face right now makes me think it has something to do with you." All Alva's irritability was gone, replaced with a more curious gleam. "I don't want to speak out of turn, or break any confidences, but I will say we've been getting together weekly since she moved to the island over a year ago, and only recently she finally opened up about her life in Chicago. Her personal life, I mean. She's a happy, outgoing, smart, and capable woman, and yet she held that in for close to two years. Tells you something. That's all I'm going to say about it."

Quinn's expression was half smile, half frown. "I can't tell if you're encouraging me, or warning me off."

Alva smiled, and there wasn't the slightest bit of calculation in her old eagle eyes. Just honest affection. "I'm not right sure myself. All I know is leaving things simmering, whichever way they're to go, isn't the same as resolving them. Can't leave the house as long as you've got a pot still on the stove, if you get my meaning."

Before Quinn could comment, Alva's attention perked up and moved past his shoulder.

Quinn's neck tightened, as did other parts of his body. Had she spotted Riley? He knew they might cross paths at some point, he just hadn't counted on it being at Laura Jo's . . . with Alva playing chaperone, and half the island in attendance. Something told him Riley wouldn't be any happier being the topic of Alva's conversation than he'd been on the receiving end of it.

When he glanced over his shoulder, he saw that Walter, Dwight, and two more of their town council cronies had stepped up to the counter. Quinn looked back at Alva. The agitation was back if the stiff posture of her tiny frame was any indication, but she wasn't paying any attention to him. "Something going on here?"

"I'm holding my annual invitational poker tournament. Maybe you've seen the flyers?"

Quinn nodded. "I have. And I think it's great. Grams, rest her soul, played a wicked game of gin rummy, but I don't know that she ever tried her hand at five-card stud." He smiled. "My bet is, she'd have been quite good at it."

Alva smiled. "You don't know everything about your grandmother." Her twinkle was back. "But it would be a good bet to make." She looked back at the foursome placing their coffee order. "Brodie Banneker has had a bee in his bonnet ever since the tournament I had last year, after the fall festival. It turned out to be quite the event, what with the whole secret auction fiasco, and Baxter making a guest appearance." She folded her hands over her purse, which was draped with her gloves, the epitome of senior citizen propriety. "Naturally, I wanted to hold a rematch."

"Naturally."

"Charlotte and her fiancé, Carlo, are going to cater. She's part of the Cupcake Club. They run their own catering business out of Savannah called Sweet and Savory. She does the sweet, Carlo does the savory. Baxter has promised another appearance. He's going to give away a few of his cookbooks (signed, don't you know) and"—she looked particularly pleased—"don't tell a soul, but he's going to give away tickets to see a taping of his show, all expenses paid. Hotel, the works." Alva leaned forward and covered his hand. "Of course, I was thinking about asking you if you'd like to contribute in some way, maybe a few signed copies of your latest? I know you're here all hush-hush, working on your next project, but since everyone coming to the match knows you—"

He nodded. "I'd be more than happy to."

Looking very pleased, she said, "And while we're on that topic, I've been meaning to ask if you can make time to have a little talk with me. For my column?"

Quinn blanched. "Me?" The single word came out as a less-than-manly squeak. "Wh-why?" He thought he'd made it past the firing squad of one.

"Now, now, don't look like a boy with his hand caught in the church plate. I don't just do advice columns. Sometimes I do human interest. In fact, my launch column was about Baxter when he first came to film his show here, in Lani's shop. Turns out it was all part of his big plan to woo her—see, there's a man who doesn't sit around and wait for things to happen—and I got the scoop." She leaned forward again, dropping her voice. "I'd be so honored to get the scoop on your next book. I've asked around, but there's been nary a word on it. Seems like something hush-hush is happening. Am I right?"

Quinn briefly narrowed his gaze, and decided if the UN really wanted to negotiate world peace, they need look no further than Alva Liles. He didn't bother asking her whom she'd spoken to, doubting Riley had said anything, but not putting it past Alva to have called his publisher. Maybe they should ask her to find out where the missing seventeen minutes of Watergate tape had gone. Or where Hoffa was buried.

"As a matter of fact. I do have some interesting news. But I can't talk about it just yet."

He thought her carefully coiffed beehive might finally come unglued as she all but vibrated in her seat with excitement. "Well, that would be very kind of you. Very kind indeed." The sweetness and cream response didn't at all match the avid gleam in her eyes, but that's what made it so much fun. "You just say the word, and I'll have you over to dinner. I think chatting over a nice meal is far more civilized, don't you? I cooked for Baxter. All my husband Harold's favorites."

"That sounds civilized and tasty," Quinn said, making a point to chat with Baxter when he had the chance, and look up that first article in the *Islander* archives. That was the great thing about being a writer, he could pass off any snooping as research.

Alva's gaze had drifted back to the foursome at the counter, and her fingers clutched at her gloves a bit tightly.

Quinn was curious despite himself. "What is the problem with the poker tournament?"

Alva dragged her gaze back to his, annoyed all over again. "Well, this year, to avoid any . . . unpleasantness, I opted to make the tournament an invitational."

"And how does one get an invitation?"

"Why, from me, of course. It's my party."

"I take it Walter and other council members didn't make the cut?"

"The tournament is only open to women. And it's not Walter, it's Dee Dee Banneker's husband, Brodie, who's the problem. He used to be a deputy sheriff, now sits on the council. I didn't invite his wife. She was the instigator of all the drama last year. And, of course, since she's not coming, her best friend Suzette is making a stink about it—her son-in-law's the fire chief, also on the council—and not coming, either. Though I'd have let her if she'd asked." Alva leaned forward. "She's not much of a player, but she makes a mean ham salad. Win-win, really."

Quinn swallowed another snort of laughter. "So, what is the council doing about it?"

"Passing an ordinance to prevent me from holding the tournament in any public facility. I had it here at Laura Jo's last year, but I was aiming for a bigger venue this year, as I've invited a few more players. I'm not limiting it to the seniors this year. Lani May and Miss Riley, for instance, are both playing. But there aren't any private places with more space. Lani would have us, but we can't squeeze in there. I booked the Senior Center annex. It's a new building we added on last year." She patted her hair. "Due to a prior misunderstanding, I'm no longer allowed to book the center itself, but there was no rule about the annex and my money is just as green as anyone else's. Besides, most of the players use the center facilities all the time. Doesn't seem right to keep them from enjoying this event. Now they're saying I can't use it for a private event, but I don't think they can do that."

"So, you're fighting City Hall, as it were."

"I'm fighting Brodie Banneker and his ridiculous group of cronies. Why, I taught them all Sunday school when they were barely out of diapers. Taught their children, too.

Seems un-Christian-like if you ask me. Keeping a Sunday school teacher from having a little party."

Quinn struggled to keep a straight face. "How many invitations have been issued?"

"Twenty-eight. Up from sixteen last fall."

He couldn't have said what provoked him to open his mouth. "Perhaps I can contribute more than a few signed books."

Alva suddenly lost all interest in the councilmen. Her hands were still clutching her gloves when she looked back at Quinn, but there was nothing innocent in those gleaming eyes. "Why, Mr. Brannigan. What do you have in mind?"

Chapter 14

"He did what?" Riley paused in the middle of scooping chocolate-pumpkin cupcake batter into rows of cute yellow and purple floral paper liners to look over at Alva.

"Who did what?" Dre asked from her perch on a stool across the room. She was preoccupied with her latest project: sugarcrafting.

"Alva just told us Quinn Brannigan is going to have the invitational poker tournament at the bungalow," Riley said.

"Cool," Dre offered, not looking up from the delicate sugar creations she was painstakingly building. Riley didn't know what they were, exactly, but they looked like exotic blown glass made entirely out of sugar.

Riley steered well clear, knowing better than to get anywhere close to that kind of fragile work. "Cool, yes," she echoed with feigned enthusiasm. "Awesome."

Alva kept a speculative expression on her face as she looked at Riley, so Riley went right back to scooping batter. She'd accepted Alva's invitation to the poker tournament back when Alva had first planned it, and there was no way to gracefully back out now. But the idea of the event being at the bungalow, spending time in Quinn's space . . . well, she didn't know how that made her feel.

Actually, she knew exactly how it made her feel. Confused, regretful, and annoyed at herself for feeling either when she very much wished she simply felt nothing. She *knew* she'd made the right call in not contacting him. She'd done what he'd asked. She'd figured out what she wanted, and, more important, what she could handle. And she couldn't handle Quinn. She just wasn't ready to take the kind of risk he was offering.

Maybe the way to look at the poker tournament at the bungalow was to treat it like a test, an assessment of her decision to continue on with the life she already had, to not take on anything more. If she passed, that meant she'd done the right thing. That the status quo was where it was best for her to stay. She'd spent the better part of last year going through the big giant test of living through the anniversary of every special date and holiday she'd shared with Jeremy. After seven years together, there had been many. This year, she'd been concentrating on making new memories and new special days. But shouldn't she have a few more under her belt before any of those new memories included someone who might put her through another "test year?"

She sighed. Maybe she could just get food poisoning or something and not be able to go. That sounded like more fun.

"I've abandoned the potluck idea after Beryl brought that torte dessert to the Independence Day picnic. Remember, the one with the exotic fruit that turned out to be poisonous?"

"We remember," Dre and Riley said in unison.

"I'm still trying to forget," Dre added.

"Aren't we all, dear. Especially Beryl. So I didn't want her to be embarrassed in any way. Charlotte and Carlo are officially on board for the catering. Isn't that fun?" Alva was clearly excited about the plans as she filled her pastry bag with whipped cream-marshmallow fluff filling. "And Franco has agreed to be our server for the evening."

Riley smiled at that. "That will get the party started."

"The ladies all adore him," Alva agreed. "It's the Gallic accent. Gets them every time." She turned one of her cooled cocoa cupcakes over and punched a hole in the bottom of the paper liner with the tip of her pastry bag, then squeezed a shot of cream-fluff filling into the chocolate cake. "And," she went on, picking up the next cupcake, poking another hole, "since we're holding it on private property, the town council and Brodie Banneker can bite my fanny."

"And a very nice fanny it is, Miss Alva." Baxter's handsome face creased in a wide smile as he entered the kitchen through the back door. He leaned down to buss her flour-coated and pink cheek. "Can I steal one of these?" He plucked the cake she'd just filled from her tiny hand, peeled the wrapper back and took a bite. He immediately closed his eyes. "The town council doesn't know what they're missing."

"My point exactly." Alva brushed at her apron and patted her net-covered hair . . . all while beaming up at him like a schoolgirl with her first crush.

In addition to the fact that Baxter Dunne was one of the industry's top pastry chefs, with a successful New York City patisserie, a best-selling cookbook, and a hit television show under his belt, he was also exceedingly tall and rangy, with a thick thatch of blond hair and sizzling hot electric green eyes. And he packed a lot of charm into that sexy British accent. They all had a little crush on him. Even Dre had stopped spinning sugar to gaze fondly at her idol. It was pretty much the only time Riley ever saw her soften up.

"Has anyone seen my lovely wife?" Baxter asked, strolling around the room and checking what everyone was working on. "Who is the lucky recipient of this week's labor?"

"Charlotte is taking all the cupcakes this week and distributing them to one of the children's wards at a hospital in Savannah," Riley told him. "The doctors and nurses will be happy campers, too, I think."

"Indeed. Lots of happy faces. That's good." He peeked over Riley's shoulder. "What are you teaching yourself this week?"

"Nothing yet, just baking the last of the cupcakes. Pumpkin-chocolate."

"Great flavor profile." Baxter nodded to the rack of cakes cooling to her right, and the bowl of chilled frosting. "What's the topping?"

"Cream cheese and mascarpone. I've never worked with Italian cream cheese, so I wanted to try." She shot him a dry smile. "This is my second batch."

"Let me guess. Overmixed it the first time 'round and the mascarpone curdled."

Riley nodded, raising a guilty-as-charged hand.

"Hey, that's what experimenting is all about." He took a small, unused spatula and scooped a dollop of the frosting on it, then scooped off some of that with a finger, which he tasted. "Creamy, well blended, no lumps. Quite good. You should let Lani sample this."

Riley laughed. "It's her recipe."

"Ah," Baxter said, with a chuckle. "Of course." His eyes warmed, as they always did at the mention of her.

The fact that he was utterly besotted with his wife made him all the more ridiculously hot, Riley thought with a little sigh. "She and Charlotte are upstairs going over details on a joint catering event they're doing in Savannah next week."

"Right, right. The charity thing. I'd forgotten about that. Delightful as always to see you ladies. Keep up the good baking." He sketched a quick bow, then ducked his head so he could go through the narrow door leading up the back stairs to the small apartment space on the second floor over the shop. It was partly used for storage, partly as an office, but still had furnishings from when it had been a living space. Dre, Franco, and Charlotte had all crashed there from time to time when their Cupcake Club sessions ran into the wee hours and they hadn't wanted to make the drive back over the causeway to the mainland.

Riley had just finished scooping out her last cup of batter when the sound of cheers from the apartment overhead echoed down to the kitchen below.

"Oh, fudge," Alva said, dismayed. Startled by the sudden sound, she'd squirted filling clear through her cupcake and shot it out the other side, where it had landed in a haphazard heap all over the rest of the cupcakes on the rack.

Riley, who had looked up at the sudden sound, glanced over at Alva's table. "Both a filling and a topping, all in one," she teased.

Alva, with a disgusted look at the pastry bag as if it were to blame, set the overfilled cupcake down to inspect the mess on the other cakes. "That will scrape off well enough, I suppose." She sighed, clearly not enthusiastic about the chore.

"I say spread out the squirted stuff over the top of each cake as a secret filling layer under the frosting. You can call them Alva's Surprise Cakes." This from Dre, who never broke her fierce focus on the crystallized . . . whatever it was she was constructing.

Alva paused in mid-scrape to ponder that. "Alva's Surprise Cakes," she repeated. "It does have a certain ring." She didn't say anything more, but Riley glanced over to spy the sly senior carefully shift her spatula so it smoothed rather than scraped.

Riley smiled privately as she carried her trays over to the oven. The only question was which new angle Alva would use to convince Lani to include the Alva's Surprise Cakes on the bake shop menu. Everyone knew Lani's cakes were Lani's cakes. She shared her expertise willingly, and even some of her standard recipes, but only her own recipes were used to keep the trays in the shop full. No guest chefs, not even her famous husband.

But that didn't stop Alva from trying.

Riley shot Dre a droll smile, knowing she'd intentionally put the suggestion out there for the pure entertainment value of watching Alva plot and plan. "Nicely done," Riley murmured as she turned back from closing the oven, her voice low so only Dre could hear.

Dre merely lifted her hands, palm to the ceiling, and pumped up twice, then went right back to work.

"Shoulders tight?" Alva asked her, catching the motion.

Riley swallowed a snort of laughter and purposefully did not look at Dre, who she knew would remain utterly expressionless. Another skill set Riley did not possess.

"You shouldn't stay hunched on that stool like that," Alva advised Dre. "Young people today simply aren't taught the life benefits of proper posture. Get to be my age, and you're thankful you can stand upright at all."

Riley scooped up her empty batter bowl, dumped the other utensils she'd used in it, and carried it all over to the utility sink. "Wonder what the cheer was all about?" she commented as she washed and rinsed.

Before anyone could respond, the door to the upper floor opened and Charlotte, Lani, and Baxter poured into the kitchen like a batch of happy, excited children.

"Awesome announcement!" Lani called out, even though it was only the three of them in the kitchen that evening.

Alva clasped her hands. "How exciting!"

Dre actually looked up at that. Of course, Baxter was back in the room.

Riley dried her hands on the towel tucked over the apron strings wrapped around her waist, and turned to face them. "What's up?"

"Great news, and Riley, we're hoping it's good news for you, too."

Riley's eyebrows climbed. "Me? Why?"

"Well, you know I'm finishing up the second cookbook, and a third was proposed, but we've never moved forward on it. With the latest season of *Hot Cakes* in the can, I've finally wrapped up the second book."

"That's wonderful," Riley said, "Great job!"

"That's not the news," Baxter said, "though thank you. It's a great relief because just today, my agent received an offer to officially contract for a third book."

Lani linked her arm through her husband's. "*We've* been offered the contract," she amended.

"I was getting to that part, luv." Baxter leaned down and bussed her on the top of the head, then beamed at the group. "This time around, they'd like me to collaborate with my brilliant wife, and put together a book that charts our culinary odyssey from working our first kitchen together in New York, through putting Gateau on the map, to coming to Georgia and starting a whole new chapter in our lives." He looked down at Lani, who beamed right back up at him.

Riley's heart stuttered . . . and her thoughts went straight to Quinn. And the way he'd looked at her. And the way she felt when she looked at him. Nowhere did Jeremy, or any part of her past life, enter into the equation. She wanted what Lani and Baxter had. There was no hopscotching over the scary parts to get to that, and no guarantee if she started the journey, she'd reach that desired destination. Riley had been convinced, standing on that beach, feeling overwhelmed by Quinn and all that he was so certain of, that she needed more time by herself. Needed to be more sure of herself.

As she watched Lani and Baxter, she wondered just how badly she was letting her fears of repeating the past ruin her chances of ever having love again in her future.

"Congratulations," Dre said, which, for her, was the equivalent of giving them a standing O.

Riley jerked her thoughts away from that path and focused on the good news, the celebration at hand. *Yes, tuck it away, ignore it, and it will just go away.*

Alva's eyes twinkled and she raised her clasped hands until they were propped under her chin. "Now then, that's just wonderful news, isn't it? And well deserved. Your love story does deserve to be told."

"We'll only be exploring the culinary part, but—"

"Nonsense," Alva said, "your culinary journey is your love affair. It's your passion for food and each other that has made you who you are."

There were more googly eyes shared between husband and wife, followed by a surprisingly hot, hard kiss on the mouth.

"Still in public," Charlotte reminded them, always the arbiter of decorum.

"My, my," Alva added, though she didn't look particularly disturbed by the display. Possibly quite the opposite.

Riley's thoughts precariously teetered once again, which prompted her to say, "Let me add my congratulations to the pile. I think it's great! And very well deserved. If you don't mind my asking, though, what does it have to do with me?"

Lani pushed at Baxter's chest, then pushed harder when he leaned down and kissed her again. "All right, all right," he said, both of them laughing. He looked at Riley, that spark still flashing in his eyes, and she felt a surprisingly sharp jab in the center of her chest.

"So, here's the deal," Lani was saying, but Baxter pulled her into a face-planting hug, muffling her voice against his chest as he grinned at Riley over her head.

"We've seen your amazing work in *Foodie*," he told her. "In fact, Lani looked it up right after you arrived. We discussed talking with you about this on the last cookbook, but you were new here, and had just left Chicago behind. We . . . didn't want to intrude. But we had trouble getting the photos for the second cookbook; we struggled a great deal with the team we ended up working with."

Lani, laughing and pushing at her husband, managed to squeak free just enough to blurt out, "So we pitched your previous work to Baxter's editor—who I guess is our editor now," she amended quite gaily. "We wanted a green light before even talking to you." She grabbed Baxter's hand when he laughingly tried to subvert her again. "We want you to be the food stylist for the cookbook!" she said in a rush, then looked smugly up at Baxter, before lifting on tiptoes and kissing his pouting bottom lip.

Baxter retaliated by pinching her backside, which prompted a wolf whistle from Dre and an eye roll from Charlotte.

"I believe there should be a new rule, effective immediately," Charlotte said. "No hanky-panky in the kitchen unless we all have equal opportunity hanky with our own personal panky."

"Says the only other person in the room who happens to have a panky," Dre grumbled.

"What's a panky?" Alva wanted to know.

It was all a buzz in Riley's ears, because she was still trying to digest what Lani had blurted out. Style food again. For a cookbook that was a surefire best seller even before it was written.

"Would you be willing to consider it?" Baxter asked.

"Obviously you'll have a lot of questions, but . . . would you?" Lani lifted up on her toes, clasping her hands together under her chin, much like Alva had earlier, but looking far more winsome. "At least consider it?"

"Wow," Riley said on a nervous laugh, skating along the edge of hysterical laughter. *Were they kidding? Consider it?* "When would we start?"

"Is that a yes?" Lani squealed.

"We'd get a production meeting set up, then figure out the filming dates," Baxter said, far more reasonable, but looking nonetheless equally thrilled. "As soon as we can swing it. A month at the most."

"Don't you have to plan it all out, test the recipes, and all of that?"

"Yes, of course," he said. "It will take some time to complete the whole project, but we need to put together a sampler, something for marketing purposes for the publisher, as soon as possible. They have some other events they want to be able to promote up front, so there will be a lot of work to do, straight off."

"We know you have other commitments," Lani added. "But, being as it's now almost October—and winter is a slow time for you, typically, right?—we were hoping—"

"I only have one winter under my belt here, but yes, it was slow last season. Given how spotty things have been already coming into this fall, I think it's a safe bet this season will be the same. I'm sure I can work around my staging jobs." Riley's brain was spinning, but she couldn't catch her breath enough to really let it all sink in.

"Actually, we'd want to have you on board full-time, for the duration," Baxter said. "Naturally, you'll be given prominent credit."

Lani elbowed him. "Don't overwhelm her." To Riley, she said, "We'll talk this all over, professionally. Hopefully tomorrow or as soon as you can make time for us. But right now, I say this is cause for a double celebration!"

The timer for Riley's cupcakes went off exactly at that moment, and everyone jumped. Their laughter filled the room.

A bottle of champagne was produced from somewhere in Lani's office, and Dre retrieved paper coffee cups from the front of the shop. "Franco is not going to be happy he missed this," she said, coming back into the kitchen.

"I'll talk to him tomorrow. He's helping Carlo and me with the fall charity ball." Charlotte smiled her little demure-but-devilish smile as she poured the champagne. "Besides, I don't think he will be too upset that he's not here."

"Is he entertaining his new young man again?" Alva inquired.

Charlotte's hand wobbled the champagne bottle, and Dre ducked her head to keep from being seen with a totally uncool smile, so it was left to Riley to respond. "Yes, Miss Alva, I believe he mentioned something about a dinner." She shot the other two quelling glares, then smiled back at Alva. "I gave him one of my recipes for pan-seared duck."

Alva smiled approvingly. "He's being a thoughtful host. Setting a good table. Good boy. I do hope they practice safe sex." She took the coffee cup from Charlotte just then, which was a good thing. Otherwise it might have ended up straight in her lap.

Riley thanked Char as she took the next cup and hid her smile behind the rim. Alva was such an odd amalgamation. None of them ever knew quite what to expect from her. Just when they thought she couldn't shock them, she'd say something like that.

"To Baxter and Lani," Charlotte said, lifting her glass.

They all sipped, then Lani lifted her glass again. "And to Riley, who is going to make our cookbook look like a million bucks!"

Everyone sipped again and the room devolved into excited chatter as a dozen questions were aimed at Baxter and Lani. Riley took the moment to turn and get her cupcakes out of their pans to finish cooling on the racks. She worked by rote, her mind reeling in so many different directions, no single thought sustained itself for more than a few seconds.

She didn't have a single tool of her trade, she'd have to talk to Baxter about meeting with the photographer; she wondered how he'd feel if she suggested they talk to Chuck and Greg. It was vital that the relationship between stylist and photographer be simpatico if they wanted shots worthy of a glossy coffee-table book, no matter the finished scale of the book itself. Richer was always better.

So lost in her thoughts was she that she jumped slightly when Baxter touched her elbow. "I know this has to seem like an avalanche of information, but Lan and I are so pleased you're considering it. Please know that, when we get the chance to discuss all the logistics, if it's not something you want to commit yourself to doing, we'll understand." He smiled. "Pout, throw a tantrum or two—"

Riley laughed. "I do have a lot of questions," she said, being honest. "I know you've done two of these now, so it's a process you're familiar with, but I have my own style and process, too. We'll really need to go over every detail before any of us should commit to doing this together. Friends and business, you know what they say—"

"You can trust your friends." He looked over at his wife. "I married my best one."

Riley's smile softened, even as that tweak pinched her heart again. "That you did," she managed. "I don't have any bookings tomorrow, and my appointment with the new bed and bath vendor canceled, so if you'll be staying on the island—or did you need me to go to Savannah?"

"No, this isn't part of my television production. We can handle this from my office here on Sugarberry. I don't have to be back on set until the first of next week to begin editing, so if we can manage it before then, that would be great. Actually, I'm getting the creative director I used with the first book, along with some of the production team, to come this way over the next few days."

"Okay, well, good. I should be able to sit down whenever you want me. Why are you bringing the entire crew here? Are you going to want to do the book shoot here?" Riley thought, given the theme, maybe he planned to use Lani's bakery kitchen, or perhaps their home.

Lani slid underneath Baxter's arm and tucked herself next to him. "Did you tell her yet?"

"Was just about to."

"Tell me what?" Riley asked.

"I had one of those brochures from when you styled the bungalow," Lani said. "I showed it to Baxter a month or so ago, because I thought about maybe leasing it for that amazing kitchen space."

"I've been thinking of perhaps filming some of the next season here on Sugarberry instead of in Savannah," Baxter said. "But I can't take over Leilani's kitchen, and our home isn't suitable for filming purposes."

"So, on his way back here tonight, Baxter thought about how the bungalow with that amazing kitchen would be perfect as a backdrop for the preliminary stuff we need to shoot," Lani interrupted excitedly. "It's upscale, modern, but reflects island life, our life. It would be great neutral territory, not disrupting either of our regular day-to-day work spaces. If it all works, who knows, maybe we'll do the whole book there."

Lani's words turned into a buzzing inside Riley's head that only got louder when Baxter ended with, "I've already had a brief chat with Quinn about setting up a meet, just to see if the logistics work. I don't know how long he's leased the place, but he's probably not going to be staying around for a long time, so if it works as well as we think it will, we'll just arrange another short-term lease after he moves out."

"That brochure was a double bonus, because Baxter's publisher loved what you did styling the place. That and your work at *Foodie*, and she was completely sold on bringing you on board." Lani took Riley's arm and squeezed. "Isn't it exciting? It's all falling into place, like it's meant to be."

Riley nodded, suddenly feeling a bit light-headed. In the span of one evening, she'd gone from firmly deciding not to pursue things with Quinn, to having to play poker in his home, to feeling jabs of doubt about her choice, and now . . . working around him. For who knew how long. "Yeah," she managed weakly. "Meant to be."

Chapter 15

Quinn couldn't type the words fast enough. When he was writing introspection, or action elements, he had to sit and work through the right thoughts or staging dynamics. But when it came to the dialogue and byplay between Joe and Hannah, it flew fast and furious. It was a challenge to write as fast as the words filled his brain.

His hands were cramping, his back and shoulders tight; he had no idea when he'd eaten last. The music he'd put on earlier had stopped some time ago, but none of that registered.

"Bam!" he grunted, hitting the final period on the keyboard. Flinging himself back in his chair, he whistled out a long, slow breath, feeling as if he'd just completed a marathon—which he had, of sorts. A mental marathon. It felt good to stop worrying about recording every word as it came into his head before it vanished, to give himself a mental break from thinking. Only then did the growling stomach, aching shoulders, and echoing silence filter back in.

He looked around and noticed the sun was already past zenith, casting long shadows across the back patio. He liked the cooler nights and lower humidity now that autumn was finally beginning to make itself known. He was probably the only one who didn't mind the days growing shorter. He wrote better in the winter, for some reason. Something to do with hibernation and cave mentality, he was sure. But it was easier to focus.

He pushed himself out of his chair, then leaned forward and snapped his laptop shut. No more tonight. But he smiled. It was a good feeling to know that he was tempted, that he had more to say. Already ideas were waltzing around in his mind, snippets of conversation, thoughts his characters needed to have. He even started to look for a pad and pen to make additional notes, but forced himself to turn and walk into the kitchen.

"It'll all be there tomorrow," he told himself, then grinned. For once, he knew it would be. Right now, though, he wanted food. A glass of wine. Maybe sit on the deck to eat, pipe some music from the house, read a chapter or two of something written by somebody other than him. "Get a life," he added to the list.

As he wandered into the kitchen his thoughts traveled straight to Riley. With her silence the past two weeks, she had made her choice clear. He really needed to stop those thoughts from getting on that train anymore. Mercifully, his new fictional friends were taking care of that for large portions of the day, but when writing time was over, his thoughts did wander.

He stared past the open door into the fridge, and thought about heading into town for dinner at Laura Jo's. He'd been doing more of that and less of breakfast lately, as he'd pretty much hit the ground running, writing almost as soon as he opened his eyes in the morning. By the time he came up for air, it was lunch. More often than not, he spent that time hitting the beach for a good mind-clearing run.

And, if he were being honest with himself, a slim hope that a certain behemoth of a dog would accost him again.

And bring his lovely owner along for the adventure. So far, no such luck.

He closed the fridge door. He didn't feel like cooking. "Diner it is." Grabbing his wallet and keys from the foyer table, he pulled the door open just as Riley was lifting her curled fist to knock on it.

Startled, she stepped back, then belatedly lowered her fist.

"Sorry," he said, almost too stunned to speak. "I didn't know you were there."

"Of course, how could you have?" she said, trying for dry humor. The dark splotches of pink in her cheeks, and along the sides of her neck, gave away the true state of her nerves. He didn't think he'd ever seen her that red.

"What can I do for you?" He leaned casually on the doorframe, pretending his heart wasn't racing a thousand miles per second. Or that he wasn't ridiculously happy to see her. All of which made him foolish and pathetic. *Shut it down, Brannigan. What part of thanks, but no thanks, didn't you get?*

Riley's brows knitted together as she noticed the keys and wallet in his hand. "I'm sorry, were you heading out? Did they change the meeting time? Isn't it supposed to be at seven?"

"What meeting?"

She frowned fully. "About the setups for the first shoot? For the cookbook? You and Baxter did agree to shoot some preliminaries here tonight when you spoke a few weeks back? Maybe I got the date wrong." Another splash of color joined to the rest.

Quinn frowned along with her, then the lightbulb went on. Baxter. Cookbook. "Oh. Right. Is it Friday already?"

She smiled, a bit as one would when looking at a crazy person. "All day."

"Good thing I didn't leave for the diner then." He

stepped back and motioned her inside, feeling discombob-ulated and anything but smooth and in control. "That would have been rude. Come on in. Let me get you some-thing to drink."

Riley waited until he stepped out of the doorway before she moved into the foyer. "I'm fine, that's okay. I'll just . . . I can wait in the kitchen until they get here." She turned back as he closed the door. "In fact, if you want to head out to eat, I can let everyone in and show them what's what. You won't need to stay." Her voice trailed off a bit as she added, "You know, if you'd rather not."

Just like that, it was awkward. He wasn't sure which thing he hated more, the awkwardness or the fact that Riley hadn't once met his direct gaze.

"I gather *you'd* rather me not."

She sighed and looked more defeated than he could re-call ever seeing her. In fact, he'd never seen her defeated. "I should have called you. Come by. Something." Riley fi-nally looked at him. "I didn't know what to say. I don't think straight when I'm with you, and I was—"

"Afraid I'd talk you into something again."

"You didn't talk me into anything. I made my own choices. I was just trying to do what I thought would be bet-ter for us both, down the line. I really . . ." She shrugged. The helpless look that accompanied it was worse than the defeated one. "You were right. I can want what I want, but that doesn't mean I'm ready to handle what I'll get."

"That's fair, and the only reason I haven't turned up on your doorstep with Brutus bribes and a list of reasons why I think you should give us a chance."

She gave a flicker of a smile at that, and a few small pieces of his heart shifted back into place. He was sad, and sure, he was hurt. Maybe even a little angry, not at her, but at the gods, or fate, or whoever thought putting her in his path had been a good idea in the first place. But none of that was her fault. She'd been trying to tell him all along that she wasn't ready.

"I appreciate that. I'm not sure I deserved the consideration." That tiny hint of smile resurfaced when she added, "Just make sure Brutus never finds out what I just turned down."

Quinn made the lock and key motion over his mouth, as she had that day on the beach.

Her expression softened then. For just a moment, real warmth crept into her eyes, mixed in with what looked like regret, or maybe he was just seeing what he wanted to see.

"What are you doing for the cookbook?" he asked, searching for the right tone, the right balance. The longer she stood there, the harder it was starting to be. He wanted to do the right thing by her, especially when the last person she'd let in had done so wrong. He still knew none of the specifics, nor had he tried to find out. The aftermath was all he needed to see, to know.

"You mean, why am I here? Oh." That seemed to set her back. "I'm sorry. I thought you knew. Wow, that just makes this even more awkward," she murmured. "I didn't mean to make it a surprise. Thought it was all—anyway, I'm styling the food. For the prelims, and if that goes how we hope it will, for the whole book."

He smiled. It was something of a relief to have an honest and sincerely happy moment between them. "That's great. I mean, I'm assuming it is. You said you loved your work."

"I did. And yes, this is a dream come true. Totally out of the blue and, well, pretty exciting."

He was happy for her. But he wasn't happy about how she was trying to downplay it, as if being happy in his presence was somehow rubbing it in his face. "Riley, it's okay to be happy, to be excited. I'm truly excited for you. I'm sorry, about the us part, okay? But that's all I'm sorry for."

She didn't speak right away; then she took in a steadying breath, and let it out slowly. "Okay. Thank you. That's . . . good."

And still so damn awkward he wanted to scream.

"How is the book coming?" she asked, always the trouper, trying to make things okay for everybody else.

"Flying. Editor's happy, publisher's happy, I'm happy, the characters are happy."

Her lips curved, and she finally looked comfortable and not so tense and jumpy. "That's great. Really." She pointed to herself. "Reader is happy."

His responding grin came fast and naturally, and so did the clutch in his chest. God, he wanted her back. He missed her so much, even though he'd never really had her. In his arms, his space, his bed . . . his life.

He let that yearning show through on his face.

And she shifted her gaze away again. "So, do you want to go—"

"Riley, listen—"

They stopped, both faltered.

He motioned to her to go first.

"I was just asking if you wanted to go eat. If this works, the book, I mean, I'll—uh, I can make up a schedule. Of when I'll be here. Just so you know."

"You don't need to do that. And I wish you didn't feel you have to tiptoe around or act like you're at a funeral. I'm not fragile and I'm not dead."

"I know, I know. I'm not good at hurting people I care about," she said. "And I know I hurt you. Maybe not a deathblow or anything, it was just a kiss, but still . . . it's not something I ever meant to do."

"I know that," he said quietly. "You did exactly what you were supposed to do. You were honest with me. And yourself. No one can ask for more than that."

She didn't say anything, as her gaze wandered the foyer,

then fell back to her hands, which clutched the small tote she was carrying in front of her in a white-knuckled grip. She remained silent for a long moment, as if trying to decide whether or not to say what was on her mind.

"Is there something else?" he asked. "No point in censoring your thoughts now."

She looked up at that. "Part of me wants to tell you all the things I've been thinking about the past few weeks, so maybe you'll understand how much I didn't want either of us to be hurt."

"And the other part?"

There was a hint of . . . desperation, almost, in her eyes. But, she squeezed them shut, and dipped her chin. For the first time since she'd entered the house, he had to curl his fingers into his palm to keep from reaching for her.

He opened his mouth to tell her he would go to the diner for the duration, but her head shot up, and her eyes were open again. Huge and . . . scared.

He stepped forward without hesitation. He took her arm, but stopped short of pulling her close. "What is it?" He was actually alarmed. "Is everything okay? Did something else happen?"

"Yes." Her voice was shaky . . . as was she. He could feel the tremors in her arm. "Something did happen."

"Riley, what—"

"God, I feel like a fruitcake or something. I thought I could come here, and do this. Okay, no I didn't. I had no idea how I was going to work here, be here, around you. Just because I decided I couldn't handle it doesn't mean the want goes away. And now . . . you're going to think I'm . . . well, whatever you think I am, I'm sure I'll deserve it."

"What are you talking about?"

"The thing that happened was me trying to figure out how I'm ever going to bridge my past to get to my future. I watch Baxter and Lani, and Char and Carlo. Heck, Alva's even been seeing Sam Shearin on the sly, though she thinks we don't know about it. Franco has a new beau. It's all around me. I can't escape it, can't stop thinking about it . . . can't stop wishing I had it." She lifted her free hand. "I know, I know. I could have it. It's staring me right in the face. All I have to do is grab for it."

She lifted her gaze to his and his heart squeezed until it about broke in two when he saw those twin pools go glassy with tears. Her lip was quivering. "I want it so badly." The words choked out on a hoarse whisper. "I do, Quinn. I do. And I haven't, for even one second, stopped wanting it." She was almost pleading with him. "But I'm so scared. I know it's dumb, and I should be strong, but I'm just not. I'm not, and the fear is real and it's big. It's swallowing me up. I'm so ready to be happy . . . but I don't know if I can go through being hurt again. I want to make that grab, but then I think about last time, and how hard I've worked just to get to where I am now. And I don't know how to get to what comes next."

He felt her shoulders jerk and her body shake, and he tugged her hard and fast against his chest, folding her into his arms, wrapping her up tight. "It's okay." He pulled the tote she'd been carrying from her hands and blindly shoved it on the foyer table behind him, not caring about whatever it was he'd just shoved off the table to the floor, then pulled her more tightly against him. "I'm so sorry you were hurt." It was the God's honest truth, and the only part of the truth he could afford to let himself think about, or he'd get angry all over again and want to go asshole hunting. "I hate it. I wish like hell I could give you a guarantee that nothing will ever hurt you again—"

She sniffled. "I know, I know. No one can."

He tipped back just enough to nudge her chin until he could look into her eyes. His heart teetered and squeezed, as big, fat tears rolled down her cheeks. "But I can make you a promise. No matter what role we play in each other's lives I will always be honest with you. Even if it hurts. You'll always know where I stand, what I feel. And if you don't, ask me. You can trust me, Riley. Today, tomorrow, and every day after that. I can't promise I'll never hurt you, because it happens. It happened on the beach to me, and I know you didn't want to hurt me. But you were being honest, and that's what I need to be able to count on. I won't play you, I won't lie to you, I won't disrespect you. You have my word on that. Those are the guarantees I can make."

She nodded, tears still gathered at the corners of her eyes, her body still shuddering a bit in his arms. "Thank you," she whispered.

That single sentiment sounded so damn . . . grateful, he felt the hot sting in his own eyes. She deserved so much more than to feel freaking grateful because someone was going to treat her the way she should automatically be treated right from the get-go. What the hell kind of number had that guy done on her?

Quinn tucked her close again, his heart pounding; then relief flooded through him when she tentatively slid her arms around his waist. When he instinctively tightened his own hold, she did the same, as if she were holding on for dear life.

And maybe she was. Because he sure as hell considered her life dear to him.

Slowly, the trembling ebbed, as did her sniffles. He stroked her hair, soothed a hand up and down her spine, and just . . . held on.

"I wish I had the answers," he said quietly, gently. "I don't. I've never been where you are. I don't know how you reach out a second time. Or a third, or a fourth. I was half scared to death trying to figure out how to do it for the first time."

Against his shirt, he heard her say, "How did you get yourself to do it?"

"Same as you did. I was honest about all of it." He smiled briefly against her soft curls. "Then I just up and kissed the girl." His smile faded. "And, turns out, I made her cry."

Riley pulled her head back at that, and lifted damp cheeks and wet eyes to his. "No, you didn't. It wasn't you who made me cry."

"Point is . . . I might. Someday. Won't mean to, but I'll hate having added to any tears that came before. Maybe you've cried enough. But for all the fear, and the being scared, and the chance of feeling the way I do right now, which is hurt, angry at the fates, at your ex, and missing you more than I thought it was possible to miss a person . . . I know I'd do it all over again."

"Why?"

"Because I made you laugh, too. And you made me feel like the cleverest guy in the room, every time you did. Because of the way you looked at me, whether it was the dry smile, the avid listener, the curious monkey, or even the eye roll of I-can't-believe-he-just-said-that. Because of that single, amazing first kiss." He smiled. "And the second one. And the hope I felt, getting a gift like that, like anything is possible after all." He looked down at her upturned face, and smoothed the hair clinging to her damp cheeks. "Maybe that's it right there. I'd do it all again, because you gave me hope I could someday have it all. I've never once felt that, but I've always wanted to."

Riley stared into his eyes almost helplessly, then finally lowered her head and pressed her cheek hard against his chest. He could feel her shake her head.

"What?" he asked.

"I just . . . wish I was worthy of all that."

He tilted her head back again, and for the first time, he

felt a sliver of irritation with her. "You don't get to judge that. I do. And saying you're not worthy of my affection, or interest, or any other damn thing I want to feel about you, is a pretty big slap at me, don't you think?"

She looked shocked by his retort, and immediately remorseful. "That—that's not what I meant."

"But it is what you said. You may not value youself, but that doesn't mean I don't. Or can't. Maybe you can't see it because you are convinced it's not there. But I can see it. And so do all your friends. How many people are going to have to value you before you stop judging yourself by the one selfish bastard who didn't?"

Her eyes widened at that, but rather than look hurt, or stung, or even insulted, she looked . . . thoughtful.

"Is that what I'm doing?" she asked, the words a hushed whisper.

"Only you can say. But . . . it sure seems that way."

"Well, it's not what I meant." Her voice grew steadily stronger. She looked like she was getting a little mad, too.

He didn't mind that at all. That was the Riley he knew, that was the Riley he'd thought he'd be getting to know better. And he was so damn thankful to see that Riley finally step up to the damn plate.

"I know I have value. I know I'm good at what I do. And I know I'm a good friend. I know I'm good to my dog. And I know I have value to all of those people, and to myself. The only thing I don't know—the only thing—is whether I'm a good partner. I thought I was." She looked at him, holding his gaze evenly, steadily. "And I was wrong. So, that's the place where I don't feel like I know anything, where I question what you see in me, where I question if I have what you think I have."

"I believe you do," he said. "I wish you did, too."

She looked disgusted, whether it was at him for provoking her, or herself for realizing how far down the rabbit hole she'd let herself sink, he didn't know. But when she looked at him, there was a fire there, one he couldn't ever recall seeing.

But one he responded to, with every fiber of his being.

"Well," she said, "I guess you're right. There is only one way to find out."

"How is that?"

"Lay it all on the line. Then just kiss the boy."

And so she did.

Chapter 16

Quinn went still for approximately two earth-shattering seconds. Then he gripped the back of her head and kissed her back.

He groaned against her mouth, and Riley gripped his head, slanted her mouth on his . . . and jumped right off the cliff.

Quinn grinned against her open mouth. "Dead cat."

"What?"

"Dead cat." He kissed and nipped along her bottom lip, her jaw, making her tip her head back in thrilling wanton abandon, of which he took immediate and full advantage. "We should have known all along." He punctuated the words with kisses, his hands very—very—busy. "We're both too curious, by nature . . . not to find out."

"Find out what?"

He turned and neatly backed her up against the wall. "This." He dove straight back in, kissing her like a man not set on claiming, or languidly exploring, but going for every bit of gusto the two of them could muster.

She wanted to laugh, she wanted to howl at the moon,

but most of all, she wanted him. "I'm still terrified," she told him, gasping when he flicked the tip of his tongue over a sensitive spot on the side of her neck, moaning when he nipped the same spot, her body jerking in response to the sweetness in him . . . and even more so to the savory. Or maybe that was the unsavory, she thought, riding a giddy high as his hands slid up her waist, his thumbs pressed against the center of her torso, his palms splayed wide, coming to stop just below the weight of her breasts.

"Join the club," he readily agreed. "Better to not be alone in the dark, though, right?" He nudged the shoulder of her camp shirt open, and continued his seductive tyranny along her collarbone.

"Right." The single word ended up a long, satisfied groan when he finally slid his thumbs up just a little higher, then dragged them across her painfully hard nipples.

She moaned in the back of her throat, and opened for him as he slid his tongue past her lips. The moan continued, long, low, almost a growl, as he rolled one nipple gently between his fingers. "I want these bared. I want to feel them, lick them, taste them."

She shuddered—hard—against him, and he pushed up against her, making them groan when the rigid length of him pressed into all the softness of her.

He hiked her up on the wall, and she slid her knees up the outside of his thighs, to his hips, pressing tight. She whimpered when his fingers left her swollen nipples so he could slide his hand between the wall and the small of her back. That whimper turned to a grunt of raw heat when he arched her back and slid himself more fully between her thighs.

He made that growling noise again, and her hips bucked against him of their own volition. But he was too tall, and she couldn't grip him tightly enough with her thighs to gain any real leverage to shift herself higher, to get herself where she most needed to be.

God, there was such a glorious freedom to be found in simply giving herself permission to stop thinking and only feel. Thinking had gotten her into panicked trouble, whereas feeling was getting her into rhapsodic amounts of pleasure. It wasn't hard to do the math.

Now that she'd opened the floodgates, the hunger, the need, was voracious. She wanted to submerge herself in it, wallow, revel, swamp, drown. From everything he was doing and the sounds he was making, he was quite willing to let her pull him under with her.

"I can't—reach—" She bucked against him.

He broke away from her mouth long enough to say, "Hold on to me." The command was rough, but coated with all that warm honey, his accent having strengthened from the moment he'd pulled her into his arms.

She couldn't let herself think about that. She couldn't let herself think about anything. The only way she was going to scale that giant wall she'd spent two years so cautiously and thoroughly erecting was to go sailing over it on the wings of lust, and want, and need. And trust, not just him . . . but herself. She'd either crash and burn all over again . . . or hit the ground running.

She wrapped her legs around him without hesitation and thought, *I guess you're going to find out!*

He lifted her from the wall and kept her wrapped around his big, hard body. As it had before, the way he swept her up so effortlessly thrilled her straight down to her toes. She wrapped her arms around his neck and pulled his mouth back to hers.

He grunted in surprise, but when she started to pull back, he halted their progress long enough to turn his head, and take her mouth in a hot, hard kiss. "Remember where we left off," he said, then tucked her against him and started for the stairs.

His foot had just hit the first riser when a knock came at the front door.

They froze, wobbling badly as Quinn turned them back around, Riley still wrapped around him.

The knock came again. "Yoo-hoo. It's just me!"

Riley and Quinn looked a bit wildly at each other. "Alva?" Riley hissed. "Oh crap!" How had they forgotten all about the meeting? Well, she knew exactly how. "Put me down," she told him, flustered to the extreme as she struggled to straighten her clothes and make a half-assed effort with her hair, which had to be totally wild. "Baxter and the crew should have been here ages ago."

"I didn't know Alva was coming," Quinn said, straightening his own clothes, raking a hand through his hair, looking a bit wild and undone himself for a change.

"I'm sure I look like I've been ravaged—"

"And liked it," he said with a grin.

She swatted at him, but her grin matched his.

"Why don't you duck into the guest bathroom off the hall and I'll find out what Our Lady of Untimely Interruptions wants?"

"Not untimely," she corrected him. "Baxter and company should have already been here. If she hadn't come by when she did, they could have walked in and found us—"

"Right." Quinn's eyes flashed all over again, and Riley had to fight the urge to fling herself at him and to hell with the rest.

"I'm going to need more than whatever is in the guest bathroom, but I'll work with what I've got."

Quinn wiggled his eyebrows as he slid a hot gaze over her. "Then you'll be more than fine."

The doorbell rang this time. "Hello? Anyone home?" Alva pressed the buzzer again.

Riley silently went through an entire string of swear words. "Stall her, for at least a minute or two. And keep a lookout for the production trucks. Big white vans, three of them."

"I think I can manage that." He snagged her arm as she went to dash off, spinning her neatly around right back up against him. He planted a sizzling hot, very short, but incredibly intent kiss on her mouth.

When he lifted his head, she dazedly asked, "What was that for?"

"We're not done with this . . . conversation. No ducking back behind barriers and stuff."

She surprised him, and herself, by smiling right back at him. "Like that's going to keep you out anyway. I don't know why I bothered trying."

His smile curved slowly into a deep, incredibly sexy grin. "That's what I was trying to tell you. Just a couple of dead cats."

She swatted him again, then tugged him down by his shirtfront for a fast, hard kiss of her own. Then she did something completely out of character for her, but hell . . . fair was fair. He'd put his hands all over her, hadn't he? Before she lost her nerve, she impulsively ran a hand down his chest . . . resting it on his belt buckle as her thumb caressed just below. His body twitched, and he jerked her against him. She slid her tongue in his mouth, and pushed it and her hips against him at the same time, before releasing him and stepping back.

"Get the door, smart guy," she said, panting as hard as he was, enjoying immensely the somewhat stunned, glazed look in his eyes. She knew the feeling. "And give me two minutes."

She ducked out, but heard him say quite clearly, "Oh,

I'm pretty sure you're going to get all the time from me that you need."

"What in the hell did you just do, Riley Brown?" she murmured on a breathless laugh as she swung into the bathroom and closed the door behind her. "What in the *hell* did you just go and do?" But she was grinning like a loon when she said it.

Chapter 17

Quinn knocked on the side of the boat before stepping onboard. "Honey, I'm home!" he called out, hoping the greeting would make her smile. Truth be told, he was nervous, though he couldn't have said exactly why.

He hadn't seen or talked to Riley since the rather ragtag assemblage had finally converged on the bungalow two nights ago. It turned out Alva had come by to talk about the poker tournament. The production trucks had been pulling into his drive when he'd opened the door to her.

Quinn was pretty damn sure that without Alva ever laying eyes on Riley, her eagle sharp senses had picked up on enough little signals to know she'd interrupted something more than a production meeting. Fortunately Baxter, Lani, and a gaggle of production crew types had rolled in as he was still chatting with Alva on his front porch.

He'd made alternate plans with Alva, which they'd completed yesterday afternoon, over lunch at Laura Jo's. While Baxter and crew had swarmed his kitchen, he'd opted to take his laptop out on the deck and pretended to do just about anything but pay attention to what was going on inside his house. He'd had no clue how well he and Riley were concealing anything from the equally sharp intellects of Baxter and Lani, so decided leaving the field of play was the better part of valor, along with the best shot of preserving Riley's privacy.

Baxter had come out at the end to set up another shoot date and confirm his plans to move forward.

Quinn knew from their preliminary talks that Baxter intended to lease the place after Quinn moved out. Had his life stayed on the planned course, it would have been by the year's end. He wasn't so sure about that anymore.

It was, in part, why he was standing on the dock next to Riley's houseboat early on Monday morning. The sun had barely crept up to cast thin, pink streamers of light over the line of sails moored on the far pier.

"Quinn?" Pushing a mass of blond curls from her still sleepy face, looking lush and warm and soft and delectable wearing an ever-so-alluring pair of pink and green flannel boxers and an old, faded Bulls T-shirt, she poked her head through the rear glass doors, blinking a few times in the spare dregs of morning light. "What are you doing here?"

He wanted to wrap her up in his arms and slowly wake her rumpled, sleepy self with a long, deep, slow kiss. He wanted to feel her come alive and alert, until she smiled up at him, that full-dimpled, rich-chocolate-brown-eyed smile. And he wanted to drag her straight back to her stateroom like a caveman and tear the clothes from her warm, delectable, voluptuous body—with his teeth—and sink every last hard inch of himself into the welcoming and ready hot, wet core of her.

He shifted his stance, and angled the slim black leather satchel he carried so it was in front of him. He hadn't known what to expect from her with this surprise visit, but he supposed he should have known better what to expect of himself. He lifted the cardboard tray balanced in his other hand. "I come bearing Laura Jo's coffee and egg sandwiches. I think she snuck two apple Danishes in there, too." He tried for an endearing, please-don't-shoot-the-delivery-boy grin, knowing Riley would see right through it, which somehow made it even more fun to try. "She took pity when I explained about my plans. I didn't know if you were a morning person or not, but she seemed to think maybe something sweet might be in order."

"I am a morning person," she grumbled. "But this isn't morning. This is just nighttime thinking about becoming morning. Eventually. What time is it, anyway? Why didn't you call first?"

"I don't have your number." And he hadn't wanted to risk her turning him down.

"Sure you do. It's on all the paperwork from the leased furniture and stuff."

"I sent all that to David, since he's handling it, and it didn't occur to me until after the fact that I'd shipped off your contact information with it." He smiled briefly. "At the time, I didn't think I'd be needing it. If something went wrong with anything at the house, I'd have had David contact you anyway. Just to spare you any awkwardness."

"Unlike now, you mean."

He shrugged and tried for abashed. "I didn't know where else to go."

"Because, what, the bungalow washed out to sea last night?"

"No, because Baxter's crew showed up before the crack of dawn this morning to start with the lighting setup and staging. I can't work with all the noise. I figured you'd be at the bungalow to do whatever is on the schedule to be done today, so I'd talk you into swapping spots for the day. Or however long you'll be over there."

"Really."

He nodded. "Truly." He lifted the coffee offering again. "I did come bearing gifts."

She didn't look at the tray of coffee and food. She was still staring rather grumpily at him. Say what she wanted, she was *not* a morning person. It should have been a clear warning to him regarding just how far off the cliff he'd already dived when he found that fact rather endearing.

"So, is that why I haven't heard from you about continuing the . . . conversation? Because you lost my number?"

"We started that . . . conversation, a little more than forty-eight hours ago," he reminded her. "We've both been rather busy during that time, with all this accelerated cookbook sampler stuff going on."

"So?"

He grinned at that. He couldn't help it.

"What's funny?"

"Not a thing." Deciding to take matters into his own hands, he slid his satchel to the deck, and set the tray down on one of the fish wells. Then he stepped over to her and simply pulled her through the door and right into his arms.

"What makes you think you can just climb on my boat and have your way with my person?" she asked, blinking up at him, making absolutely no effort whatsoever to extract herself from his hold.

"This." He bent down and kissed her.

She didn't respond, for at least the span of three seconds. Then there was a little . . . whimpering sound, and he felt her body soften against his. She gave a soft little moan in the back of her throat, then gave up entirely and slid her hands behind his neck, and molded his mouth more firmly to hers.

He'd only intended that slow, sweet, warm, good morning kiss he'd imagined earlier, but it was quickly moving along toward the caveman scenario by the time he managed to break free and lift his head. She was smiling up at him just as he'd hoped, only there was a bit of smugness there. Probably because his heart was beating like a wild man, and he looked and sounded a bit the part, as well.

"Well," she said. "When you put it that way."

He grinned at that. "You weren't changing your mind, were you?"

"I might have been." She was a terrible liar. "Of course, you wouldn't know, since you didn't bother to call, come by, send smoke signals. A tasteful carrier pigeon would have been welcome."

"I know. But if you recall, you all were at that first shoot until three or four in the morning. I didn't see or hear from you Saturday."

"I was unconscious Saturday. I haven't done that kind of work in a couple years."

"I did come by here that afternoon—"

"You did? Oh. I drove into Savannah. I had a ton of things to replace, put my tool kit back together, all the tricks of my trade. Char and Carlo asked me out to dinner. I wanted to call you, tell you to come meet us . . . but I didn't have your number, either. And I hadn't heard anything. Where were you yesterday? I came by the bungalow."

"You did?" He grinned. "You know, we might want to avail ourselves of some modern technology."

"I was thinking the same thing."

"Good. I had to drive to Atlanta to do some press stuff for the book that's out now. I didn't get back until late last night."

"You were in Atlanta yesterday?"

He nodded. "Being away was torture—which should appease your need to punish me if you feel the need to do so."

"I'm not disagreeing with that part, but next time, punish yourself some other way, will ya? Depriving you, deprives me."

"Well," he said, echoing her earlier statement. "When you put it that way."

And the caveman scenario won.

She squealed when he scooped her over his shoulder. "You can't haul me off my feet and—"

"Can too. And I prefer the more romantic *sweep*, if you don't mind."

"Well, I don't sweep easily, either." She giggled when he slid his hands up her waist and adjusted her so they could make it down the narrow passageway to her stateroom.

Sliding her down his body, he ducked and cleared his head through the opening to the stateroom.

"I have no idea how you managed that," she said on a breathless laugh. "I can hardly make it down that hall without elbow bumps and bruises to show for it, and probably would even if this thing didn't bob and sway."

He smoothly whirled her into his arms and around in a tight circle, without either of them clearing a thing off any surface. "That's why you need me around. I'll keep you safe from all the bobbing and swaying."

She looped her arms around his neck and let him whirl her again. "Is that right?" She squealed again when he scooped her up against him so her feet left the floor.

"In fact, it's possible we can find a way to make the bobbing and swaying work to our benefit." He wiggled his eyebrows and made her laugh again. Then he slid his hands up and under the edge of her flannel boxers, cupping the soft, delectably full curves of her buttocks, turning the laughter into gasps.

"What time are you due at the bungalow?" he said, nuzzling her neck.

He felt her fingertips dig into his back as he continued nuzzling, which tugged the thin cotton across her plump, hard nipples.

"Eight," she breathed.

"Good." He stepped up so he could lower them to the bed. "It's possible you might still get there on time."

The boat rocked just as he was lifting her onto the bed, which landed her closer to the middle. She laughed again, and covered the top of her head to keep it from bumping the headboard. Quinn tugged off his polo shirt and levered himself up . . . and over her.

"You have way too many clothes on," he said, bracing himself above her.

"The same could be said about you," she replied, sinking back into the tousled linens of the unmade bed she'd just crawled from.

He grinned. "We could probably fix that."

"Probably." She started to reach for the hem of her tee, but he stopped her.

"That's no fun."

"No?"

He nudged her hands away and levered himself so he could sprawl on the bed next to her. The bed itself was wide, though a bit short for his long legs. "Well, more fun for me, if I get to do it—which may mean more fun for you."

She lifted her hands away and let them rest over her head. "Really? Huh," she said, trying for insouciance, but the gleam in her dark eyes betrayed her anticipation. "Who knew?"

"I could explain—"

"You are very good with words."

"—but as writers, we're taught to show, rather than tell."

"Is that so?" She lifted one hand to toy with his hair, just above where it brushed his ear. "This would be another one of those things about your work that fascinates me." She ruffled his hair. "It's grown. Since you've been here."

"I haven't found a barber. Or looked, really."

"Don't." She smiled when he lifted his eyebrows. "Not on my account, anyway. It makes you look—"

"Heathenish?"

"I was going to say a little rough around the edges. Less like that book jacket guy." She teased his hair with her fingertips. "You're always so effortlessly groomed. This makes you seem, I don't know . . . more like us mere mortals."

"Good to know. Being godlike can be such a burden." He leaned down and placed his lips over one plump nipple, making her gasp and her hips buck up.

"I can only imagine," she managed, her hands falling limply next to her head when he shifted his attention to her other nipple. "Oh . . . God," she gasped, when he used his fingers to gently rub and massage one nipple, while suckling the other hard through the thin cotton of her shirt.

"Yes?" he said, lifting his head and giving her his best celestial leer.

She snorted out a laugh, then almost choked on a sharp indrawn breath, her hips bucking again as he went back to teasing and tormenting first one tight tip, then the other.

She fisted her hands in the loose linens as he nuzzled the hem of her shirt up, exposing the creamy white skin of her tummy. "You have the softest skin."

"With freckles galore," she said. "Everywhere. If you squint in the right light, they look just like a tan."

"I like them just the way they are," he said, kissing one, then another. "In fact, I think I'll make it my mission to catalog each and every one." Quinn lifted his head to look at her. "After all, I'm very good at research and keeping track of lots of tiny details."

She lifted her head to look at him, whereupon he

dropped his mouth to one freckle, then another and another, all while keeping his gaze intermittently focused on hers.

"Hmm," he said. "I've a quandary."

"That's a good word," she said, moving restlessly beneath him. "Quandary," she repeated, drawing it out, rolling her hips in a sinuous motion as she did so. "Who knew vocabulary could be so hot?"

That got a chuckle out of him.

"What is your quandary, sir?" She rolled her hips again.

"Well, it seems I've gotten to all the freckles in my immediate research area. I'm torn now between exploring northward"—he nuzzled her shirt up another few inches, until the plump undersides of her breasts were exposed—"or taking a more leisurely southern route."

She let out a long, satisfied groan when he nudged the wide elastic band of her boxers down below her bellybutton, then farther down, until they clung to the faint crests of her hip bones. "I hear the south is lovely this time of year," she croaked out as he kissed and teased his way lower . . . then higher, then back lower again.

"There's another skill that writing and researching has helped me to hone."

"Hone," she repeated, drawing the word out and making it sound remarkably earthy.

He was already rigidly hard almost to the point of pain, but that got another surge and twitch out of him, making him swallow his own groan. She had absolutely no idea how utterly carnal she was. Goddess in her own right.

"Go on," she urged.

It took him a moment to recall the thread . . . he was sidetracked by how decadent it was, seeing her sprawled half beneath him, a hint of those voluptuous breasts exposed, threatening to spill out of that thin, worn cotton. And that wide, flat band of flannel-covered elastic, caressing the softly rounded swell of her stomach, exposing the creamy freckled sweetness to his hands and mouth. Teasing him, so close to revealing the truth of her blond hair, downy and waiting for his tongue to toy, part, and plunder.

She was all but vibrating beneath him, a coiled spring, as he continued to linger around her navel, dipping his tongue in, then drawing it out, then darting it in again, until her hips moved in unison and her soft moans became urging growls.

"Multitasking," he murmured against the sweet, freshly exposed skin below that elastic band, which he pulled down farther . . . and farther still, taking advantage of the way her hips pumped up hard in shock when his fingers slid under her tee and closed over her swollen nipple. He gently rolled and caressed it while tugging her flannel shorts down with his free hand, so she could kick them loose.

"Move up," he urged her, shifting them so they lay diagonally across the wide bed. He kicked off his worn Docksiders and shucked his shorts down and off, as she wrestled off her tee. "You're glorious, Riley," he said, easing his body between her legs. He had to keep his long legs bent slightly, but he could prop his toes against the stateroom wall, which gave him leverage. "Scoot back, just a—yes, right there." He leaned down and kissed the sweet, tender skin of her inner thigh. "Hold on," he said, then slid his tongue deep into her.

Her surprise shout of pleasure ended on a long, shuddering groan, as he began to toy and tease, stroke, and caress. He stopped long enough to slide two fingers into his mouth, then returned to his slow, languorous exploration. He slid his hand back up her body, reaching her nipples with his slick fingers, toying, flicking, and rolling them with a bit less gentleness as her hips started to buck in earnest.

"Quinn," she panted.

"Right here," he murmured against her slick, sweet flesh.

She shuddered hard as she went over, her body jerking beneath his questing and plunging tongue, as he pushed her longer, higher, harder.

"Can't, can't," she panted.

"Can," he said gruffly, focusing on the throbbing nerve center with the gentlest of swipes with the very tip of his tongue . . . while sliding a finger, slowly, deeply, inside her.

She cried out loudly, and thrashed beneath him.

Then she was grabbing his hair, leaning up to claw at his shoulders, her body still bucking and quaking with the aftershocks of her release. "Here," she commanded, pulling him up and over her body. "Now."

"Now?" he asked, poised over her.

Her eyes were so dark, the pupils had all but swallowed the sweet dark chocolate of her eyes. "Now," she growled almost angrily.

He grinned, even as he throbbed almost in pain he was so hard. "I like a woman who knows what she wants. Let me grab—"

"No," she said, which made him lift a brow. "I'm—I'm safe. Pill. We don't need, I mean . . . unless you want—"

"I only want one thing." He gripped her hips and dragged them up and off the bed so he could drive himself between them, sheathing all of himself inside every last sweet, hot, wet inch of her in one smooth, steady plunge.

She cried out, bucked hard against him again, and he realized she was climaxing. Again. Thinking of her he thrust again, and again, and she almost sobbed as she cried out, her nails digging into his shoulders, then his buttocks, as she urged—no, demanded—that he keep on. Faster. Deeper. Harder.

Her command was absolutely his wish. He'd have gone longer, for as long as she wanted him to, but her tight muscles throbbing around him ripped him to release before he even knew it was going to happen. He'd been on the brink since he'd slid his tongue inside her. Or, more honestly, since she'd stuck her head out the sliding glass door, all sleepy and flushed in those ridiculous flannel shorts.

Panting heavily and trying to find his breath, he moved to roll away, so he could take his weight from her, only to have her hook her ankles around the backs of his calves and pull his head down to hers.

"I'm heavy," he said, his voice sounding like that of a drugged man.

"Stay," was all she said. Then she pulled his head down the rest of the way and kissed him.

They'd coupled more like wild beasts than lovers. There hadn't been anything intimate about it. He knew that because the kiss . . . her kiss . . . the one she was tenderly giving him, so sweetly exploring, and soft, as if she'd never kissed him before, as if they hadn't just mated like wild jackals—was truly intimate. Not the way she'd responded to his slightest touch, not her multiple orgasms which had, in fact, made him truly feel somewhat godlike. No. It was this genuine and pure kiss, freely and fully given, all vulnerabilities laid bare.

He knew enough about her, understood enough about what scared her, to know that this was the true gift of herself. It was that, more than anything that had come before, that completely undid him.

He slid from her then, and eased his weight off her, pulling her with him when she would have ended the kiss to protest the shift in position. He kept her with him, tucked her against him, and continued to glory in the most amazing gift he'd ever received.

As he pulled her closer, sheltered her with his body, as if protecting her was and would always be his natural, default directive, he knew he'd do everything in his power to always be worthy of that one, single kiss.

Chapter 18

"What time is it?" Riley murmured, coming awake slowly, realizing as she became aware of being wrapped up against Quinn's big, hard body, that they must have dozed off—while still kissing, if she recalled it properly. She smiled against the warmth of his skin as it all filtered back.

She rolled her head just enough to see the bolted wall clock. Just after seven. Good, she had a little more time before embracing the real world.

"Is someone else on the boat?" Quinn's deep voice was even sexier when rough with sleep and a little honest fatigue. "I hear footsteps."

"That's just Brutus."

Quinn's eyes cracked open. "Brutus is onboard? How did I miss that?"

She laughed. "Where did you think he was? Out in the backyard, treading water?" She started to roll over and sit up, but a very strong arm hooked her right back up against an equally strong body. Since that was exactly where she wanted to be, she let him. "He sleeps up on the front of the boat, and nothing wakes him until the sun comes up."

"What if it's raining?"

"He goes under the awnings."

"Never in here?"

Riley grinned. "Let's just say he goes wherever he's most comfortable. That storm we had last week? I found him wedged between the barbeque and the life preserver bins. I try to get him to stay in here, but I think he just likes being outside. If it's really cold, he stretches out in the main cabin in front of the little space heater. Mostly I don't mind him not being underfoot."

"I can imagine." Quinn grinned and rolled his head so he could press a kiss against her hair. "I liked you being under me." He toyed with the long tangle of curls that spread across his chest, sending delicious little tingling sensations skittering all over her skin. She really thought this was perhaps the best use of an early morning she'd ever had.

"Yeah," she sighed. "That I didn't mind so much."

There was another thud from somewhere onboard.

"He's jumping down from the front of the deck to the side rails."

"Sounds like he's really gotten accustomed to boat living." Quinn drew his fingertips through her curls, slowly untangling them. "I guess you both have. How long did that take? Do you take it out much? I've never been on one of these—how does it maneuver in open water with the waves and all?"

She laughed. "Curious monkey and silly wabbit. I have no idea how to even turn the thing on, much less steer it anywhere. You don't honestly think Chuck and Greg would want me to take their big expensive toy out for a spin, do you? I mean, they have been around me for more than five minutes. It's a testament to their inexplicable affection for me that they agreed to let me even step onboard."

"How did you get it up here from Jekyll then?"

"The same way any self-respecting klutz would. I paid Chuck's uncle to do it."

Quinn chuckled at that. "Well, given my extensive, if youthful, life aboard ships of various sizes and modes, what do you think the chances are your very dear friends would let me take us out for a spin?"

She lifted her head to look at him. "I'm sure they'd be delighted to, but . . ."

"But what? Do you get seasick?"

"No, I don't think so. I didn't on the boat ride here, anyway."

"Is that the only time you've ever been on a boat?"

"Yes, why?"

He grinned. "It's funny to think someone who's never been in or around boats, lives on one."

"I know. I feel the same. And yet, here I am. I have to admit, I have come to really like it."

"So, why don't we take her out for a spin?"

"Because I finagled a space on the docks here by promising I wouldn't stay long. No one has said anything, but I'm afraid if I take it out they won't let me back."

"Don't you have a contract or something?"

She shook her head. "Just month to month. I dump an envelope in the slot at Biggers' and they leave me to my own devices."

He surprised her by sliding her body over and more fully on top of his much bigger body, making her feel lithe, and petite and anything other than how she'd always felt before. "Well, maybe I could put David on that for you. He's very good at making things happen."

"Why?" she asked. "I mean, thank you. I would feel better if I had something in writing."

"You're welcome. It's purely selfish. I'd like a sunset

cruise around the sound with you. That's where my grand-father and I sailed in the evenings after work. I'd like to share something of that with you."

She softened, and her heart teetered dangerously. This was the intimacy she wanted, the kind of opening up and sharing. "That sounds very lovely. If David can work his magic, I accept the invitation."

"Good." He looked inordinately pleased.

Riley braced herself, mentally anyway, for the fears to kick in. Making Quinn happy—she wanted to do that, and much more—but the fact that she could implied she mattered to him. That should scare her.

It did . . . but it didn't make her want to hide. She considered it forward progress made, and left it at that. "Fair warning, though. I don't know if I'll make any better a first mate than I do a captain."

He slid his hands down and cupped her bottom, then lightly pinched the soft flesh. "You're doing really well on the mating scale so far."

"Ha, ha," she said, but felt the warmth of pleasure at his comment fill her cheeks. She leaned down and kissed him. "So are you, Captain." She moved to roll her weight off him, but he wrapped his arms around her and kept her there.

"Few more minutes. You don't have to go yet, do you?"

She shook her head. And probably would have stayed, even if she knew she'd be late. Just a few more minutes sounded like heaven.

"I have one other request."

She slid her hands down his sides and pinched the side of his butt. "Getting awful cheeky," she said, enjoying the surprised snort of laughter that got from him. "What is the request?"

"Will you mind if I stay here to work while you're at the

bungalow? Tell me honestly, because I can find another place—"

"No. I kind of like the idea of you being here. Uh, could I maybe ask a favor in return? Would you mind if I left Brutus with you? Say no if you'd rather not. I know you need to concentrate. But he's really no trouble. Just walk him down to the end of the pier to the grassy area every once in a while. He'll let you know."

As if on cue, there was a jarring thud overhead, then a big, panting dog face appeared in the tiny window in the wall above their heads.

"Would that constitute letting me know? And how the hell did he get up on the fly deck?"

"There's a ramp. Sort of."

"A sort of ramp. I probably don't want to know."

"I think he likes the windier breeze up there. Or maybe he just likes playing king of the world." Riley grinned. "But right now I need to get the king out for his royal stroll. It'll just take a minute. And I . . . need to shower, before I go. I'd ask you to share, but it's tiny."

"Asking was nice." He tugged her down for one last fast, hard, and very hot kiss before letting her crawl off him and off the bed to search for her shorts and T-shirt.

Riley's thoughts flashed back to that hot and hard kiss Baxter had dropped on Lani the night they'd announced the cookbook deal. The one that had got her wondering all over again, and really questioning what she wanted in her life— who she wanted in it—and how she was going to get to where she could have it. She smiled privately to herself as she quickly pulled on her clothes. Maybe what she had with Quinn wasn't the love affair of the century, like the Dunnes' was, but, for what it was right now . . . it would do. It would certainly do.

"A shame," Quinn said.

Riley looked over her shoulder to find him sprawled back, sheet half over his naked body, arms propped behind his head. She was surprised she didn't outright drool, but it didn't keep the *you lucky dog* thought from skimming through her mind. "What is?" she asked him, wondering what he thought when he looked at her. He certainly didn't seem put off.

"Putting clothes on that body. When we take our sunset cruise, can we have naked sailing time?"

Her responding grin was swift and honest. He made her feel good about herself, and just . . . good in general. Even swifter than the grin was the infusion of warmth his sincerity gave her . . . not to mention the healthy boost it gave her ego. Maybe she shouldn't need that, but after everything she'd been through, and all the self-examination that had followed, she was too human to deny it felt pretty damn good.

"Only if you have five billion level sun block."

"I'll take that as a yes then."

She shot him a dry smile. "Of course you will."

Brutus scratched at the window.

"I'm coming, I'm coming. Keep your collar on."

"When you come back down, why don't you grab the stuff from the diner. We can nuke it, have a little reheated breakfast, and—"

"Uh-oh."

"Uh-oh what?"

"I forgot about that. About the food. Someone distracted me."

Quinn grinned, quite broadly and somewhat smugly. "And?"

"And I'm pretty sure I won't have to feed Brutus this morning."

It was entertaining how quickly Quinn's smug grin turned into a droop of disappointment. "Oh."

"Right. But I can put something together for you."

"Do you have eggs, some bacon? I can fix us something quick while you walk the dog. I've cooked onboard before."

"Which is dandy, because I have not. Hence no eggs, no bacon."

"You're in a cupcake baking club."

"We keep the spoilables in the shop kitchen so we don't have to haul everything back and forth. Char, Dre, and Franco come over the causeway from Savannah, sometimes straight from a job or school, so it helps to keep all refrigerated stuff on-site. I just bring the dry ingredients, or replace what I use of Lani's."

"Makes sense. But I wasn't referring to the lack of eggs. You're a food stylist. You have culinary training of some kind to do that, right?"

"I'm a trained chef, yes, though I didn't work in the field as one. My slant was always the photography aspect, though I ended up in design and styling." She grinned and shrugged. "I love food, trying new things. Not so much preparing all the intricate and involved dishes myself, but I have great respect for those who do, as well as for the final result of the food itself. When I figured out I could combine my love of photography with my love of international cuisine, and make a living at it, it seemed like a no-brainer to me."

"So you don't cook," he repeated. "At all?"

"I said I don't cook onboard." She gestured to herself. "Clearly I'm not wasting away here, so I manage. I either nuke stuff—you'd be amazed how much cooking you can actually do in a convection microwave—or I beg, pout, and say pretty, pretty please, and Carlo sends in with Char on club nights whatever dish he's experimenting on."

She held up her arm so he could see the Bullwinkle Band-Aid on the back of her tricep. "Rope burn from tying down the deck stuff before that storm—when the water was still flat as glass and there was no wind." She turned sideways and lifted the hem of her shorts to show a faint, almost healed bruise. "Banging against the dining room table, off-loading bags of groceries. The boat barely even rocked. No way am I turning on anything with the potential to catch fire."

"I suppose that makes sense." He sat up, stretched, and the sheet slid farther . . . and farther, down his lap. "Would you mind if I gave it a go?"

"Knock yourself out—not literally, of course—but like I said, there's nothing in the pantry to be cooked. Nuked, yes, Grilled, fried, or scrambled, not so much."

He slid from the bed, making her entire body wobble with want, and walked to her buck naked, simply too good to be true. He framed her face, bent down, and kissed her soundly on the mouth. "That's why they make markets. I'll go pick up some stuff and make us dinner. You'll be back by then, right?"

All she could do was nod, and whimper a little. How could she ache all over again? She should be a walking collection of sore muscles in need of great recuperation time. But had he even nodded toward the bed, she might have been the one to drag him there. Or to the floor. Or the nearest wall.

A huge, thundering *woof* made them jump.

"Right. Sorry, Brutus," she called out, then looked back at Quinn, whimpered again, turned and fled. It was that or attack him.

That she heard him chuckling all the way as she dashed through the main cabin and out the back sliding door didn't help matters any. She really needed a better poker face.

She checked that thought and changed her mind as she clipped the lead on the dancing dog. Did it matter if Quinn could read her every thought if he seemed to be of like mind?

Brutus leaped from the boat to the pier. Riley tried her best to keep him from dislocating her shoulder on his mad dash to the grass, but her thoughts were still back on the boat. And with Quinn. She definitely hadn't seen this morning happening . . . not like it had, anyway. But she was thankful and relieved. If he'd called and asked to see her on some kind of official date, she'd have been a nervous wreck. She'd have overthought her choice of clothes, overthought how she should act, overthought how the whole transition from date to possible sex might go, not to mention the getting naked part—speaking for herself anyway—followed by spending far too much time worrying about every single aspect of that dynamic.

Instead, he'd just shown up, been funny, charming, sexy, and somehow made her feel the same, despite being in dorky sleep clothes with massive bed head. He had literally swept her off her feet and taken her to bed, where they'd had the most amazing sex she'd ever experienced.

It had been thrilling and fierce. He made her feel like a femme fatale siren goddess. For that alone, she'd be forever in his debt.

Brutus bumped his head against her leg and she got a bag, cleaned up after him, then started back to the boat after depositing it in the big trash can.

What she and Quinn had done hadn't been anything like lovemaking, not really. It had been hot, but not necessarily intimate. Of course, for a first time . . . She paused as Brutus sniffed some particularly intriguing fishy smells, and her thoughts drifted to after, when he'd pulled her close to him, and then after that, when they'd kissed.

She sighed deeply. Her body felt all warm and achy—in a good way—just thinking about that kiss. Hands down, that had been the most intimate act they'd shared. It had gone on and on, and she'd felt truly connected to the part of him that mattered.

He knew his way around a woman's body—like a violinist intent on making a Stradivarius weep. But he'd been the first one to admit that his relationships never got past that part.

She'd loved the snuggling, the banter, after they'd woken up together, and how he'd wanted to keep her there with him. He'd made her feel alive and desirable in her own skin, not just comfortable, but sexy and naturally at ease. He was a hedonist, making her aware of every single cell in her body at all times, and making her feel good about it.

She remembered how he'd laid himself bare to her, standing in his foyer, when she'd cracked under the pressure of her own fears. She knew he could open up and be more than a very skilled lover. A whole lot more. Would those two parts of him eventually blend? Could he open himself up fully and make love to her?

And, more important, would he want to?

She shook her head, and smiled dryly at her own thoughts. "He makes you feel like Cleopatra and Sophia Loren all wrapped into one exotic package and you're already worrying about what happens next?" She let Brutus lead her back to the boat, thinking about the irony that Jeremy had loved her for her mind, her offbeat humor, and her skills with the work they shared. He'd made her feel strong, respected, valued . . . but he'd never made her feel comfortable in her own skin. In fact, she'd always suspected that while he claimed to love her body, the lushness of it had always been a little too much for his true personal taste. He was taller than she was by a few inches, but slender. In fact, they weighed close to the same. She'd never sprawled herself across his body as she had Quinn's. As years went by, they learned to satisfy each other's needs and their sex life remained a healthy enough one. Was it any surprise she'd assumed he'd come to love her body as he'd come to love her? Just like she'd come to love his skinny, long, bird legs and the complete lack of hair on his chest?

Wasn't that what a couple did?

She thought again about how Quinn had brought every part of her body to a feverish pitch, kept her there, vibrating on the edge, then effortlessly teased her up and over, again and again, to a series of the strongest climaxes she'd ever had. Or known she was capable of having. She was not a screamer. She smiled privately. *I am now.* That had certainly not been in the repertoire with Jeremy. Their lovemaking had been ardent at times, but much more . . . staid. Jeremy wasn't particularly earthy.

Riley let Brutus hop onboard, then followed him along the walkway and on deck. Something smelled amazing. She'd thought it had been coming from one of the other boats, but almost all of them were battened down for the winter.

"Quinn?" She climbed down the companionway and found him in the galley.

Tousled hair, rumpled khaki slacks, no shirt, towel tucked sideways in the waistband of his pants like a short apron. He looked up, spatula in one hand, and grinned. Her heart fluttered, flipped, then did a lovely little freefall—which made no sense. He always looked hot. And had shot her that sexy grin more than once.

Of course, this time he was half naked in her own kitchen, but still. She thought her heart had higher standards than that. Or at least more integrity than to be swayed by a hunky chef. *Who plays your body like a violin,* her little voice reminded her. Needlessly.

"Come taste this," he said, lifting up the spoon.

Rather than duck past the galley for her shower, and the very wise distance and time it would give her to sort through her jumbled thoughts, she walked right over to him. "What did you even find to make?"

He carefully tipped the spoon to her lips. "Rice, cheese, and mushrooms. Some flour from your baking supply stash, milk, and a few of your spices to make a sauce. Here, try."

She took a nibble, then felt her eyebrows climb halfway up her forehead as the rich, creamy, incredible flavors burst all over her tongue. She closed her eyes and groaned as she finished off the nibble. "Where did you learn to do that?"

He shrugged. "Necessity. I hate eating out all the time. And you forget, I was chief biscuit cutter in Grams' kitchen."

"Right, right. Never underestimate the culinary powers of Grandma."

"Did you learn to cook from yours?"

"What? No. I never knew my grandparents. Two of them were alive when I was born, but infirm. We were stationed overseas." She shrugged. "They were both gone by the time we returned stateside."

"Military brat then?" he asked.

She nodded. "My dad was killed by a land mine when I was little. I don't remember him."

"I'm sorry, Riley."

"It's okay. I lived on base, so I wasn't the only kid who went through it. Maybe because of that it was—well, it wasn't normal, of course—but it was part of the culture of that life. You got yourself through it, as those around you did."

"And your mom?"

"Also military." When he looked surprised, she said, "That made it hard—she was gone a lot. I got shuffled around a lot. But I kind of liked the freedom I had . . . and the security of knowing I lived on a military base. It was an interesting combination."

"And now? Your mom? Still serving?"

Riley shook her head. "She passed when I was in college. Complications from pneumonia."

Quinn's expression was tender and sad. "I'm sorry for that. I know what it's like."

"Thank you. It's okay now. I was thankful—very—that I'd grown up as independent as I had. Helped me move forward and be okay."

"It explains a lot about you," he said.

It was her turn to look surprised. "As in?"

"All good," he said, echoing her words from the beach that day, when she'd been describing how she saw him. "You have this innate strength and you've definitely tackled life, even when it hands you rough stuff. You hung in, you pushed through. Maybe there is something about losing parents young that makes us wary of allowing ourselves to want something, or to let someone else contribute to our feelings of security. We know, quite literally, how fleeting life can be."

She thought about that, and nodded. "You probably have a point. I think, in my case, though I avidly pursued my career, I was too eager for the sense of security that came with someone suddenly being there for me. Maybe because my parents largely hadn't been, even when they were alive? I don't know. I do know that I sucked it all in, draped it all over myself, and paraded it around. I loved everything about being half of two, rather than only one."

"I can see that. Reacting that way. It helps me understand how you went the other direction after it was over. I'm glad you told me."

"Good," she said. "I don't want it to be awkward."

"If you mean your past relationship, I don't want it to be either. For the record, I don't need to know about it. That's your business. I understand the general dynamics enough to understand why this leap was hard for you to take. I don't need or want you to mine your own pain just to help me understand you better."

"I—thank you." Riley ducked her head for a moment, surprised not only by his words, but by this welling of . . . she didn't know how to label the emotions he was making her feel. Except to know that instead of scaring her, they made her feel good. As if she was on solid ground. And that was . . . a lot. "You promised me you'd always be square with me. I promise you the same thing. So, if you want details, I'll give them to you. But I feel . . . sturdier, with you. Than I thought I would. I very much like being in the present, especially this one right now, with you."

"Then the present is where we'll stay. Though I do have one last dead cat question."

She didn't exactly brace herself, because that teasing gleam had come back into his eyes. She realized not only how well she'd come to read him . . . but that she'd also come to trust that what she found there was real. "And what would that be?"

"Where did you learn to cook? Or what made you want to learn?"

"Oh, that's easy." She laughed. "Military base food. I never had family cooking, even when staying with other families. It was always my luck to get stuck where meals were prepared much as ours were—leftovers and quickly thrown together potlucks. I remember watching TV and seeing families on those shows always gathered around a big table, enjoying all that food together. I wanted to be an honorary Walton." She laughed, and a bit of pink warmed her cheeks.

He grinned. "Well, if it makes you feel any better, I'll call you Riley Sue."

"Thanks, Quinn Bob."

He laughed outright at that. "If you're going to grab a

shower, you might want to do it now. I'll put a plate together for you."

"Okay." she said, grinning, too. "Thanks." But she didn't make a mad dash to the shower. She stood right where she was for a few moments longer. As soon as she moved, he took her arm in a gentle hold and turned her back to face him.

"Everything okay?"

"Amazing." There was nothing about the last hour and a half that had been anything short of that. And she had a lot more than hot sex to base that judgment on.

"But?"

She dropped her chin, which he lifted right back up. "You always do that," she said.

"What, not letting you hide? Or wanting to know what's bugging you?"

"No, reading my mind so you know there's something bugging me in the first place."

"More of my godlike skills." He offered her a crooked grin. When she didn't smile back, his faded. "Come here."

"I should really—"

"Come here, is what you should really do." He gently cupped her head and tilted her face up to his. "Did I do something wrong?"

Another part of her simply melted. "No. You're everything that's right."

"Too much still?" His gaze searched hers and she realized that maybe he needed reassurance as much as she did.

That it mattered to him, that she mattered, did reassure her . . . even as it made her nervous. "I—" she began, then faltered, not sure how to put her thoughts into words.

She was falling in love with him.

"We probably should have waited," he said, "given everything else. We should have spent more time getting to know each other with our clothes on first."

That got a spontaneous laugh from her. "You might be godlike in many ways, but neither of us is superhuman. Given what happened this morning—and in your foyer, and on the beach—just how long would we have been able to hold out?"

"Well"—a teasing light came into his beautiful blue eyes—"when you put it that way. We were simply victims of the primordial order of things. There was nothing else to be done but surrender to the inevitable."

"Something like that," she said with a wry smile. "Maybe that's the way the whole thing is going to be with us. Explosive and primordial and completely incapable of going at any other speed than full tilt." She paused, and dipped her chin.

After a moment he very gently tilted it back up again until their eyes met.

"So, yes. It's still too much," she said softly. "But I'd rather have too much, too fast, than nothing at all."

"I don't know if this helps, but it feels that way to me, too. It's all a new roller-coaster ride for me. So, hell yes, it's too much right from the starting gun. But you're right. I'd rather hurry and play catch-up than ditch the ride altogether."

Her lips curved.

"What is that smile all about?" he asked.

"What a pair we are, Quinn Brannigan."

He leaned down and kissed the tip of her nose. "Finally," he teased. "That's what I've been trying to tell you all along." Gathering her in his arms, he kissed her the way a man did when maybe, just maybe, he was falling, too.

Chapter 19

"It's coming along really well, Dad." Quinn stretched his feet out on the deck in front of him as he leaned back in his chair for leverage, and launched the huge stick toward the pergola. Brutus dutifully watched it hurtle and fall into a large palmetto, then hauled his butt up and trotted over to retrieve it. Quinn shook his head and smiled, then shifted the phone to his other ear. "It's a departure from what I've been doing, so I'm excited and a bit nervous to see how it will be received."

"Sounds good," his father said, which was the same response he'd have given if Quinn had told him he'd decided to paint his body blue and jump out of a plane. "I've got a meeting. Good to catch up."

"Yes, Dad, you, too. Love you," he said as his father signed off. His father wasn't comfortable with expressing emotions, or receiving them. He was a policy wonk on Capitol Hill, which suited his sober, serious nature and allowed him to avoid pretty much all emotional ties. If his dad didn't regularly play racquetball and golf, most often with a small group of guys who dated all the way back to his far more social frat days, Quinn would worry about him more. But, all in all, he seemed content with the status quo. Quinn knew his father loved him, and he figured his dad could put up with hearing it expressed occasionally from his son.

He looked over his shoulder into the breakfast nook off the kitchen. Still a busy beehive of activity going on in there. Baxter and Lani were baking up a storm, along with a handful of assistants; then there was the art director, the photographer, Riley, and who knew who else. They were finishing up principal photography for a glossy booklet that would be stuffed in bags and handed out at huge, regional cooking shows around the country.

Quinn laid his phone on the side table next to his closed laptop. He'd been on the boat earlier, but had decided to come back here. It was a gorgeous day, above average temperature, but no humidity, so he figured he'd camp out in the pergola and enjoy the perks of making his living on a mobile device. He heard a squeal, then something crashed, but he didn't turn around. He smiled to himself and leaned down to pick up the slobber-covered log Brutus had deposited. "Ten-to-one your mom just busted something expensive," he told the dog, who offered a baleful stare in return. "I know. That's what I said." Laughing, Quinn launched the log across the back yard again, and watched as Brutus made his slow and steady trek toward it.

Quinn had come to have a great appreciation for the way Brutus observed life. He was all for balance and not sweating the small stuff, which the mammoth dog seemed to have down to a science. "It doesn't hurt that you get regular meals and lots of love from a beautiful woman. I'd take that life."

Quinn's cell phone chirped and he picked it up.

That wasn't my fault.

He grinned, but before he could text Riley back, another one came through.

This time.

Brutus returned and dropped the log, then sat and let his tongue loll to the side as he stared at Quinn. The tongue lolling meant he'd had enough of the game. Quinn reached in his pocket and pulled out one of the superdog-size Milk-Bones he'd stashed away there, tossed it into the gaping maw that was Brutus's mouth, then watched with bemused pleasure as the dog sank into a boneless heap and munched on his treat, as if it were nothing more than his due. He picked up his phone again, smiled . . . and typed out a message.

What are you wearing?

A moment later: You're such a guy. And then: Thank God. Come out and play with me.

I can't. I'm drizzling glycerin all over the top of this nice, plump red cherry so it looks all sticky and sweet.

You play dirty.

And sticky, she wrote back, which made him bark a laugh out loud. It even startled the dog.

Fine, fine. Me and Brutus will just sit out here in the garden and eat worms.

Nothing came back after that, which meant she was busy making pastry look naturally sumptuous by using a blowtorch, or motor oil, or spray deodorant. Who knew what? As she'd explained it to him, under the unrelenting heat of the lights, hot foods still cooled, cool foods grew warmed, frozen foods melted, greens wilted, and moist foods went dry.

It wasn't enough to keep fresh duplicates on hand to swap out. Staging one individual dish could take hours all by itself, so swapping wouldn't work. Good stylists learned all kinds of tricks to sustain and extend the original look of the food by using a few less than natural—or even edible—items to create the necessary illusions.

She'd caught him looking through her Supergirl Tool

Belt the other day after climbing out of the shower, and—after copious curious monkey comments—had given him quite the education on how stylists made the food in those magazines and print ads look so luscious. She almost put him off chocolate sauce for life.

He tossed the phone back on the table, and stretched his legs out again. He'd told himself he'd come back to the bungalow to work, and let Brutus have a bit of a romp, but he knew he'd come back so he could be closer to Riley. He missed her—which was kind of crazy, since they'd shared their mind-blowing, life-altering morning together only two days ago. At least, that was how he'd viewed that morning in the grand scheme of things.

They'd spent zero time alone together since. Not all her fault. Or his. She'd gotten hung up that day through the evening and into the wee hours planning the initial shoot with Baxter, Lani, and the art director. The following morning she went back to Savannah, frantically searching for specialty gadgets she needed for the first shoot and ordering the rest of the equipment she'd need.

He'd likely passed her on her way back to Sugarberry, as he'd had to go into Savannah to meet with a producer and screenwriter who'd been dogging him for rights to his current release. David had tried to keep them at bay, but when they'd offered to bring the meeting to him, Quinn had finally agreed to have a dinner meeting and be done with it. That dinner meeting had gone to the wee hours. In the end, though, it had been worth it for all parties involved.

He'd come back to the bungalow after the meeting instead of going to the houseboat, thinking he would just show up with breakfast at the boat in the morning and see if he could start their day in the same spectacular fashion he had two days before.

He'd zonked out and slept straight through his alarm. By the time he'd gotten himself together and out the door, the vans were already pulling in for the day's shoot. Riley showed up right behind them, leaving little time for any private conversation. She'd told him the boat was his as long as he wanted, that they'd definitely be running long that day, and apologized for being so rushed. Someone had called her name and off she'd dashed. He hadn't even given her a kiss good morning. Or gotten one.

The desire for her kiss had hovered over and around the edges of his mind the entire morning as he tried to write. He'd managed to pull a few decent pages out of his distracted brain, then had spent another hour digging into some research about horses for the book, but had finally given up and decided maybe he'd get his concentration back if she were at least within viewing distance.

"So much for that, big guy. Right? At least we have modern technology on our side now."

Brutus responded by heaving his weight to his side and stretching his legs out more fully as the late afternoon sun warmed his half-exposed underbelly.

Quinn smiled to himself as he admitted that he'd developed a whole new appreciation for the connective powers of text messaging. He might not have spent any alone time with Riley in two days, but since she'd hopped off the houseboat that morning with his cell number in her back pocket, they hadn't been apart-apart for more than a few hours at a time. They hadn't used their phones for actual talking yet. With her being on set or him being in that meeting almost the whole time, they hadn't been able to.

Tapping out secret little messages to each other tickled some other place inside him that he was coming not only to appreciate, but to enjoy as its own, separate way of having fun with her. There was a kind of passing-notes-in-class, breaking-the-rules vibe to it that felt a little naughty and rebellious.

"I promise this tastes better than worms."

Startled, he looked up to find Riley standing over him with the most amazing, piled-high version of a napoleon he'd ever seen.

She had her hair pulled up in a messy knot on her head. Glasses he didn't know she wore were shoved up into the tangle of curls. Her face was flushed, he supposed from the heat of the kitchen and the lights. She was wearing what he'd come to think of as her standard uniform—loose khakis, long tee, with an open camp shirt thrown over it. The new addition of her Supergirl Tool Belt was slung low around her hips, but he wasn't really paying attention to that. Or the amazing napoleon, for that matter.

The way the breeze caught and lifted the front panels of her camp shirt away from her body, revealing just how perfectly the long tee hugged her amazingly beautiful breasts, made his body stir. He'd had those breasts under his thumb, under his tongue, between his lips . . .

He groaned under his breath and reached out to pluck off the cherry from the top of the dessert, then dragged it through the thick and foamy frosting. It wasn't going to come close to the taste of her bare breasts, but it would make a decent second choice. He paused with the treat halfway to his open and waiting mouth and lifted a single brow in question.

She raised her hand, palm out. "I swear, no glycerin has been used in the making of this dessert."

He plopped the cherry in his mouth, then closed his lips over it and groaned. Still not naked nipples, but . . . "My God," he said, his mouth still full. "That's amazing."

She set the plate down on his side table, along with silverware tucked inside a rolled linen. "Don't talk with your mouth full."

"Okay." Still savoring the last of the frosting, he elicited a squeal from her when he tugged her down across his lap. "You can keep me from talking for a few minutes."

"My tools," she cried out, as various things jangled and clanked.

"Will be fine. I have a big lap." He pulled her in for a long and languorous exploration. The kiss was heady and sweet and better than any napoleon could hope to be.

When he finally lifted his head, her eyes were dazed and sparkly, and he suspected his might look the same.

She smacked her lips. "You taste yummy and creamy."

He grinned. "Bring a few pieces of that back to the boat and I'll make you taste yummy, too."

Her eyes went dark and he was pulling her back down for another round, when he spied the rather large bandage on her elbow. He lifted her arm up in front of them. "What happened?"

"It's nothing, just a scrape, and before you mock me—"

"I would never mock." He leaned down and pressed a kiss next to the bandage. "I understand my role here is to kiss the boo-boos, confirm that it really wasn't your fault"—he reached down beside him and fished blindly in his leather computer bag, then brandished a small box in front of her—"and provide copious quantities of cartoon character Band-Aids."

The way her expression instantly softened, as if he'd given her flowers, or diamonds, for that matter, made him glad he'd given in to the impulse. He'd hoped she'd be amused rather than offended.

"You're such a guy, though."

"A nice guy," he amended, handing her the box.

"Spiderman?" She offered him a wry grin. "Was your manhood threatened by getting Hello Kitty or Powderpuff Girls?" She tucked the pack in her tool belt, but he didn't miss the sweet smile she privately allowed herself as she did.

"It was all they had. Well, it was that or plain brown, and on your lovely skin, a plain brown wrapper simply wouldn't do."

She laughed. "Well, I appreciate your attention to aesthetics and I take it all back."

He slid his palm along the back of her neck, nudging her closer again.

"The whole crew is still in there. I have to get back," she cautioned.

"You know, I didn't get the chance to kiss you good morning earlier."

"That's true. I don't guess you did. But we just kissed two seconds ago. Doesn't that count?"

He shook his head. "You have to call it first. Official make-up-kiss rule." His smile stayed in place, but he caught her gaze and held it intently. "I missed getting to do that." He reached up and traced a finger along her lower lip, following the motion with his eyes, then lifting his gaze back to hers. "I missed you." He felt a fine tremor shiver through her, and his body responded with equal enthusiasm.

"Boy"—her voice was a little shaky, though she was striving for casual and light—"give a guy a nooner before breakfast and he gets all needy on you."

"Spectacular as that was"—he traced her upper lip, delighting in the way her body instantly responded—"I've missed you every day since I met you." That was the simple truth of it. She hadn't left his thoughts since the day she'd first entered them. He leaned in and replaced his fingertip with his lips, taking her mouth softly, sweetly, working hard to get a grip on the more ferocious needs that ignited the instant he tasted her again. "And I missed kissing you," he said against her lips, "before I ever tasted you."

She sighed, and he felt her body relax and soften on his. He continued the slow, steady exploration, urging her to open to him, languidly sliding his tongue into her mouth. Both moaned as he coaxed her tongue into his mouth, then pulled it in more deeply.

He kept his hand cupped on the back of her neck as she lifted her mouth from his, keeping her close, in the intimacy of the moment they'd created. "Good morning."

She smiled at him, and it wasn't just the obvious parts of his body that responded to the affection and light that entered her eyes. He also felt a tightening in his chest and throat. And he couldn't stop the thought that he could easily stand to see that look in those eyes every single day for the rest of his life.

"Good morning," she responded. "I missed that, too. I'm sorry I didn't know about the rules sooner."

"Well, I would have told you that morning on the houseboat, but you went and distracted me with your wicked, wanton ways."

She laughed. "Right, because baggy shorts, a basketball jersey, and crazy bed head just shout *take me!* to a man."

"You don't need to shout," he said, pulling her mouth back to his.

"Why is it you always say the absolute perfect thing?" she asked, on a sigh against his lips.

"You forget, you're playing with a professional," he told her, making them laugh even as their mouths stayed fused together. He shifted his kisses to the side of her jaw, then along the side of her neck. "You could be wearing a cardboard box with holes cut out for arms, and I'd still want to rip it off you."

She gave a mock shudder. "Ew. So would I." Then she surprised him by turning her head and catching his mouth with hers for a fast, hard kiss. "But I like your reasons much better." She lifted her mouth and leaned back.

"Not to intrude on the poolside canoodling here, but do you think maybe you could let her come back inside to work sometime soon?"

Startled by the close proximity of the new voice in the conversation, they jumped, but it was the poleaxed look on

Riley's face that got Quinn's attention. He'd completely forgotten no one had seen them together yet. "Uh-oh," he whispered, though he was sure Lani could hear him. "Looks like
Mommy and Daddy know you have a boyfriend." When
Riley merely narrowed her eyes at him—though there was a
distinct threat of a smile hovering around the corners of her
mouth—he silently mouthed *sorry.*

Quinn glanced up at Lani, but kept his arm locked
around Riley's waist. "Did you know that four out of five
people on a survey I'm sure has been taken somewhere say
workers who spend at least fifteen minutes a day canoodling
perform at a much higher standard than those who don't?"

Lani's lips twitched. "I hadn't heard that. I'd have to do
some independent research analysis on that, and get back
to you."

Quinn looked at Riley. "I like her."

"Yeah," Riley said. "She makes it hard not to."

"In the meantime," Lani said, "could we have her return
to her slave labor job?"

Quinn consulted his watch. "I believe we need at least
three more minutes. You know, for optimal performance."

Lani gave him a dry smile. "We'll risk her being slightly
subpar."

"You both realize I'm sitting right here."

"Oh, I'm very aware of where you're sitting," Quinn
said, making Lani bark out a laugh. It had the unfortunate
affect of startling Brutus from his doggie dreams.

Belying his more usual speed-of-sludge style, he heaved
himself up, blinking and swinging his head around, as if
looking for the source of the noise. He also heaved the top-
heavy deck chair over, sending both of its occupants directly into the pool.

Quinn reached instinctively for Riley, and pushed her to
the surface first, following her a second or two later.

Lani was standing poolside, hands on her hips, with a

very innocent-looking Brutus sitting ever-so-politely beside her. "You know, some people will do anything to get their extra three minutes." She grinned. "Of course, if it cools off some of the steam rising off that deck chair when I came out, then maybe it's for the best. Kitchen's hot enough."

Quinn guided Riley to the edge so she could hold on while scraping a mass of wet, blond curls from her face. "I lost my scrunchie."

"I hate it when that happens." Quinn smiled when she stuck her tongue out at him. "Careful where you aim that thing," he warned, then helped her pull her heavy, wet hair away from her face.

"I'm pretty sure no one has seen me so consecutively at my worst, ever. This is now officially a record."

"You look like a mermaid with bed head." He leaned in and kissed her smiling mouth.

"Oh my God," Lani said. "You're soaking wet and still there's steam. I'm surprised there's not fog over the water. Not that anyone is listening to me."

"I am," Riley said. "Just let me find my way out of this pool with a tiny shred of dignity, if that's possible. This tool belt weighs a ton wet and it's possible I may have a serious wardrobe malfunction with my pants as I try to exit the pool area."

Quinn scooted behind her. "I believe I can be of some assistance with that."

"Oh, brother." There was laughter in Lani's voice. "I'm going back inside before I see things I don't need to be seeing. Still in public!" she called out in a dead-on impression of Charlotte as she headed back to the house.

"Says the woman who is the cause of all Charlotte's constant admonitions," Riley shouted back.

Lani turned at the French doors and sketched a bow. "I may be the reigning queen of Kingdom Gettaroom, but I

believe you may be in the running to topple my crown."
She waved her hand in a swirly motion in front of her forehead as she bowed. "Sim-salah-bim. Now please get your
most excellent, wet, royal fanny inside as soon as you can.
The semifreddo is melting . . . melting." Wavering the last
word, she cut loose with a fairly excellent Wicked Witch of
the West cackle as she ducked inside.

"Her skill set is even broader than one would imagine,"
Quinn stated, staring at the closed patio door.

"You have no idea. Whatever you do, don't get her
started on boy bands of the nineties."

"You don't like boy bands? Huh. I'll make a note of that.
No impromptu Backstreet Boys medleys under the moonlight during our naked time dinner cruise."

Quinn had guided them to the set of wide stone steps
leading out of the small pool, but Riley turned back. "The
fact that you're even aware of who the Backstreet Boys are
is disconcerting and oddly hot."

Quinn leaned down and put his mouth close to her ear
and sang the first two lines of the chorus from "I Want It
That Way."

Riley clamped a hand over her mouth, whether to stifle
peals of laughter or utter shock, he couldn't be certain. Her
eyebrows probably would have climbed just as high either
way. She flung her arms around his shoulders, bussed his
cheek with a loud kiss, and whispered in his ear, "If you
ever sing that to me while we're in bed, I will either die in
sure-to-be mood-killing laughter . . . or you'll be able to
have me any way you want me. I can't decide."

"I'm thinking it might be worth the risk just to find out."

She caught his gaze, and they snorted. Quinn put his
hand over his heart as if he were about to break out into
song again, which sent Riley into snickering peals of
laughter. They were full-out laughing as they dragged their

wet, soggy selves from the pool. Water ran from her tool belt like its own miniature waterfall.

She looked down and pouted. "It took me a full day of hunting to find all my special Supergirl stuff."

Quinn looked down at the soggy nylon pockets. "If you give me a list, I'll be happy to help out. I've got some time tomorrow." Frowning, he reached in and pulled out a package that read ICE POWDER. He looked at her and lifted his eyebrows.

She wiggled hers in response and snatched it back. "If you're really nice to me, I'll show you a few of its many uses. Only some of which are for photographic purposes."

Grinning, he impulsively hooked his hand on the front of her tool belt, tugged her against him, and dropped a hard, fast kiss on her mouth.

"What was that for?" Riley asked, looking a bit dazed.

"My life is so much better with you in it."

She chuckled. "Yes, well, it's not every man who dares to live in Calamityville."

He framed her face. "Actually, I meant that." He dropped a softer, sweeter kiss on her lips. "Before you say anything, or get nervous, I just mean you make me happy, that's all." Worried he'd pushed a little too much, he said, "Let's get inside. I'm sure I have something you can pull on. At least you'll be dry. I know you have work to do."

Inside was only a notch or two below utter and complete chaos. He brought down an old sweatshirt and sweatpants for her to change into, but that was the last he saw of her until the chefs and crew packed up shop on the far side of midnight.

By half past twelve, he'd gone upstairs after texting her to come find him to say good night before she left.

He woke up when he heard the vans backing out of the drive. Thinking Riley would show up at his door shortly, he

debated the relative merits of talking her into staying with
him, if for no other reason than it was the more expedient
route to getting some sleep after what he knew had been a
very, very long day for her.

He heard another vehicle engine start up, and managed
to look out his bedroom window in time to see her pull out,
with Brutus enthroned in the passenger side of the Jeep.

He glanced at the clock, and saw it was just after two in
the morning. He supposed he couldn't fault her for not
coming up and disturbing him. She'd likely assumed he'd
gone to sleep. He checked his phone. No text from her, either. He'd never thought of himself as a pouter, but he
pushed out his bottom lip a bit right then.

He didn't like his chances of getting right back to sleep,
so he went downstairs to grab a bottle of water. He was
more than a little stunned to see that what had looked like
the aftermath of a nuclear bomb the last time he'd popped
his head in had been restored to his nice, clean kitchen.
There were still cables, lighting, and cameras everywhere,
but the immediate cooking area was spotless.

"Well done," he murmured, in what he thought wasn't a
bad Baxter Dunne imitation. He'd come to know the famous chef fairly well in the brief time he'd been loaning
out his kitchen to him. Baxter was a likable guy, as tall as
Quinn, with an effortless kind of affable charm, but there
was also an intense edge about him. Quinn supposed it was
the latter that had made him the rock star chef he was.

Quinn had enjoyed the few chats they'd had, and had
been surprised to find they had a lot more in common than
he initially thought. Not just the books, and dealing with
various aspects of celebrity—though Baxter dealt with way
more than Quinn did—but also making adjustments to life
on Sugarberry after city dwelling for a long time. Not to
mention their involvement with two of the island's more

prominent citizens. In Baxter's case, he'd married her and was now a full-time resident himself.

Quinn wondered how inappropriate it would be to ask Baxter if he had any advice where Riley was concerned. He didn't regret the comment he'd made to Riley by the pool, about his life being better with her in it. He wished he knew how to convey those happy feelings without making her nervous. He was probably overthinking it, just as she had said they both had a tendency to do. Of course, he probably wouldn't be having wee-hour musings at all if she'd left him some kind of good night message.

"Oh yes, old chap, you're in veddy, veddy deep, indeed." He popped open the door to the fridge, and spied the bone-in roast he'd optimistically moved from the freezer that morning to thaw. The stray thought that he'd better save the bone for Brutus had him shaking his head. "Deep end, deep," he murmured. Unlike Riley . . . the nerves he felt about where their relationship might be heading bred more excitement and anticipation than any sort of dread or concern. Standing in front of the open fridge door in the wee hours of the morning, he knew he was in for the duration.

It wasn't some revelatory epiphany. It was thinking about that spontaneous kiss by the pool, and what had motivated him to do it. His life *was* better with her in it. He was happy. Deep-down happy in a place he didn't even know existed. She made him happy.

It was that simple.

He had to hope and trust that Riley would give herself a chance to get to that same place.

That's when he found the note.

Grinning so broadly he thought he'd pull a facial muscle, he plucked the small, handwritten note off the top of the carton of eggs, which was stacked on top of the pound of bacon he'd bought at the market the day before. He straightened as he scanned what she'd written.

I didn't want to wake you. I was thinking maybe a round of pirate and wench at sunrise? I'll bring the pirate ship. Your job is to bring our hearty apres-pillaging repast. Oh, and I call dibs on the good night kiss we missed. And where to deliver it. It could have something to do with my tongue being forced to walk a certain . . . plank. Hope you dreamed good stuff, matey. Har har.
         —Riley

"I don't have to dream it," he murmured, his heart tripping right over the edge into that fast slide straight into love. He closed the refrigerator door and shuffled back upstairs to bed, note still in hand. He propped it on his nightstand where he'd see it first thing when he opened his eyes, and buried his stupid-grin smiling face into his pillow. "I'm living the good stuff."

Chapter 20

Riley woke up to the heavenly smell of bacon, decided she was clearly still dreaming, and rolled back over so she could enjoy it a little longer, delaying the harsh reality of the cold, dry breakfast cereal that actually awaited her. But, snuggling in more deeply, she still smelled bacon. Then she abruptly sat up. *The note!* Bacon, eggs . . . and a pirate.

She grinned. "Har har, indeed." She hadn't known if Quinn would see the note, much less in time to do anything about what it said. She looked down at the baseball jersey and pajama pants she'd dragged on when she'd come home in the middle of the night to a chilly stateroom. "Not exactly wenching clothes."

Of course, bacon was already on the griddle, so perhaps there would be no time for pillaging. They were apparently going straight to the hearty après pillage repast portion of her proposed morning's activities. She pushed her hair out of her face and checked the clock. Seven. Fortunately call time had been moved back to eleven that morning, as Lani had no one to cover Cakes by the Cup. She had to open the shop until Alva was done with her weekly set and starch (as

Lani privately called it) at Cynthia's. Of course, Quinn probably didn't know that.

Hmm. A slow smile spread across her face as she wondered what Quinn's schedule looked like that morning. And just what kind of wenching attire she could throw together in hopes of enticing him into a bit of raid and pillage.

She slid her feet out of the covers and over the side of the bed, felt the cold air, and pulled them right back in, deciding wardrobe planning would be better undertaken while staying warm and tucked in.

She stilled when she thought she heard something coming from the galley that sounded like . . . She grinned. Quinn was singing. Not loudly, but still. She strained to make out the tune, then covered her face with a pillow so she could laugh out loud when she heard him bust out the refrain to New Kids on the Block's "The Right Stuff."

She flopped back with the pillow still on her face, but found herself wiggling her hips in the tangle of sheets as the song flooded her mind. "Oh, oh, oh," she sang along. Flinging the pillow aside, she took a full slide into the second refrain, singing a heartfelt, "All that I needed was you!"

"Ahoy, matey," came a deep voice from the door.

She slammed the pillow back on her face, immediately starting to snicker, which led to full-out laughter.

A second later the pillow was gently peeled back from her face, sending her into a fresh peal of laughter when she spied Captain Jack Quinn looming over her, complete with handmade black patch strapped over one eye and red bandanna wrapped around his head.

"If it's dancin' in the sheets ye wanted"—he gave it his best Jack Sparrow—"I believe I can be of some assistance." He tossed the pillow aside. "But first, let me usher my worthy sidekick to his observation post off the portside bow."

He straightened and glanced to the side, drawing her gaze downward . . . where it landed on Brutus, who was also sporting an eyepatch. A bandanna bowtie was attached to his collar.

"They were out of parrots at ye olde pirate shoppe," Captain Quinn offered by way of explanation when she lifted her gaze to his in openmouthed disbelief.

"I can't believe he let you do that."

Brutus looked up at Quinn, and his tongue lolled to one side.

"Okay. Yes, I can." Riley flopped back on the bed, the laughter making her breathless. "First pirates who sing sea chanteys complete with a solid bassline and synchronized dance moves, and now this. I've no restraint left." She flung one arm wide and the other dramatically over her eyes. "Have your wicked, wanton way with me, Captain Quinn. I know I've stirred your manly ardor with my wicked, wanton attire."

She cracked one eye open and spied Quinn sliding off Brutus's patch and nudging him out the stateroom door, which he promptly closed behind him. A moment later, they heard a thud, indicating Brutus had parked himself in his standard boneless heap just outside the door.

Quinn turned back to Riley. "No one can save you now, my pretty." She felt his weight on the side of the bed a moment later. "And if it's restraints ye be wantin' . . ."

She lifted her arm slightly to look at him. "Wait—"

He just grinned, and reached for his patch.

She grinned. "Leave it on."

"Aye aye, Cap'n," he said, and rolled on top of her.

He pushed her hands over her head, pinning them down as another breathless laugh escaped her. But that laughter quickly faded as he ran his hands down her arms, and straight over her breasts. She moaned and arched up hard against him as his fingers closed over her nipples.

"Oh, aye. A wench ye are indeed." He slid down and shoved her shirt up . . . and suddenly things shifted from light and funny to lusty and hot. He suckled one nipple and tore her shorts off as she yanked the white linen shirt he'd worn, thankfully open to the waist, from the waistband of his pants. In seconds she was naked and he was pulling on the buckle of his belt and dropping his pants on the floor.

She drove greedy hands into his hair and dragged his mouth to hers as he fell on top of her, parting her legs with the weight of his body. They growled as she shoved her tongue in his mouth just as he yanked her thighs up high on his hips and drove into her.

It was hot and wild. His mouth never left hers and he plundered it in the same rhythm and thrust as he plundered her. She didn't even try to keep from shouting as she came . . . and neither did he.

He collapsed on top of her while still throbbing inside her. She shuddered in the throes of rippling aftershocks. They were breathing so hard, neither could speak. He finally rolled off, tugging her hard against him, her body half splayed across his torso and legs as they dragged air into greedy lungs.

With her cheek pressed against the damp, hot skin of his chest, she felt his hands slide into her hair, stroking, toying. He tucked her foot around his ankle, and slid his other arm over the small of her back. Little things, instinctive things, they were the things that made her know he was always aware of her. Always. And he wanted her to know it.

She slid her hand up his chest, and cupped her palm to the side of his face. That was all, just pressed it there. With a little tilt of her head, she pressed a kiss over his heart. Because she wanted him to know it, too.

As their pounding hearts slowed along with their rapid intake of breath, he let the fingers that were teasing the ends of her hair wander slowly, lightly, across the tops of her shoulders, then traced a path along the length of her spine.

She moved the hand cupping his cheek so her fingers could slide into his thick hair, toy with it, tracing her fingertips around the shell of his ear.

And slowly her body began to stir all over again as she felt his begin to do the same.

Silently, wordlessly, he eased her to her back. Pushing her hair from her cheeks, he caught her gaze. The patch was gone, and his eyes were like blue crystals, dark and flashing, belying the exquisite gentleness of his touch and the protective way he sheltered her body with his own.

He cupped her face, and she felt the finest of tremors shaking his fingers. He tipped her mouth up to his, keeping his gaze locked on hers as he lowered his lips. The intensity was something she'd never seen in him before. When he kissed her it was as if her body, her mind . . . her heart—everything she was, or had ever wanted to be—opened to him. He'd laid her utterly bare, but in doing so, had bared himself to her as well.

As he took the kiss deeper, she gave herself over to him. In what was the most intimate act she'd ever experienced, it was the most vulnerable, honest, and elemental way she knew how.

He finally moved on top of her, and took her slowly, almost reverently. His rhythm was steady, powerful, claiming . . . just as it was nurturing, compelling, protective. He took her up, higher, sweeter. The only sounds were her gasps, as he took her right to the brink, and kept her there, winding slowly, ever tightening, until she thought she'd splinter into a thousand pieces if he didn't give her release—which was exactly when he jerked her gently over the edge. Pleasure cascaded through her like a waterfall, gently flowing until it went thundering over the edge and into the abyss.

He kissed her again, framing her face as he pushed deeper, and harder, and she could feel his heartbeat, thundering like her own, pressed against her.

"Riley." He said just the one word, the only word he'd spoken. She locked her gaze on his as he pushed one last time, hard, deep, and claimed her mouth as his body bucked, shuddered, and shook.

And that, she thought as she wrapped herself around him, holding the weight of him on top of her and him inside her, was how you made love.

They drifted, slept, and when she finally opened her eyes fully again, it was to discover at some point he'd pulled the covers over them. Quinn was on his back with her curled against him, her head on his chest, her leg entwined between his. His arm around the small of her back held her to him, and his other hand was tangled in the lengths of her hair as it draped across his chest.

His steady, even breathing didn't change as she slowly came awake, and she knew he was still deep in sleep. Staying where she was, which was right where she wanted to be, she let her thoughts wander where they would.

She closed her eyes and listened to the beat of his heart. *Well, you don't have to wonder if he's capable of being vulnerable with you.* She had no idea where that thought had come from. Maybe the intensity of their first time had left them with nothing to protect their more vulnerable selves.

She didn't know what she was feeling. But she knew she was herself with him, utterly and fully, all the time, in every moment they shared. And that apparently wasn't going to change.

She realized her ability to be so relaxed with him, so herself, was because she'd never had to strategize, or worry, or plan. She might wish she'd not been a klutz here or a dork there, but it went far deeper than that. At first that had been scary, had made her feel exposed, like her guard was constantly down. Thinking about it, she realized it wasn't because she was stripped bare of her defenses . . . it was because she had no need of them.

If she could purely be her true self there was nothing to defend, no inner part to protect. That begged the question . . . protect against what? What had she been so afraid of? Jeremy hadn't been harsh or critical. She had wondered what his true thoughts or feelings were at times, but he'd never overtly made her feel defensive.

She thought more about that. Though it might seem odd or wrong to be thinking back over personal times, intimate times, spent with one man, while lying in bed in the arms of another, it wasn't. She was so comfortable, relaxed, at peace, she could finally peel back some of those painful layers and put aside the hurt brought on by betrayal. She could finally look at what her life had been then in a more rational, objective, maybe even impersonal, way.

It was true that Jeremy had been somewhat picky about certain things—particular, he called it. She had known there had been a certain amount of passive-aggressive manipulation on his part, to get what he wanted from her. But it had been so benign. She was, by nature, a pleaser, and she'd loved him, and he'd loved her, so she'd never thought of it as anything other than what someone does when they're in a relationship.

With the luxury of dispassionate hindsight, she played back moments, and comments, reactions, interactions. Patterns of behavior began to emerge. Not just his, but hers as well. She'd never really asserted her opinions or her wants with him. She'd been so happy to be part of that pair her focus had been on making it a happy, joyful world to exist in. If she'd been asked then, she'd have said she had everything she wanted. If he was happy, so was she. Certainly, he had habits that annoyed her, routines that didn't mesh with hers, opinions she didn't share, but those were all things she knew were just part of their yin and yang. It was normal. What wasn't necessarily normal, and what she saw now, was while Jeremy wasn't the type to directly point out her flaws or shortcomings as he saw them, he found a way to make it known to her that maybe it would be better—for her—if she changed this, or did that.

Even that was part and parcel of a relationship. She didn't have to make any of those adjustments, though she always had. Making him happy had brought her joy. But, she realized, she'd never let him know about those same sorts of little things that bugged her. Not because she'd been afraid of making him angry. He was the most even-tempered person she knew. She had loved that about him, in fact. It had made her feel safe and secure knowing he'd never fly off the handle. No, that wasn't it at all.

She realized she hadn't pushed any of those opinions, or wants or needs at him, because she'd suspected he wouldn't have been moved to do for her what she so happily and willingly did for him. It wouldn't have mattered to him. Making her happy in that way was not something that motivated him, especially if it meant doing something he didn't want to do.

She'd been so busy making both of them happy, and maintaining the status quo, it had never occurred to her he wasn't really having to do much of anything. She'd felt needed by him, vital to his happiness. She supposed she had been, but not in the way she'd thought, or the way she should have been.

It wasn't until the images and memories finally began to

coalesce into an accurate picture of what their lives had really been that she understood the real, painful truth: he'd never loved her. Of course, it might have been the only way he knew how to be a partner, how to love. What did that say? What she saw so clearly was that he hadn't loved her the way she'd assumed he had, or in the way she'd counted on him to. Much less the way she'd loved him.

What she'd thought of as their inseparableness had been Jeremy's neediness. He'd relied on her for everything. It had made her feel wanted. Strong. Equal. Loved. But when had he ever been there for her? Those times when he appeared to anticipate her needs, brought home dinner—or got her a spa day—she saw that he was really serving his own needs.

That led her to a more personal, painful truth. She'd spent most of the time after their breakup wondering what had been lacking in her, where had she gone wrong, what hadn't she done right, or what did she need to improve about herself. The only person she'd been letting down and disappointing, whose love she hadn't been living up to . . . was her own.

What she'd needed to do to improve herself was, essentially, grow a pair. Value herself. Acknowledge she had needs that were at least as important as his. Stand up for herself. *Be* herself.

Somehow, somewhere along the way since coming to Sugarberry, she'd become that woman. The woman she should have been, and should have lived up to, all along.

That woman wouldn't have put up with Jeremy's "particularness," at least not without asserting some "particularities" of her own. That woman would have seen through the affection and recognized it as clinginess. In fact, had she been then the woman she was right now, she'd never have fallen in love with Jeremy Wainwright in the first place.

Riley's eyes blinked wide open. *Wow.* When, exactly, had she stopped loving Jeremy? And how?

Had it come from finally making choices purely for herself? Had it come from making new friends, real friends? From gaining confidence in who she was, merely by getting up every day and being that person without having to make adjustments for any other person? On the heels of that realization was another revelation. While Jeremy definitely made it known what he expected from her, she realized she'd made a lot of personal adjustments in anticipation of what he'd want. That was entirely on her. Oftentimes, he'd never even asked. She'd made sure he didn't have to— which meant keeping expectations that, in essence, she'd created herself.

Not that Jeremy wasn't a complete and utter *bastarde!* for what he'd done to her, but if she'd been remotely the person she was now, she'd have seen through his bullshit so early on, he'd never have had a chance to pull that selfish stunt on her. She'd have dumped his self-centered ass long before.

She laughed silently at herself, wondering why on earth if felt so good to realize what a ridiculous, blind, needy, clinging dork she'd truly, truly been. Finally . . . she got it. She really got it. She knew exactly who she was. And therefore . . . who she'd never, ever be again.

That brought her to Quinn.

She shifted, propped her chin on his chest, and watched him sleep. Had he been part of the transformation? She knew the answer to that. And it was a relief. No. She'd already become who she needed to be, a better woman, a better friend. She'd done that for herself, no one else.

She thought about Quinn's words that day on the beach, about her valuing herself, trusting herself, and finally she understood what he'd been trying to tell her. She'd been that better woman. She just hadn't tried her new confidence out yet. He'd given her the chance to see herself for who she was now . . . and to put that newfound knowledge to work.

Just as her friendships with Lani and Char had helped her to see her value as a friend, Quinn had allowed her to realize her true value as a partner. He had been that final piece falling into place, showing her what a real partner was in return. It was what she'd seen with Lani and Baxter, Char and Carlo. Quinn was someone who would be there for her, see her for who she really was . . . and support that person. Maybe even love that person. He'd encouraged her, pushed her to believe in what he knew to be true, to believe she was the woman he was falling for. And trust that woman could handle falling right back.

And she had. Oh yes. Yes, indeed she had.

Chapter 21

Quinn had been awake for some time before he let Riley know about it. He lay there, almost hearing the singing of the wheels as they spun around, furiously, inside her head.

He wished like hell he knew where those spinning wheels were taking her. He couldn't see her face, so he had no easy gauge.

He hadn't forgotten a single, heart-searing moment of what they'd done together in that bed this morning, and he knew she hadn't either. It had been wild and raw, driving him so far past anything he'd experienced in the way of pure, unadulterated pleasure. They'd given themselves over to it with utter abandon and intensity, and had been amply and exhaustively rewarded.

He knew there was trust in that, to let go and to reach like they had. It wasn't just about heart-slamming, body-pounding sex. What they'd done was possible only because they'd given themselves to each other, trusting the other to match them shout for shout, thrust for thrust.

And then there was that second time . . . He squeezed his eyes more tightly shut against the sudden hot sting he felt as tears welled.

He loved her. Hard. Complete. Epic. It was his grand-parents' love story. It was the reason Joe and Hannah's love story was thumping out of him. And it was going to be his own love story . . . . if he hadn't just scared the living beje-sus out of her while he'd let everything bottled up inside him come pouring out in one steady flowing, never-ending stream of gushing emotion.

For the very first time, he understood the depths of the soul-chilling fear that had kept Riley from reaching for love again. It would hurt more than a little if she left him now, if she decided, nope, this wasn't going to be it for her.

She was it for him. If she walked away, she'd be ripping out everything that was good inside him, and taking it right along with her.

How did anyone go on after something like that? How did anyone even think such a risk was anything other than the most insane act they could ever willingly embark upon? Who in their having-ever-loved mind would put themselves in that place, knowing firsthand the risks they were taking?

Riley had, his little voice snuck in and whispered.

She had at that. She'd taken the initial leap. She might not land where he wanted her to, but the respect he had for how innately strong she truly was had grown to strato-spheric heights as he'd lain in bed. He doubted he would ever be able to do the same.

It also gave him a new understanding of his father's choices. Riley might not understand what she'd done in moving forward, but Quinn understood it. His father had chosen the opposite of Riley. He'd chosen to completely close himself off from feeling anything for anyone. He'd turned inward, focusing on things meaningful to him, like his work, that he could walk away from at the end of the day.

Riley hadn't done that. She thought she'd closed herself off from risking her heart. But look what she'd done. She'd taken her dog and run away to hide, yes. But she'd made a home for herself here. Made friends, good friends. Made a place for herself in the community, cared for people, as they'd come to care about her. Started, in essence, the family that her fiancé's choices had robbed her of having. To take it one step further, she'd taken on a job that allowed her to turn house after house into home after home, to pour all of what she wanted into everything she did. He wondered if she realized that instead of closing any part of herself off, she'd put herself out there.

He hoped he'd have done the same. He thought about his life. He kept people at arm's length. Friends were casual, or more associates and peers than real buddies. He'd tried to reach out to his father; it wasn't that he didn't want family. The bottom line was, the people who presently had the deepest entrée to his personal life were on his payroll, for God's sake. Not that they hadn't developed an honest respect and affection for one another . . . but was that the best he could do when it came to building a family?

And there was Riley.

Maybe he'd just needed someone to show him the way. How to bridge the gap between himself and his father . . . to his grandparents.

Thank God for her all over again. He'd been correct, believing that when it was the right thing, it became more all on its own. Important and special, there was no other way for it to be. It was the most mysterious thing, and the simplest thing in the world to see—when he'd finally seen it.

What in the hell could he do so she'd love him back?

He felt her subtly shift her weight, and felt her gaze, even with his eyes still closed, steadily on his face. He debated on how to handle this morning. What he wanted to do was open his eyes and tell her he loved her, straight out. He realized that he was dying to tell her, to share it with her . . . as he did every other thing that happened as his days bumped along. She'd so swiftly become his friend and his lover, his companion and his cohort. How could he keep something so important from her?

He cracked one eye open, and her brown eyes were shining right into his. A smile immediately curved those beautiful, lush lips. Everything inside him relaxed.

Calm down, Brannigan. He had time. Thank God. No need to rush things and blow it. She was happy and smiling. That was enough. For now. He'd tell her when she was ready. He could wait for that. He'd waited his whole life, after all.

He opened his other eye and let himself enjoy the simple and exquisite pleasure of drinking his fill of her, understanding he was already half buzzed on love.

"Morning, Cap'n," she said, all double dimples, and looking like the cat with the proverbial canary.

His grin was slower, but curved just as deeply. He lazily wrapped one of her blond curls around his finger and tugged her gently closer. "So"—the word came out as a gravelly drawl—"I can't wait to play doctor and naughty nurse."

She snorted a little giggle, which made him chuckle. "Can we take turns with the roles?"

He lifted his eyebrows, but pretended to give it some thought. "Okay. But candy stripes really aren't my color."

There was a scratching sound at the stateroom door.

Riley lifted a warning finger. "No stethoscope for Brutus. He'll just eat it."

Quinn laughed huskily. "So noted." He glanced at the clock. "Uh-oh. Somebody is really late for work." He lightly slapped her butt. "Naughty pirate wench."

"I didn't get the chance to tell you earlier, as you were too busy ravaging my lusty and voluptuous pirate booty. I don't have to be there until eleven."

"That might be the second best news I've had so far today. What say we go avail ourselves of that hearty repast?"

"That sounds heavenly. I'll take your pirate matey out there in the hall for his walk if you'll do the reheating."

"Deal."

She started to shift so she could sit up, but stopped and leaned down, kissing him, not on the mouth . . . but on his chest. Right over his heart. She looked up, and there was a spectacular shine in her eyes. "What was the first best news you've had today?"

All of his carefully laid plans went right up in smoke.

"That I love you."

She froze.

He closed his eyes. *Seriously, Brannigan?* The single most important thing, the *only* thing he had to get right, and—

"Good," she whispered.

He froze.

"Quinn."

He opened his eyes.

She was smiling, dimples winking, brown eyes dancing, freckled cheeks blooming pink. Her hair was a wild halo around her head. She had a Bullwinkle bandage on her elbow, and her massive dog was heavily snort-breathing under the bedroom door. "I didn't want you to have your eyes closed the first time I told you I loved you."

Suddenly it was the Fourth of July inside his head, his heart, and he was pretty sure all over the universe as he knew it. He rolled her to her back, framed her face with his hands.

"You do." Making it more statement than question, he needed to make sure he hadn't gone to some parallel dimension in his head after blurting out his own admission. "You're sure?"

She placed her hand over his heart. "I, Riley Brown, love you, Quinn Brannigan, with my whole messed-up, beat-up, but resilient-as-all-hell heart."

"How?"

She spluttered a laugh. "*How*? What do you mean, how? Hopefully really, really well."

He tried to get his galloping heart and his even more unruly thundering thoughts under control. "It wasn't that long ago that you couldn't even—"

She touched his lips with her finger. "You helped me figure it out, to see who I'd already become. You pushed me, you believed in me, you badgered me . . . and this morning you loved me. At least that's what it felt like to me."

"It was. I am so head over heels in love with you."

Sudden tears sparkled on her lashes, but the light in her eyes was a joyous one. "That's what I knew I wanted to get to. I watched you sleep this morning, and I thought over everything, and I have clarity now. I see what it was with Jeremy. What I was. And what I wasn't. I know who I've become, Quinn. A woman who wants to love and be loved, and who finally understands how. Then I looked at you . . . and realized I'm already there."

"Would you have told me? Had I not—"

"I don't know." He appreciated that truth. Because it helped him to believe the rest.

She smiled again. "Were you planning on telling me?"

"I wanted to. I wanted to shout it. But I wanted you to have time and space. I wanted you to be more sure. Of me. Of you."

"What happened?"

"You kissed my heart, and then you smiled at me with your heart in your eyes. When you asked me what the best news was, there was nothing to say but the God's honest truth. I couldn't *not* say it."

Her eyes grew extra shiny and the self-deprecating laughter that followed was sweet music. "I'm pretty sure that's what I would have done, too. But I'm glad you said it first."

"Sure, sure," he teased, "piggyback on." Just like that,

everything slid back into place, that rhythm, that space they'd carved out just for the two of them, that only they understood, where only they existed.

"Look at it this way," she said. "You got to hear it like I did, all curled up in our bed, happy and satiated after an amazing morning of hot sex and wonderful lovemaking. Left up to me, you know I'd have probably blurted it out at the most inappropriate time, in God only knows what place, or in front of who knows who." She lifted her head, and kissed his mouth. Gentle, sweet, pure. "I'm glad we got to have it right here on our little pirate ship, just between the two of us."

A bellowing, door-rattling *woof* reverberated around the stateroom.

"Three of us," she amended, and they laughed.

"Can I tell you the third best news?"

"You don't have to be the one to take him for a walk?" Riley guessed.

Quinn rolled to his back and slid her on top of him. "You said our bed."

"Well, it is our bed. Wait, you don't think we're going to share it with—" She nodded to the door.

He barked out a laugh. "Uh, no. He can sleep on the floor if he wants though." He nestled her more snugly on top of him. "I just liked that instead of yours and mine . . . there's an ours now."

"Yeah," she said, and leaned down. "Yours," she breathed, as she kissed him long and slow, bringing all those banked embers back to life. "Mine," she panted, sliding his hand down until it covered her breast, where he rubbed, rolled, tweaked.

He lifted her hips even as she started to do so herself, sliding her body down over his, until they were fully, completely joined.

"And ours," they said together.

* * *

Outside the door, Brutus rested his mighty head on his paws as he made himself more comfortable. He'd wait. It was okay. After all, he had a family to look after now.

With that in mind, he rolled slowly over to his side, letting out a long, sleepy sigh as he relaxed his back against the door. Yep. It was a job he planned to take very, very seriously. As laughter pealed on the other side of the door, and someone burst into song, he closed his eyes . . . and let his tongue loll happily to the side.

Epilogue

Riley glanced at the clock in Quinn's kitchen, and sidled over to the crystal cupcake display. Half past one in the morning. The poker tournament had finally wound down and was officially over. Thank God.

"Lost twenty bucks," Quinn said as he came in through the door from the deck.

"How'd that happen?" Riley eyed one of Lani's few remaining dark chocolate and raspberry cupcakes, but decided it was just too late to give in to temptation.

Quinn bent down and pressed a kiss to the side of her neck. "There was a pool going as to whether the police would be summoned before or after midnight. Person picking the closest time in a fifteen-minute interval wins."

"The police weren't here, were they? What did I miss?"

"Nothing," he said, turning her into his arms. "That's why I lost the twenty."

"Ah," she said, smiling. "Sucker."

"Apparently." He leaned down and trailed his tongue along her jaw, to her ear. "And yet, you never seem to complain . . ."

As tired as she was, he stirred her body to life. She

should be used to that by now. Or dead. She had no idea where their stamina was coming from. She figured it was a good thing they both had jobs to do or they might never wear clothes. Turned out naked sunset cruise time was pretty fun.

"How did that last part of the scene you were working on go?" she asked. "Did you get all the right info for the dressage stuff, for the horse show?"

"I did. Then they ended up not going."

"Why?"

He grinned. "Never could get them out of that damn hayloft."

"Ungrateful characters. After you did all that research."

He shrugged. "That's okay. It didn't suck to be me today, either way."

"Well, when you put it like that." Riley leaned up and kissed him. "Although I'm beginning to see a trend with this sucking thing and you, today."

"Day's not over either." Quinn plucked a cupcake from the display and dangled it in front of her. "Pirate's ship or knight's castle?"

"I'm so tired, I don't know if it's going to matter. So don't go dangling your . . . cupcakes at me."

"Still in public," Char sang as she swooped into the kitchen with another bag of trash.

Riley looked past Quinn's shoulder. "You said get a room, you didn't specify which one."

Quinn turned her around and pulled her back against him, looping his arms around her waist as he rested his weight on the breakfast nook table. Only Riley understood the real reason for his snuggled pose. It was presently pressed against her backside.

She wiggled, just slightly, and his arms tightened like steel bands. He leaned down and pressed a kiss near her ear. "Careful what you wriggle for," he whispered.

"Do you need a hand with that?" Riley asked Char, then wriggled, just a tiny bit, once more.

"No, this is the last round."

"Outstanding menu," Quinn said to Charlotte, who was scooping up the last few disposable plates and cups and adding them to her trash bag. "The savory and the sweet. Please give my regards to Carlo. I'll pass the word to my agent and publisher. They often have to entertain at things like regional book fairs, writers' conferences, that sort of thing, and are always looking for the best and most interesting."

Charlotte smiled. "Thank you. That's very kind." To Riley, she said, "Okay, we'll keep him." Adding the full trash bag to the ones already lined up along the wall, Char snatched up another empty tray and bustled to the door, at which point she glanced over her shoulder.

But Riley beat her to it. "It's only still in public because the public isn't leaving."

Quinn chuckled as Charlotte sailed out.

"She's just grumpy because her panky isn't here," Riley told him.

Char's catering service had been double booked at the eleventh hour. By stepping in and taking over a birthday celebration bash for one of the mayor's closest aides when his caterer backed out at the last minute, Char and Carlo were likely to get many other bookings, not to mention being owed a favor by the mayor. It meant Charlotte had run Alva's event, while Carlo had done the birthday party.

"What's a panky?" Quinn asked.

"Long story," Riley said, just as Dre hustled in with another loaded tray. Because of the double booking, she'd stepped in to help serve.

"She was dealing off the bottom," Dre was saying. "Hey, Riley. Hey, Quinn." Dre turned back to Franco as he came in behind her. "I saw her with my own eyes."

"No one said a word to her," Franco responded, and Dre leveled a look of disbelief at him. "Okay, fine," he went on, "but if Alva was dealing from the bottom, why wasn't Beryl getting better hands? Suzette took half the pot tonight."

"I said I saw her deal from the bottom. I didn't say she was any good at it. And, if you noticed, Beryl won the trip to Baxter's taping *and* one of Quinn's books."

"This is true."

Charlotte came in again. "This is the last of it." To Quinn, she said, "Are you certain you don't mind me coming back tomorrow to get all my stuff? Carlo is stuck in Savannah. The party is going way over, and I won't get our van back until—"

"It's fine, really," Quinn assured her. "Is there anything I can do to help?"

"No. I'll have some helpers with me tomorrow. We need to come get all the equipment for another event the day after tomorrow."

"It's an anti-versary party," Franco added. "For a group of divorcées. Should be interesting."

"Interesting is certainly one word," Charlotte said. "Can you still drive me back tonight?"

"Of course, *ma petite.*" He looked at Dre. "You ready?"

"As ever." Dre took off her Sweet and Savory server's jacket.

"You are godsends, both of you," Char said. She turned back to Riley and Quinn. "We leave you in privacy."

"You did good," Riley told her. "All I heard were raves."

"Except for old Mrs. Lauderberg," Dre added. "But considering she was sampling all the garnishes and not any of the actual food, I don't think that counts. She kept complaining how bitter everything was. I tried to tell her parsley snips weren't part of the serving menu, but she smacked my hand when I tried to take her plate." Dre examined the back of her left hand. "Turns out she wears a lot of rings. Heavy ones."

"Tough audience," Quinn offered.

"You said it."

Saying their good nights, they all headed to the door.

"We'll see ourselves out," Franco said.

Char was the last one out, then turned back. "Oh, I almost forgot. When you see Lani tomorrow night—tell her I'm sorry I won't be there. I have to get all this transition and prep done, but let her know I think I have the perfect person for her to talk to."

Riley frowned. "About?"

"The mail-order business she's thinking about starting, as an adjunct to the cupcakery. Requests for mail orders keep flooding in every time the *Hot Cakes* road trip show is repeated. With Baxter being a constant draw to the area, and their joint cookbook coming out sometime next year, she thought it would be a good idea to get the mail-order division up and running. I'm surprised she hasn't said anything about it, with all the time you've spent working on the cookbook."

"She mentioned it. I just didn't realize she was going to move on it so fast."

"Well, only if they can find someone she can trust who can handle it, and hit the ground running. Anyway"— Charlotte fished in the pocket of her chef's jacket—"I'll just put her card here. Her name is Kit Bellamy."

"I'll make sure Lani gets it. I know she was bummed she couldn't be here." At one time, Riley had hoped she'd get sick so she could miss the tournament, but Lani actually had.

Char smiled. "Between you and me, I don't think she was that bummed."

Riley's eyes widened. "Are you saying she played hookey?"

"Maybe. Baxter got back from New York a day early. But you didn't hear it from me. Okay, I'm really leaving now." She looked at Quinn, then back at Riley. "Nice panky, I will give you that. Have a good night."

"What is it with this panky business?" Quinn said, barely waiting for the front door to close before he turned and neatly pinned Riley between him and the breakfast nook table behind her.

"No hanky-panky in the kitchen on club night unless everyone's hanky has a panky. Or something like that."

"Ah. That clears it right up."

"It made perfect sense at the time."

"So . . . I'm your official panky, am I?"

"That you are."

"Well, it's awfully convenient that we're in a kitchen. And you're the only hanky here."

"Hmm. You make a good point."

He pressed against her, and she grinned. "More than one, it would seem."

He lofted the cupcake again, then peeled the paper liner off with his teeth. "Did I mention that I'm plagued by this fantasy I've had? It involves you, a cupcake, some amazing chocolate frosting . . . and me getting the chance to lick it off."

"Funny, sounds like I've heard that story before."

"All but the licking it off part."

She pretended to think about that. "No . . . that was definitely part of the story." A slow smile spread across her face. "At least that's how I remember it playing out. And I remembered it . . . a lot."

"Funny, so did I."

"Huh. What should we do about that?" she asked.

"I think we should compare stories. See how they . . . stack up."

"Hmm. I think you're the one who told me that writers should always show . . . not tell."

"It really is the best way." Quinn popped open the buttons down the front of her blouse one at a time with his free hand.

Riley looked down. "You're very good at that."

"I'm very motivated at the moment. I'm really good when I'm motivated." He pushed her back onto the table, her blouse sliding down her arms as she braced herself. He flipped open the front catch of her bra on the first try.

"I've noticed that." Her breathing started to hitch a little as he spread her legs with his thighs . . . and dragged his finger through the thick, dark chocolate ganache frosting.

"Now, in your version of the story did I paint the frosting on?" He drew his frosting-covered finger down the center of her torso. "Or did I decorate the cupcake with a little . . ." He pressed the top of the cake onto her nipple, making her gasp.

"I—can't remember. Maybe . . . refresh my memory?"

Quinn pushed her all the way back on the table and leaned down over her, so he could retrace his actions . . . with his tongue.

"Still not sure," she managed, and earned a wicked chuckle as he lifted her hips off the table and slid pants and panties off.

"What time are you meeting Chuck to look at final brochure prints tomorrow?" he asked, as he reached for his pants buckle.

"Eight."

He grinned. "You might make that." Then he dipped her other nipple in frosting. "Or not."

She smiled up at him, then reached up and yanked him down on top of her. "I'll just blame it on the cupcakes."

In *Sweet Stuff*, Lani has Quinn and the rest of the Cupcake Club crew taste-test her newest creation, the Reverse Caramel Apple Cupcake. Just like a caramel apple, but with the caramel coating on the inside as filling. Now, this was a fictional cake—I just made it up—but it got me to thinking . . . hmmm . . . that *would* be yummy! So, as part of my ongoing research into all things cupcake, I set about figuring out how to make my own.

Naturally, the first step was to call my mom and find out if we had any great apple cake recipes in the family, and sure enough, we did! She sent me her Johnny Applesauce Cake recipe, which I adapted from loaf pans to cupcakes. Next, I had to figure out the caramel filling. I'm envisioning getting caramels and melting them, or using ice cream topping heated up—something like that. Color me surprised when I found out that you can make your own caramel. From scratch. I mean, of course *someone* had to make the first caramel at some point, but I thought it was kind of like Oreo cookies, i.e., you can't make them yourself. Wrong! You can. And I did! (And lived to tell!)

Of course, as soon as I saw words like "candy thermometer" and "360 degrees Farenheit," I immediately put my local hunky EMT on speed dial. Partly because, if you've read my cupcake research blog at www.cakesbythecupblog.com, you know that I've learned a local hunky EMT can come in really (really) handy at those times when you're trying not to blow things up or burn things down. And partly because, if you have a hunky EMT in your life for any reason, why not keep him on speed dial?

So, below is my "every baker" version of Lani's Reverse Caramel Apple Cupcake. You don't even have to be a big-time fancy pastry chef to make them. Enjoy!

Reverse Caramel Apple Cupcakes

Johnny Applesauce Cake

$^1/_2$ cup butter (1 stick, cut into pieces)
$1^3/_4$ cups sweetened applesauce (1-pound can or jar)
2 cups flour (not self-rising)
1 cup sugar
1 teaspoon salt
1 teaspoon soda
1 teaspoon cinnamon
1 teaspoon nutmeg
$^1/_4$ teaspoon ground cloves
1 cup raisins or chopped nuts (*optional*)

1. Preheat oven to 350 degrees F. Line 20–24 muffin tins with paper liners.
2. In a small saucepan, melt cut-up pieces of butter over medium heat.
3. In a large mixing bowl, combine all dry ingredients except raisins or nuts.
4. If you're making the cake, add in raisins or nuts and stir thoroughly. (For the purposes of caramel-filled cupcakes, I left out the raisins or nuts.)
5. Add in the applesauce and melted butter, and stir until well blended.
6. Spoon the batter into the paper cups until each is two-thirds full.
7. Bake 20–22 minutes until test toothpick comes out clean, or until a cupcake springs back when lightly touched in center.
8. Let cool in pan for 5 minutes, then transfer to wire rack to cool completely.
9. Use a paring knife or apple corer to remove the centers of each cake. (Reserve the cored pieces.)

Salted Caramel Filling

2½ cups sugar
⅔ cup water
1 tablespoon light corn syrup
¾ cup heavy whipping cream
2½ teaspoons sea salt

1. Heat sugar with the water and corn syrup in a heavy saucepan over high heat, stirring occasionally, until syrup is clear; clip a candy thermometer to the side of the pan and stop stirring.
2. Cook until syrup comes to a boil.
3. Boil until mixture is caramelized and just reaches 360 degrees F. (You can swirl the caramel in the pan as it boils to keep it from sticking to the sides, but be very careful as this mixture is very hot.)
4. Remove from heat and slowly pour in cream, stirring with a wooden spoon (plastic can melt at this temperature) until smooth.
5. Stir in sea salt.
6. Fill cupcakes immediately. If caramel begins to harden, heat again until soft.
7. Use a spoon to fill each cupcake with the caramel filling. The caramel will seep into the cake, so add a bit more to fill.
8. Plug the top of the cupcake with a piece of the cored filling before frosting.

Vanilla Buttercream Frosting

1 package powdered sugar (approximately 4 cups)
$\frac{1}{2}$ cup butter (1 stick), softened
3 tablespoons milk
2 teaspoons vanilla

1. Beat sugar and butter together, then add milk and vanilla with an electric mixer at low speed until well blended and smooth.
2. If the frosting is too thick, add more milk, one teaspoon at a time, until the frosting is smooth enough to frost the cupcakes.

Makes about $2\frac{1}{2}$ cups frosting for 20–24 cupcakes.

As part of my research for the Cupcake Club Romance series, I've been learning all about baking cupcakes. Beginning back in January 2011, I started sharing my adventures in baking with everyone via my author blog at www.donna kauffman.com/blog, as well as my designated research site, www.cakesbythecupblog.com (named after Lani's bakery, of course!) It's become a fun cupcake recipe destination for both readers and cupcake bakers alike. So, last summer, my wonderful publisher, Kensington, decided to amp up the cupcake excitement by launching the Original Cupcake Recipe contest. The prize? One very lucky reader would see his or her recipe published in an upcoming Cupcake Club Romance book. The contest was on!

Word spread quickly, and recipes started coming in from all over the world. Then Amazon.com heard about the contest, and asked if they could be part of the cupcake fun and judge the final round. Of course, we said yes! It was very challenging narrowing the field down to the final three, but we did, then sent off samples of the finalist cupcakes to Seattle for Amazon's final decision. They were so torn between Chocolate Meringue, Sweet Peach Tea, and the Fluffy Elvis that they asked to have the recipes sent their way for an in-house bake-off! In the end, it was close . . . but see the winning recipe below, submitted by Stephanie Gamverona, all the way from South Korea. (And if you're curious about the other two finalists, see the blogs mentioned above for those recipes.) We were thrilled with Amazon's choice. Stephanie's Sweet Peach Tea cupcake recipe truly embodied everything we thought was perfect for *Sweet Stuff* and the Cupcake Club Romance series, from the wonderful Georgia locale of the books to the complexity of the flavor profiles in the cake itself. This recipe is truly worthy of a cupcake that would be featured at Lani's Cakes by the Cup bakery. Enjoy! (I certainly did.)

Sweet Peach Tea Cupcakes

Sweet Tea Butter

1 cup unsalted butter
32 grams (about ⅓ cup) whole-leaf or loose-leaf black* tea

1. In a small saucepan, melt butter on medium-high heat until just melted.
2. Add tea leaves.
3. Continue heating mixture for about 5 minutes on low heat. Make sure mixture does not reach simmering point.
4. Remove from heat and allow to stand for another 5 minutes.

5. Pour mixture through fine sieve, pressing hard on tea leaves to squeeze out as much butter as possible.
6. Let tea-infused butter cool to room temperature and refrigerate until solid.
7. Use for Tea Cupcakes recipe below.

Tea Cupcakes

$1\frac{1}{2}$ cups sugar
Zest of 1 medium-size lemon
$\frac{2}{3}$ cup Sweet Tea Butter
3 eggs
$\frac{1}{2}$ teaspoon ground ginger**
$1\frac{1}{2}$ cups all-purpose flour
$\frac{1}{2}$ cup milk
1 cup finely chopped overripe peaches***

1. Preheat oven to 350 degrees Fahrenheit.
2. Line muffin tins with paper or foil baking cups, and spray lightly with cooking spray.
3. In a small mixing bowl, mix sugar and lemon zest. Allow to sit for at least 30 minutes.
4. In a large mixing bowl, stir Sweet Tea Butter with lemon sugar until mixture is smooth.
5. Beat in eggs, one at a time.
6. Beat in ginger.
7. Beat in flour, one cup at a time, alternating with tablespoons of milk.

   * Earl Grey may be substituted.
  ** Cinnamon may be substituted.
*** Canned lightly sweetened peaches, drained, may be substituted, but of course they don't taste as good as the real thing.

8. Gently fold in peaches.
9. Fill prepared cupcake liners two-thirds full.
10. Bake 18–23 minutes.
11. Frost with Peach Whipped Cream Frosting when completely cooled.

Peach Whipped Cream Frosting

1 cup heavy whipping cream
1/2 teaspoon pure vanilla extract
1 tablespoon sugar
1/2 cup lightly sweetened peach puree *or* peach preserves

1. In a large mixing bowl, place whipping cream, vanilla extract, and sugar, and stir with wire whisk to combine.
2. Cover bowl, and chill in refrigerator for at least 30 minutes.
3. When chilled, beat the mixture until soft peaks form.
4. Add sweetened peach puree a little at a time, beating just until stiff peaks form when whisk is raised.
5. Taste, and fold in more puree, if required.
6. Frost Tea Cupcakes once cupcakes are completely cooled.

Makes approximately 18 cupcakes.

Did you miss the first book in the Cupcake Club series?
Go back and read SUGAR RUSH!

"Take charge," she said flatly. "With Baxter. How often has anyone been successful doing that? Oh, right. Never."

"I'm simply saying—"

"Charlotte has a point," Franco chimed in. "At least you can let him know that you know what's going on, and set the tone for how you're going to handle it with him. You don't work for him anymore, you don't run his place anymore, you aren't beholden to him for anything, Leilani. Think about it. He has no hold on you."

Oh, if only that were true, Lani thought, then paused, hands ready at the squeeze. Franco did have a point, though. She really hadn't thought about the situation like that. Not in a purely professional sense. She'd been confronting the news like the woman she'd been before leaving New York, the one still pathetically half in love with a clueless man who'd have never even noticed her if it weren't for her crazy mad baking skills.

But she wasn't that woman any longer. Not entirely, anyway. It hadn't been all that long since she'd left New York for good, but so much had happened since she'd come to Sugarberry. Her entire life had changed. She had changed. "You know, maybe you're right."

A short cheer went up on the other end of the line.

"I want to hear every detail," Charlotte said.

"You go, *ma chérie amour!*" Franco sang out.

A series of buzzers going off came through the speaker. "I've got to go, the cakes are coming out," Charlotte said hurriedly.

"We've been making solidarity cakes this morning in support of you, *ma chère*," Franco said. "We're featuring your to-die-for black walnut spice cakes with cream cheese and cardamom frosting as today's special."

"Thanks, you guys," Lani said sincerely.

"Every detail! Call me!" Charlotte ordered before clicking off.

Lani stood there, pastry bag still at the ready, and looked at the racks in front of her. And thought about her friends in New York. Solidarity cakes. Salvation cakes. "Healing the disgruntled, displaced, and just plain dissed," she said, smiling briefly. "One cake at a time."

She and Charlotte knew a lot about that. They'd been friends since culinary school. Charlotte had more actual business experience than Lani, as she'd gone straight to work post-graduation as a pastry chef for a small boutique hotel in midtown, while Lani had gone overseas to continue her studies in Belgium and France. Lani's mom and dad had moved from D.C. to Sugarberry shortly after that.

It had been a time full of transition and change, but also one of promise and excitement. Lani's best friend had been launching her career in earnest while Lani was grabbing the chance to learn at the hands of Europe's best. For her dad, it had been retirement from the D.C. police force and taking on a very different challenge in Georgia . . . and for her mom, who'd grown up in Savannah, it had been a chance to go back home again, to a place she'd always missed dearly.

Lani and Char had kept in touch throughout that time, their friendship only deepening as their separate experiences widened their respective paths and boosted their dreams. When Lani had come back, Char was still in New York, having already worked her way up to executive pastry chef at the same hotel. Franco was on board by then as her right hand and had quickly become Lani's other best friend. Lani had gotten an offer in the city, as a staff baker for a well-known restaurant in a five-star, Upper East Side hotel. The same hotel that had just brought on board the hottest import from the U.K. America was the new playground for the young and impetuous, and ridiculously charismatic Baxter Dunne.

He'd risen quickly, and had taken Lani with him, plucking her from the ranks to make her his personal assistant and protégé when he'd opened Gateau a miraculous eighteen months later. His had been a rare, meteoric rise in a very challenging and competitive industry. By the time he'd made his move to the television cooking world three years later, his immediate dominance hadn't surprised anyone.

Lani blinked away mental images of him, how he'd been then, how totally infatuated she'd been with his charisma and his talent almost from the moment she'd first set foot in that Upper East Side kitchen. Okay, the lust had started before then. She'd known a lot about him, more than most, having heard quite a bit during her time in Europe. He was three years younger than her, and light-years ahead in every way measurable in their field. The baker in her wanted to be him when she grew up. And, the woman in her wanted to be with him *as* a grown-up. It had been harmless idolatry and fantasy.

Then she'd gotten the opportunity of a lifetime.

She'd been convinced the heavens and fates were sending her a direct message when she'd tried for, and gotten the job working under him.

Under him.

Lani made a face at that unfortunate double entendre and moved to a fresh rack of cupcakes, forcing her thoughts back to the job at hand.

The pathetic irony was that she'd wished she had been under him. In every possible sense. Then everyone else had speculated, quite nastily, that the very same thing was actually happening. When it wasn't. Lose-lose.

The competition in any kitchen was fierce, but with a rising star like Baxter running the show, the battle to dominate his kitchen was downright apocalyptic, the chance to make a name and launch huge careers the spoils of winning the war. He was the epitome of the golden boy, from his looks to his demeanor, to his unparalleled talent. The speculation regarding their relationship was the hot topic of the day, every day. Fueled by jealousy, fear, and paranoia, the chatter was nasty and vicious. And not particularly quiet.

In order to keep up with the chaotic pace and the insane demands, every kitchen had to work like a well-oiled machine, which meant teamwork in the most basic sense. It was a close, if not close-knit, environment, where you worked all but on top of each other. There was no place to go, no place to hide. And certainly no place to speak privately. Not that the gossips would have bothered to, anyway.

Every chance they got, at least when Baxter didn't have her working right by his side, they'd done everything they could to undermine her.

As her esteem had risen in his eyes, and he'd given her more and more preferential treatment, the gossip had just gotten uglier and uglier. What could he possibly see in the mousy girl from D.C. who was too nice to know better? What made her so special? That Lani was certain she'd looked at Baxter like the pathetic little smitten kitten she'd been only made the whole ordeal even more painful to recall. She'd tried to rein that part in when she'd realized what was happening, heard what was being said. She knew she was only hurting herself further with her stupid crush, personally and professionally.

Of course, at some point, as it all escalated, she'd privately thought—hoped—that Baxter would ride to her rescue. He was the white knight, after all, wasn't he?

So many illusions had been shattered, so rapidly. She was tougher than any of them had thought, her time overseas preparing her in ways many of them couldn't have imagined. She was calm and well mannered because she chose to be, not because she was some silly ninny who couldn't defend herself. She simply chose not to, as any attempt would be drowned out by the chorus against her, anyway. She'd rather hoped her hard work and Baxter's faith in her would speak for her, but that hadn't been the case. So, ultimately, she'd figured out that if she wanted to survive there, the easiest path was simply to stay in her own world, build a certain kind of calm around her, where she could focus on learning. And on Baxter. Preferably doing both at the same time. But . . . not always.

She'd endured almost five years of that constant bedlam. And, in doing so, had learned more, professionally, from Baxter, than she'd ever hoped. She had no regrets. So what if Baxter never had come to her rescue? So what if he had, in fact, thrown her directly to those very same wolves when he'd left for the bright lights of his own brand-new television show, and put Gateau, his baby, essentially in her hands? She'd done it, hadn't she? She'd shown them all.

Though it had come at a cost. No matter how calm and

centered she remained, that kind of life took a toll. She thought about all the baking therapy she and Char had done together during that time. Usually in the wee, wee hours. Those sessions never had anything to do with their respective jobs.

And everything to do with salvation.

Their worlds might be uncontrolled chaos, but baking always made sense. Flour, butter, and sugar were as integral a part of her as breathing.

Lani had long since lost count of the number of nights she and Charlotte had crammed themselves into her tiny kitchen, or Charlotte's even tinier one, whipping up this creation or that, all the while hashing and rehashing whatever the problems du jour happened to be. It was the one thing she truly missed about being in New York.

No one on Sugarberry understood how baking helped take the edge off. Some folks liked a dry martini. Lani and Char, on the other hand, had routinely talked themselves down from the emotional ledge with rich vanilla queen cake and some black velvet frosting. It might take a little longer to assemble than the perfect adult beverage . . . but it was the very solace found in the dependable process of measuring and leavening that had made it their own personal martini. Not to mention the payoff was way, way better.

Those nights hadn't been about culinary excellence, either. The more basic, the more elemental the recipe, the better. Maybe Lani should have seen it all along. Her destiny wasn't to be found in New York, or even Paris, or Prague, making the richest, most intricate cakes, or the most delicate French pastries. No, culinary fulfillment—for her, the same as life fulfillment—was going to be experienced on a tiny spit of land off the coast of Georgia, where she would happily populate the world with gloriously unpretentious, rustic, and rudimentary little cupcakes.

"That's me." She lifted her pastry bag in salute. "Cupcake Baker Barbie!" She aimed the silver tip, and bulleted a row of raspberry shots with rapid-fire precision, then another, and another, before finally straightening, spent pastry bag cocked on her shoulder like a weapon. She was a take-no-prisoners Baker Barbie, that's what she was. "Yeah. Welcome to the Cupcake Club," she said, giving it her best Brad Pitt impersonation. She grinned at that, and tried to convince herself she was ready to take on the true test of her newfound toughness, the real proof of her independence.

The phone call.

She could do it. She would do it. She didn't need to bow down to the whims of Baxter Dunne any longer. Wasn't she standing right there, in her own kitchen, working for her very own self?

"Damn straight I am." She moved to the next tray, discarding the spent bag for a freshly filled one, then positioning it like an expert sniper lining up his next kill shot. "Hear that, Chef Hot Cakes?" She completed the next three rows with deadly precision. "I . . . don't . . . need . . . you." She punctuated each word with another squeeze.

She straightened. And swore. "Yeah, that's why I'm standing here at the crack of dawn, shooting raspberry truffle filling like a woman armed with an AK-47." But, she had to admit, it felt good. Powerful, even.

Salvation cakes, indeed.

So, she went with it. Moving to the last tray, she shot another squirt of raspberry, picturing his smiling, handsome face as she did so. "*Why* are you doing this to me, Bax?" *Pow, pow, pow.* "Why are you invading my world?" *Bap, bap, bap.* "*My* world, *my* kitchen, *my* home." So many questions scrambling her brain. Making it impossible to think straight, impossible to concentrate on anything except—

"Dammit!" Lani glared at the oozing, overly truffled

cupcake like it had committed an unspeakable cupcake crime.

She blamed Baxter for that, too.

She might have growled, just a little. It was stupid to be so upset about this. Like Franco said, she was operating from a position of strength here. Who cared why he was coming to town?

Or what laying eyes on him again might make her feel?

She'd handled worse things, she reminded herself. Far, far worse things. Losing her mother two years ago. Almost losing her father ten months ago. "I can handle Baxter Dunne," she muttered.

But as she stood there with flour powdering her hair, a smear of raspberry truffle across her chin, a spent pastry bag in her hand—happily content in her own element—she thought about it all, and tried to harness her inner Smackdown Baker Barbie . . . she really did. But she kept picturing his face, hearing his voice, seeing his hands move so precisely perfect, so beautifully efficient as he worked, making every step look so effortless, so simple . . . and wishing he'd put those smart and clever hands on her . . . and found herself failing. Miserably.

The sound of the delivery door slapping shut behind her made her spin abruptly around, the flailing pastry bag sending at least a half dozen freshly filled cupcakes skittering to the floor.

The sight that met her eyes sent her heart skittering as well. As only Baxter could.

He was very tall, with long arms and legs that would be gawky and awkward on anyone else, but were graceful and elegant on his lean, muscular frame. He had a wild thatch of wheat-blond hair that was forever sticking out in all directions, brown eyes so rich and warm they rivaled even the most decadent melted chocolate, and a ridiculously charming, crooked grin that always made her secretly wonder what trouble he was about to get into . . . and wish, desperately, that she could join him.

"Hello, luv. Happy to see me? My God, you look a fright."

And, always—always—too late, she remembered the trouble she was forever getting into . . . was him.

Can't wait to get back to Sugarberry Island
and the Cupcake Club?
You're in luck!
BABYCAKES is available now!

Here's a taste to whet your appetite.

Sugarberry Island.

If a person was going to start her life over, Kit had to admit there was a storybook feel to the name alone, with a happily-ever-after implied, if not guaranteed. But she couldn't imagine what a happily-ever-after would even look like. She'd be happy to get through the days feeling as if she was contributing something important to something that mattered. Of course, if her business friend, Charlotte, was to be believed, Sugarberry offered her all that and more.

It had been two weeks since the courts had handed Teddy and Tas-T-Snaks their final victory. Fourteen days since Mamie Sue's officially no longer belonged to a single Bellamy. And almost the same number of months since she'd had regular employment. That she still had this particular job offer, one that was pretty sweet no matter how you defined it, was nothing short of miraculous. Charlotte had come to her with the possible offer right after the sale to Tas-T-Snaks hit the news the year before. But Kit had turned the job down when she'd decided to fight Teddy and Tas-T-Snaks.

A year later, that fight was over. After delays of her own, Leilani Dunne was still interested in finding someone to run Babycakes, the planned shipping and catering business that would adjoin her successful cupcakery, Cakes by the Cup.

Kit knew she should be jumping at the chance and thanking her lucky stars the offer was still on the table. The position was so important to her prospective employer though, Kit wouldn't have taken the position unless she'd stick with it. The last thing she could handle was disappointing someone else.

Hence the five-hour drive to the little barrier island off the Georgia coast—a big change from Atlanta, former home of Mamie Sue's pies, and, if all went well during the on-site job interview . . . former home of Kit Bellamy.

Charlotte had warned her Sugarberry wasn't anything like the city, or even like the ritzier islands down in the central and southern part of the barrier chain. Being one of the northernmost islands, it was still largely a wilderness area, only partly developed and inhabited. As she had defined it, it was a traditional small Southern town, with a distinctly unique island flair. That part had sounded perfectly fine to Kit. Disappearing to a wilderness island after being front-page news in Atlanta for the past year sounded downright heavenly. It was the rest of it she was uncertain about.

Kit felt confident she had the skills for the job, but in every other possible way, it was about as different from the life she'd had at Mamie Sue's as it could be. She thought about all the stories her mom, Grandma Reenie, and Grammy Sue had told her growing up, about how her great-grandmother, as a young military bride, had started the company in the Bellamy House kitchen during World War I.

Kit loved those stories, had never tired of hearing them. They were inspirational and motivational, but she loved them mostly because of the reminiscing smiles they brought to the faces of the three women as they recalled the fond memories they shared. Kit had loved being a part of that bond, the passing down of so many traditions, feeling connected to something so important, the fruits of the hard labors and talents and dreams of those very same women.

Dreams she'd managed to shatter in the span of six short years.

Kit forcibly tamped down the guilt and anger living inside her. The day was about next steps and new possibilities. Her thirtieth birthday was on the near horizon. She'd sort of made that her mental deadline for getting her act together and having a new plan in place. If all went well, she'd be ahead of schedule on some of it, anyway

"And we always like being ahead of schedule!" she said, a slight smile ghosting her mouth as she intoned the chipper phrase Reenie had been so fond of repeating.

If it wasn't for the grief and anger, Kit might have been truly excited about the idea of tackling a small, independent business and having her hands in on the initial growth and development. Being part of a new story with its own lore and legends was both an opportunity and a potential blessing. As she bumped over the grid at the far end of the causeway and turned onto Sugarberry, she imagined what words of wisdom, encouragement, or concern the Bellamy women might have offered.

"I know I let you all down," she said softly. "Horribly. Unforgivably. I trusted when I shouldn't have. I took my eye off the ball, because I thought it was safely tucked away. But if there's a way to make you proud of me again, you know I'll find it."

On that, the most optimistic note she'd managed since walking, stunned, out of that boardroom a year ago, she wound her way around the tiny, but charming town square and pulled into the little lot off the alley running behind the row of shops that included Cakes by the Cup. "Here goes nothing." *And everything.*

She tapped a quick knock on the frame of the screen door at the back entrance as instructed. She could hear music playing through the partially opened door behind the screen. The song was "Theme from a Summer Place," which made Kit smile. Mamie Sue had loved that song, mostly because she adored "that handsome Troy Donahue," who had starred, along with Sandra Dee, in the film of the same name in the late fifties. In addition, someone was talking quite animatedly over the music, making it impossible not to inadvertently eavesdrop.

"Well, I was as stunned as anybody, except maybe Birdie. Could have knocked me over with a feather when she told me that Asher's younger brother had claimed custody of her little grandbaby. But now that Morgan is actually here on Sugarberry, I just don't know what to think."

"Well, I think it's good," came a second voice, younger, steadier. "Great, even. I assume he's here because he wants Birdie to be part of Lilly's life."

"So he says," the older woman responded. "But can you really trust anything a Westlake says?"

Kit had lifted her hand to knock again, but froze at the sound of that name. *Westlake.* She shook her head. Coincidence. Surely the Westlakes who had helped dismantle four generations of hard work and dedication weren't the only Westlakes in Georgia The older woman had said the names Morgan and Asher. Neither rang a bell with Kit, but that didn't mean much. She hadn't done any research on the firm Teddy had hired. She hadn't needed to.

The Westlakes were an Atlanta institution, as was their generations-old law firm. Despite any successes her pie company might have achieved, the Westlakes ran in very different circles from the Bellamys. They were old money. Very old. Everyone knew of them, like everyone knew of the royal family.

Kit had never paid any attention to them or their frequent mentions in the political and social pages. They'd never been of any personal interest to her. Until they'd sat, with smug superiority, across the courtroom from her, she couldn't have named any one of them. All Kit knew was that Teddy had been a frat brother of one of the Westlakes, hence their prestigious name and power lent to Teddy's, and Tas-T-Snaks' cause. Trixie, on the other hand, probably knew their entire detailed history. Kit didn't think she'd be giving her sister a call on that anytime soon.

"I heard he bought a place on the north end of the loop," came the younger voice. "Which means he plans to stay. That has to count for something."

"We'll see," the older woman said. "We all just want what's best for the child, but given how Delilah let the Westlakes trample all over her and shove poor Birdie—her own mother—aside like they did . . . I don t trust this sudden change of heart."

"Didn't you mention something about Morgan being the black sheep of the family? By their standards, anyway. I've been so busy with all the craziness leading up to the cookbook release, I'll admit I haven't paid as much attention to the local gossip as I usually do. But what I have heard . . . well . . . I don't know. It sounds like he's trying to do the right thing. We can at least give him the benefit of the doubt, can't we?"

"Oh, he'll get a warm Sugarberry reception, all right."

The younger woman's tone was affectionate, but with a warning note. "Alva—"

"Don't Alva me, Miss Lani May. I don't have a single say in this."

"Other than being Birdie's closest friend for the past forty or so years."

"I just don't want to see her hurt again. Delilah was a late-in-life baby for Birdie, long after she'd given up hope of ever having a child. Everyone on this island knew she loved that girl with everything in her heart. What that same child handed her in return . . . and now she's gone as well . . ." The woman's voice trailed off.

Her voice was a bit more wavery when she continued. "I simply couldn't bear it if that family were to ruin things again. I've never met Olivia Westlake, and God help her if

I ever do. I have more than a few words for that bitter old prune."

"She's not planning a visit so soon, is she?"

"Not that I've heard, but we need to be prepared. I wouldn't put anything past that—" The older woman broke off, and Kit found herself leaning closer to the screen door to hear the rest of what she was saying. "Birdie's been through enough. No mother should outlive her own child. She didn't attend the funeral, you know. Made the trip to Atlanta in her own time, paid her respects in private."

"Probably for the best, but a shame it had to be like that. I'm glad she has you looking out for her, Alva."

"She certainly does, and I've let everybody know about it, too."

"I'm sure you have," came the somewhat dry, but compassionate response. "And, of course, all of us will be rooting for her and little Lilly to hit it off. Have they reunited yet?"

"Not yet. Supposed to have a picnic or some such, but Mr. Morgan is taking his time."

"Well, given all they've been through, maybe that's not a bad idea. It's a lot of change in that little girl's life. And a picnic, whenever it happens, sounds lovely. It's been so warm this fall. I can't believe it's almost November and we're still having weather in the upper seventies every day. Not that I'm complaining." Lani laughed. "Neither Baxter nor I are missing those New York winters. Let me know if I can contribute anything to the picnic when the time comes. A few cupcakes could add some smiles."

"I'll mention it to Birdie. She loves your strawberry shortcake cupcakes. That might be just the thing."

"Done. Consider it my homecoming gift to Miss Lilly."

"Imagine not having seen your own grandchild since the day of her birth. Lilly just turned five, you know."

"I heard. Well, I still say we should give her uncle the benefit of the doubt going in. Sounds to me like he's trying to do what's best for the child, giving her family, a home, and roots. And, apparently going against that bitter old prune you mentioned, in order to do it. Pretty commendable if you ask me."

"I suppose you're right. He's unmarried, no kids of his own, you know," Alva added. "To turn your whole life upside down like that . . ." She gave an audible sigh. "If it were anyone other than a Westlake, I'd be heading the welcoming committee. As it is, I'm still doing some digging."

"On?"

"Him. For Birdie's sake, of course."

"Of course," came the dry response. "You're not thinking of putting him in one of your columns, I hope. I don't think anyone would benefit, least of all Birdie."

"Now, now, I wouldn't do that," the older woman said.

Even Kit, who hadn't met the woman yet, wasn't sure how sold she was on that score, and she didn't know what the "column" was they were talking about. With the comment about a funeral in Atlanta . . . there was no doubt which Westlakes they were talking about. Even during the trial, she knew the Westlakes had suffered a tragedy when one of the Westlake scions and his wife had died in a car accident. Kit had been too overwhelmed with what was happening to her and her employees—not to mention losing loved ones that way struck a little too close to home—to pay attention, especially when the name Westlake was involved. But . . . she was almost certain that was the situation Alva and Lani were talking about. And that situation had come to Sugarberry, too. Right along with her.

Crap.

"What I know is that he's thirty-two, wealthy, educated, and quite the looker as it happens. So," Alva said, sounding all conspiratorial, "what I wonder is, why isn't a man like that married? Must be something wrong with him."

The younger woman laughed. "Not everyone thinks marriage has to go hand-in-hand with the rest of that list."

"Well . . . we'll see. If he thinks he's bringing his playboy ways to Sugarberry—"

"He brought his five-year-old niece. I hardly think that would be his intent."

"Well, those rich folks usually pawn off child care to a nanny, so until we know what's what, we can't be certain of anything," Alva said, sounding quite put out. "And be assured, if it's there to be found, I'll find it."

"I'm sure you will," Lani said dryly, "but, if he is a playboy, I doubt he'd have come to Sugarberry. The island isn't exactly teeming with single women."

"Speak for yourself, missy," Alva said. "Besides, all the rest aside, nice scenery is never a bad thing."

The younger woman laughed outright. "Now that's the Alva I know and admire."

Kit knew she'd been standing at the screen door way too long, but her mind was spinning with all the Westlake talk. The doubts she'd had about moving to Sugarberry suddenly tripled. But she could hardly walk away without saying hello. She owed Charlotte that much for going to the trouble to set up the interview. At the brief break in conversation, she rapped on the door without further delay. "Hello?" she called out, over the conversation and the music. "It's Kit Bellamy."

The door suddenly opened and Kit had to lower her gaze almost a foot to meet that of a tiny, senior-aged woman as she popped into view.

"Well, hello there!"

"Hello." Kit smiled fully for what felt like the first time in ages. It was pretty much impossible not to. The woman—Alva, she presumed—barely topped five feet, with twinkling eyes and a welcomjng smile, pearls clasped to her earlobes and strung around the starched Peter Pan collar of her lemon-colored blouse, which she'd paired with a moss green cardigan sweater. Pearl buttons, of course.

All of what you'd expect from a grandmotherly type, except, perhaps, for the hair, which had been teased into a spectacular beehive of curls and waves, and was a rather shocking, unnatural shade of red. Add to that, the entire ensemble had been topped with an apron that was essentially a movie poster for *Pirates of the Caribbean*—namely its star, Captain Jack Sparrow, as played by the very swash-buckling Johnny Depp. Kit couldn't help staring.

Alva followed her gaze, then looked back up, beaming. "I like pirates."

"I-I do, too," Kit stammered.

"Well then, I like you already." Alva stepped back and waved Kit inside. "Come on in. Welcome to Sugarberry."